PRAISE FOR JEREMIAH HEALY AND
SPIRAL

"Healy's writing is vivid and the assortment of believable characters is fascinating."

—San Antonio Express-News

"Packs an emotional wallop as it exposes the basest of human emotions—greed, jealousy, lust, and unbridled ambition. Another strong entry in a fine series."

—Booklist

"Hidden motives surface as this very compelling tale unfolds. . . . [Features] one of the more ingenious murder methods I've read about, in real life or fiction."

—Pittsburgh Post-Gazette

"As usual—in the modern bestselling mode—Healy populates his novel with strong and interesting characters. . . . Healy fans will enjoy SPIRAL."

—Lincoln Journal Star (NE)

"A scintillating saga."

—St. Petersburg Times (FL)

"With a sound ear for dialogue, Healy lets his characters speak for themselves, revealing more than they realize in their own words."

—Boston Herald

THE ONLY GOOD LAWYER

"[Jeremiah Healy] looks ready to join the honors class of private-eye writers that includes Robert B. Parker."

—*USA Today*

"Moves at a fast clip, punctuated with surprises that continually keep the reader off balance. . . . Healy does not scrimp on the quality readers have come to expect from this award-winning series."

—*Sun-Sentinel* (Ft. Lauderdale, FL)

"Healy has quietly labored for the better part of two decades to make the John Francis Cuddy novels among the best in the hard-boiled subgenre. This, the twelfth in the series, is one of the best."

—*The Pilot* (Southern Pines, NC)

"Healy puts a rapid pace on the story. . . . The writing is strong and clear and the characters are believable."

—*San Antonio Express-News*

"There are vicious gang members, sleazy attorneys, easy women, and hidden truths galore. . . . Another brilliant effort by a superb crime-writing craftsman."

—*Lansing State Journal* (MI)

"Noteworthy for its byzantine plot as well as the usual Cuddy strengths: characterization, dialogue, and explosive action."

—*Booklist*

INVASION OF PRIVACY

"The plot evoked vintage Ross MacDonald: the detective's search reveals old secrets that spawn new horrors years later. Cuddy is always good gritty company."

—*Publishers Weekly*

"As always, Cuddy is a good man on Boston's mean streets. The dialogue crackles, the plot is complex and clever, and Cuddy's relationship with his long-time lover faces a crisis in which machismo won't help.... An excellent series."

—*Booklist*

"This may be Jeremiah Healy's best Cuddy adventure yet.... Fascinating."

—*St. Petersburg Times* (FL)

RESCUE

"Healy at his best—a richly textured, superbly unfolded tale.... Cuddy is a beautifully rounded character: tough, resourceful, witty, and not afraid of deep feelings."

—*Houston Chronicle*

"Brilliant.... I've always wished Jerry Healy well, but not *this* well."

—*Robert B. Parker*

"A doozy.... The story unfolds beautifully.... The tension is palpable, the writing elegant yet clipped, the action, when it comes, [is] violent, vicious, and explicit.... This is exciting, thoughtful, wily fiction."

—*The Washington Post*

Other John Cuddy novels by Jeremiah Healy

Blunt Darts
The Staked Goat
So Like Sleep
Swan Dive
Yesterday's News
Right to Die
Shallow Graves
Foursome
Act of God
Rescue
Invasion of Privacy
The Only Good Lawyer

Published by POCKET BOOKS

JEREMIAH HEALY

SPIRAL

A John Francis Cuddy Mystery

POCKET BOOKS

New York   London   Toronto   Sydney   Singapore

This book is a work of fiction. Names, characters, places and
incidents are products of the author's imagination or are used
fictitiously. Any resemblance to actual events or locales or persons
living or dead is entirely coincidental.

 POCKET BOOKS, a division of Simon & Schuster, Inc.
1230 Avenue of the Americas, New York, NY 10020

ISBN: 0-671-00956-7

First Pocket Books paperback printing December 2000

10 9 8 7 6 5 4 3 2 1

POCKET and colophon are registered trademarks of
Simon & Schuster, Inc.

Front cover photo montage by John Vairo, Jr.;
photo credits: Tomek Sikora/The Image Bank;
Susan Van Etten/Picture Quest

Printed in the U.S.A.

For all our friends at the Tennis Club

ONE

From the passenger's seat, Nancy Meagher said, "Ted Williams used to play some sport, right?"

Behind the wheel of the Honda Civic, I didn't glance at her or the white-on-green traffic sign as I turned us into the new tunnel to Boston's Logan Airport. "Sacrilege, Nance."

"Because I insulted a public-works project?"

Even without looking, I could feel the playful smile, like a model on a postcard from County Kerry, as she needled me oh-so-subtly about the difference in our ages.

Traffic in the Ted was light, the reason we'd taken Nancy's car instead of mine on that cold Wednesday evening in early January. A prosecutor in downtown, she lived in my old neighborhood of South Boston, and the political deal on the tunnel project was that Southie residents could get a windshield decal that let them use the new route when it was otherwise restricted to commercial vehicles. Which made driving to the airport—usually an unpredictable nightmare—into a milk-run of no more than ten minutes.

Nancy said, "John?," the playful smile still in her voice.

"What?"

"It's not as much fun to needle you if I don't get timely responses."

"Ted Williams was the best outfielder the Red Sox ever had, and—"

"Better even than that Bill Russell guy?"

The Hall-of-Fame basketball center for the Celtics. "I'm

beginning to understand what teachers mean by 'not educable.'"

Nancy shifted in her seat, but didn't change her tone. "You're just jealous."

"Of what?"

"My going to San Francisco."

An educational conference for prosecutors was being held there, and Nancy had been chosen by her boss to be the assistant district attorney attending from Suffolk County, a genuine feather in her professional cap. But I'd promised another private investigator named George-Ann Izzo that I'd help her with an industrial surveillance, and she was estimating a solid week for the job. Frankly, George-Ann would probably—

"John?," now a different tone in Nancy's voice.

This time I did turn my head toward her. "Only half right."

"About . . . ?"

"About your going to San Francisco. The part that makes me jealous is I won't be there with you."

Nancy brought her left hand up to the back of my neck, very gently drawing her thumb and forefinger along the strands of hair at my collar. "Me, too."

"Of course," I said, "there's a good chance this 'El Niño' thing will wreck the weather out there for you."

"Funny, I heard the warm currents were actually reaching the beaches, almost like Los Angeles."

"The TV news said those same warm currents were also bringing sharks up from the south."

"John?"

"What?"

"The sharks won't get me lying in the sun on the sand."

"Then again," I said, "you'll more likely be spending your days taking copious notes in some conference room."

Nancy tugged a little on a couple of my neck hairs. "I was thinking more of how I'd like to be spending my nights."

"But I promised George-Ann, and—"

"—a promise is a promise."

"Always," I said.

Nancy started grazing my skin at the nape ever-so-lightly with her fingernails. "John Francis Cuddy, consistency is not always a virtue."

I leaned my head back against her hand. "You keep doing that, and the concept of virtue will probably fly off our agenda."

The nails dug a little deeper. "Imagine, making love in a tunnel named after a famous hockey player."

"Nance?"

"Yes?"

"You sure know how to kill a mood."

She slid her hand out from behind me, but she was laughing softly doing it.

"This is the final boarding call for Flight Number One-thirty-three to San Francisco."

In the brightly lit departure lounge, Nancy and I watched the airline's gate agent put down his microphone. The flight seemed only about half-full, so the boarding process had gone quickly.

A little too quickly for me.

Nancy said, "You'll call me about the decision on your apartment, right?"

Around the time we'd met, I started renting a condominium in Boston's neighborhood of Back Bay from a doctor leaving for a residency in Chicago. The doctor had called me the prior week, saying she was going to extend another year and asking if I wanted to stay on as a tenant.

Nancy was the first woman I'd cared anything about since my wife, Beth, had died young from brain cancer. Nancy and I had been through a lot, and we'd finally begun talking about living together. She was renting the top floor of a three-decker from a Boston Police family named Lynch, several generations of whom lived on the first two floors. But Nancy wasn't sure the older Mrs. Lynch would swing for a "living-in-sin" arrangement in her house, and I wasn't sure the doctor's one-bedroom condo would be big enough for us and Nancy's cat. Her pet went by "Renfield," after the madman in Dracula who ate small mammals, but he'd—

"John?"

"Sorry."

"I really worry when you zone out on me like that."

"I'll call you about the condo."

Nancy slipped both her hands up under my arms, her palms firmly planted on my shoulder blades as we hugged each other. "The Lynches will feed Renfield, but he might like you to come play with him once or twice."

"I'll stop at the pet store first, pick up a couple of canaries."

The gate agent looked at us rather pointedly as he reached for his microphone again. "*All* passengers should now be . . . "

I put my lips close to Nancy's right ear. "I'm going to miss you, kid."

"What, you aren't already?"

Kissing the lobe above her earring, I got a whiff of her shampoo and perfume, but even more a scent that was so specifically, definably Nancy that I thought I could find her by sense of smell the way a momma dog can identify one of her puppies in the dark.

Turning to go, Nancy said over her shoulder, "Call me at my hotel.

"I will."

"But don't forget about the time-zone difference."

"I won't."

A last smile just before the gate agent closed the jetway door behind her.

I turned and began walking back toward the main terminal, an emptiness welling up inside me. Nancy and I had been together most of the holiday season. Just before Christmas, we attended the Chorus Pro Musica concert at the Old South Church on Boylston Street. We celebrated New Year's Eve by going to three First Night events: medieval carols at the First Lutheran on Marlborough, a saxophone tribute to Duke Ellington at the First Baptist on Commonwealth, and a salsa show at the Church of the Covenant on Newbury.

Nancy had called it "a very yuppie-scum evening."

Reaching her Civic in the Logan parking garage, I realized there was another reason for my emptiness. Because of Nancy's trial duties as a prosecutor, usually she was the one staying in Boston while I traveled somewhere. It was a different feeling, her leaving me behind.

A feeling I'd had years ago, with someone else I loved.

Shaking that off, I turned the key in the ignition.

When I got home, the little window in my telephone tape machine was glowing a red "1," meaning I had a message. Playing it, I heard George-Ann Izzo's voice tell me that our job for the next day had been cancelled, but that the client had called her only "a few minutes ago." Then the machine's atonal voice recited the time George-Ann had called me. Four-ten, or a good fifteen minutes before Nancy and I had left her apartment for the airport.

In other words, if I'd just checked my messages by remote from Southie—or even from the gate at Logan itself—I could have gotten a ticket on that half-empty flight and spent the long weekend with Nancy in San Fran'.

Picking up the phone, I tried her hotel out there. The desk clerk I drew told me he indeed had a reservation for a "Ms. Meagher, assuming that's 'Nancy Eugenia,' sir." I laughed silently that she'd use her middle name for the hotel when she never did usually, then realized that probably the District Attorney's office would have made the reservation for her. The desk clerk also said Ms. Meagher hadn't checked in yet, which didn't surprise me, since I figured her flight would still be hours east of the city. I left a message for Nancy that I might be able to join her after all and would call back at a reasonable hour in the morning.

I remember going to bed that night feeling pretty good.

For the last time in a long time.

Nancy's boss had bought her plane ticket in addition to making her hotel reservation, so the airline contacted the D.A.'s office first. A secretary there who knew about us reached me at 6:50 A.M. Eastern Time on Thursday morning, just before I would have awakened to the clock radio.

And the frantic bulletins about Flight #133, en route from Boston to San Francisco.

Trying to look back on it with some objectivity, the people at the airline were pretty good about handling what had to be their worst nightmare, too. They made every effort to contact each passenger's family/friends/lovers and shepherd us to a ballroom in one of Boston's bigger hotels. They set up bottomless urns of coffee and laid out a buffet for every meal. And all the while, they marched a rotating cast of experts to the podium on a raised stage "for the purpose of providing information as it becomes available."

The exact sequence of the next twenty-four hours is still

pretty hazy. And for someone who supposedly makes his living by being observant, I have almost no memory—almost no inkling, in fact—of the other stunned and grieving people sitting or standing with me in that ballroom. All I remember doing is watching the experts ascend the platform, each contributing one more piece to a puzzle that couldn't be solved.

Somebody told us that bizarre wind and rain conditions caused by El Niño made the San Francisco control tower ask incoming flights to stay aloft a while longer, finally forcing many to circle over the ocean off the peninsula. Somebody else said the problem for Nancy's plane was almost certainly caused by El Niño as well, perhaps in a parallel way to the incredible turbulence that had rocked a Japanese airliner only weeks before, even killing one person on board.

However, nobody was sure just what the problem for Flight #133 actually had been.

The tower tapes of radio transmissions from the aircraft held the voice of a man (identified to us as the copilot), screaming, "We're tumbling!" A woman (the pilot) then gave half an order to "Kill the—." After that came an earsplitting noise, like a car shredder ripping an old wreck apart for scrap.

Probably the sound of the starboard wing shearing off.

Somebody in a uniform explained why weather conditions kept rescue planes and helicopters on the ground out there until almost twelve hours later. A different somebody in a similar uniform described how the boats that could brave the wind and rain got bounced around "like so many apples in a punchbowl." A genuinely empathetic somebody related how hard it was on the crews to find the floating, often mutilated bodies of eighty-six passengers, and—to his credit—he nearly cried when he let slip an acronym for the other seventeen people who'd been on board Flight #133.

"BNR" was the acronym, by the way. Standing for, "Body Not Recovered."

A nerdlike somebody at the podium said the reason so many bodies weren't found is that they might have been carried away by the crazy currents churning off the coast. A pompous somebody else felt more strongly that given the likely magnitude and uncertain angle of the aircraft's impact on the water, some of the bodies ("... and believe me, I know how hard it is for all of you out there to hear this...") were probably dismembered to the point of being ... pulverized. Finally one somebody had the guts to climb the ballroom's platform and say that, in her opinion, the warm waters brought in by El Niño probably contained roving schools of sharks.

All I really cared about, though, was that "Meagher, Nancy Eugenia" had been listed among the BNRs.

The following days were, if possible, even worse. After I'd lost Beth to her cancer, I'd "adjusted" with alcohol, to the point of nearly creaming a kid on a bike with my car. This time around, I was a lot smarter.

No establishments beyond walking distance.

Bellied up to one bar or another, I'd stare raptly at the screens of their television sets, usually with the audio muted so that sporting events or CNN became pantomime experiences. Only a few news stories not about Flight #133 registered on me, and even they had to be somehow related to each other. I watched reporters in California cover the funeral for then-congressman Sonny Bono, who had joined one of our own Commonwealth's premier political clan in dying on a ski slope. I watched different reporters in Florida cover the homicide-by-drowning of the young daughter of another former rock star, still-shots of the JonBenet Ramsey tragedy from Colorado apparently being used for comparison. Broadening my horizons, I watched footage of massacres in Bosnia and Rwanda. Graphs of the Hong Kong stock market starting to rise while the South Korean one continued to slide. Even a nearly incomprehensible piece on the renaming of countries over the last twenty-five years.

I sobered up—briefly—for Nancy's memorial service, arranged by the D.A.'s office. Collectively, we who had known her nearly filled Gate of Heaven church in Southie. There were classmates of hers from New England School of Law and coworkers from the courtroom, even a number of opposing attorneys from Nancy's trials. I sat in a pew near her landlords, the Lynch family, as good and accurate things were recounted by a priest I'd never met. He then asked if anyone wished to come forward and offer their thoughts as well. Everybody waited for me to go first. When I didn't, others went up to the altar rail, and then everybody waited for me to go last. When I didn't do that, either, there was a final, short hymn, and the service was over.

Walking out, I saw people who'd come more for me than because they'd known Nancy well. Robert Murphy, a black lieutenant commanding the Homicide Unit; Mo Katzen, a crotchety reporter for the Boston *Herald*; Elie Honein, a Nautilus club manager; and even Primo Zuppone, a mob enforcer. Each tried to talk with me or get me to agree on a date to talk. I fended off all of them.

I'd gone through all this before, you see. I "knew" how to grieve. Or at least how I grieved.

Once I'd driven myself home, I went back to hitting the watering holes. On bitterly cold nights, understanding bartenders poured me into cabs if they were concerned their self-absorbed patron might die from exposure.

And, frankly, that's probably a little bit of what I was doing. Trying to die in a way that wasn't exactly suicide, because I wasn't putting a gun to my head or diving off a bridge. But I would have been deliriously happy if something beyond my control had conveniently, mercifully taken me off the board.

For what it's worth, the capper came exactly eleven days

after the crash of Flight #133. I was in a nearly empty bar late on a Sunday night, even more hammered than I'd gotten the previous ten. I remember thinking, I can't talk to Nancy anymore, because she's gone. Then, ordering what I was firmly told would be my last round, I had a brainstorm.

I could call her apartment in Southie and get the outgoing tape message.

Hear her voice.

I remember leaving my fresh drink on the bar top and stumbling into most of the few people in the bar as I weaved my way back to the pay phone. I even remember putting in the quarter—Jesus, the feel of it leaving my fingers—and how warm the metal buttons were on the keypad, I guessed because somebody else had just made a call. After punching in Nancy's home number, I counted the rings—three—before her machine kicked in. And then her cheery but no-nonsense announcement started, and I could feel the dam break behind my eyes. I tried twice to hang up the receiver but couldn't quite manage it.

I did manage to stagger out of the place and back home to my empty condo.

The next night, from just inside the front door of his three-decker, Drew Lynch said, "John?"

I watched the young police officer relax his right arm, the revolver in that hand now visible against his sweatpants and hanging down loosely at his thigh. "Sorry to bother you, Drew, but there're some things I'd like to get from the third floor."

"Sure." He stepped aside to let me come in. "How're you doing?"

"Not great, but I'm functioning."

It was almost twenty-four hours since the dam had broken in that last bar. I'd spent the morning and afternoon working through the accumulated paperwork at my office and drinking lots of water chased by aspirin for the hangover. As Drew stared at me, though, I realized I wasn't quite functioning on the amenities level.

"How's your family doing?" I said.

"Okay. Mom's still taking it pretty hard, and on top of that she's gotten some kind of flu. Nothing that'll kill her, but—"

You could see Drew wince as his own words struck him. "Christ, John, I'm sorry. I didn't—"

"Don't sweat it. We're all a little off from this thing."

"Right." Then a hesitation before, "Yeah."

He turned, and I followed him up the front stairs.

At the second-floor landing, Drew opened his apartment door. "And don't worry about Renfield."

Jesus. Not only hadn't I been worrying about Nancy's cat: I'd completely forgotten the poor little guy existed.

Drew said, "We've been feeding him and doing the litter box. My wife even carries him down to our place sometimes so he has somebody to play with, and Mom cuts up scraps from the table."

I cleared my throat. "He likes that."

"Yeah." Drew hesitated again. "You, uh, need any help up there?"

"I don't think so, but thanks."

As Drew closed his door, I climbed to the third floor. At the landing, I could hear scratching sounds coming from the other side of Nancy's door.

Renfield.

I turned the knob and pushed slowly. As soon as the door was ajar, a gray tiger head was forcing the issue, scuttling out crablike on rear legs that had some kind of congenital defect requiring them to be literally, clinically broken and reset by the vet. Because Nancy had been flying—

God, it hit me hard enough, I nearly went down.

I closed my eyes, steadying myself. When I opened

them again, I could see Renfield, now trundling toward his food dish in the corner of the kitchen. He sat back on his haunches and looked up at me, meowing once.

After Renfield's operation, I'd had to pick him up from the animal hospital because Nancy was . . . away. Given what he'd been through—including having his hindquarters shaved down to the skin for the surgery—the cat had kind of imprinted on me as a substitute parent. At least, that's how the vet explained it. When I was around Renfield, he paid unusual attention to me, including licking my hand and always trying to crawl into my lap by rearing up awkwardly and pawing my pant leg with his clawless front feet.

Right now, though, he just cried again.

I walked over to the food bowl. Full of the dry cereal stuff as well as some fresh-looking canned glop.

As soon as I was near him, I noticed Renfield stopped crying and began chowing down. When I turned and started to walk away, he cried a third time. Turning back around, I saw the cat was staring at me.

I turned for good this time and went past Nancy's bedroom to the living room in the front of the third floor. It was exactly as we'd left it twelve days before. From behind me, I heard a rhythmic, bonking sound.

The noise Renfield's rear knees made against the hardwood floor, his legs churning like the linkage on a locomotive's wheels.

As soon as he crossed the threshold into the living room, Renfield stopped before looking up and crying some more.

I went over to him and bent down. He started licking my hand, his tongue like sandpaper. Then an almost fierce purring began.

"Renfield, I'm so sorry."

I walked carefully past him as he tried to move between my shoes.

In Nancy's bedroom, I opened her closet door to get the one suit I left there. That scent of her rocketed my memory back to the departure lounge for Flight #133.

I grabbed the hanger holding my suit and closed the door, trying not to inhale.

Renfield, now at the bedroom sill, cried again.

I kept only a few other things at Nancy's place. Two shirts, three pairs of underwear, five (for some reason) socks, all in "my" drawer of her dresser. And a dopp kit on top of her bathroom's toilet tank.

Renfield was at the bathroom threshold now, crying some more.

I stepped over him and toward the kitchen. Above the sink, Nancy had thumbtacked a photo she'd gotten some obliging tourist to take of us when we were at the beach together the prior summer. Judith Harker was the name, from somewhere in Arizona, I knew, because I had to give her my business card so she could mail the print to us. In the shot, Nancy and I were on a blanket, sitting with our knees up and touching each other, my right arm around her shoulders, Nancy's left hand resting on my left wrist over my left knee. I wore a yearbook smile, Nancy the same but with her eyes crossed, mugging for the camera.

I tried to remember another photo of just us, together. I couldn't.

Almost two years, and only the one shot.

Setting down the clothes and toilet kit on Nancy's kitchen table, I very carefully pried the thumbtack out of the photo and the wall as Renfield began crying again behind me.

The cemetery is on a harbor hillside only a few blocks from the Lynches' three-decker. There's a gate that's kept open, even at night, so folks can visit when they get off work. I walked down the macadam path to her row, stopping at the gravestone with ELIZABETH MARY DEVLIN CUDDY carved into the marble.

John, what's the matter?

She could always tell. Always.

John?

"It's Nancy, Beth."

Trouble between you?

I shook my head before lifting it away from her and toward the inky blackness of the water—Jesus, the ocean water—at the foot of the—

Oh, John. No . . . no. . . .

Just a nod this time.

She paused. Then, *How?*

I told her. At first, in short, choppy phrases that an English teacher probably wouldn't count as sentences. Once the words started coming, though, I began to get more detailed, even glib.

Beth waited me out before saying, *This is the first time you've talked it through, right?*

"Right."

Do you feel any . . . better?

I took a deep breath. "No more than I did after losing you."

Another pause. *John, I think you have to accept that Nancy's death is going to be different for you.*

"Different."

Though I hadn't said it as a question, Beth answered me anyway. *You knew for a long time that I was sick, that I was going to—*

"Goddamnit, Beth, it's just not fair!"

The thought jumped out before I was conscious I'd spoken it aloud.

A third pause. *If you're waiting for life to be fair, John, I think you're in for a very long siege.*

I looked down toward the water again, then immediately back at her stone. "It's not just that Nancy was taken so young, or so . . . abruptly. It's that because they didn't find her body, she doesn't have even a grave."

And you don't have any special place for visiting her.

Beth was right. "Nowhere she wasn't . . ."

Alive?

I tried to take a deep breath again. Couldn't.

John?

"You're right. I don't have Nancy anymore, and I don't have a place I can be with her that doesn't remind me of . . ." I shook my head.

This may not help, but there's a reason why you weren't on that plane.

"Sure there is. I didn't check my messages in time to—"

Not what I mean, John. There's some reason why you were spared.

I thought back to one of the first visits I'd made to the graveyard after Beth had died. "You know that."

I do.

"Mind letting me in on it?"

A short pause this time that passed for a small smile. *If only I could.*

Suddenly, I started to feel the cold. "Do me a favor?"

What?

"Keep an eye out for Nancy. I think you'd like her."

I was back in the condo—finally opening almost two weeks of home mail—when the phone rang. I thought about letting the tape machine handle it, then realized nobody had called me, morning or afternoon, at the office. Odd for a Monday.

"John Cuddy."

"*Buenas noches desde Florida,* John."

"Justo?"

"The one and the same."

Justo Vega was a friend from my military police days in Saigon. He'd been practicing law in Miami most of the time since, helping me some months before with a case down in the Florida Keys that had blown sky—

"John?"

"Sorry, Justo. Something wrong with the Keys thing?"

"No. No, unfortunately I disturb you on a holiday for another matter."

"Holiday?"

A hesitation on the other end of the line. "The third Monday in January. Martin Luther King."

No wonder there'd been no calls at the office. "Sorry—" I decided I had to stop saying that. "I've been kind of stuck on another matter."

A longer hesitation. "John, there is also something else, no?"

When you soldier with someone during bad times, there's a certain connection that's beyond even good friendship. "Yes, but I've gotten a little tired of talking about it."

"Of course." The longest hesitation yet. "I am not sure I should be burdening you with what I will say now. Yet, if you were calling me, I would want to know of it because of an old debt we both share."

"Being?"

"The Skipper, John."

Shit. Back in Vietnam, "the Skipper" was the nickname the lieutenants like Justo and me used affectionately for Colonel Nicolas Helides, our commanding officer. Though we were Army, not Navy, we called him that because his real love outside the military was sailing. Helides graduated West Point while most of us came from ROTC programs, but the man treated us all as sons. And in a bar one night when he wasn't around—the Skipper drank alcohol but never cursed and didn't suffer gladly those who did—six or seven of us took one of those expletive-laden, drunks-in-arms oaths to watch out for him like we would our own fathers. In the end, of course, Helides was the one who watched out for us, especially during the all-night horrors of the Tet Offensive, keeping us together—and almost sane—as we lost whole squads of our troopers behind barricades of Jeeps, the MPs standing their ground against Viet Cong armed with AK-47s when all we had were the .45 calibre Colts drawn from our hol—

"John, you are still there?"

"Sor—" Last time with the apologies. Last time.

"John?"

"I just kind of . . . zoned out for a minute. The Skipper died?"

"No," said Justo. "No, he has had his share of health problems, but that is not why I am calling you for him."

For him. "What's the trouble then?"

"If you do not know already, I think the Skipper would want to tell you this himself."

If I didn't . . . Shaking my head, I finally started focusing. "He's in Florida, then?"

"Yes, but not Miami. Up in Broward."

"Broward."

"The county, which for you is the Fort Lauderdale area, twenty miles and a little north of here."

"Justo, the Skipper wants me for something . . . professional?"

"Correct."

"You might remember, I'm not licensed down there."

"It will not be a difficulty in this situation."

"What situation?"

"As I said, if you do not know already—"

"—the Skipper wants to tell me himself."

"Yes."

"And not over the telephone."

"For a good reason, I believe."

I considered it. Surrogate father, surrogate son. And then I realized something else.

For the first time in almost two weeks, I hadn't thought about Nancy for five minutes.

"John, if this is truly a bad time . . ."

"No, Justo. No. I'll be there."

"I am very glad you will come." A different tone of voice now. Relief, maybe? "And do not worry. We will fly you into Fort Lauderdale, and I will have you picked up by Pepe—you remember him, yes?"

"Tough guy to forget."

A musical laugh. "And he has become only more so. However, my Alicia and our three daughters love him, and I could not do without his help. When can you leave Boston?"

In my mind, I went back over what I'd seen at the office that day. "How about tomorrow morning?"

"Excellent. You have a preference among the airlines?"

"One flight's about the same as another," I said.

Which did make me think of Nancy, and of how stupid my last comment would forever sound.

TWO

In fact, until the plane was ready to leave, I wasn't sure I'd be able to walk onto it.

Things weren't helped any by the people around me in the shared departure area at Logan, either. Across from my row of seats sat an elderly man in a wheelchair, wearing a cardigan sweater and a watch cap, booked on a later flight to Miami than mine for Fort Lauderdale. Flanking him were his sixtyish daughter and son-in-law, whose conversation seemed fixated on coffee.

She said to her husband, "What are you buying him coffee for now?"

"Your father wanted it for the plane."

"They seat him, they'll bring him coffee."

"He told me they don't bring it when he wants it."

"Of course they don't. It'd spill when the plane moves."

I watched the old man, smiling happily, his head following the conversation like a spectator on the sidelines of a tennis match.

"So," said the son-in-law, "this way your father'll have it first."

"No, this way he'll spill it first."

"It's just a small cup."

"So, that means it won't spill?"

"No, that means he'll finish the thing by the time the plane's moving."

The daughter upped the ante. "How's my father gonna finish that much coffee without having to go pee-pee?"

"Now I've got to worry, will they take him to the bathroom?"

The old man's smile broadened. One of his remaining joys clearly was watching two experienced opponents pound away at each other.

The gate agent called my own flight. Walking toward the jetway, I found myself thinking, After this reduced, elderly man, it will be good to see the Skipper again.

I'd never flown into Fort Lauderdale/Hollywood International Airport before, but I had flown over it on the case in the Keys. The view of Lauderdale from the air is more than a little disorienting as to the scale of the snaking Intracoastal canal system that gives thousands of people postage-stamp lots and deep-water moorings for boats bigger than their houses.

I was pretty sure of the perspective issue, since I'd decided after my plane took off that I was going to watch out the windows when—and if—we landed safely.

Which, as luck would have it, this particular aircraft did.

"Hey, Mr. John Francis."

The slight alias I'd used when he'd met me before. "Pepe."

I watched the slim, six-foot-tall man come off his leaning position against the wall opposite my arrival gate. Pepe had gotten a little more bald since I'd seen him last, the black hair receding from front to back. The mustache was black, too, but trimmed down from the bandit-style he'd favored back in September. His current outfit more than compensated for the conservative cut, though. Pepe was wearing clothes of enough different colors to pass for an Easter egg.

He began walking toward me. "How you doing, man?"

His words came out, "How chew dune, mahn." I said, "Fine, Pepe. Just fine."

When he drew close enough to study my eyes, his own went a little off. "You sure you okay?"

"Just a rough flight."

A bit more study, then a shrug. "Okay, Mr. John Francis, I suppose to pick you up, take you where Mr. Vega at."

As he turned away, I said, "Pepe?"

He turned back to me. "Yeah, I figure you got the luggage. We pick that up down the stairs."

"Not what I meant."

The study look again. "You don't got no luggage?"

"I've got luggage. What I wanted to tell you is, I'm not sure which name I'll be using down here."

A cocky grin. "I remember that about you, man. Always somebody you are not, huh?"

Grunting as he hoisted my suitcase into the trunk of the older Ford Escort in the parking garage, Pepe said, "You ain't gonna need all this clothes down here in the sunshine."

I watched him as he looked around at the other cars quickly, then unfastened the shirt button just above his belt buckle with the thumb and middle finger of his right hand. Pepe used the same fingers to lift up the trunk mat next to my suitcase, his left hand pulling a Glock ten-millimeter semiautomatic from underneath. After another look around, he slipped the gun into the gap in his shirt and under his belt, leaving the button above the buckle undone for a left-handed cross-draw.

"I guess some things don't change," I said.

Pepe's right hand closed the trunk lid while he patted the bulge his Glock made in his clothes. "You mean the piece, man?"

I waved at the Escort. "And the two-door stick-shift, so you don't get taken for a rent-a-car tourist by the bad guys."

"Hey, Mr. Whatever, you up in Broward now. Not like Miami in the quiet suburbs."

"Then why the gun?"

"I still maybe got to drive to Miami after Mr. Vega see you."

"See me about what?"

"I don't know, man." Pepe shook his head as he moved to open my door. "I just your driver."

Not from what I remembered of him.

* * *

Windows closed and air-conditioning on against an almost eighty-degree, muggy day, we bumped along a service road before Pepe turned us north onto Andrews Avenue. "Most times, you want to take ninety-five."

"Interstate 95?"

"Right, be faster. But Mr. Vega say he want you to get 'ori-*ent*-ed' on this town."

The first thing I noticed about Fort Lauderdale was that its airport was a snap to negotiate, especially compared to Miami's.

"Anything special I should be 'orienting' myself about?"

"Mr. Vega, he tell you that."

Okay. Trying to make small talk, I said, "Things still bad back in Cuba?"

"Worser than when you here last time. They got these old American cars—like a Packard, a fifty-seven Chevy with the big tail's fin—but they don't got no gas for putting in them. They got old women volunteer to serve the meals in the hospitals, but they don't got no food for the patients. Then the Pope, he supposed to come this month, so Fidel let everybody have Christmas couple weeks ago, like the first time since '*la Revolución*.'" Pepe slewed toward the curb. "Only gonna take more than some fiestas and church candles, change things for the people."

The Escort came to a complete stop, and Pepe gestured forward and sideways. "We on Andrews, and that street go across is Broward, a boul-e-vard. In Lauderdale, you got everything like the compass thing."

"Compass?"

"Yeah, like north, south, you know it? Where Andrews and Broward cross each others here, this is center of everything."

I thought I got what Pepe meant by looking at the street signs on each side of the avenue. The ones to the right said

S.E., the ones to the left, S.W. Across Broward Boulevard were N.E. and N.W., respectively. "So, northeast of this intersection is N.E., southwest is S.W., and—"

"—like that, right. You got somebody's address you want to find, all you got to do is know the compass part, and the number of the house. So two-five-oh Northeast Fourth Avenue gonna be past Second Street and before Third Street in the northeast."

"Sounds easy enough. But maybe we ought to go see Justo, be sure I need to be oriented much more."

Nodding, Pepe shifted into first and feathered the clutch.

"This boulevard here, Mr. Whatever, they call it 'Las Olas.'"

"Spanish?"

"For 'the waves.'"

We were heading east on a Florida version of Boston's Newbury Street, with tony bars and boutiques crowded together. "I don't see any water, much less waves."

"You wait a couple minutes, you see all the water you want." After another ten blocks or so, there were quaint little bridges like the one over our Public Garden's swan pond. These spanned some kind of canal, however, and the first two spinal roadways were named Hendricks Isle and Isle of Venice. Pepe finally turned left and over a bridge that said ISLE OF ATHENS on its convex wall.

I said, "Colonel Helides lives here?"

Pepe nodded.

After passing a number of mansions—each with frontage on perpendicular canals and many with yachts lashed to docks—Pepe pulled toward a clump of people at the side of the road near a gate. The gate was part of a fence with twelve-foot-high metal spikes enclosing a sprawling, Art Deco home. The people were carrying cameras—some video, some professional photographic, some just little disposable jobbies.

On the other side of the gate stood a guy who acted like a security guard, but not one of the retired scarecrows the cheapjack companies hire. Except for the casual shirt and hiking shorts, this guy was more Secret Service, with the kind of blond buzz-cut and build that you associate with fullbacks from Nebraska.

Pepe drove slowly toward the clump, who turned and began shooting footage of us. When the Escort's nose approached the gate, the guard pointed an electronic device of some kind at the lock. As the gate opened, he returned the device to one of the front pockets in his shorts. There was a bulge visible in the other front pocket that I somehow thought would be measured less in amperage and more in calibre.

The camera people shouted questions at us, but they were mangled by each other and mostly lost through the closed windows and air-conditioning hum. We pulled up the drive past the guard's station, designed to look like a gazebo matching the house. The grounds were carefully landscaped with exotic plants and flowers.

The drive curved and ended at discreetly hidden garage doors for five bays, the cars in front of them ranging from a mud-spattered compact pickup to a Lincoln Continental. Beyond the cars, a multimasted sailboat rocked against its ropes, telling you where the grassy yard had to end.

Pepe killed the engine, then turned to me. "The TV and newspapers, they been at this place ever since."

I looked at him. "Since what?"

Pepe shook his head. "I still just the driver, man."

He got out, and I followed suit. We walked toward the steps of a "back" door that could have been lifted off hinges at Buckingham Palace.

Pepe said, "Is easier this way."

"Because of the media people out front?"

A shrug as the door opened, and I assumed the gate guard must have radioed ahead about us. When I looked up, Justo Vega was smiling at me.

"John, it is so good to see you again."

Justo hadn't lost any more hair, but he'd started growing a mustache under the wide nose in his moonish face. As tall as I am, Justo wore a light gray business suit with a white, collarless shirt underneath, top button fastened. His broad shoulders moved under the jacket in a swaying motion that always reminded me of a man making up his mind to ask somebody for a dance.

Climbing the steps, I went to shake hands with him. "Justo, it's—"

He came forward, enclosing me in a bear hug. "Truly good to see you, John."

"Same here."

Justo broke the hug. "No problems with your flight?"

If my eyes gave anything away, Justo's didn't. "Fine. Just fine."

He nodded once, then spoke in a grave, modulated tone. "I am afraid the Skipper hates pity, so please, brace yourself for seeing him."

I closed my eyes, then nodded once, too, as Justo led me into the house.

As the rear foyer yielded to real rooms, I blinked, but less from the lighting and more from the contrast. While the architecture viewed from the street was modern, the inside felt like a Maine hunting lodge. Each room seemed to have its own cathedral ceiling, with exposed beams of rough-hewn, stained wood. Same look to the walls, and even the parts of the floor not covered by thick rugs or carpeting.

Taste is a personal thing, and I found myself warming to the interior of the house in a way I never could to its exterior.

"To the right, now," said Justo, as though comforted by giving directions.

We turned into a massive den, fully twenty-by-forty, another cathedral ceiling looming overhead. The colors red and buff dominated—on leather sofas, plaid chairs, and seascapes-at-sunset hanging from the walls. Two men were in front of a stone fireplace I could have entered without bumping my head on the mantel. One was standing, no more than five-five and slight of build. His black hair ran to medium length, parted on the right side but so straight it didn't quite lie flat against his skull. A long-sleeved rugby shirt swam on his torso over shiny athletic pants that had a designer logo stitched into one pocket. It was more his features that caught you, however. Vietnamese, I'd have bet, with piercing eyes that didn't smile despite the nod and upturning of the corners of his mouth. I ballparked his age at early thirties.

When I looked into the face of the sitting man, I thought, Jesus Christ.

"Good to see you again, Lieutenant," said Nicolas Helides from the chair to the Asian man's right.

The voice was still there, the intonation a rounded baritone that caught your attention without having to demand it. But the words came out garbled, as though someone were pulling down his right cheek, making it into a jowl. That sagging cheek caused some of his teeth to show, both too pearly and too big for his mouth, kind of like a ventriloquist's dummy. His hairline had evolved into a long, narrow widow's peak, the hair itself gone a dusty gray though the eyebrows were still a bushy black. And the hands—large and strong in my memory—were both nearly skeletal, the right one crabbed enough that the fingernails nearly touched the underside of his wrist. Doing a quick calculation in my head, I realized that the Skipper would be only about seventy, but somehow he looked more reduced than the elderly man in the wheelchair at our departure lounge back in Boston.

I realized Helides was waiting for me to reply. "It's been a long time, Colonel."

"And nearly as long since I merited being called 'colonel,' though I appreciate the courtesy and would understand if the old way is more comfortable for you."

"Thank you, sir."

Helides gestured with his good hand. "Quite the view, eh?"

Until then, I hadn't looked to my left. Through a picture window twelve feet long and nearly as high, I could see a big yacht putting along the canal behind that moored sailboat. Even moving slowly, the yacht created a three-foot wake that rolled toward us.

Helides said, "The Intracoastal Waterway, Lieutenant. A water taxi could pick you up from here and deposit you at the Jackie Gleason Theater in Miami Beach, a good twenty-five miles south." He looked up at the Asian man. "Mother Goose, I'm forgetting my manners."

Mother Goose. The man who never cursed.

Helides gestured with the crabbed right hand. "This is Duy Tranh. He's been with me since the Fall."

I didn't have to ask whether the Skipper meant our prior autumn or the last helicopter out of Saigon in seventy-five. "Pleased to meet you. Is 'Tranh' your family or given name?"

"We can talk about that when you have a paper and pencil so you can get it right."

His accent gave the words a clucky overlay, but the man spoke without inflection, so I couldn't tell quite how insulting he was trying to be.

"Stroke," said Helides.

I turned back to him.

He waved with the good hand this time. "Thought you should know. Happened in the summer, out on Court One at the tennis club. Went to swing my backhand and remember the green clay surface coming up to hit me instead. Had a greenish-purple tint to my chin till Christmas, something about the dye in the clay." Helides exhaled through his nose. "Not the worst news, either. When I woke up in the hospital, the whole right side of my body was paralyzed."

I pictured the Skipper in action—in virtually constant motion—during the nightmarish time of Tet. Then I pictured that poor man at the airport departure lounge again, watching the debate over his coffee, and I think I realized for a moment how humiliating this scene had to be for Helides.

He said, "They call them 'brain attacks' now."

"Sir?"

"Strokes. I suppose to remove some sort of stigma, make the brain seem more like just another organ subject to nature's aggression. Heart attack, gall bladder attack." The Skipper paused. "Every minute in this country somebody suffers a stroke. Every four minutes, somebody dies from one. There's even an 800 number for those of us who survive, and a few, like me, regain some degree of . . ."

He raised the crabbed hand again, a tremor passing through it.

To change the subject, I said, "Justo mentioned you wanted to see me . . . professionally."

Helides shot his eyes up at the lawyer.

Justo shrugged. "I followed your instructions, Colonel, and I am sure Pepe did as well."

The Skipper came back to me. "They told you nothing about my problem?"

"Nothing."

"And you don't know about it from the media jackals?"

"Only what I saw a few minutes ago in front of your gate."

Helides changed the focal point of his eyes somehow, and I felt as though I were a side of beef being scanned by an experienced meat inspector. He said, "Something's wrong, isn't it?"

"Sir, I've just been out of touch for a while."

The Skipper wasn't buying that, but his eyes changed again, as though he needed other answers. "My older son is Spi—short for 'Spiro'—Held."

I didn't get it, and Helides clearly expected that I would. "Your son changed his last name?"

Justo said, "John?"

"Yes?"

"The news coverage on the killing of Very Held."

"Her name was 'Veronica,' Lieutenant."

"Sorry, sir," said Justo.

I must still have looked like a dunce to the Skipper, because he said, "My son's daughter, Veronica, was . . . performing as the singer in his rock-and-roll band, 'Spiral.' She died in this house on my birthday."

Rock band and . . . "Your granddaughter was the little girl who drowned in a pool?"

Helides flared. "No, Lieutenant, she did not 'drown.' She *was* drowned, and not in *a* pool, but in *my* pool. And I would greatly appreciate your helping me identify the . . . bastard who did that to my family."

The first time I could ever remember the Skipper cursing.

Justo had just finished helping Tranh make drinks for all four of us. I sat in a brass-tacked, red-leather chair, Justo on its matching couch. The Skipper had never left his seat, and Tranh remained standing, having taken one small sip after his boss had raised his glass in the good left hand and said, "To old soldiers."

I lowered the vodka/rocks in my crystal tumbler. "Colonel, are you sure you want to hire one as a private investigator?"

To drink, Helides tilted both his glass and his head slightly to the left, enlisting gravity in the fight against the slack right cheek. "I've tried everything else. Lieutenant?"

Justo took his cue. "John, the Colonel has met with the investigating officers on the police force and spoken with the State's Attorney's office, our prosecutor here. He has even—"

"—hired a profiler," finished Helides. "As in that horrible JonBenet Ramsey situation from Colorado. Golly Moses, Lieutenant, the man charged me fifteen thousand dollars to generate a report that said we should be looking for some orphaned drifter driving an old station wagon."

I said, "Who may have broken in here?"

"What?" said the Skipper, clearly confused.

Slowing down a little, I chose my next words carefully. "From the things I've heard about profiling, the killer is usually a loner who wanders a great deal, partly for his own reasons, partly to throw off any—"

"You don't understand, Lieutenant," from Helides, shaking his head in a motion that more resembled a shudder. "Veronica wasn't killed by some transient maniac peeping through a window." The Skipper swallowed hard. "She was murdered by someone attending my . . . birthday party." Now just a hollow stare, the right side of his face like a Halloween mask. "By an invited guest in my home."

I gave it a long beat before, "Colonel, I think you could do better hiring someone other than me for this."

"I don't, and I'll tell you why." Helides straightened himself in the chair. "After retiring from the service, I went into investment advising. I even took my own advice, to the point where I don't need it anymore. I have a lot of money, Lieutenant. For present purposes, an unlimited amount.

Which can be a dangerous . . . distraction in South Florida."

"Distraction?" I said.

"Yes. That profiler only confirmed what I already suspected, that I'd be seen as a doddering old fool who could be ripped off by any charlatan offering his snake oil with some snappy patter. I need an investigator I can trust absolutely, someone who'll treat me loyally rather than royally."

Out of the corner of my eye, I thought Tranh flinched at that. Then I looked over to Justo. "Sir, it seems that you have the right person already."

"Agreed, but only for certain aspects of this situation. Lieutenant Vega is an excellent lawyer with exceptional judgment, but he hasn't been an investigator since our time in Saigon together." A pause. "Also, he has a family himself."

I wasn't sure I understood that one. "Meaning?"

The Skipper sighed, the right side of his lip flapping a bit, some spittle running down onto his chin. As Tranh moved toward him, Helides swiped at it with the back of his good hand, then swiped again. "Blasted stroke, makes me drool like an infant." He refocused on me. "Lieutenant, I'm more than a little concerned that any investigation I commission could make the killer take another life."

I turned that over. "Another reason to stay with the police investigators already assigned to the case. Not many killers would go after a badge."

The Skipper closed his eyes a moment, the right lid fluttering when he reopened them. "Lieutenant, the police have had this case for over a week, and if they are telling me the truth, they've discovered nothing. I need a fresh approach, and I need it . . ." Another hard swallow. ". . . soon."

I was pretty sure that this time I got what he meant. "Colonel—"

"At least let me walk you through what we believe must have happened. Then decide."

I owed Nicolas Helides that much. And a lot more.

THREE

Since the stroke, I pretty much confine myself to the downstairs rooms."

Not hard to understand, as I followed the Skipper and Duy Tranh along a wood-paneled corridor, Justo staying behind in the den. Like someone with polio, Helides grasped a single aluminum brace in his left hand, but he used it more as a ski pole than a crutch, pointing it forward and then vaulting a little when its white rubber tip made contact with the beige carpet.

"And now to the right."

The Skipper turned as he said the words, that dank smell of chlorine noticeable as I reached the branching hallway. The carpeting gave way to tile laid in a blue and ivory checkerboard pattern, and Helides preceded me into a gleaming, humid space with a glass wall on the side facing the Intracoastal and the moored sailboat. We moved more deliberately on the damp tiles, coming to a stop near the end of a pool that was Olympic-size in length and four lanes across.

"Before the stroke, I used to swim every day. Now Duy helps me walk through the water at the shallower end. Physical therapy for the muscles that still work." The Skipper pointed his wobbling brace at the far corner of the pool—the northeast one, if the Intracoastal ran due south by the house. "Veronica was found there."

"By who, Colonel?"

"By me," said Tranh.

I glanced at him, got a neutral stare from the dark eyes. "How long had she been missing from the party?"

Helides shook his head. "Not that kind of a party, Lieutenant. Not so formal, I mean. People drifted in and around the house all afternoon, and just about everyone had been in the pool at some point before Duy came in here."

I looked away from Helides. "Were you going for a swim yourself?"

Tranh maintained the neutral stare. "No."

"You just happened to—"

"I realized the Colonel's granddaughter had not been in my sight for some time. I thought I should look for her without alarming anyone."

"Veronica wasn't a good swimmer?"

"The Colonel's granddaughter was an excellent swimmer," said Tranh. "But she was also a thirteen-year-old girl who would run about, and the floor here can be slippery."

"So you were afraid she'd had an accident."

"I was not afraid. Only concerned."

"And when you found her?"

"From here I saw her bathing suit on the edge of the pool."

"You saw her suit before you noticed Veronica?"

"I noticed it first. It was . . . neon chartreuse, in the pattern of a tiger's skin."

Something in my reaction made Helides break in. "I told you my son Spiro was using Veronica in his band."

"Spiral."

"Yes. Apparently Spiro commissioned a series of outfits—provocative outfits—for her to help with their 'comeback.' But the police believe the bathing suit was off her that day because she'd been . . . molested."

Nobody said anything for a moment.

The Skipper spoke his next words in a monotone. "The autopsy gave reason to believe that she was raped while the killer held her underwater."

Quietly, I said, "Forensic evidence?"

Helides shook his head. "The chlorinated water—and Duy's efforts to save Veronica—destroyed what might have . . ." Suddenly, the Skipper sounded very tired. "The police can give you any further . . . details."

I went back to Tranh. "A minute ago, you said you'd noticed Veronica's bathing suit before seeing her body."

"Correct."

"So, you believed she was dead?"

"Veronica was facedown in the pool and not moving."

"What did you do then?"

"I jumped into the water and swam to her. When I pulled her out, she was not breathing, so I ran to the phone. There."

Tranh tipped his head toward an arrangement of patio furniture and wicker sideboard with some towels the colors of the tiles. I could see a cordless phone on one of the wicker shelves.

Without looking back at Tranh, I said, "You didn't try to give Veronica CPR?"

"I was never trained to do it."

Now I turned my face back toward his. Throughout my questioning, I couldn't remember Tranh so much as blinking.

"Lieutenant?"

I glanced at the Skipper. "Sorry, Colonel."

"Don't apologize for doing your job."

Helides said it in a way that sounded like a hint. I glanced around the room, finally seeing the bracketed mount high on the wall behind us.

A video camera. "You have the attack on tape?"

Helides shook his head. "The camera was generally engaged, as a safety monitor on anyone in the pool. However, that day it had been turned off."

"Why?"

"Buford Biggs—one of the players in Spiro's band—has a son who is intrigued by filmmaking. Kalil wanted to take footage of the party toward editing it into a video."

"I don't understand, Colonel. Wouldn't that mean the camera up there should have been working?"

"No," said Helides, sounding even more tired. "No, Kalil—and Veronica—wanted only his *own* footage."

"So, no tape from the pool camera."

"Nor from any of the others in the house."

I looked to the glass wall, steamed by ambient humidity to the point of being translucent instead of transparent. "And no one on the waterway or across it would be able to see in here."

"That's right. In the winter, we keep the door closed."

"The door?"

"That glass expanse is more door than window, Lieutenant. It's designed to allow the entire pool to be used in summer."

"What do you mean by 'entire'?" I said.

"You're looking at only half the surface area. The rest is outdoors, the glass wall dividing the warmer, interior water from the colder exterior."

I stared at the point where the glass wall met and extended down into the water, seeming to be sealed shut against the bottom of the pool. "Can the wall be opened?"

"Only from the inside," said Helides.

I was about to say something more when a subtle, skittering sound came from behind us. I turned around but didn't see anyone.

The Skipper spoke to me. "That was just David."

"David?"

"My other son. He's younger than Spiro by ten years. Nina . . ." A twinge of pain crossed the good side of his face. "Their mother died bearing him."

"Where does David live?"

"Here."

"He came home to be with you?"

"What?" said Helides, another look of confusion replacing the pained one.

"After your granddaughter died, your son came here to be with you?"

A tone more tired than any so far. "David never left home, Lieutenant."

Before I could ask why, Nicolas Helides shivered. "It's chilly here. Let's go back to the library."

Afternoon sunlight slanted through the big window opposite the fireplace, near where Justo Vega was speaking quietly into the telephone, his shoulders rolling a little with his internal music. Tranh repositioned the Skipper's chair so that the rays from outside fell across the old man's torso without shining in his eyes. Even so, a plaid stadium blanket materialized from behind another chair, Tranh spreading it over Helides's legs.

The Skipper waited until he was finished, then motioned me to the brass-tacked couch. "The party was on January eleventh, a Sunday. Because my pool is indoors, we held it here so people could enjoy themselves despite the cold weather. The television forecasters say this winter's so lousy because of El Niño. You getting any consequences of that up by you?"

"Yes," I said, trying not to show any further reaction.

Helides just nodded. "Well, we'd had a fine time. Wet bar, buffet, a lot of people playing in the pool. Veronica even sang 'Happy Birthday' to me, sitting on my lap, before everybody else joined in for a verse." The Skipper shivered again, as he had in the pool area, then cleared his throat. "The house was teeming with guests who all knew each other. Nobody could have gained access past Umberto without being noticed as a stranger."

"Who's Umberto?"

"The security guard at the gate. Cuban despite that blond crewcut. He arrived during the Marielito boatlift, enlisted in the army, and came out an MP, too. Made something of himself, and a good man."

I glanced at Justo, but he didn't give me any signals. "Umberto's last name?"

"Reyes," said the Skipper. "He's Delgis's brother."

"Dell-*hees*?"

Justo spelled it for me. "She was the au pair for Veronica, John. Delgis lives at Spiro Held's house."

I thought about the granddaughter being thirteen. "Wasn't Veronica a little old to need an au pair?"

"I didn't think so," said Helides.

Topic closed, I guessed. "And Delgis was here for the party?"

"Yes."

"Umberto the only security?"

"My other security man—Jack Byrne, also an ex-MP— had moved to Tampa, take care of his aunt."

"That's been verified?"

"By the police here and there," said Justo. "No way Mr. Byrne could have committed the crime."

"And his being away was known to the people you'd invited?"

The Skipper nodded. "We'd talked about Jack having to leave for—oh, a few weeks, anyway."

"Who actually attended the party?"

"Spiro and his wife, Jeanette. The other members of his band."

I tried to dredge up what little information I'd retained about Spiral from twenty-some years before. The couple of hits the band had enjoyed. Some crazy drummer, and "Spi Held" as lead singer. "I never knew he was your son, Colonel."

"While I was overseas, Spiro ran away from the housekeeper I'd hired after his mother died. He was only fifteen, but it was the late sixties, remember, so a lot of kids just disappeared into the hippie/rock culture." Helides seemed able to speak about it without any bitterness clinging to his garbled words. "Spiro came to South Florida and changed his name—supposedly to distance himself from me and the 'establishment' I represented, but more I think to make him marketable as 'Spi,' founder of 'Spiral,' rather than the offspring of Greek immigrants."

Some irony in the voice now, but still no bitterness. "Anyone else at the party that we haven't talked about?"

Justo said, "I can give you a list, John, with names, addresses, and telephones. But the band's manager was also here. And Mrs. Helides."

I looked at the Skipper. "You remarried?"

"Yes. You may as well know now, Lieutenant. My wife's name is Cassandra, and her tennis instructor came to the party as well."

Some bitterness now. "This tennis pro—"

"Lieutenant?" said Helides, but not to me.

Justo seemed uncomfortable. "His name is Cornel Radescu. From Romania, originally."

I didn't say anything.

The Skipper nodded. "You find it a bit odd that my wife's tennis instructor would be attending her husband's birthday party, don't you?"

After a moment, I said, "Yes."

A crooked smile, only the left side of his face changing. "I'm glad you still have the capacity for speaking awkward truths, Lieutenant. But in fact, it was Veronica who insisted that Mr. Radescu be invited to my party."

"Your granddaughter?"

"Cassandra had been taking Veronica to tennis lessons at the club we belong to, and Veronica had grown to like Mr. Radescu enormously." A pause. "When you meet him, I think you'll see why."

"No other family at the party?"

Now sadness. "David, briefly."

When Helides didn't continue, I tilted my head toward the man standing next to him. "And Mr. Tranh."

The Skipper grew a little stern. "In fact, Lieutenant, I do consider Duy 'family,' but we'd already mentioned his attendance."

I let that leach from the air for a minute before saying, "Colonel, what happened here is a tragedy. If you're right about the security aspect, the killer does have to be somebody invited to the party. But since that's a finite list, I still don't see what I can do for you that the police can't."

Justo said, "Everybody has lawyered up, John."

I looked at him.

Helides said, "My 'guests' took their lesson from the Ramsey case in Colorado, Lieutenant. Everyone has hired an attorney, or refuses to speak to the police without one."

"And that's . . . working for them?"

Justo shook his head. "The police cannot force any of the people here that day to speak with them, because each can reasonably claim to be a suspect."

"Lieutenant Vega, I find the use of the word 'reasonably' to be offensive in this context."

"Sorry, sir."

"Colonel," I said, "offensive or not, if the police can't crack the circle, what makes you think I can?"

Helides came back to me. "There wasn't a man, woman, or child at that party who isn't beholden to my fortune for a significant part of his or her well-being. I've offered each a simple choice: Speak with my chosen investigator privately, or have the resources at my disposal devoted to the destruction of the person involved."

Not bitterness now, nor irony. Just determination, a force of will that transcended the physical limitations imposed on him by the stroke.

I said, "Colonel, I'm not licensed in Florida, and even if I were, the police wouldn't tolerate my having access denied to them."

"Lieutenant, those resources of mine put a United States congressman and three state senators in their seats. Behind the scenes and quietly, but they know who buttered their bread for them. Mother *Goose*, if they can't hand-carry the application for a private investigator's license through the bureaucracy, I'll see to it they don't get to take home with them so much as a paper clip when they lose the next election."

Quietly, I said, "That still leaves the police problem."

Helides grew still, almost serene. "The police 'problem' is that in nearly two weeks, they have not found diddly, because I've received personal briefings every other day. We were MPs together in Saigon, Lieutenant Cuddy. You know what the passage of so much time does to the odds of their ever determining who killed my granddaughter, much less being able to prove it in a court of law."

"Colonel, at best the police would wait till I'd gathered information they want themselves, then subpoena me to provide it."

"Lieutenant Vega can protect you in court, though I'm

not sure I'd mind your sharing what you'll have learned with the police. And we have ten thousand in cash for you, plus a credit card in your name and a cellular phone. Duy?"

How Tranh brought the things into his own hands without my noticing, I don't know, but there were the stack of bills, the card, and a tiny black object with a corded socket adaptor, held out in his palms like the proverbial horn of plenty.

"I don't think I—"

"Lieutenant." The Skipper cleared his throat again. "Please?"

A word I'd never heard Colonel Nicolas Helides use before.

I looked from Justo Vega to Duy Tranh before returning to the Skipper. Watching his eyes, I thought of standing at Beth's graveside the night before, about her thoughts on my being spared from Nancy's flight for a purpose.

Helides just watched me back. He'd said all he could on the subject, and he knew I realized that.

"I'll do my best to help you, Colonel."

A tear trickled down the sagging right side of his face. "Thank you, Lieutenant Cuddy. For my granddaughter's memory."

"Mr. Vega said he will be back to take you to dinner tonight. He also will arrange for you to see the police tomorrow. But now, the Colonel wishes me to show you the rest of his house for . . . orientation purposes."

Duy Tranh spoke the words like a jaded tour guide. He and I were standing by ourselves in the corridor outside the den, the Skipper feeling he needed some rest after reliving "his birthday."

"Mr. Tranh, when I asked you those questions in the

pool area, I wasn't trying to single you out. Anyone investigating a homicide would focus first on the person finding the body."

"Do you wish to start with a certain place in the house, or just have me take you around?"

Tranh's tone hadn't changed. "I was thinking of a given room."

"Which, please?"

"Yours."

A faint twitching of the lips, almost a smug smile, as if he knew all along that's where I'd begin. "Come."

I followed him down the corridor to a staircase and up that to the second floor. He took a key from the pocket of his athletic pants and stuck it in the knob of the first door we came to.

"You keep your room locked?"

"I often have important papers of the Colonel in my suite."

His suite.

As Tranh swung the door open for me, though, I saw he wasn't kidding.

The large room had a living area partioned by a low bookcase, a collection of exotic knives on the longest wall. To the right of the shelves were a love seat and an armchair separated from each other by a coffee table. Off to the left, the floorplan dog-legged right and back to create a sleeping L with a nice double window over the bed. Next to the bed was a fairly elaborate computer system occupying a hutch designed to hold all the different components. The bathroom door was ajar, two towels hanging from their rack next to a shower stall that looked big enough for a barbershop quartet.

"Nice digs," I said.

"The Colonel is a generous man living in a large house."

"Can we sit a while?"

Tranh motioned me to the love seat. He took the arm-chair.

I pointed at the computer. "What do you use that for?"

"The usual things."

"How about some details?"

Tranh watched me for a moment. "You do not know much about computers, do you?"

"Honestly? No."

He said, "Then I am probably not skilled enough to explain them to you."

"Mr. Tranh, let's cut the shit and talk about what you use that computer setup for."

The smug smile, maybe his reward to himself for getting a rise out of me. "Surfing the Net, crawling the Web. E-mail, data- and word-processing, spreadsheet analysis—I notice you are not taking notes. Should I go on?"

"What kind of work do you do for the Colonel?"

"On the computer?"

Disingenuous. "Overall."

"I am his personal assistant." Tranh began ticking his duties off raised fingers. "I coordinate the household here. I maintain the Colonel's checkbook. I help him in the online execution of his investment decisions. I replace physically some of the faculties he lost due to his stroke." Tranh had reached his pinkie finger. "And I am his confidant, because while I am not blood, I am family."

The Skipper had said as much downstairs. "How did you come to know Colonel Helides?"

"In Vietnam. My father served as an undercover 'operative' for Colonel Helides in the black market. A 'business rival' assassinated him just before the fall of Saigon to the Communists. They would have put me into a re-education camp, but the Colonel felt he owed something to my father, and so I was brought to the United States and raised in the Colonel's home."

"This home?"

"Not originally," said Tranh. "The Colonel built here only after Mrs. . . . After he married his second wife, Cassandra. We moved to Florida twenty-two years ago."

"So you've been with Colonel Helides . . . ?"

". . . since I was six years old. He became my surrogate father, putting me through secondary school and university."

"Where?"

"P.M.I. and V.M.I."

Both military schools. "You went into the service, then?"

"No."

I gave Tranh a chance to follow that up. When he didn't, I said, "How come?"

"I have an arrhythmic heart, Mr. Cuddy, but it was not discovered until I collapsed during a soccer game my senior year of college."

I glanced up at the wall of knives. "Is that when you began collecting?"

Tranh followed my eyes. "Yes, though not all of those are merely decorative." He pointed toward a matched trio of quarter-moons about a foot long each, made of something like tungsten steel, with different diameter circular holes in the handles. "Those, for example, are for throwing."

"Which doesn't hurt your heart?"

"Mr. Cuddy, we can learn to live with all kinds of limitations."

"And you help Colonel Helides live with his."

A pause, like Tranh was measuring something on the inside before responding. "The Colonel has not been lucky in the children his first wife bore him. Spiro—the one who calls himself 'Spi'—came back to his father only when money was needed. David has never been able to leave."

The Skipper had mentioned that in the pool area. "Why?"

"Why does David still live with us?"

"Yes."

Another measured pause. "David is chronically, clinically depressed, Mr. Cuddy. He has never been able to . . . function normally in the world. So, we—and now I—must take care of him."

Interesting, but maybe more interesting was the way Tranh identified with Helides in the royal "we" format. "David's under a doctor's care?"

"Yes, a psychiatrist. More so now."

"Now?"

"Since Veronica's death. Even with Dr. Forbes at the party, David was very upset by the incident, and by the police interrogating him afterward."

"I don't recall Colonel Helides mentioning this doctor as one of the guests."

"Since his stroke, the Colonel does not always remember every detail."

As I thought about that, Tranh said, "If you wish to see David's psychiatrist, it can be arranged."

"What about patient confidentiality?"

"The Colonel can pierce that."

I wouldn't bet against it. "Mr. Tranh, what do you think happened here that day?"

A long stare, the man gauging something that required a string of discreet measurements. "I believe that someone very carefully planned the killing of a very difficult girl."

"Difficult how?"

"Perhaps it would be best for us to start with the 'careful plan' first."

I decided to let him have his head. "Whatever you think best."

Duy Tranh rose gracefully from the armchair. "Come."

* * *

"The Colonel refers to this as 'Central Control.'"

We had walked back downstairs and now stood outside a solid-looking door, Tranh fishing another key from his pocket. He used it on a lock about a foot above the knob.

As the door swung open, you might have thought you'd stumbled into a television studio. Monitors ringed the level just below the ceiling, several chairs and desktop machines positioned at various angles. The monitor screens showed different intersections of the house, both interior and exterior.

I said, "The video cameras must be pretty well camouflaged."

"Because you did not notice them?"

A subtle challenge there. "Partly. They record as well as display?"

"Usually." Tranh passed his hand over a vertical stack of VCRs.

I moved toward them. "Meaning, not always."

"The Colonel has already explained to you about his acceding to Kalil's request."

"On the interior locations. But only because Veronica insisted."

"Yes."

Again nonjudgmental in tone, though the curtness of his response seemed to carry Tranh's seal of disapproval. I said, "How about the exterior cameras?"

"All functioning perfectly."

"And showing nothing unusual during the party?"

"Correct."

I glanced back at the door Tranh had opened for us. "This room kept locked?"

"Unless someone is inside it, as we are now."

"And who has access?"

"If you mean by key, I have one, the security staff—Mr.

Jack Byrne and Mr. Umberto Reyes—each were given one, and of course the Colonel has his own."

"So somebody with a key—or access to one—could have tampered with the external video stations."

A slight shrug. "Yes, but not with the tapes recorded from each."

"Because?"

Tranh glanced at the stack of VCRs. "Each camera is chronometered by day, date, and military time. None of the videos had been altered, according to the police, who told us they examined each rather carefully."

"So the external ones show—"

"—precisely what our outside security, Mr. Umberto Reyes, maintains. That no one entered the grounds during the party."

"Up till the time you found Veronica dead."

"Correct."

I looked around the room again. "Who knew about Kalil wanting to shoot his home movie?"

Tranh gave me his smug little smile. "I believe everyone. It was announced with the invitations weeks before."

"Announced as in printed on something?"

"No, nothing so formal. Everyone was simply told the party would be 'filmed' that way."

"And that the other, security cameras on the inside of the house would be turned off?"

"If not everyone was told directly, everyone could have heard about it."

I watched Tranh. "Which is your 'careful plan' part."

He watched me, too. "Yes. Whoever killed Veronica had carefully planned her death for the one time many people would be *in* the house without being watched *by* the house."

"You also said in your suite that she was a 'very difficult' girl."

"I did."

"Difficult how?"

Tranh paused. "Veronica had learned too much too quickly."

"About what?"

"How to get what she believed she wanted."

"Like having her grandfather order the interior cameras turned off during his party?"

Duy Tranh paused again, then said, "Perhaps you should speak with Mr. Umberto Reyes now."

FOUR

We walked through the house and out the front door toward the gate. The guy in the blond crew-cut was standing next to his little security gazebo, most of the media and gawkers gone from the street.

Duy Tranh waited until we were an arm's length away from the guard before saying, "Mr. Umberto Reyes, this is Mr. John Cuddy. The Colonel has hired him to look into the death of Veronica."

"I know."

Reyes's lips barely moved as he looked at Tranh, and I got the distinct impression there was no love lost between them.

I turned to Tranh myself. "Thanks for your help so far, but I think I can take it from here."

He hesitated, then said, "Please advise me if you need anything further."

When Duy Tranh disappeared around a corner of the house, I turned back to Reyes. "I'm told you were in the MPs, too."

"That's right."

Still terse, any accent buried. "Then we both know there are two ways of doing this."

Reyes moved his tongue around inside his cheek. "I'm 'Umberto' by birthname, but you can call me 'Berto.'"

"And I prefer John."

I stuck out my hand, and we shook on the truce. Reyes let me speak next, though.

"Tell me about the day Veronica Held was killed."

"You want overview first, then detail?"

I nodded.

He took a breath. "Big picture, a lot of people came on the grounds for the party, but once they got here, they all stayed inside the house because of the cold, and nobody else came in behind them."

"Or around them, Berto?"

Reyes pointed to the gazebo. "I've got six video monitors in there. Small screens, but they do the job. Four exterior corners, two interior intersections. Since both the interior cameras were nonoperational—you been told why?"

"Yes."

"Okay, that left me just the four exterior ones, and I knew everybody who came through that gate for the party."

"Meaning?"

"Meaning I just had to glance up at their faces to recognize them."

"So, you didn't have to spend much time looking away from the screens."

"Right. Nobody else came in. Or out."

"None of the guests left early?"

"Or even went outside. Like I said, it was cold that day."

"How cold, Berto?"

"Fifty, maybe even forty-five."

Everything's relative, but at least Reyes was warming up

to me a little. "You pretty familiar with the video monitor-
ing equipment in Central Control?"

"We had the same system, my last post in the service."

"And?"

"Worked fine back then, worked fine that day."

"You keep a guest list for the party?"

"Negative, man. Like I told you before, I knew everybody."

"Can you name them?"

Reyes reeled off a dozen or so, both first and last, some I
recognized from my talks with the Skipper. Impressive, or
well rehearsed. "How about your logbook?"

"The police took the entry page for that day. Evidence."

I was about to ask him if he'd copied it first when a
Porsche Boxster convertible screeched to a halt outside the
gate and a young woman with platinum hair leaned into
the horn on the wheel in front of her. Through the car's
windshield I could see opaque blue sunglasses and a wide,
Kewpie-doll frown.

"Berto, you bastard, open this fucking gate."

Reyes took a long, slow step toward the gazebo, and then
he flicked at something. The gate swung outward, and the
woman burned a little rubber moving her car the twenty
feet to where we were standing.

She wore a placket-collared shirt over a tennis skirt that
rode about eighty percent of the way up her thighs. The
veined hands and facial lines also brought her a little closer
to forty than to twenty. "And just who might you be?"

"John Cuddy."

"Ah, Nick's dick from Boston. You'll want to talk with
me. Duy can guide you to my suite."

The woman took off, leaving a little more tread on the
driveway as she spun the convertible around the corner of
the house toward the garage doors.

I said to Reyes. "Let me guess. She refers to herself as 'moi,' too."

"And to the rest of the world as 'bastards.'"

"Well, she's got some standing to be upset."

Reyes looked at me oddly. "I don't get you."

"The woman just lost her daughter."

Umberto Reyes started to grin, then iced it. "That's not Jeanette Held."

"It isn't?"

"Uh-unh. That's Mrs. Cassandra Helides, the Colonel's wife."

I just closed my eyes.

"You found your way."

I'd knocked on the door at the end of a second-floor corridor, and Cassandra Helides's voice had told me to come through it. She stood hip-cocked—and nearly six feet tall—in front of a four-poster bed, wearing a powder-blue terry-cloth robe with some emblem on the left breast.

Helides said, "I've got to take a shower, or I'll be late for a drinks date. Sit down and you can yell to me through the sliding glass door."

"That might be kind of awkward."

Without the sunglasses, her eyes were big, white showing around both irises. "Then maybe you should join me?"

I gave it a beat. "That would be more than awkward, Mrs. Helides."

She wagged her head, the tip of her tongue sticking out between her lips. "My Nick sure can pick them."

I wasn't thinking the same thing.

Helides stood hip-cocked a moment longer. "So sit. Won't be two minutes."

She broke the pose and swayed under the robe, entering

the bathroom without closing the door. As water began drumming against tiles in the other room, I moved to a chair and looked around me.

Helides had a suite with the same floor plan as Tranh's but maybe a third again as large. The living area where I sat included pink upholstered chairs and a settee that might have been an antique but struck me as schlock. The color motif was carried over to the four-poster, the cloth skirting the box spring bordered with white lace, though the pink bedclothes themselves lay tousled, pillows at domino angles to each other. Full-length mirrors rose on either side of a walk-in closet, and the wall paintings were all of flamingos. The entertainment center contained components of so many sizes and shapes, I could identify only about half by function.

"Told you I could do it quickly when I had to."

Turning toward the bathroom again, I realized I couldn't hear the water anymore. Cassandra Helides's platinum hair was plastered against her skull, and she wore only a large towel wrap this time, her breasts pushing forward more dramatically through the tucked towel than they had under the robe.

Helides smiled slyly. "Caught you, didn't I?"

"Caught me?"

"Licking your chops over my little babies here. Want to see the wonders modern surgery can wreck?"

I guessed she meant "wreak." "You always come on this strong?"

Helides pouted, the lips seeming glossed. "Strong is what I never was before."

"Before what?"

"Before marrying Nick." She stopped and pouted again, putting a bit more into it. "No, that's not right. It was after I seduced him but before I married him that I felt it."

"Felt what?"

Her sly smile again. "The power." Helides raked a hand through wet hair. "I've got to dry this, but the portable's pretty quiet. So, what can I tell you?"

As she rummaged through the unmade bedclothes, I said, "You're the one who said I'd want to talk with you."

Helides turned back around, a Star-Wars appliance in her right hand. She clicked something on it, and the thing came to life, even though I didn't see any cord running to a socket.

"About who killed Very, right?"

"Your husband seems to prefer 'Veronica.'"

Helides began running the snout of the dryer back and forth across her hair. "Nick's 'preferences' aren't exactly uttermost in my mind."

Another Norm Crosby malaprop, for "uppermost" this time, but I decided to go with the spirit. "And why is that?"

A theatrical shrug. "You ever see the TV shows about the old bastards playing softball?"

"I'm sorry?"

"They're all over the place down here, especially on the Gulf Coast. The geezers have leagues, uniforms, and all that other guy stuff."

"Must have missed the coverage."

"Yeah, well, let me tell you then. They pull on those cleats and pick up a bat, they think they're kids again. Or at least young. But you watch them take a swing or try to run the bases, and it's pathetic, you know?"

"Pathetic."

"Yeah." She switched the dryer to her other hand. "That's kind of my problem, too."

"Your problem?"

"Nick. When I married him, it was like I got a new daddy, but one with real money who I could sleep with and not have it be some kind of crime."

Christ. "You married the Colonel for his money."

Another switch of the dryer. "Hey, even the sex wasn't bad at first. Only problem is, when you marry your father, nobody warns you that ten years later you'll be stuck with your grandfather, you know?"

From what Duy Tranh had given me as chronology, I thought it had to be over twenty years, but I also didn't want to hear any more on the subject. "Maybe if you'd tell me what you can about Veronica's death, I won't make you late for your date."

"Oh, I don't know." The sly smile. "That might be kind of fun."

"What might?"

She clicked off the dryer. "You making me late for my date."

Relentless. "Veronica's death?"

Helides tossed the dryer back onto the bedclothes. "I don't know anything about it."

"What?"

She turned and shook her head like a horse does to settle its mane. "You deaf? I don't know a fucking thing about it. I got drunk pretty early that day."

"Why?"

"Hey, Nick living out another birthday isn't exactly a reason for me to celebrate, you know?"

I spoke slowly. "But you told me out in the driveway that I should talk with you."

"That was just a fucking line, boytoy. When did you fall off the turkey truck?"

"'Turnip truck,'" I said before standing up and walking away.

From by the bed, Cassandra Helides asked, almost meekly, "You sure it's not 'turkey'?"

* * *

As I closed her door behind me, I registered a flash of movement in my peripheral vision. By the time I turned my head, I had only one frame of a man with shaggy hair in dark clothes disappearing around the corner to the stairway.

"Just a second," I called out. When I didn't hear any footfalls on the steps, I went over to them. Empty, and no other sounds I could hear.

At the bottom of the stairway, I got my bearings and walked through the living room toward the corridor leading to the den. From the door, I could see Justo, speaking into a telephone, the Skipper sitting in the same chair again, Duy Tranh standing at his side.

"Lieutenant Cuddy," said Helides in his garbled voice. There was something in his eyes that told me he wasn't completely in the present. Then I noticed his hands on the binder of a photo album in his lap.

"Colonel."

"Come in, please. Duy and I were just looking at some old photos from our time over there."

I approached them, Helides using the good hand to swing the album toward me on his bent knees.

He said, "A shot of you and Lieutenant Vega."

One look, and I remembered. It was during the Tet Offensive, probably somewhere into our twentieth hour on duty that night, some jerk from *Stars and Stripes* magazine snapping pictures of us coming in off Tu Do Street and appearing impossibly young. I had the blood of a private first class all over me, an MP whose name I never got because most of him had been blown away before I pulled him into the relative safety of an alley mouth. Justo was forced to empty his forty-five into two of the "enemy" rushing us with grenades, neither of the kids more than twelve years old. I could recall seeing the photographer, grinning from ear to ear as he got a shot he was sure would bring him some kind of prize. Or maybe just a ticket home.

If the Skipper hadn't been there, I would have taken that jerk's camera strap and—

"Lieutenant," said Helides, "I'm the one who's supposed to be going senile."

"Sorry, sir."

A different expression came over the good side of his face, the black, bushy eyebrow arcing in concern. "Are you all right?"

"Just kind of a flashback."

The Skipper nodded once, chin almost touching his chest. "We all have them. One way or another." Then he straightened in the chair. "Have you satisfied yourself that the killer had to be someone invited here?"

"Almost."

"Meaning?"

"I was pretty much convinced until I just saw a man on the second floor that I couldn't account for."

Justo hung up the phone and joined us. "A man?"

"Shaggy hair, dark clothes. He got a look at me, then—"

"David," said the Skipper. "My son's painfully . . . shy. From his depressive condition." Helides inclined his head toward Tranh. "I've instructed Duy to have David's doctor speak with you. Henry Forbes is from an old-line family down here, and he's a third-generation psychiatrist himself. Once you've talked with Henry, you can approach David."

Approach. "If that's what you think best, Colonel."

"I believe it's what Henry will. The business with the police investigators threw David into an episode. His behavior with you just now, for example."

I caught myself stifling a yawn.

"Lieutenant, I must be slipping. We're not the young soldiers we used to be, eh?" The Skipper looked to Justo. "If

you could take over, I think Lieutenant Cuddy would benefit from a good meal and a soft bed. Duy?"

Tranh moved smoothly to help Helides out of the chair
and onto the single brace. Arrhythmic heart or not, a sign of
significant strength under the rugby shirt and athletic pants.

The Skipper extended his good hand to me. "John
Cuddy, I'm much in your debt for deciding to help with
this tragedy."

For better or worse, we shook on it.

Justo Vega said, "I would take you to my house for dinner,
because Alicia is anxious to meet you, and our little girls
must be seen to be believed."

We were in his Cadillac coupe, a small Cuban flag
standing proudly on the dashboard, its fabric fluttering in
the breeze from the air vents. Justo maneuvered us over the
quaint little bridge spanning the canal and turned right
onto the boulevard Pepe had called "Las Olas."

"But you have had a long trip, John, and a longer day,
and Miami is at least an hour away during the best of rush
hours."

From the passenger's seat, I thought about the Skipper's
concern for attracting danger from his case to Justo's family.
All I said, though, was, "A raincheck, then."

"Only as to the home-cooking. Tonight we eat out, just
the two of us."

"Alicia won't mind?"

Justo glanced over at me. "She was one of my calls from
the Skipper's library."

"They do seafood well here, but many places in the area
can boast of that. And the baby-back ribs are to die for."

We were in a restaurant called Flanigan's, on that
Andrews Avenue divider road. It had light-wood walls, with

fishnet as hangings and small floats hooked into the nets. Photos of what appeared to be an extended family posed with various kinds of saltwater trophies on decks and docks. A blond waitress in a green polo shirt with the restaurant's name and a bearded man's face on the front took our order of a bucket of Killian's Irish Red and two full racks of ribs, with cole slaw.

Writing on her pad, she said, "Fries with that?"

There was a touch of Southern accent in her voice, but it was her choice of terms that made me begin to question Justo's choice of place. "They worth the cholesterol?"

"This is South Florida, hon'. Cholesterol's right up there with fruits and grains as one of our major food groups." But she was smiling wisely as she spoke the words.

"Fries, then. Thanks."

"You won't be sorry."

After she'd walked away, Justo said, "*Cubana*."

I looked in her direction. "How can you tell?"

"Those in the first generation born here have no Spanish accent, but neither do they develop the full Southern lilt."

I decided to take his word for it, then thought about the little flag on his dashboard. "Pepe talked with me about conditions on the island. How are things going here in South Florida?"

"For Cuban-Americans, you mean?"

"Yes."

The shoulders rose and fell an inch. "The census bureau says that in fifty years, one quarter of the United States population will be 'Hispanic,' but that is mostly because of the high birthrates among Mexican-Americans. *Cubanas* contribute only about two percent of those babies, so we will always be a small minority within a large minority. However, here in Florida, we prosper. Our own businesses, social circles, even country clubs. One of us was again the mayor of Miami, and he a graduate of the Harvard Law School. Those of my parents' generation—who gathered up their children and fled to this country when Castro's Revolution overwhelmed them—the old ones still dream of a *Cuba libre,* but those our age? We are Cuban-Americans, John, but now more the latter than the former."

"And the Marielitos?"

A small smile. "Some of us still think of them that way, but the bad criminals Castro inflicted on President Carter and this area are now mostly dead or in prison forever. And many of the others have become as successful as our generation of immigrants. It seems hard to believe, John, but the Marielitos have now been here nearly as long as my parents had been when the Marielitos arrived."

Justo was right. It was hard to believe that so much time had passed so quickly.

Our waitress arrived with the pitcher of red ale and poured about ten ounces into each frosted mug.

After she told us the ribs would be out shortly, I lifted my Killian's. Thinking of our time together in Saigon, I clinked the rim of my mug against Justo's. "To absent friends."

At which point, Nancy's loss hit me like a ton of bricks.

"And to present ones," said Justo, I think before he saw my face. "John, what is the matter?"

I debated inside for what was probably too long.

"John?"

I set down my mug without drinking from it. "Since Beth died, there's been only one other woman in my life."

"The assistant prosecutor you told me about the last time you were in Florida."

"Yes."

Justo sipped his ale. "Troubles?"

"She died, too."

He froze, the mug only halfway back to the table. "John, no."

"That plane crash, off San Francisco."

Justo blinked. "But the catastrophe was only . . . ten days ago?"

"More like twelve."

Finally, he set his mug down, too. "And yet, my friend, you are here."

"Because of the Skipper. Mostly, anyway. But partly also for a change of scene, to keep my mind occupied."

Reaching his right hand across the table, Justo squeezed my forearm. "Does the Skipper know about your loss?"

I shook my head. "I haven't told him, though I'm probably showing it."

"Only to one such as I, who has seen you recently."

Get off the subject. "Justo, a question about the case?"

"Of course."

"Anybody benefit financially from Veronica Held's death?"

Justo's turn to shake his head. "Not that I can see. Her presence in the band was an advantage to everyone, and any other money flows from the Colonel downward, not from his granddaughter upward."

"Another question then, about the Helides house."

"If I can answer it, I will. But remember, I was not there on the day of the party."

"I meant more about the current conditions."

Justo darkened a little. "Go on."

"Putting aside what we just talked about, I was basically propositioned by the Skipper's new wife."

Justo darkened more. "Not so 'new,' John. And not even 'news,' in its own right." He paused. "Did she invite you for a shower at her tennis apartment?"

"Her tennis . . . ?"

"Apartment. Cassandra—or the Skipper, as a matter of record—owns a condominium at the Tennis Club of Fort Lauderdale."

"She was wearing tennis clothes when I first saw her."

Justo nodded. "The woman . . . propositioned me as well. Some time ago." A frown. "Apparently, her shower there is . . . large enough for two."

I pictured the ones in the suites I'd seen at the Helides house. "You have any reason to believe we're the only ones?"

"That Cassandra has approached?"

"That's what I mean."

"No. No, I fear it is endemic with her."

"Does the Skipper know?"

Justo seemed to weigh something. "A man reaches a certain age, John, he tends to see only what he wants to see."

"And hear only what he wants to hear?"

"Do you mean, did I advise him about Cassandra targeting me?"

"Or has anyone else?"

"Not that I know of. The Skipper is a proud man, but perhaps the stroke has caused him to . . . ignore what even his senses try to tell him." Justo looked away for a moment. "Also, his condition is causing him to become nostalgic."

"The album from our service days?"

"An example, but such began even before Veronica was killed. In early January, Colonel F. J. Kelly died. Do you remember him?"

"The Special Forces commander in Vietnam?"

"Exactly so. When the Skipper read Colonel Kelly's obituary, he called me."

"Why?"

"To talk with someone about all the soldiers in his generation dying."

"Wasn't Kelly older than the Skipper, though?"

"By seven or eight years. But they knew each other, and his passing hit hard." Justo smiled sadly. "So, it may be the Skipper is concerned about more things than his wife's time at an athletic club."

I thought about the roster of party guests. "That tennis pro at the birthday party?"

"Cornel Radescu."

"Do you think he's been one of Cassandra's targets, too?"

"I cannot say, but I believe she is at the club every day for several hours. You will want to see Mr. Radescu, I assume."

"Yes, but I'll need a car first."

"Of course. We will rent you one at the hotel."

"Fine."

The waitress brought our ribs, not leaving the table until I tried one of the fries and pronounced her advice sound.

When we were alone again, Justo attacked his rack with a knife and fork. "It is as I remembered. At the slightest touch, the meat falls off the bone."

When he finished chewing his first mouthful, I said, "Would you have some time tomorrow to introduce me around?"

"Introduce you . . . ?"

"To the investigating officers on the case."

A nod. "After breakfast, Pepe or I will drive you to the Fort Lauderdale station." Justo Vega paused before resuming his meal, the darkening coming back over his features. "I can tell you now, though. You will not mistake its Homicide Unit for the Welcome Wagon."

FIVE

I was kneeling in the bow of a black inflatable boat, the kind commandoes use, at least in the movies. But the people in it with me were men and women of all ages and dress codes, even some children, which made no sense at all.

And each of them, youngest to oldest, was crying.

The fog around us hung thick, shrouding everything but your hand in front of you. A nautical bell tolled nearby, and I somehow knew it was a lighthouse.

Suddenly, through a narrow rift in the fog, I could see Nancy, right by the side of our boat. She was at the surface, her head bobbing some in the chop. I leaned over the rubber gunwale, reaching out and calling for her to take my hand. But Nancy just smiled at me—a wry little smile—and then she began to sink, her black hair billowing up behind her head like seaweed in a current. I screamed her name now, the bell tolling louder and—

I sat bolt upright, the bedsheet, heavy from sweat, peeling off and falling into my lap. When I picked up the telephone, the electronic voice told me it was my requested wake-up call and to be sure to have a nice day, now.

Before showering that Wednesday morning, I ordered breakfast from room service. Shaving while I waited for the knock at the door, I thought about my dream. Or nightmare.

I hadn't had any during the whole time in Boston after Flight #133 went down, despite all the nights I'd passed out from the booze. So why now? Maybe it was the reduced alcohol intake the last few days, coupled with sleeping in a strange bed after a long day of flying and dealing with the Skipper's problem.

I hoped that was all it was.

Breakfast arrived as I wiped my face free of residual shaving cream. When I opened my door, the bellman was tugging a local paper called the *Sun-Sentinel*—packaged in a plastic bag—off the outside knob. After I finished eating and read the first section of what appeared to be a pretty good daily, there was still half an hour until Justo or Pepe was to meet me, so I decided to rent a car while I waited.

Before leaving the room, though, I walked over to my bureau and touched the photo I'd unpacked. The one of Nancy and me, her mugging for the camera.

"I remember how you like the old-fashion guns, maybe you like old-fashion cars, too."

Pepe had been sitting on a lobby chair near the rent-a-car counter when I walked up to it. As he came over to me, I said, "You could have called me in my room rather than wait here."

A head shake. "Mr. Vega, he say to me, 'Let the man sleep after his hard trip.'" Pepe gave me a different look. "How you feeling, Mr. Whatever?"

"Better," I said automatically, then realized—despite the nightmare—that I really did.

A nod before Pepe glanced at the woman behind the counter. "What I say before about the old cars is true. In Havana, we have them, but no gas, like I told you yesterday. Here, we got the old cars, but with the gas, too. You want a sixty-four Caddy convertible, I got this friend—"

"Pepe, thanks, but I think something less conspicuous might be better."

"Less con-spic-u-*ous*, huh? So, like some little shitbox, four doors and no performance package."

"Like that, yes."

"Okay. You see the nice lady behind the counter, I wait on the chair, then drive you to the police station."

"I'll have my own car, Pepe. Can't you just lead me in yours?"

"Mr. Vega, he tell me to drive you this morning so he can meet you there. I don't argue with Mr. Vega, you don't argue with me, okay?"

"Okay."

"This Fort Lauderdale, she's a pretty nice town, you don't mind the murders now and then."

We'd left my Chevy Cavalier—four doors of teal-blue anonymity—in the garage beyond the hotel's pool. With the air temperature hovering around eighty again and a cloud-patched sky smothering us in humidity, I'd shrugged out of my suit jacket before getting into Pepe's Ford Escort. When we turned onto West Broward Boulevard, he set the air conditioner on high, its motor or fan rattling a little.

"Thanks," I said.

"I figure, you still on Boston weather, Mr. Whatever, you need it. But you better get used to this Florida stuff, you gonna be down here a while."

I turned sideways in my passenger seat. "Pepe, a question?"

"Sure, man."

"You know any of the people at the birthday party for Colonel Helides well enough to give me your take on them?"

"My 'take'? You mean like, do I think they maybe not right, somehow?"

"We can start there."

Pepe thought a moment. "I see a few of them, but the

onliest one I talk to is Berto—Umberto Reyes, the security guy? He is *cubano*, too, so I think he okay."

"Would you bet your life on it?"

Another moment of thought. "No, but I would bet the life of a very good friend." Pepe grinned at me.

He eased the Escort over to the center lane, then turned left into a parking lot that ran the length of a sprawling, multilevel building. Light gray exterior walls sported powder-blue trim and awnings while palm trees swayed above tended beds of brightly colored flowers.

I said, "This is the police station?"

"You got it."

"Looks more like a resort hotel." I opened my door, but Pepe stayed put. "You're not coming in?"

"Uh-unh," he said, gazing out the windshield at the traffic on Broward. "Police places remind me too much of *Presidente* Castro's Courtesy Inns. Mr. Vega meet you on the second floor, though. You got to go first up to the counter, then they buzz you in the doors."

"Pepe?"

"Yeah?"

"You don't like being in police stations, how come you know so much about the layout of this one?"

He turned toward me this time. "Mr. Vega tell me." Turning back and glancing in his outside mirror, Pepe said, "And remember, in this country, the policeman is your friend."

The interior of the building didn't look like a resort hotel.

In a lobby of gray cylindrical pillars and gray formed chairs, one wall was hung with glass cases bearing yearbook-like photos and captions such as POLICE EMPLOYEE OF THE MONTH. Another wall had a different array of more candid photos marked PLEASE HELP—MISSING CHILDREN.

I walked to the INFORMATION counter on the left as a uniformed officer in a chocolate-brown shirt and gray pants with brown piping passed me, the small radio on his epaulet squawking. Two women were behind the counter, enclosed in thick—and probably bulletproof—glass. One of them got me through two security doors, the second of which led to a staircase.

I climbed the flight and wound up in a smaller reception area with a beige metal door and a window covered by the kind of roll-down grating you'd see over a pawnshop. The window was closed most of the way down to its ledge, an elderly woman sitting sidesaddle behind it and an equally old sign saying something about "It's freezing in here."

Justo Vega rose from one of the chairs in the reception area. "John, you slept well?"

"Pretty much."

A grave nod. Reaching into his suit coat, he came out with a folded paper. "This is the list of all who attended the Skipper's birthday party, with addresses and telephone numbers."

I took it from him. "Thanks, Justo. Are we ready to go in?"

"The detectives will see you, but only if I am not present."

"Wait a minute. They'll see me but not you?"

"For several reasons, I think, though they mentioned none to me. First, I am a lawyer, and they are sick to death of lawyers on this case. Second, I believe if I were in charge of the investigation, I would want any 'discrepancies' in recollection from your interview to be a verdict of two against one."

Made sense from their standpoint. "How do we proceed, then?"

Justo tilted his head toward the counter behind him. "We give your name to the nice lady, she buzzes you in, and the detectives spend as much time with you as they like. I will wait for you out here."

"Okay. What are these people's names?"

The squad room at the end of the corridor measured maybe thirty-by-thirty, with lots of old wooden desks and black swivel chairs dragged toward modernity by a couple of computers. High, clerestory windows let in surprisingly little of the Florida sunshine, the air smelling of moldy documents, possibly in the light brown folders or dark brown accordion files. The parts of the walls not playing host to bookshelves were the same beige as the metal security door, and the overall impression I drew from the room was one of dreary routine.

Sergeant Lourdes Pintana sat behind a desk covered by papers the way snow covers an alley in Boston. Her complexion was the color of honey, her hair two shades darker and pulled straight back but long enough to brush her shoulders. She wore gold-framed half glasses partway down her nose, watching me over the tops of the concave lenses. Her suit jacket shaded toward light green, and I thought from the texture it might be linen. The desk hid whether Pintana was wearing skirt or slacks, but her torso was slim, and the hollows under high cheekbones gave the woman a fashion-model look well into her thirties.

Detective Kyle Cascadden, on the other hand, looked as though he swung from tree to tree via strong vines. Standing to Pintana's left against one of the bookshelves, he had a craggy brow under sandy hair that was short on top but tumbling over the back of his collar. The fish-pattern tie was tugged down almost to the second button on his shirt, a short-sleeved Kmart special that showed tattoos on each forearm including the eagle-and-anchor of the Marine Corps. At the right side of his belt I could see a badge and some kind of magnum revolver. His nose had led the charge more than once, a scar line running through the left eyebrow as well.

From the visitor chair in front of the desk, I gave them my best smile. "A pleasure to meet you both."

"Pity we cannot say the same," said Pintana, an icing of Spanish on her words.

"I'm glad to see we're off to such a good start."

Cascadden pushed his butt away from the shelf. "I throw you through one of those windows up there, just how far you think you'd bounce?"

Southern country accent. "Probably from here to the nearest federal courthouse, where civil-rights suits eat civil-service pensions."

Cascadden showed me some teeth, rottweiler fashion, but Pintana raised her hand in a "Down, boy" gesture. "Mr. Cuddy, we are meeting here instead of my office because it is more comfortable."

"Doesn't give me much hope for your office."

Pintana lowered her hand. "Do you know why we are meeting with you at all?"

"Because somebody you respect was told by somebody you don't that this was to be a command performance."

"A what?" said Cascadden.

Pintana canted her head at me but spoke to her partner. "Like when Elton John plays for the Queen, Kyle."

He showed me more teeth. "Yeah, well, nobody fucking 'commands' me to do anything. We don't just have this Held killing. There's a whore got herself slashed to death in a hot-sheet joint, maybe because she wouldn't do some *john's* 'joint.' Then there's a vehicular over on Federal Highway, hit-and-run of this tourist from—"

I said, "No offense intended, Detective. I was military police for a while, and I know how it can be in a department."

"How far did you get?" asked Pintana.

"In terms of rank or geography?"

Just the barest twitch of a smile. "I had a brother went to Vietnam, and you're the right age, so how about just rank."

"Lieutenant mostly, captain for a while."

Cascadden said, "And that's supposed to make you some kind of expert?"

I leaned forward in my chair, elbows on knees, hands spread. "Look, we can spar, and probably you can win this round. But that means I go back with thin soup for a report, and you'll get told to entertain me all over again, only with a little more enthusiasm. So, why don't we just get to it, save everybody another sit-down?"

Cascadden glared at me. Pintana picked up a pencil and began tapping its eraser against gleaming, even teeth.

She said, "Let's see your identification."

I passed the Boston version across the desk, Cascadden leaning over her left shoulder to read it. I could see his lips moving as Pintana said, "We were told you'd have Florida papers."

"My guess is that Justo Vega will be able to produce them for you by the end of the day."

Cascadden shook his head, the hair at his collar picking up dull light from the windows. "I say we throw this bozo out till he comes up with righteous ID."

"We could, Kyle," Pintana rising partway to hand my identification holder back to me. She had carefully manicured nails, short enough so that computer keyboards and gun trigger guards wouldn't present a problem. "But as Mr. Cuddy said, it would only postpone the inevitable. I say we talk with him and be rid of it."

Cascadden didn't reply for a moment. Then, "You're the one passed the sergeant's exam."

Pintana nodded to me. "What do you want to know?"

"Might save all of us time if I got to see your file on this."

"Not while I'm in this chair," said Pintana.

"All right, then how about your view on what happened."

She folded her hands on top of the desk. Or, more accurately, on top of one of the papers covering it. "Held, Veronica Janis, white female, was killed by drowning in the pool at her grandfather's home. There were bruises on the ankles suggesting someone held her down there and forced her head under the water."

"Prints?"

"Not thanks to the water. And the chlorine in it."

Cascadden said, "Plus that houseboy fucked the crime scene all to hell."

I looked over. "I don't think Duy Tranh is a houseboy." Going back to Pintana, I asked, "Any trace evidence?"

"Pool, pool area, and filter checked carefully for fibers and hair. We found a catalog of them, which isn't surprising, since just about everybody at the party or the house in general used the pool in the preceding twenty-four hours."

First no evidence, now too much. "I understand the girl was sexually assaulted."

Pintana gave a sidelong look at Cascadden, but apparently her partner had learned at least something about sensitivity, because he didn't say anything. She came back to me with, "Sí. Evidence of violent penetration, no semen or other fluids."

"Because of the pool water again?"

"Possibly, but the Medical Examiner did find traces of latex in the vagina, torn though it was."

"A condom?"

"That is my belief. When I joined the unit as a detective, we were still responsible for child molestation and sexual battery as well as homicide."

"Anything further from the autopsy?"

"Given lung and vaginal tissue, the M.E. feels the penetration probably occurred while the girl was struggling underwater."

The Skipper had said that, but it was still troubling. "She was raped while the killer was drowning her?"

Cascadden laughed. "Or the fucking perp' was getting his jollies, and he never noticed the kid wasn't breathing real good."

I looked at Cascadden again. Police work, and especially homicide investigation, can harden you. But this ex-Marine seemed more amused than callous.

He said, "What're you looking at, Beantown?"

"Nobody there calls it that."

"Huh?"

"Nobody in Boston calls it 'Beantown,' any more than I'd call somebody down here a 'redneck.'"

Cascadden clenched his fists. "That what you're calling me?"

"Kyle," from Pintana.

"Huh, boy?" coming forward a step with the fists still clenched but not yet up. "You calling me—"

"Kyle," from Pintana, but with a little more juice behind it. "Enough, okay?"

Cascadden glanced at her, but kept his eyes mostly on mine, to make sure I knew he could still handle me if his partner weren't around. Then he stepped back, shoulders against the wall, arms folded across his chest so that the eagle tatt' was eyeing me, too.

I said to Pintana, "You were first on the scene?"

"No. Road patrol responded to the nine-one-one. I got called out."

"Meaning you were off duty?"

"In my apartment."

Not just "at home." "How about your partner here?"

Cascadden grunted. "Sergeant's not my partner."

I looked at her. "You're not?"

"No, Mr. Cuddy. I run the unit."

"In Boston, that'd be a lieutenant's slot."

"In Lauderdale, we don't have that rank. It's sergeant or captain, and I'm years away from a promotion."

"Maybe not after this case."

Pintana watched me. "The Held murder was so high-profile from the get-go that I've been riding with Kyle on it since he wasn't partnered up at the time."

That came as no surprise. To Cascadden, I said, "So, you were here at the station?"

"What difference does it fucking make?"

"You won't let me see the logs and files, I'd like to have some idea how long people in the house would have had before the police in general and Homicide in particular got things under control."

Cascadden started to say something, but Pintana spoke over him. "That makes sense. Road patrol was there within five minutes after the nine-one-one."

"And how long after the girl was found did somebody think to call it in?"

"Given the confusion at the scene—family, the band members, everybody milling around—hard to say for sure, but Mr. Tranh said he 'ran' for the phone."

Same thing he'd told me. "So say it takes him one or two minutes to get her out of the pool and dial for help. How long after the girl was killed does the M.E. estimate she was found by Mr. Tranh?"

Pintana gave me an appraising look. "Given the temperature of the pool water, that's pretty hazy. But most of the guests say she left the party about an hour before the body was found."

So, adding in even the rapid police response, the killer had plenty of time to hide any evidence of condom—or even gloves to hold her. . . . "Were there any latex tracings on the girl's ankles?"

Cascadden glanced at Pintana, but she watched me with the appraising look. "Lab says yes, in some of the cracks in the skin caused by her thrashing around."

I thought back to what Duy Tranh had said to me about planning. "Premeditated rather than opportunistic."

Cascadden seemed confused. Pintana picked up her pencil again before adding, "Worse than that."

"How do you mean?"

"Drownings are generally tough cases to make. Hard to determine whether it was intentional or accidental."

"But I'm told the Held girl was an excellent swimmer."

"Even excellent swimmers drown, especially if they get high before they hit the water."

"High?"

"Lab reported cocaine in her system."

Christ. "We know where she got it?"

Cascadden said, "Her shitbird father, probably."

I stayed with Pintana. "But the lab also reported those latex tracings from both—"

"Think about it, Mr. Cuddy. You just want to kill the girl, you leave her swimsuit on and keep her under the water by holding it. Chances are, little or no trace evidence, and the death is closed as accidental."

I did think about it. "But by taking off the suit, and using a condom and gloves, the killer makes it obvious."

Pintana nodded.

I said, "We were supposed to know it was intentional."

Cascadden grunted. "Less the perp' just had to get his jollies, like I said before."

Neither Pintana nor I acted like we'd heard him.

I said to her, "And the killer knew in advance that the birthday party would provide perfect timing . . ."

Pintana pointed at me with her pencil. ". . . because the band member's son wanted the house security cameras off when he made his video."

"That's what I'm thinking, too."

When Pintana didn't break eye contact with me, I said, "Any chance of my getting a look at Kalil's video?"

Cascadden said, "Oh, sure thing, Beantown."

His sarcasm was still dripping when Sergeant Lourdes Pintana tapped the pencil eraser against her front teeth and said, "Why not?"

Kyle Cascadden threw up his hands and left the room. Either he'd forgotten his sports jacket or he didn't believe in wearing one.

I said, "The party's already under way."

"*Sí.*" The only Spanish word Pintana seemed to use. "Buford and Kalil Biggs did not arrive at the very beginning of it."

We were in her small office now, each of us with half our rumps on respective front corners of the desk, both of us staring at the monitor above her VCR.

I said, "The house cameras were turned off by this point?"

"Approximately thirty minutes earlier. We were told that Veronica wished it so, and her grandfather made it so."

I watched the silent images on the screen.

"Audio?"

"Kalil told us he forgot to engage it."

The images bounced and shifted as whoever was carrying the camcorder—Kalil, probably—tried to pan the living room and the party-goers in it.

Pintana said, "You have seen the interior of the house?"

"Yes."

She pointed to a corner. "That is the entrance to the corridor leading to the pool area." The focus shifted away. "Unfortunately, the entire tape is like this. Plenty of time for one of the guests to enter the pool area without being on camera."

"Veronica, too?"

"Yes and no. I think he preceded her there, though."

"You're assuming a male did the killing?"

Pintana kept her eyes on the screen. "I would not like to think that a woman—the ones at the party, anyway—would mimic a rape in killing another female."

I thought about Cassandra Helides's apparently avid interest in sex, but kept my own counsel on it.

Then I started counting the people onscreen that I could recognize. The Skipper and his wife. Duy Tranh. And now a brash, sassy girl with cornrowed, reddish-blond hair that I vaguely remembered seeing pictured on the television in a Boston bar the week before. Her gold lamé blouse was tucked into the waist of spandex tights, the material stretching over her upper thighs and buttocks. She looked at least seventeen.

"That's Veronica?" I said.

"Sí."

"I thought she was only thirteen?"

"Twelve and ten months, actually."

Veronica and a number of adults ebbed and flowed across the none-too-steady lens. "You've analyzed how much time each person is offscreen?"

"To the tenth of a second. It is hopeless. Apparently Kalil Biggs was striving for a 'stream of consciousness' in his cinema verité."

"James Joyce meets Martin Scorsese."

After a moment, Pintana said, "Kyle would really hate you as a partner."

Within ten minutes, there was food and drink being taken from a lavishly stocked buffet table that Kalil's camera panned in the adjoining room. I could see what Pintana meant about the tape not being very helpful in locating who was where when.

Then we were back in the living room, focused on Veronica Held. Suddenly, she tore off her own blouse, showing a tank top underneath, budding breasts pushing against it. And Veronica began a suggestive, languid dance, her mouth and throat cords implying that she was singing.

I said, "Is there any—"

"Kalil Biggs remembers now to click on the audio."

And suddenly a piercing, achingly adult voice filled Pintana's office. It wasn't that the volume was turned up too high; it was more that Veronica's voice carried so well. Maybe the reddish hair spurred the memory, but I was reminded of the signature song from *Annie*, "Tomorrow," I think it's called.

Except the a cappella lyric coming from Veronica Held's mouth was anything but naively optimistic.

I said, "She's singing a song about sex with an older man on her grandfather's birthday?"

Pintana said, "Not for long."

You could hear the thunder of the Skipper's voice even through the garbling caused by his stroke. And while Veronica pouted—in a pretty fair imitation of Cassandra, her "stepgrandmother"—the girl did stop singing before stalking off, the camera following her until she was lost in the broader adult bodies. A stocky man in his forties with a Fu Manchu mustache hurried after Veronica, a woman in her thirties with flowers in her hair—literally—following behind him.

"The parents?"

"Sí. Spi Held and Jeanette Held."

"Can you identify the others for me?"

"If I hurry." Pintana leaned forward, pressing the pad of an index finger to the screen over the face of a thin African-American man. "Kalil's father, Buford Biggs, the band's keyboardist." The finger moved to a fat, bald man and a stolid, sandy-haired woman. "Gordo Lazar, the band's bass player, and Delgis Reyes, Veronica's au pair."

I watched Lazar and Reyes. "They seem closer than just joint guests."

"Each told me they are involved with one another." A pause before, "Romantically."

Another skinny man—white, with a bad hair transplant—came across the screen, a drink in his hand.

Pintana said, "The band's manager, Mitch Eisen."

Cassandra Helides followed him, also carrying a drink, this one sloshing over the sides of her glass.

"And she is the wife of Nicolas Helides. Cassandra."

Next I got a couple of frames showing a guy in his twenties, the hair wildly platinum and orange, before the VCR made a clicking, whirring noise, and the screen went to snow abruptly.

"Who was that last one?"

"Ricky Queen, the band's drummer."

"Kalil have to switch tapes?"

"No. You have seen all he gave us."

Didn't seem right. "How many minutes of running time after Veronica left the room?"

"One minute, thirty-two seconds. The reason I told you I would have to be quick to identify the other guests."

I checked the digital timer on Pintana's VCR. "That says we've seen a total of only twenty-five minutes of tape?"

"Right."

"You ask Kalil Biggs why he stopped rolling on his epic?"

"Sí. He said to me that he got bored with the party."

I looked at Lourdes Pintana. "Shortly after Veronica left it."

The homicide sergeant just nodded.

"Let me give you my cellular number so you don't have to play phone tag with the voice mail, okay?"

We were in the corridor leading to the metal security door by the reception area. I watched Pintana in front of me take a business card from the side pocket of her green, maybe-linen jacket.

At the door, she handed the card to me. I read the information on it, then looked back up at her. "Good cop, bad cop."

The twitch that was almost a smile. "Polite cop, difficult cop."

"Use whatever adjectives you want, but I have the feeling you and Cascadden were kind of playing me, him stonewalling so I'd be even more appreciative of whatever you gave me."

Pintana did smile this time. "I am playing you, Mr. Cuddy, but Kyle is not. He is what he seems, but he took a bullet for the city once, and he came back from it maybe a little harder than wiser. So I try to temper him, but I do not pretend to control him."

"Yet he stays on Homicide?"

"The politics of heroism."

"That's pretty blunt."

Her smile grew wider, as though my comment were a compliment. "Then allow me to be blunter still. The reason I am playing you is that this is the most problematic killing I have seen in my time in the department, much less running Homicide. The captain I report to dumps on my head all the shit which is dumped first on his. I would like to really work this case, not shuttle to another press conference every time one of our esteemed politicians has a 'promising lead' for the police to follow. The force in Miami Beach suffered from the Cunanan-Versace media circus, and I myself have studied the Ramsey case in Colorado until my eyes cross. The fact is, though, that every one of the people at the Helides party may have put in the same amount of study, because they all either have gotten lawyers or claim to be dumb as fenceposts, and the forensic evidence doesn't give me squat to use as leverage with any of them. If you can make better progress, I would welcome it, and I would hope you would share your results with me."

"With you, not Cascadden."

"Do not underestimate Kyle, Mr. Cuddy. A man who would step in front of a bullet is capable of many things."

"He *stepped* in front of one?"

"*Sí.*" She pushed open the security door, ushering me into the little second-floor reception area. "One meant for me, in fact. And Kyle does not appreciate another male showing him up before the woman he saved."

By the time I turned around, the beige metal door was closed enough that I couldn't see Lourdes Pintana's face.

"And who are you showing up?" said Justo Vega as we went down the stairs toward the first floor.

"Long story. Will Pepe be outside?"

"I have never known him to fail in an instruction I have given him. Where do you wish to go?"

"Back to the hotel, pick up my rent-a-car."

"You feel sufficiently familiar with the area now?"

"I can still read a compass."

Justo gave one of his musical laughs. "What did you think of Sergeant Pintana?"

"Smart and tough. Maybe even smart enough not to feel she has to show just how tough."

"And a genuine beauty, a woman who grows more attractive the more one speaks with her. If I were not married already, she would be a good choice."

I looked back at Justo before being aware of how my face must have looked to him.

"Oh, John. Forgive me, please. I—"

"No forgiveness is necessary among friends."

The grave nod. "Perhaps not, but an apology is still appropriate, and I extend it."

My turn to nod, and then we went through the doors that could remind you of an airport terminal and into the heat of the nearly midday sun.

SIX

After Pepe dropped me back at my hotel, I stopped by the front desk to see if there were any messages for me. The clerk seemed a little nervous, but dutifully checked his computer before saying yes, a "Mr. Tranh" had called a while before.

I thought I should return it from my room, so I went up there. Once inside, I touched the beach photo atop the bureau again on my way to the bed. Using the mattress as a seat, I dialed, and Tranh's voice answered midway through the second ring.

"John Cuddy, returning your call."

"You are at your hotel?"

He sounded miffed. "Yes."

"Before trying you there, I dialed your cell phone, but without success."

I stared at bottom drawer of the bureau, where I'd left the portable. "I didn't have it with me."

"Mr. Cuddy, do you even have it turned on?"

Now a sardonic tone to Tranh's voice. I waited a moment before saying, "No."

He took an equal amount of time, then said, "I dialed your cellular as a test, to be sure the Colonel could reach you if necessary. As he cannot always be available himself for a return call from your hotel room, could you please keep the cell phone fully charged and with you—power *on*—at all times?"

"I'll do my best."

"Thank you again. I see no need to trouble the Colonel with the reason for my reminder to you."

Favor supposedly owed. "I appreciate that."

"Good-bye, Mr. Cuddy."

I started to say the same before realizing that Duy Tranh had already hung up on me.

Rising from the bed, I went over to my bureau and retrieved the cell phone from its drawer. When I pushed the button marked PWR, the tiny window lit up with a pale green background, telling me the phone's own dialing number. A bar graph on the right-hand side showed the battery as fully charged.

I slipped the unit into my inside jacket pocket and went to the door. When I pulled it open, something like a battering ram hit me square in the chest.

Backpedaling, I registered Detective Kyle Cascadden's following through with an open right hand to my breastplate. Granted I wasn't expecting it, he'd still managed to drive almost two hundred pounds of me to the edge of the bed eight feet into the room.

I stayed on my feet as the back of my knees hit the mattress. Cascadden had slammed the door with his left hand

and kept coming, bringing his right up to my throat and grabbing hold. Not choking me, just getting my attention and keeping it.

"All right, Beantown, now here's the program. I got the room clerk by the short hairs, account of he's got an old drug conviction I know about but the hotel don't. So he called me soon's he knew you were back up here. I got that kind of stuff on enough people, I can find you wherever you go in my town. We clear on that?"

I gave what I thought Cascadden would take to be a weak nod.

"Rest of the program. I don't much like you coming into my squad room, showing me up with your high-handed Yankee power-trip. You were working for some dogshit defendant, I'd have to give you a mite of leeway, account of the courts won't let me tell witnesses not to talk with the 'accused's investigators.' But you're just butting your nose in where it don't belong, and I don't like that either. Fact is, I don't much like anything about you. So, I catch you even just a bitty-bit dirty—like maybe you carrying unlicensed?—and Beantown, I'm gonna be on you like flies over horseshit. We clear on that, too?"

Another weak nod from me.

Cascadden started to squeeze harder on my throat. "And I don't mean formal, neither. I mean I come out and see you personal, like now, only maybe you gonna walk away with worse than some ache in your Adam's apple." A grin. "Or, maybe you don't walk away at all."

Sagging a bit in my shoulders, I flopped my left hand up toward his right elbow under the shirtsleeve, my thumb and middle finger lightly probing on each side of the joint for the right spot. The one the unarmed-defense sergeant showed us in the sawdust pit back in Military Police Officer Basic.

When Cascadden squeezed harder still on my throat, I pinched my fingers into the flesh.

His right hand went limp against my collarbone as his eyes bugged and his face drained of color. Then he folded over at the belly, drawing in a ragged breath. When Cascadden let out the breath, he wheezed.

I said, "This amount of pressure, you almost can't think from the pain, right?"

One abrupt nod.

"A little more pressure, and you'd drop to your knees, maybe throw up all over my carpet here. Are we communicating?"

Another nod, more abrupt.

"All right, Cascadden, the difference between us is, I'm doing this to you only because you ran your routine on me first. I didn't ask for the job I'm doing here, but I'll do it, and things might be better for both of us if you could see your way clear to cooperate. If you can't, though, just stay the hell away from me, and save the rousting for the college kids come Spring Break. Okay?"

An even faster nod than the first two, almost as though his head wanted off his neck.

I let go of the elbow, and his arm drooped to his side.

Still doubled over, Cascadden stumbled backward a few steps, his left hand going up to the right elbow, massaging it tentatively. "Mother-fucker . . . Mother-*fuck*-er."

"Sticks and stones, Cascadden. Now get out of here."

He turned and awkwardly used his left hand to open the door, letting the spring carry it shut behind him rather than slamming it as he had on his entrance.

That was when I caught myself in the mirror over the bureau. Grinning in a way I never thought I would.

The way that says you enjoyed what you just did.

* * *

I recognized him, but I also realized I'd have had a hard time describing him.

The nervous desk clerk was handing an older woman an envelope across the counter, using his hands to give her some kind of directions. He was about five-nine, with fine features and hair slicked back with some kind of gel. I waited until the woman walked away before going up to him. When he caught my movement, he looked up, smiling professionally.

But only briefly.

I said, "Busy morning for you, huh?"

"Uh, yes. Mr. . . . uh—"

"Oh, come on now. You can't have forgotten already? You had it right ten minutes ago when you spoke with Detective Cascadden."

"I don't think—"

"Unfortunately, though, Cascadden is a little free with his information. He let slip how firm you were about a certain personal . . . conviction."

The clerk flinched.

I said, "What's your name?"

"Damon."

I leaned into him over the counter. "Damon, the problem with information about any kind of conviction is, once you share it, things can get out of hand."

A nod.

"I don't intend to share this information any further, but I want something in return."

"They don't pay me enough here to—"

"Different coin of the realm, Damon. All I want is advanced notice from you."

Hope and confusion both. "Notice?"

"Of any trouble headed my way that you sniff out first."

"Trouble."

"That's right. Either Detective Cascadden or anybody else. You think you can do that for me?"

Damon glanced around before nodding. Vigorously.

"I'm going out now."

"Uh, have a nice day."

"I'll try to, Damon. I'll really try."

Mitch Eisen's office showed an address in what I thought of as the southeast quadrant of Fort Lauderdale. I used the shore route A1A to reach it, partly because I wanted to get the hang of handling the Cavalier but mostly to clear my head of the feelings Kyle Cascadden and Damon had left in me. Watching people jog, race-walk, and roller-blade along the oceanside path helped, especially with the beach, turquoise water, and swaying palm trees as backdrops.

South of Broward Boulevard, I turned back west until I found a strip mall lying between the right avenues. There was no sign on the three-story building that read like the business name of a rock group's manager, maybe because the Dunkin' Donuts and Mail Boxes, Etc., on the ground floor had taken up all the available advertising space. I parked the Cavalier across from the short line buying fresh-brewed coffee and fresh-baked health food.

Between the two establishments, I found a glass and chrome door with three apartment-style mailboxes inside it. The middle one showed a piece of masking tape with "M. Eisen, Ltd.," so I climbed the flight of stairs to the second floor.

There was only one door, a plastic faux-grained plaque not quite centered on it but reading "M. Eisen, Ltd." as well. Knocking, I wondered why the manager of even a faded rock group couldn't spring for at least a second plaque downstairs.

A muffled "It's open" came through the door, so I turned the knob. A man was sitting at the secretarial desk in the outer office, a threshold behind it leading to an inner one. I recognized the hair transplant from the video of the birth-day party that Sergeant Lourdes Pintana had shown me back at police headquarters. It looked like nursery rows of Christmas trees, planted at identical intervals.

Eisen glanced up at me. "Yeah?"

I went through the formalities anyway. "Mr. Eisen?"

"No, Mick Jagger. The fuck are you?"

I realized that it hadn't been so much the door muffling his voice as the voice itself. There was a breathy quality to it that wouldn't carry five feet in an empty church, even though he didn't seem older than fifty or so. Eisen looked thinner than he had in the video. I'd always heard that the camera adds ten pounds, but in this case, the subtraction made the guy almost emaciated, the name SPIRAL over a tornado logo on his black T-shirt almost completely cover-ing his narrow chest.

"My name's John Cuddy. Nicolas Helides thought I should talk to you."

"Oh, the private eye, right?"

"Right."

"Tranh told me I might get a visit. How come you didn't call, let me know you were coming?"

"Thought I'd just drive over."

"Yeah, but why not use your cellular from the car?"

"Tranh told you he'd given me a cell phone?"

Eisen blinked. "No. No, he didn't. I just—shit, man, everybody who's anybody has one now."

"I wonder if we could talk about Veronica Held."

A frown this time. "You know, my lawyer doesn't think I should be talking to you at all."

"But Nicolas Helides does."

The frown evolved into a shrewd grin. "John, I like a man knows when he has leverage for negotiating." Eisen glanced behind him. "Let's go into my office. I can't stand the fucking clutter out here."

The desk Eisen rose from sported folded correspondence and waxy faxes, eight-by-ten photos and tape cassettes. "Secretary out sick?"

"Huh?" he said over his shoulder as he led me through the inner doorway.

"Your secretary. He or she out sick for a while?"

"Oh, I don't have what you'd call a formal secretary. Got this single-mother chick, used to work for a temp agency, but she got tired of having to go to different places all the time. So I pay her less to come here more. Only one of her yard-apes is sick with something, so I'm up to my ass in shit from people I don't even know."

"I'm surprised they can find you, Mitch."

Eisen waved me to a seat before collapsing as heavily as his weight would let him into a high-backed judge's chair behind a desk at least as cluttered as the one we'd just left. "Find me?"

"Without any advertising downstairs."

"Oh, that doesn't stop the wanna-bes. I could change my name and move to Tahiti, and I'd still be getting demo tapes recorded in somebody's fucking garage."

"You ever find new clients that way?"

"What, off the street, so to speak?"

"Yes."

"Once in a great while." Eisen pursed his lips, which somehow caused the hair plugs to march like a drill team toward his forehead. "Was how I found Spi Held, tell you the truth. Or how he found me."

"And when was this?"

"Back in seventy." Eisen swung in his chair, waving this

time at the wall of photos to his left and my right. "That's us, whole first row there."

I followed his hand gesture to a vertical line of framed shots, some posed, some candid. Most had a younger, heavier version of Eisen in them, with four even younger men around him. I recognized Buford Biggs despite the Jimi Hendryx Afro and husky build. I also recognized the fat, bald one called Gordo, but you would have been hard-pressed to pick the man Lourdes Pintana identified to me as Spi Held, and the fourth man with dishwater-blond hair falling onto his shoulders was clearly not the young drummer I'd seen in the video of the party.

I said, "Who's the guy with the long blond hair?"

"The . . . ? Oh, that was O'D."

"Oh-Dee?"

"Tommy O'Dell. Original drummer in the band. Called him 'O'D' for short, because of his last name." A cough that I realized stood for a grunted laugh. "Or because of how he checked out. Always thought that's how the stone should have read."

"I don't follow you, Mitch."

"His tombstone. O'D died of an 'OD,' get it?"

Beth's own grave flashed behind my eyes as I said, "O'Dell died from a drug overdose?"

"Yeah. Fucking would have killed the band, too, disco didn't do them in first."

"Why is that?"

Eisen sized me up. "You're old enough, John, you would have been listening to their music in the early seventies, right?"

"I remember the name, anyway."

"Okay. Spiral had a couple of hits, mainly songs that Spi and O'D wrote together—Spi on the music, O'D the lyrics, which is funny for a drummer, you think about it."

"Funny?"

"Drummer, he's got to keep the beat when they play a song, you don't usually peg him as a word guy."

"Got it."

"Okay. Well, even with those couple of hits, Spiral as a band never had enough name recognition once they fell off CHR."

"What's CHR, Mitch?"

"'Contemporary Hit Radio,' top-40 tunes, follow?"

"I think so."

"CHR is different from AOR."

"Which is?"

"'Album-Oriented Rock.' Or 'Radio,' doesn't matter. What matters is, groups like Pink Floyd or even Black Sabbath could make it without top-40 hits, because those bands got played on AOR."

"The album stations."

"Right, right. A band like Spiral, though—with no superstar, only don't let Spi know I said that—needs play on the CHR outlets to stay popular. Otherwise, it's out of hearing, out of mind, follow?"

"And this O'Dell had a knack for writing lyrics that CHR stations liked."

"Yeah. But once—look, John, how much do you really know about the music?"

"Like you said, I listened to it, but I never studied it."

"Okay." Eisen settled deeper in his chair, like a kid visiting Dad's office when the old man was attending a meeting. "The history of rock-'n'-roll, short course. Fast forward through Elvis, the Beach Boys, and the British Invasion. Stop at the late sixties, when you had the whole San Francisco scene. Jefferson Airplane with Gracie Slick—God, what a voice she had for the psychedelic sound. Then the second wave of Brits: Elton John, Peter Frampton—talk about a guy should have become a legend, but that's another story. Weave in Carlos Santana and his salsa-rock, the Allman Brothers and their Southern-rock, the Eagles and their country—"

"How about Spiral, Mitch?"

A pause and another lip purse, the hair plugs marching forward again. "They had a kind of raunchy-rock sound. O'D was a genius at writing lyrics just this side of what a record company *wouldn't* put on albums. Nice counterpoint to Fleetwood Mac and their romance-rock, E.L.O.—that's Electric Light Orchestra—and their symphony-rock, etc., etc."

"So Spiral found its own niche and filled it."

"Right, right. But like I said, only CHR play, not the album stations."

"And then Tommy O'Dell died."

"Right, though he was getting so drugged out even before he took the big one, I don't know how much longer he could have produced new lyrics. Didn't really matter though, because in seventy-six, seventy-seven, along came . . . disco!"

I had the feeling Eisen had delivered this speech before. "Which . . . ?"

". . . fucking killed the CHR-driven rock groups like Spiral. I mean, all you heard was Donna Summer, Barry White, Evelyn 'Champagne' King—funny, a lot of the performers were black, but most of the fans weren't. Even so, *Saturday Night Fever* with John Travolta gets released, and the ballgame was over for Spiral and twenty other bands like them."

"What happened then?"

"Late seventies, we got punk-rock as a kind of a 'death-to-disco' protest. You had the Ramones, the Sex Pistols, not to mention—"

"I meant more, what happened to Spiral."

"Couldn't get them gigs, man. Or only little store-front clubs. No decent promoter wanted their sound anymore. At most, the middle-road rock fans who couldn't stand punk had migrated to corporate-rock, like Journey, Air Supply. Not too harsh, not too sweet, kind of Baby-Bear music, follow?"

The fairy tale. "Baby-Bear, as in 'just right.'"

"Exact-a-mundo, John. Even quality bands like—that accent, you're from Boston?"

"Yes."

"Okay. Bands from up there—J. Geils and Aerosmith—were monster-big in the early seventies, but even they struggled against the tide. And it was like Spiral forgot how to swim."

That brought back an image of the Skipper's pool, and Veronica Held. But I wanted more background from Eisen before asking him about the birthday party. "You were the band's manager from the beginning?"

"Yeah. In fact, they wouldn't have had the little name recognition they did, wasn't for me."

"How so?"

"I came up with the name. I mean, can you imagine? A lead singer in seventy with the same first name as Nixon's veep?"

Spiro Agnew. "You changed it to 'Spi'?"

"No. No, he'd already done that himself, running away from home and all. But I'm the one came up with 'Spiral.' Spi tends to remember that different, but the idea was mine. 'Spi,' lead singer of 'Spiral.' Get it?"

"Catchy."

"Subliminal signature."

"Sorry?"

"It's like an actor does, make a role his own by some kind of little mannerism or bit of business. I figured to get positive name bounce from the jazz-fusion group Spyro Gyra, then

have 'Spi' and 'Spiral' and even the logo"—he pointed to the
tornado symbol on his T-shirt—"reinforce each other sublim-
inally in the fan's mind, follow me?"

"I think so. Is that why you thought the band could
make a comeback?"

"No," said Eisen. "No, I was the one thought they
couldn't."

"How come?"

"Back to that difference between CHR and AOR. It's the
same today, John. The album-oriented stations that never
played Spiral's old stuff wouldn't play any new music they
came up with, and the contemporary-hit stations never
heard of them."

"So why did Spi Held think the comeback would be a
success?"

"Boils down to one word. Very."

"Meaning his daughter."

"Meaning Lolita with a mike in her hand. You ever see
her live?"

I didn't think Eisen meant "alive," but I still shifted a little in my chair. "No."

"Wait a sec." He started shuffling through a stack of
unboxed VHS cassettes on the corner of his desk. "I think I
got one of their—yeah, here it is. Watch."

My day for videos. "What's that?"

Eisen was already pedaling his chair over to a VCR
under the monitor on a side table. "Dry run for a music
video. Unedited, which is probably how I'd want to see it, I
was you."

Eisen picked up a remote device and pushed some buttons before inserting the tape. "Okay, John, fasten your seat
belt."

The screen came alive with color, a kaleidoscopic background constantly shifting shape and shade. Then some

yelling offstage, and the camera zoomed in on Veronica Held and her cornrowed hair. There was some blurring of the men in the background before the camera operator caught on and evened out the range, Spi Held and his band members becoming clearer.

That's when Veronica said, "What is this bullshit? Like, the fucking camera's supposed to be on me, right?"

Eisen's breathy, grunted laugh. "Lovely, isn't she?"

Not the word I'd have used. Veronica Held was dressed in a spandex outfit again, at least below the waist. Above it, bare midriff, a gold ring through her navel, and a leopard-skin bikini top that did its best to give her thirteen-year-old chest some cleavage.

I shook my head.

"Wait," said Eisen to me. "It gets better."

Veronica stomped over to her father, him letting the big, flashy guitar sag against the strap around his shoulders.

She said, "The fuck did you get this clown? The cunt doesn't even know who's the star?"

Spi Held said, "Very, honey—"

"Fuck you. She goes, or I'm like gone yesterday."

The screen went to snow.

Eisen said, "This next take really captures her."

When the picture resolved again, there was no doubt who "the star" was. Veronica Held fondled a bulbous portable mike between her hands, the fingers looking delicate, even fragile against it.

Until she began to sing. Or wail.

As with the party tape, the voice wasn't a schoolgirl's. Nor were her hand movements on the mike.

"Lolita," said Eisen. "Crossed with her namesake."

"Her namesake?"

"Janis, Very's middle name. After Janis Joplin. You know, Big Brother and the Holding Company, then—"

"I remember Joplin."

"That Bette Midler in *The Rose*, she did a better-than-okay job, but Very's the closest I've ever seen. The sex-kitten looks of a Spice Girl, but the voice, the voice . . ."

All I could think was, Thirteen years old.

Veronica Held gyrated through the rest of the tune, the lyric a poorly rhymed stanza of barely disguised sexual desire for a teacher, her hips grinding against the microphone she rubbed along her thighs during the instrumental sections. After a crescendo of wail and music both, the screen went to snow again.

"I didn't recognize the song, Mitch."

Eisen gave his breathy grunt as he pressed another button on the remote and swung back around to me. "I'm not surprised. It was one of the new ones Spi wrote for the comeback."

"Not very good lyrics."

"No, but what do you want from an eighth-grader?"

I stared at him. "You're not serious."

"So, okay. She had a tutor the last few months, not a real school and classroom, but—"

"Wait a minute. Veronica wrote those lyrics?"

"Yeah." Eisen seemed surprised now. "Like I said before, Spi was the music guy, and O'D wrote the words."

"And Veronica replaced O'Dell?"

"Hey, they're not so bad, John, you compare them with the current crop of crap out there. Nothing you'd mistake for Paul Simon or Carole King, maybe, but—"

"I also don't remember hearing about any 'tutor.'"

"Hearing about? Shit, man, you already met him."

"Who?"

"Very's tutor. Tranh."

That stopped me a minute.

"Hey, John, you okay?"

"Fine." I gestured toward the now-dark screen. "Was Veronica always like that?"

"Like that 'cock-tease,' or like that 'bitchy'?"

"Both."

Eisen pursed his lips again, the rug doing its little glide on his forehead. "Depended on the circumstance."

"Meaning?"

"Meaning—look, I gave you Rock-'n'-Roll 101, let me give you the same about Very. She knew how to use it better than most women I've ever met, and believe me, you're the personal manager of a rock band, you've seen them all ages and sizes."

"Use what?"

"The hint of sex, John. You might say Very was 'mature beyond her years.' She knew what worked with her father, and her grandfather, for that matter."

I felt myself starting to bristle, tried to keep it out of my voice. "Nicolas Helides?"

"Yeah. Oh, I don't mean the real thing, like incest or whatever. Shit, man, I protested the war back then like everybody else I know, but with the old man financing the comeback, I finally got to know him a little, and you got to feel sorry for the guy. Was a stand-up hero over there, what I heard."

"You heard right."

"Meanwhile, back in the states, his one son—Spi, now—goes druggie on him and runs away from home. His wife'd already turned up her toes giving birth to the other son—David—who turns out to be a fucking zombie. And then he marries a—"

"I've met Cassandra Helides."

"Then enough said about her, except that after the old man stroked out, she got worse. But even Cassie could take a lesson from Very. The little vixen knew just how high to turn up the candlepower, get her own way about things."

"Go on."

"All right." Eisen settled back into the big chair. "Very could light the super-bitch candle for Spi, the super-sweet candle for the Colonel, and the super-student candle for Tranh, though I can't say I ever saw that. She could even get that David to come out of his shell a little, which I did see once or twice."

"How?"

"I was there, John, in the house."

"I meant, how did Veronica get David 'out of his shell'?"

"Oh. Well, she'd get him to show her his computer stuff, and play on it."

"I always thought kids knew more about computers than adults."

"Most times, I'd agree with you. But David—you know computer nerds, right?"

"A few."

"Okay, David's a computer . . . zombie, like I said before. He stays in his room most of the time, and his father's house just about all of the time. The poor schmuck's whole world is that computer setup. Have him show it to you."

I made a mental note. "Back to the day of the party?"

"Okay."

"What happened after Veronica made that scene with her grandfather?"

"When she sang him the 'come-fuck-me' song?"

"Yes."

"All hell broke loose. I remember Spi and Jeanette running after Very. I'd had a few drinks, so I decided to hang around a while, sober up before driving home. Must have been twenty, thirty minutes later, we hear Tranh yelling from the pool."

Pintana had said most guests timed it as closer to an hour. "You could tell the yelling was coming from the pool?"

"Well, yeah, with the echo. And his voice was in the right direction for it. Anyway, we all run in there—to the pool—and what do I see but Very lying buck naked on the tiles and Tranh running for the phone."

"What did you do?"

"Me? I went back to the living room."

"Why?"

"Get another drink."

"I thought you were sobering up to drive home."

"Not with the case of nerves that came over me."

"From seeing Veronica's body."

"From dealing with somebody croaking her." Eisen stopped. "No, no that's not right. I—we didn't know then that it was baby-rape and murder."

"The autopsy report showed cocaine in Veronica's bloodstream."

"I'm not surprised, the way she acted with that song."

"Where do you suppose she could have gotten the drug?"

He didn't hesitate. "No idea, John. But just the fact of Very being dead is bad enough for Spiral, you know?"

"Tell me, Mitch."

He shrugged. "What happens to the band now depends on what spin I can put on it."

"Spin?"

"Yeah. You know, like Clinton's spin doctors in Washington, try to take all the shit he's done and turn it around to his advantage. I mean, hell, Nixon tried it, too, but his keepers were Dark Ages compared to what—"

"You mean, put some kind of spin on Veronica's death?"

"Yeah. I tried it with O'D when he bit the big one. Back then, it was almost fucking fashionable for a band member to die from drugs. Look at Keith Moon from the Who, or Jimmie Morrison of the Doors, or even—"

"What kind of spin can Spiral put on Veronica's death?"

Eisen stopped. "Remember when Slowhand's kid fell from that window?"

Christ. "Eric Clapton's child."

"Right, right. Now, I'm not saying the two situations are identical or anything, but he writes a number-one song about it. And then there's Elton John with the Princess Di stuff."

"Mitch, Spi Held is going to write a song about his daughter's murder?"

Eisen came forward in his chair, his hands nesting on the desk in front of him. "Look, John, let me spell it out for you, okay? Spiral's comeback didn't just kind of 'hinge' on Very. She was the only hope of a comeback, pure and simple. But now that she's history, maybe—just maybe—I can weave gold out of straw here."

I watched him for a moment. "Are you saying that the band could have a *better* chance at a comeback now that Veronica's dead?"

"No, I wouldn't say that at all." Mitch Eisen spoke very evenly. "And neither would my lawyer."

SEVEN

Back in the Chevy Cavalier, I went over the list of names and numbers Justo Vega had given me outside the Homicide Unit. I used my cellular phone to call ahead to Spi Held's house.

"Hello."

A woman's voice, overlaid by an accent. "I'd like to speak with Mr. Held, please."

"He is not available."

With more words, she reminded me of someone from the Philippines I'd met in an earlier case. "His father told me he would be. Tell him John Cuddy will be there in thirty minutes."

A pause. "You are Mr. Cuddy?"

"Yes."

"I look forward to meeting you."

She broke the connection.

Held's home lay northwest of downtown Fort Lauderdale, maybe in a suburb, since I noticed the street signs change suddenly from "N.W." to "S.W.," as though I'd passed into another municipality's quadrant system. The house itself was painfully contemporary, with white stonework on the exterior walls and a castle turret rising above the roof like the proverbial sore thumb. The lot couldn't have been more than half an acre, though, so it looked as though the mansion-sized structure had been shoehorned into the space between its neighbors. As I entered the circular drive-way, I noticed four other cars already parked, with two more at the curb. I left the Cavalier behind the last one on the street, a yellow Toyota Celica, and went up the path to the house's front door.

Or doors.

They were the size you'd expect on a barn, with massive pull-handles in brass mounted vertically and shaped like a tornado. The logo of Spiral that Mitch Eisen had shown me.

I pushed the bell on the jamb. An electronic chime inside played chords of a song I remembered from the old days but wouldn't have known belonged to Spi Held's band if I hadn't been standing on his front steps.

The left door swung open, a man in a long-sleeved T-shirt and cutoff jeans looking out at me. The dog at his feet was wagging its tail, tongue lolling. Until it got a good look at me, that is, at which point the dog's face drooped, and it began to back slowly into the house.

The man stayed put. His eyes were bleary, the little remaining hair on his head mussed, as though he'd spent the night tossing and turning in bed. I would have recognized him from the videos I'd seen with Lourdes Pintana and Mitch Eisen, but the Fu Manchu mustache helped.

As did the Day-Glo portrait of his younger self on the front of his T-shirt.

"Mr. Held," I said.

"Spi, man." He ran the index finger of his left hand in a practiced, efficient way under his nose as he sniffled. "You're the guy used to soldier with my dad, right?"

The term "used to soldier" seemed a bit forced coming from his lips. "John Cuddy."

He extended a meaty hand. A sweaty one, too, as we shook.

"Come on in, John. We can talk in my writing loft."

Held led me into a massive foyer, brightly lit, with white tile on the floors and white, glossy walls. It was hard on the eyes, almost to the point of snow blindness, and the air smelled reconditioned and somehow artificial.

The dog was still walking, ten feet ahead of us and down the hall. It looked a little like a border collie, but its coat was gray with black patches, its paws like white socks, and I'd thought at the door that one of its eyes was blue, the other brown.

I said, "Is that a particular breed?"

Held turned to me. "What, Bowie?"

The dog's ears perked up, and it stopped to look back at us.

"As in 'Jim'?" I asked.

"Un-unh. As in 'David.' Very named him Bowie account of Australian shepherds having that one blue eye and one brown. You know, the Ziggy Stardust shtick."

I didn't get the allusion. "Bowie looks kind of sad."

"He is." Held shook his head. "Ever since Very got killed, the dog comes to the door whenever the chimes ring, figuring maybe she's finally coming home again for him."

The dead girl's father spoke heavily, but more like he was refining the line than feeling it.

As Held and I started down the hall, Bowie turned right into a doorway. When we passed by, I could see it led to a sunken living room, where an unfamiliar woman's voice spoke in hushed tones.

A little further down the hall, Held jerked his head back toward the living room. "My wife, Jeanette. This whole shit with Very really has her down."

"Understandable," I said to his back.

"Fact is, we're all kind of down." Another swipe at the nose and a sniffle. "Up here."

Held began to climb the staircase—a "spiral" one, no surprise. I followed him toward what I guessed would have to be the turret I'd seen from the street.

At the top, an opened door brought us into a circular room maybe fifteen feet in diameter with a ceiling nearly as high, a big paddle-bladed fan hanging a body-length down from the center and turning slowly like a ship's propeller at low speed.

"This is my sanctuary, man."

The walls displayed framed posters tacked up in no discernible order. Some were colorful album covers, a silhouette of the band or provocatively posed women drawing your eye. Others were mostly lettering, concert advertisements with dates and places. All had the Spiral name and logo somewhere on them.

To make conversation, I said, "Quite a museum."

"Museum? Uh-unh." Held moved to an ergonomic

chair near a computer hutch. In front of him was a guitar resting in its stand, a wire snaking from the base of the instrument around to the back of the computer. "You're looking at the future, not the past."

Taking another ergo chair, I gestured toward the guitar. "You can compose from that onto the computer?"

"Yeah. Amazing, huh? In the old days, I had to like pluck away for hours, getting the music fixed in my head without writing down any notes on sheet paper. Couple times, I had heavy tunes—*moto*-heavy, man—all up here." Held pointed to his left temple before swiping at the nose again. "But then the snow would fall up, take it all away."

"Snow as in . . . ?"

"Cocaine, man. Not that I use that shit anymore, other than maybe medicinally." Another sniffle. "What with Very and all."

"I'm sorry for your loss."

"Oh, man, 'loss' don't quite cover the situation, you know? I was ready for a comeback—the fuck's the word? *Poised.* Yeah, yeah, I was *poised* for a comeback. Mitch wanted to call it 'The Spiral Revival Tour,' 'cause he thinks he's got this talent for naming shit." Held looked at me. "Mitch called here, said he talked to you already this morning?"

"We talked."

A sly look. "Yeah, well, Mitch told you he came up with the name for the band, right?"

"Something like that."

More of the sly look. "You don't give away much, do you, man?"

"I'm more in the finding-out business."

"Yeah, well, let me help you find *this* out. Mitch got me started back then, all right. I had no connections, and he had some. But I was the one came up with the name Spiral, just like I changed mine."

A minute ago we were mourning his daughter. "From Spiro Helides."

"Right. To Spi Held. Then everybody started doing it. That guy Sting from the Police, you think that's his real name? Fuck, I'm surprised my dad didn't change his, too."

I wasn't. "You were talking about the 'Spiral Revival' idea?"

A frown now. "Mitch's idea, the rhyme gimmick. But in the trade, 'revival' kind of—the fuck's that word, too? Oh, yeah, *connotes*. In the trade, revival *connotes* just going on the road with your oldies, like some washed-up group from the sixties. Not for Spiral, man. I was composing new tunes, something to make everybody in the biz stand up and take notice."

"A comeback."

It was like Held's whole body nodded. "Now we're riding the same wave."

I thought about his daughter's body in her grandfather's pool.

"You cold or something, man?"

"No," I said. "How solid was this comeback idea of yours?"

"Solid? I had seven tunes finished. In the can, as the Hollywood types would say. Very and the band did one of them as a demo video. I figured to add two more fresh tracks, then fill out the CD with some of our big seventies numbers, like maybe 'Downward' and 'Upward,' you know?"

"You wrote these new songs?"

His body language went a little defensive. "Yeah."

Time for some quality control on what Held was feeding me. "Does that mean the lyrics, too?"

A moment before, "Uh-unh." His eyes went to the guitar. "I hear the music better than the words, man. O'D used to do our lyrics, but Very helped out some on the newbies."

"How important was your daughter to the comeback itself?"

Held closed his eyes now, and two tears—one on each side of his nose—began rolling toward the mustache. "God, she had the talent. I saw it maybe two, three times my whole professional life. Joplin, Mama Cass, Benatar. Very's middle name was 'Janis,' out of my respect for the lady, you hear me?" Held's head shook without the eyes opening. "Very, Very. You saw her on stage, you'd forget about everybody else up there. They say it comes down through the genes." His left hand cupped the cutoffs at his crotch. "I'm talking the DNA shit here, not dungarees." A solemn tone now. "Very could have taken Spiral back to the top, man."

"I know this is hard for—"

"*Hard?*" The eyes flapped open violently, like old-fashioned window shades. "What's hard is it's so fucking . . . *unfair*. All those years, watching guys with half my talent ride the crest of disco. Stupid music for greasers in polyester suits trying to dance like Fred and Ginger under whirling globes. Man, I could write the real shit, the real music, and I could play guitar better'n anybody except maybe Clapton and a couple others."

"Mr. Held?"

He seemed to catch his breath. "What?"

"After you followed your daughter from the living room at the party, what happened?"

"What happened? What do you think? Jeanette and me caught up to her in that hallway near the pool. I asked Very what the fuck she was doing, going on in front of my dad like that. She told me to fuck off. Her own father."

Imagine that. "And then?"

"Jeanette could see I was ripshit, so she dragged me back toward the living room, talk with my dad."

"And the next time you saw Veronica . . . ?"

"Was when Tranh's yelling brought a bunch of us to the pool. I was there second behind Ricky, and—"

"Ricky Queen?"

"Of course, Ricky Queen. How many—never mind. There was Tranh, laying my little girl, naked and dead, on the pool tile. Telling us he has to call nine-one-one."

"You know the lab report said Veronica tested positive for cocaine."

"Yeah," said Held, running an index finger under his nose again, "and even without my lawyer coaching me, I don't know where the fuck she got it."

"You said you have some for medicinal—"

"Shit, man. The stuff I'm using now I didn't even score till after Very was dead. There wasn't any in the house before that, because we were working. Working on the comeback."

"Mr. Held, do you know of anybody—at the party that day or not—who would want to kill your daughter?"

Spi Held rocked his head from side to side and made a sound like exasperation. "That's what I been trying to tell you, man. Very was our chariot back to the stars. Why would anybody want to kill that?"

"Jeanette, this is . . . Hey, Jeanette!"

The woman with straight, reddish-blond hair on one end of a caramel couch in the sunken living room finally turned her head slowly toward the doorway where Spi Held and I were standing. Bowie the Australian shepherd was lying at her feet. A second woman—with long, black hair—sat on the other end of the couch and had looked up as soon as she'd seen us. Asian features, olive skin, and eyes that didn't leave mine.

I was thinking of the voice on the phone when Spi Held said, "Jeanette, try to like snap out of it for fifteen, okay?" The dog growled, but Spi Held ignored it. "This is the private eye my dad hired. John Cuddy, my wife, Jeanette."

I stopped looking at the Asian woman long enough to walk down the three marble steps and cross the room to Veronica's mother, who up close had her daughter's hair color but none of the dead girl's vamping quality. "Mrs. Held, I'm truly sorry for your troubles."

She just stared up at me, like I was some harmless barnyard animal who had somehow wandered into her house. "Malinda is helping me with that."

I looked to the other woman now, who stood. Only about five-two, she'd looked taller sitting down.

Malinda said, "My last name is Dujong, Mr. Cuddy. D-U-J-O-N-G."

The Philippine accent.

Dujong extended her hand. Taking it, I felt a little ripple of energy, almost an electric jolt. "You're a grief counselor?"

"Not as such," she said, releasing my hand. "More spiritual advisor."

Spi Held sounded impatient behind me. "Jeanette, Mr. . . . Jeanette!"

Another slow turning of the reddish-blond head toward the doorway.

Her husband said, "Mr. Cuddy wants to ask you some questions about Very."

Though I wasn't watching him, there was a definite pause in the impatient voice before he added, "Alone."

Jeanette Held said, "I don't see how I can talk about that without Malinda."

As her husband began to fume, the dog growled again.

Dujong broke in with, "Jeanette, I have a very strong feeling about Mr. Cuddy." The "spiritual advisor" spoke her next words directly to me. "He has suffered, too, and recently. This man will not harm you intentionally."

I felt a little lump in my throat as Malinda Dujong walked toward Spi Held, who left the doorway before she passed through it. After Dujong was gone, I realized I couldn't have described to you what she'd been wearing.

When I turned back to Jeanette Held, she said, "If Malinda trusts you, I trust you, too."

I took an armchair the same caramel color as the leather couch. "Mrs. Held—"

"Please, call me 'Jeanette.' The media people all scream 'Mrs. Held' at me, like as long as they're polite enough to use my last name, they can follow it with any question that pops into their filthy minds."

As Bowie resettled himself across her feet, I started to revise my initial assessment of Jeanette Held. Hammered as she'd been by what had happened to her daughter, there was intelligence behind the shock shield raised around her.

"Jeanette, I want to make this as easy as possible for you."

A resigned smile seeped through the shield. "Too late, but not your fault." The smile retreated back inside her. "Ask your questions."

Start with some easy ones. "How long have you and your husband been married?"

"Fourteen years. He was thirty, clean and sober. For a while. I was twenty-five."

Making the Helds forty-four and thirty-nine now. "How did you meet?"

"Through the program."

Based on what she'd said, I tried to fill in the blank. "Alcohol rehab?"

"For me. Both drugs and booze for Spi. He loved to mix and match in his 'youth.' I'm more a one-addiction woman, and unfortunately I kind of transferred that from bourbon to Spi. Then, when he started getting back into snorting and drinking, I transferred from him to Very."

Pretty frank, so I decided to go with it. "Did you and your husband think of getting a divorce?"

"Spi? Hunh."

I thought that last part might have been Held's way of laughing, but there was no smile on her face now.

"No, John. Spi's father—the great field marshal himself—kept either one of us from even raising the possibility."

"How?"

Jeanette Held let her right hand drift to her lap, then closed her fists, watching them with something approaching interest. "The Colonel had Spi by the balls, John. The money Spiral needed for its comeback had to 'come' from somewhere."

"And his father wouldn't have financed a divorced son—"

"—who'd deprived a little girl the principal male figure in her life."

I let it hang there for a moment before saying, "Your husband was a good parent to Veronica?"

"Hunh." A genuine laugh this time, if the resigned smile was any indication. "Spi's idea of being a 'good parent' is . . . *was* to buy Very expensive stuff on her birthday and then ignore his daughter the rest of the time as kind of a drag on his life."

"What kind of 'drag'?"

"What kind of 'life' would be a better question. Spi and some sidemen Mitch Eisen came up with would—you met Mitch yet?"

"Briefly."

"That's the best way, if you can't avoid meeting him at all."

The smile seeped back through her shield. "Spi and these sidemen would tour as 'Spiral, the great raunch band of the seventies.'" Held looked down at the carpet.

"Christmases were the worst. He'd always want to be away for the holidays, avoid having to see his father. Then money got so tight that we'd barely get by, and even Spi knew he couldn't take off for Aspen or the Alps."

"I thought Colonel Helides was financing this big comeback."

"Only recently, when Spi 'discovered' how Very could put across a song. He'd ever attended shows in her elementary school here, my husband would have known a lot sooner."

"Someone else told me that Veronica was being tutored privately."

"Privately, yeah. By my father-in-law's wonderboy, Duy Tranh." Held softened just a little. "And I have to say, Duy was doing a good job by her, even if it was one more way the Colonel ran our lives."

"So, no problems between student and teacher?"

"Not that Very told me about. It was more, 'Duy showed me this way-cool nature video.' Or, 'David taught me this awesome computer game.'"

"David being the Colonel's other son."

"Yeah. Very liked him, too, even through the 'extreme weirdness.' But no matter how much she learned from those two, it still wasn't normal."

"What wasn't?"

"Her not being in school just so she could rehearse with the band."

"You didn't approve of the comeback?"

"The truth?" Held said sharply.

"That would be nice."

"The truth." Less sharply, the shield seeming to lift. "Well, here's what I heard of the old days. When the band started getting eaten alive by disco, this drummer I never met named O'D committed suicide. Spi went into a free fall. The other players—Buford, Gordo—they hooked up with other bands or got day jobs."

"Like what?"

The straight hair shook. "Don't know, because I didn't even know Spi himself then. Oh, I knew *of* him, of course, at least from the glory days in the early seventies, cause I'd hear Spiral's sounds on the radio back then. But by the time I met Spi, I'd been through one bad marriage with no kids, and a bout with the bottle that kept coming up knockout every round. So, I got off the booze, and did what I could to get Spi's monkeys off him, too. And I did, so long as everything was going good."

"Everything with your family life?"

"Hunh. No. No, I'm afraid that after a fantastic honeymoon and maybe three more months of 'wedded bliss,' Spi started missing things."

"Missing things?"

"About being in a rock-'n'-roll band, on tour in one of those stupid buses thinks it's a Winnebago." A stalling sound from her throat, then, "Being the alpha wolf with the groupies, letting the other members of the band scratch for sloppy seconds."

Franker than frank.

Held said, "Hey, John, don't be too shocked. After you're around a rock band for a while, it's just kind of hard to stay polite in mixed company."

I waited a minute.

The straight hair shook again. "If you don't have any more questions, I'd like to get back with Malinda, take my mind off things with what she can do, which is so good but so scary, too, that I almost have to brace myself for it."

I waited a minute longer.

Held said, "Hello?"

"Jeanette, I don't think you answered my question."

"I don't think I even remember it."

"I asked you whether you approved of Spiral's comeback attempt."

The shield came down again, hard. "Wasn't a question of whether or not I 'approved.' Very was the heart of the comeback."

"You were her mother, half of her parents."

"Hunh." Definitely a laugh this time, but no resigned smile. No smile period. Just the beginning of tears, the dog whuffing through its nose.

"I was Very's mother, John. I remember giving birth to her in a shiny delivery room. I remember breast-feeding her and teaching her to walk. I even remember encouraging her to sing. Sing in the bathtub, sing in the yard, sing whenever there was nobody around to bother. I remember all these things, but that doesn't mean I was her 'parent.'"

"Jeanette, I truly don't follow you here."

"Then let me spell it out. After Spi and I got married, we decided to get me pregnant real quick because his father had disowned him after my husband—'Spiro,' then—folded his underwear into a hankie and tied it on a stick. Spi's running away from home tore the guts out of the old man, especially since his first wife'd died a couple of years before—having David, who turned out to be worse than no kid at all. You met David yet?"

"Not really."

"Hunh. I don't know what that means, but it's probably a pretty good answer where David's concerned."

"I'm more concerned about—"

"Then let me finish, okay? Spi and I decided to have Very because we figured it was the best way to get ahead."

"Get ahead?"

"Yeah. The Colonel's second son turns into something out of the Twilight Zone, we figured the way to get Spi back into his father's good graces would be to 'present him with a grandchild,' as Martha Stewart might say."

I thought I finally saw it. "You had Very to heal the family wound."

"More to steal the family treasure." Held softened again. "Or not steal it, really. I mean, Spi just wanted what was his, and we would have put David in a real good home somewhere."

Off the beaten track and out of their "normal" life. "Jeanette, why are you telling me all this?"

"Because none of it fucking matters anymore." The tears started rolling now, and Held tore some tissues from a dispenser she must have had on the far side of her, since I hadn't seen it before.

"Why not?"

"Very was supposed to be our tunnel to the Colonel's money, and she was doing a great job of digging it."

"At least until the song at the birthday party."

"Which I still don't get. I mean, Spi and I ran after her, find out why she'd done it. And she just told the two of us to fuck off."

"Traces of cocaine were found—"

"And Spi denied Very got her junk from him, right?"

"Right."

"Yeah, well." The straight hair shook again. "You haven't known Spi very long yet, so maybe you can believe him on that."

"Jeanette, what happened after Veronica told you two to let her alone?"

"At the party?"

"Yes."

"I thought Spi was going to blow his lid, so I got him back to his father in the living room, try to patch the hole a little."

"And?"

"And everybody seemed to be doing that, drifting toward the old man. But when Tranh found Very, and I saw her, lying there . . ."

"Jeanette—"

"It was just so stupid! Very always knew how to behave around her grandfather, buttering him up even before she knew how sexy she was."

Reluctantly, I thought back to Mitch Eisen's "incest" comment. "Are you saying there could have been a sexual aspect to Veronica and the Colonel's—"

"Oh, shove it, will you?" said Held, loudly enough to start the dog growling and even barking. "Shush, Bowie, shush." Then, back to me with, "No, John. No actual sex. Very would have told me." That laughing sound. "Flaunted it, actually. Once she learned about sex, she was fascinated by the concept, by what she could get from teasing with it."

I tried to remember that I was talking to the bereaved mother who needed a spiritual advisor. "Do you mean Veronica was sexually active with somebody else?"

Jeanette Held suddenly hung her head, tears dropping visibly onto her lap. "God, I can't believe we're talking about this. It's really bringing me down again."

"I'm sorry if—"

Her face snapped back up at mine. "Look, let me just give you the bottom line, okay?"

Bowie began growling some more, and I didn't think I'd get much more from Held, so I said, "Okay."

"Very as a gimmick was the ticket to Spiral's comeback, and not just the onstage part as 'Lolita, lead singer.' The old man bought this house for us thirteen years ago because 'No grandchild of mine will grow up in a two-bit apartment.'" Held had lowered her voice a few octaves for that last part. She went back to her own with, "The generous gramps even put up enough cash for the band to get back on its feet—almost a quarter of a million for the production costs of the CD alone. And you know why he laid out that kind of money?"

I thought back to Kalil's wanting to video the party. "Because Veronica asked him to."

"That's right. And now we don't have Very anymore, so even if Spi can come up with a decent set of songs, I don't know what the *ex*-gramps is going to do about backing the band. Or backing us, for that matter."

"Us."

"In this house, the cars and all, too. Without a real comeback for Spiral, I could lose my whole life here."

I was about to say, "On top of your daughter," before remembering that Malinda Dujong had made my own life a little easier by telling Jeanette Held that I wouldn't intentionally hurt her.

Leaving the sunken living room, I didn't see Dujong, but there was an African-American male crossing the intersecting hallway at the back end of the entry corridor, a soda can in his left hand. He stopped awkwardly and turned my way.

Buford Biggs, from the videos.

"Help you with something?"

I nodded. "Mr. Biggs."

He cocked his head to the right. "You the man Spi's daddy send?"

I nodded again. "John Cuddy."

Another cocking of the head, this time to the left, as Biggs showed me a pack of cigarettes he'd palmed in his right hand. "Just going outside for a smoke, babe. You want, we can talk while I'm having it."

Given my day so far, a little semi-fresh air sounded good. "Show me the way."

Biggs waited until I reached the end of the corridor. In

person, he was about six feet tall and more stick-skinny than just slim, a sleeveless sweatshirt and contrasting sweatpants almost falling off him. The hair was stylishly razored half-an-inch off his scalp. His face looked drawn, though, the whites of his eyes sallow around the brown irises. Almost ebony in skin tone, Biggs had several irregular blotches on his neck that looked purplish in the hallway lighting. A single gold earring pierced the lobe of his left ear, and what I at first thought was an insignia on the sweatshirt turned out to be the looped and pinned red ribbon of AIDS Awareness.

"Most times, now, I take my nicotine break out by the pool." A pause. "Family don't use it much no more."

I didn't nod this time, but I did follow him through another corridor of white tile and walls into a matching kitchen with a large central island and murals of mountain scenes over the wide counters. Biggs slid open half of a double glass door onto a patio that acted as an apron around a pool with water the color of a glacier. Everything else—tiles, lounges and chairs, resin cocktail tables—was white, though, Biggs seeming like a piece of abstract art as he crossed to a shaded alcove with a pair of chairs and one of the small tables between them. The air felt warm but kind of . . . real, after the antiseptic, reconditioned atmosphere in the house itself.

Lowering himself into the chair farther away from the pool, Biggs said, "Not crazy about the sun myself, but you want, pull this other one out a ways."

"Shade's fine with me, too."

Biggs set the soda can on the table, then lit up as I sat down. "Expect you want me to talk about Very."

"Eventually. I'd rather start with how you came to join Spiral."

A frown as he took a long drag on the cigarette. "You mean, like, way back?"

"Right."

A shrug, the smoke coming out his nostrils like a cartoon of a raging bull. "Might be this'll turn into a three-butt break." After tapping some ash into the soda can's opened top, he looked at the smoldering end of the cigarette. "Man, but that first puff, it always the best."

"The Helds don't want you smoking inside the house?"

Another shrug. "Don't nobody want us coffin-nailers smoking inside anywhere. I hear out in California now, they went and outlawed it every which place—even bars, man. You a nicotine-fiend, how you supposed to enjoy a drink, you can't smoke, too?"

"Don't know, Mr. Biggs. Never picked up the habit."

He eyed me, then a cagey smile. "Second time you call me that, babe."

"What?"

"'Mr. Biggs,' like I'm some kind of record-company honcho and you my ass-kisser."

"Just trying to be polite."

"To the house nigger."

Biggs sent two more plumes of smoke out his nose.

I said, "You weren't black, and used that word, I'd ask you not to use it again."

Head cocked again, but a little differently. "You in the war, right?"

"Vietnam, anyway."

"What other one there been, babe?"

"Persian Gulf."

"No," said Biggs, shaking his head as he drew another lungful. "You too old for that one, and besides, you got the look."

"The look."

"Yeah, like what some of my homeboys used to get, they come back from over there and I use 'honky' or 'offay' in front of them."

I heard a sudden, buzzing sound to the right, and turned that way. Someone had suspended a hummingbird feeder on what looked like monofilament fishing line from the outside beam of the alcove. One green hummingbird was hovering over the red cover of the feeder, about to land on the clear plastic rail around the bowl part, when another hummingbird strafed it from an oblique angle, both zooming off in different directions.

Biggs said, "Bother you to talk about the war?"

I turned back to him. "Bother you to talk about how you came to join Spiral?"

A raspy laugh, then a cough before another deep drag on the cigarette. "You got a little of the bulldog in you, babe. But I admire that, so we cool." More exhaled smoke. "Okay, here's how the shit happened. I was doing studio work—you know what I'm saying?"

"Teach me."

Another raspy laugh. "Studio musician, he play for a recording session with a singer don't got their own band. Producer find out you can lay the tracks down fast and clean, he keep hiring you, account of you save him money."

"By shortening the session and the rent on the studio?"

"Now you got it." Biggs dropped the remainder of his cigarette into the can, but didn't light another right away. "So, like I was telling you, I'm working this studio, and Mitch Eisen—he Spiral's manager?"

"We've met."

"Mitch, he say to me, 'Buford, I got this white kid, wrote a couple songs I think might fly. You want in?'"

"Just like that?"

The frown. "Just like what?"

"Eisen has you match up with another musician you'd never met?"

"Oh, babe. You in the war, but not some time capsule,

right? Back in the early seventies, everything be real loosey-goosey. Wasn't no 'courtship' kind of thing. Some bands, now, they been messing around since they in junior high, but lots of groups, they got put together by the front office, you dig?"

"Go on."

Biggs shook another cigarette from his pack. "Anyway, I go in this session, and Mitch already has Gordo lined up for bass guitar—I tell you what I play?"

"Eisen said you were the keyboardist."

"Okay, then. Spi, he was lead guitar and lead singer, and I did backup vocals. This spaceshot name of Tommy O'Dell, he on drums—not to mention more drugs than you could find at twenty Walgreens."

"I know O'Dell died of an overdose."

"Yeah, yeah. But that's a long time later." Biggs lit his second cigarette. "You want the early days, right?"

"Right."

"Okay. Mitch gets us four together, and fact is, we don't sound half bad. Mitch, he has like a talent for that."

"For the right mix of people."

"Yeah, but more than just the music." Another cocking of the head. "Name me one brother who play in a rock band, you can."

"Jimi Hendryx."

"The main man. Name me another."

"You."

The cagey smile. "How about a third one?"

I thought about it. "Tapped out."

Biggs inhaled some smoke and settled deeper into his chair. "Don't feel too bad, babe, ain't many remember the others. There was a brother played with the Allmans—which was a hoot for another reason. And then the bass player for the Doobies—notice any pattern?"

"Black musicians in 'brothers' bands."

"You got it. Make the groups seem like real 'family.' The world of rock just one fine rainbow of a place."

"Which was Eisen's idea for Spiral, too?"

"Bet on it. He sure did."

"Meaning?"

"Meaning Mitch, he bankroll our first album—which in those days was a hell of a lot more bread than the four of us could of raised. This was way before Spi's daddy got himself rich."

"Go ahead."

"Okay, so we cut this album, and it hit." Biggs came forward in his chair. "Oh, babe, how it do hit. We climb the charts, all of a sudden everybody be calling Mitch, want us to play their venue."

"Venue as in concert hall?"

"Yeah. Venues, they get measured by the number of seats in the house. At our best, we couldn't fill no Yankee Stadium. But our first concert gig, we sell out a forty-five-hundred place called 'Winterland' by San Francisco, and then Boston Garden and the Cow Palace—also San Fran'—and they like fourteen-, fifteen-thousand seats each."

I blocked out the Bay Area references. "So, success came early."

"Yeah, babe." A long thoughtful drag on the cigarette. "Early, but not often."

"How do you mean?"

Biggs settled back into the chair again, watching me. "Probably should've told you this up front. I ain't hired no lawyer for this Very thing."

I didn't reply.

Biggs said, "And the way I heard it from Spi, his daddy want us to be straight with you, right?"

"I believe that would be appreciated."

The raspy laugh. "Okay, babe. 'Appreciate' this, then. Manager, he supposed to get only ten, maybe twenty percent of the gross a band make from every kind of thing it does."

"Meaning albums, concerts—"

"Meaning everything that's entertainment. Well, since Mitch put the band together, he own the name, he own the logo, he practically own *us*. We have three, four great years, then the bubble go 'pop' like a little kid with his chewing gum."

I thought back to Eisen's short course on the history of the music. "Other groups pushed you off those charts."

"Not just other groups. Hell, babe, we could rock with the best of them. Problem was other sounds, other kinds of shit. The music was evolving, and Spi, he couldn't evolve with it. He stuck with his sound."

"Which was?"

"Raunchy-rock."

Eisen's term, too. "But even after you stopped making albums or doing concerts, you still got royalties or whatever, didn't you?"

The cagey look behind a cloud of smoke. "Mitch, he tell you that?"

"We didn't spend much time on the money side."

"That don't surprise me none. Mitch, he spend his own time on the money side, but the man don't share much of it with the rest of the world."

I turned that over. "You think he cheated you?"

"Oh, he cheat us all right, but he do it by contract, dig? Or by law. Contract say, he own the name and shit. Law say, only the writer of the song get money from ASCAP or BMI when they collect it from the stations."

"So only Spi Held got royalties from radio play of Spiral's songs?"

"And Mitch."

"I don't follow you. Eisen wrote some of the songs?"

"No, babe. Our 'personal manager' had us all do wills, with him as the winner."

"The winner."

"One of us die, that share go to him."

I got it. "So when Tommy O'Dell died . . . ?"

". . . all O'D's royalties for writing the lyrics go to Mitch."

"With nothing for the other musicians?"

As Biggs started to speak, the hummingbirds came back to the feeder. This time, the two arrived nearly simultaneously and chittered at each other before a third dive-bombed them, the sound now more of clashing wings before all three zoomed away.

Biggs said, "That's what break up bands, too."

I turned back to him. "Fighting over the goodies."

"Right on. Those birdies, they just learn to share, everybody get plenty to eat, account of Jeanette, she keep that bowl just as full of sugar water as it can be."

"Kind of like a 'royalty bowl'?"

The eyes behind another cloud of smoke went sad for a minute. "Band usually got just one songwriter. Couple bands—Beatles, now, best example—they had two or three doing it. Spiral, for most of the good tunes, it was more like a collaboration."

"Meaning you all contributed to the writing."

"Some more than others."

"And you more than Gordo Lazar?"

"Right on again, babe." The sad look still. "I didn't know jackshit about this royalty stuff back then. None of us really did, and I mean most every player from the sixties, early seventies. Wasn't till some bands got lawyers to watch their managers, and then other lawyers to watch their first lawyers, any of us knew what the hell was going down."

I waited a moment before, "Yet you signed on for the comeback."

The cagey look again. "I sign on for the money. Mitch, he track me down through the union, tell me he got Spi's daddy to bankroll us for another album—or CD, shit, it's still just music for the masses, dig?"

"So your heart's not exactly in it."

"Wasn't never my heart." A change of tone. "You get to be good foxhole buddies with some brothers over in Vietnam?"

I thought back, more to the streets of Saigon than the bush. Dave Waters during Tet, Calvin Mildredge losing an arm, Luther—

"Hey, babe?"

"Yeah, I had black friends there."

"Well, then, you got a lot farther along the road of racial harmony than Spi. He was one major pain in the butt, that way."

"Racist?"

"More just resentful. He knowed how much I help him out on the keyboard with the arrangement of his tunes, but he also knowed he don't have to share none of the royalties. So there always be this . . . curtain, like, between us."

"Same with the others in the band?"

"Have to ask them, babe." Biggs stubbed out his cigarette on top of the can before dropping it through the hole. "I got to be going."

"What about that third smoke?"

Biggs looked up, the eyes now more baleful than sad. "You see these here things on my neck?"

The left hand went toward his collar.

"I see them."

"You know what they are?"

"I'm not a doctor."

"No? Well, you know what this is, right?"

Pointing now at the red ribbon on his chest.

"I do."

"Got diagnosed two years ago." A pause. "Don't know how I got it, except I hadn't been doing no horse for a long while, so I don't believe it was from a needle. But the doctors, they don't really know shit about that. They do know one thing, though. There's these pills can keep you healthy."

"Veronica Held had a drug in her body that wasn't so healthy."

"Not from me, babe. Onliest drugs I take now are that AIDS cocktail and my nicotine. Plus"—his hand went toward the water—"I swim every day in that pool, hour at a time. Ever since we all moved in here."

That stopped me. "Moved in?"

"Spi's daddy, he hire you, but he don't tell you we all bunking at his son's crib?"

"No."

The raspy laugh. "Rich man know how to save money. He backing the band, but he also paying on this house for Spi. He figure his boy's band can stay here, not run up the room service at some hotel, or maybe trash the place like the old days." Now the baleful look again. "You ask me before about my 'heart' not being in this comeback. Let me tell you where my heart is, babe. I doing this gig for the money, account of the money let me buy the pills and leave some left over for my son."

"Kalil."

A pause. "Kalil. I take those pills and I swim the laps, keep me strong so I can stay around long enough to maybe see him growed up." Another pause. "And maybe not. But I tell you the truth here so's maybe the money train don't stop running."

"Meaning, so that Nicolas Helides keeps backing the band."

"Babe, you work for him, I work for him. I help you out, you don't upset my applecart, dig?"

"I can't promise that."

Biggs rose from the chair, but a little unsteadily. "Wasn't looking for no promise. Just an understanding."

"I could use some more answers."

"Later, you want. I got to go pick up my son at the specialist."

"Specialist?"

"Another reason I need this gig. Kalil see a speech specialist."

"What's the impediment?"

"Don't use that term no more. 'Stigmatizes,' they say. Only they still call themselves speech 'pathologists,' which seem to me 'stigmatizes' more than anything else, account of it sound like you gonna die from what you got."

The keyboardist stared down at me. "And the one thing Kalil *ain't* gonna do is die. He gonna live as good a life as my music can make for him."

And with that, Buford Biggs picked up his soda can, tossed it into a white plastic barrel at the end of the alcove, and walked off the patio and around the house toward getting his son.

I waited in my chair another five minutes, but the hummingbirds never came back.

EIGHT

When I opened the sliding glass door into the kitchen, there was a stolid woman with long, sandy hair at the center island. When she turned, I realized she also appeared on the birthday video. Delgis Reyes had pale skin and blue eyes that picked up one of the minor colors in her simple print dress. I could see the makings of a sandwich on the counter behind her.

"Who are you?" said Veronica Held's former au pair, in a demanding tone and with a Spanish accent.

"John Cuddy, Ms. Reyes."

The blue eyes measured me as she put her fists on her hips. "What you want here?"

"Colonel Helides asked me to investigate the death of his granddaughter."

"I am sorry." The fists became hands again and dropped to her sides. "We are told you will come. You want, I find you someone to talk to?"

"Actually, I'd like to talk with you."

She did a half-turn toward the counter. "But I make sandwich for Gordo."

"I think he can wait."

Reyes was clearly troubled but said, "We sit here?"

"Fine with me."

There were bar stools around the central island, and we each took one.

Reyes said, "I don't know what I can tell you about this thing."

"Let's start with how you came to be Veronica's au pair."

A degree of relaxation from Reyes. "My brother, Umberto, is the guard for the Colonel's house. I go there sometimes, help with the meals. The Colonel see I am a good worker, so he hire me for Veronica."

"It was Nicolas Helides and not Spi Held who hired you?"

Reyes tensed again. "Yes, just so. I live here, but the Colonel is the one to pay me for the watching of her."

I turned that over. "When you say 'watching' Veronica, what do you mean?"

More tension. "When she alive, Veronica is a . . . diffi-cult girl."

Duy Tranh's term for her, too. "How?"

"How she is difficult?"

I nodded.

Reyes started rubbing her hands in her lap. "Veronica do not listen to her father and mother too good. She do what she want."

"Can you give me some examples?"

"*Ejemplos*." Reyes closed her eyes. "She want to go places by herself they don't want her to."

"What kind of places?"

"Clubs they play music, sing songs."

"Do you mean bars?"

"Yes."

"But she was only thirteen years old."

"There are some places, they don't sell the alcohol."

"Even for those, though, wouldn't she have to be—what, eighteen?"

Reyes became agitated. "She wear the makeup, Veronica look as many years as me, and I have now twenty-five."

"Wouldn't they check her identification, though?"

More agitation. "You ask questions, I try to help you, but I don't know all these things."

"I'm sorry. You're right."

Reyes took a breath.

I let her take another before, "Can you give me some other examples?"

"Of when Veronica don't listen to her parents?"

"Yes."

A third breath. "She like to be at the tennis place."

"Veronica enjoyed the sport?"

Some embarrassment now. "She like the teacher there."

I thought back to Kalil's video. "The pro who was helping Mrs. Helides?"

"The Colonel's wife, yes."

"Do you think there was anything . . . sexual?"

A darkening more than embarrassment. "I do not know what the Colonel's wife does."

Sometimes you get an answer when you didn't realize you'd asked the question. "I meant, anything sexual between the pro and Veronica?"

Now Reyes hung her head as the hands twisted a little in her lap. "This is most why the Colonel hire me, I think. To be the . . . chaperone?"

"How did Veronica feel about that?"

"She no get mad at me or anything. She make it more like a game."

"A game?"

Reyes lifted her head before nodding. "Veronica try to leave with me no seeing her. I catch her, she laugh, then next day, try a different way."

"What about when she went to school?"

Tension again. "After the band start to make the come-back, the Colonel don't have her in school no more."

The Skipper again, not Veronica's father. "And Duy Tranh became her teacher."

"At the Colonel's house, yes."

"Why there?"

"My brother is guard at the gate, and there is security system in that house. More hard for Veronica to get away than here."

"Did you go with her when she saw Tranh?"

"Yes, I go to house, but not in room."

"Why not?"

"I cannot help with teaching," said Reyes, "but I can help with kitchen or cleaning."

"Did you ever sense anything was wrong between Veronica and Mr. Tranh?"

"No. She tell me she play games on him, too."

"What kind of games?"

"She no tell me. Just say Mr. Tranh is no smarter than any other man."

"Meaning?"

"I tell you already, I don't know."

Time to ease off. "What else can you tell me about Veronica as a person?"

"*Como persona?*" The hung head again. "Veronica think she very smart. And she no is stupid. But she no is so smart as maybe she think."

"In what ways?"

Reyes didn't lift her head this time. "Veronica think she already know things about . . . men. She do not know enough."

"Examples again?"

"When she go to tennis place, sometime I drive her, sometime the Colonel's wife. Then, one day, the Colonel's wife tell me she no drive Veronica anymore."

"Do you know why?"

"Why the Colonel's wife no drive her?"

"Yes."

Reyes kept her head down. "I think maybe because of the tennis teacher."

"Veronica did or said something to him?"

The agitation again. "I tell you, I don't know all these things."

Back to more stable ground. "Was there someone who would want to hurt Veronica?"

"No." Reyes lifted her head again, the blue eyes tearing up. "I ask this question to myself many times, but there is no one I can think to do this to her. We are at the

Colonel's party, there is food and drink and music. A fiesta."

"Until Veronica sang that song?"

A nod, the tears welling over now. "She must be crazy to do that, I think, but I see her do it. Then she run out, and her father go after her, and I walk to the kitchen, try to make more food so people be happy again." Reyes began to sob. "I don't think anybody be happy again forever."

I was looking around for some tissues or napkins when a voice from the doorway said, "Delgis, where the fuck's my food?"

I looked up at a heavyset man in a leather biker vest and bulging black jeans. His head was shaved, some scarring on the cheeks that looked like poorly healed knife wounds from long ago.

"The fuck are you?" he said.

"John Cuddy."

"That supposed to mean something?"

Word didn't seem to travel very fast in the Held house. "I'm investigating Veronica's death for her grandfather."

A grin as he stroked a scar on his right cheek. "The guy we all got to talk to, right?"

"Right."

"Well, I'm Gordo Lazar. I don't know enough to need a lawyer, but you want, we can talk back in the studio while Delgis fixes my fucking lunch. Sandwich for you, too?"

I looked at Reyes, who had torn a paper towel off a dispenser and was blowing her nose into it. "If there's enough."

"Hey," said Lazar as he turned and beckoned to me. "I may be fat, but I haven't eaten everything in the place." His voice carried in from the corridor. "Yet."

I thanked Delgis Reyes for her time, told her a sandwich and a soda would be fine, then left the stool I was on and followed after Gordo Lazar.

* * *

"Hell of a setup, huh?"

I watched Lazar reach down for a large guitar, unclipping the strap up near the tuning pegs, then hitching the strap over his left shoulder before reclipping it. We were in a cubelike room with lots of instruments on the floor, microphones coming down from the ceiling on elbowed steel components, and cushy green blocks on three walls. An expanse of glass comprised most of the fourth wall, a picture window into what looked like a control room, though no one was occupying the chairs there.

I said, "Spi Held gave me the impression he did most of his work up in that turret room."

"The Spi Tower." Lazar's fingers went to the guitar, a pick of some kind causing three different notes in a do-re-mi pattern to strum out a bulky hi-fi speaker on the floor next to him. "That's where the genius does his writing. Here's where we try to make the shit he brings down into something that'll play."

A few chords this time, more complicated and dissonant. I said, "You're not crazy about the band's new music?"

A gruff laugh that mixed with the next run of sounds from the speaker. "The fuck of it is, I wasn't that happy about the original shit from the seventies."

There was a resin folding chair near one of the octopus mikes coming down from the ceiling, so I took it. "How come, Mr. Lazar?"

"Hey, man. Mr. Lazar was my fucking father. Call me 'Gordo.'" A wink. "You know what it stands for?"

"No."

"Actually, it's just short for 'Gordon,' which was my father's name, too. But around the house, my mom always called me 'Gordo' to let us know which one she wanted. Then I kept it 'cause the word means 'fat man' in Spanish.

Helped me like differentiate myself from the rest of the bass players of the world."

"I don't think you've told me why you weren't all that happy about Spiral's original music."

"Huh, guess I didn't. Thought we should have turned more away from raunch and more toward straight heavy metal. There's a cult market for that shit that keeps you going, no matter what the top-40 stations are passing off."

"Meaning Spiral might have had a longer run than it did?"

"Back in the 'good old days.'" Lazar got a fire in his eye. "And man, they *were* good. I got to see the country, do things you probably never even heard of."

"Such as?"

"Playing gooseshit bingo out by Idaho. A guy'd scratch this humongous bingo card in the dirt behind a bar, and everybody'd bet on which squares the geese would squat over. Or up in Baltimore, I went rat-fishing, these crazy fucks there going out with peanut butter as bait, smeared on glue pads. When the rats'd 'bite,' the guys reel them in and beat the shit out of them with baseball bats. And then there was the time in Michigan, we had Christmas Day off between gigs. Spi always carried a machine gun in the luggage compartment of our bus, and—"

"A machine gun?"

"Yeah. You know, one of those tommy-guns like The Untouchables used on the bootleggers in Chicago, big round drum of bullets? Well, like I said, this one Christmas, we didn't have fuck-all to do, and we're in the middle of nowhere, so Spi drives the bus to a little, like, glade of woods. Peaceful as shit, snow on the branches of the pine trees. Only then Spi takes out his own 'snow,' and once he's in the clouds, he takes out the tommy-gun, too, and he shoots the branches all to shit."

"On Christmas Day."

Lazar shrugged and stroked his scar some more. "Spi always did have a problem with holidays, man. Family baggage."

"And his supply of snow?"

Lazar used an index finger to tap the bridge of his nose. "Toward the end there, cocaine was everywhere. Used to be we'd snort it through rolled-up hundred-dollar bills as straws."

"And now?"

"Now?" An evasive look. "I wouldn't lay out my own money for the shit, but I wouldn't turn down a free line, either."

"I was thinking more where Veronica Held might have gotten some."

"Never saw her snort, so I can't help you there. In fact— Delgis! About fucking time."

I turned as Reyes came through the padded door of the studio carrying a tray. I got up to make space for it on a plastic table littered with soda cans and candy-bar wrappers. When she set down the tray, I could see three sandwiches, three Sprites, and a bowl of corn chips.

I said, "Delgis, you going to join us?"

"Hell, no." Lazar came over to her, though, and ran his pick-hand down through the hair on her neck. "Even if she had time, there's just the two for me and the one for you." More stroking of the hair. "Besides, Delgis's been sort of off her feed since Very got dunked and crumped in the pool."

Reyes hadn't recoiled from the stroking, but now she turned away toward the studio door. "You want some more, you call me."

"Some more what?" said Lazar, the leer in his words as well as in his eyes.

Reyes left the room without looking back in our direction.

Lazar watched me as he walked to the food tray. "Been punching that chick for the better part of three months now, and I can still embarrass her. Must be the Catholic upbringing."

After a beat, I said, "You and Ms. Reyes have been seeing each other?"

"Well, yeah." Half a sandwich disappeared into Lazar's mouth, and he spoke as he chewed. "Not exactly senior-prom stuff. In fact, not half as good as we used to see on the road, our best tours."

"Back in the seventies."

"Man, you never did a trip—even as a roadie, the guys help us set up and break down?—you got no idea. Every chick in the audience wanted to be a real groupie, ride with the band."

I reached for a sandwich. "On your bus?"

"We had a nice setup: little kitchen, closet bathroom with a shower. For sleeping or fucking, it was bunks mostly, but they'd do. And if the band was staying in the town overnight, Spi might be off somewheres, and we could maybe get his."

We. "Spi's what?"

"Bed, man." Lazar popped a fistful of corn chips, washed them down by chugging one of the Sprites. "He had a real bedroom in the back. Oh, you could sit on the center of the fucking mattress and touch all four walls without moving, but it gave a hell of a nice ride for the chick of the night. In fact, I remember this one time, Mitch was on the road with us. Him and Spi had just counted our cash from the last gig, spreading it all over the bedsheets in back—twenty, thirty thousand wouldn't have been unusual. And before we left the concert, the two of them picked up a couple of blondes from somewhere in Minnesota. Twin sisters, like the Twin Cities, get me?"

I opened one of the other two Sprites. "Mr. La—"

"Anyway, we're driving toward Minot, S.D., only vehicle on the whole fucking road, with Mitch and Spi planking these twins on a comforter of cash in the back, when all of a sudden, the tires start going thump, thump, thump. Like we're getting a flat everywhere at once only without losing our steering."

"Mr. Lazar, I—"

"But we figure we got to pull over, and at the side of the road, we can see we been hitting toads."

That stopped me. "Toads?"

"Yeah." The other half-sandwich disappeared, and Lazar reached for the last one with his right hand and for more chips with his left. "When Mitch and Spi come up front, find out what the fuck's going on—I guess the thump-thumps made it better for them back there on the hump-humps—we see all these toads, hopping across the road. And one of the Minnesota twins says they're some special kind like salmon."

After a swallow of sandwich and Sprite, I said, "Salmon."

"Yeah." Lazar spoke around his food. "These toads migrate back to the exact pond where they were born before they'll breed with another toad from the same place. Amazing, huh?"

"Amazing. You never had any trouble from the women who rode on the bus?"

Another evasive look as he snagged the last Sprite. "Well, sometimes your standard chick turned into a raging bitch."

I took another bite of sandwich. "How do you mean?"

"Coming on the bus and not expecting to do all of us."

I'd let the "we" part alone once. "You'd expect her to have sex with all of you?"

"Well, yeah." A confused look. "I mean, that was kind of the purpose of the enterprise. Unless we took on a chick for each of us, which happened too."

"Any indictments happen?"

"Nah, not back then." More corn chips and Sprite. "I mean, remember, this is post-pill and pre-AIDS, with free-love as a real established concept. Bitch wanted to cry gang-rape instead of gang-bang, she'd look awful silly explaining how it was her come backstage after a concert and onto a rock band's bus in the first place. And besides, the bitch factor was maybe one, two percent. The rest of the chicks loved doing it, probably at least as much so they could brag to their friends."

"The police believe Veronica was sexually assaulted as part of the murder."

"Yeah, well, that girl was a—the fuck did Mitch call her? Oh, yeah. 'Vixen.' A real little vixen."

"Did Veronica ever hit on the other members of the band?"

Lazar finally looked shocked, crushed the soda can in his hand. "She was Spi's fucking daughter, man."

"Did Veronica flirt with you guys?"

Now a measured look. "Spi said, we're supposed to tell you the fucking truth, right?"

"That's my understanding, too."

Lazar tossed the crushed can onto the empty food tray. "Okay, man. Truth is, Very couldn't turn it off. She'd be touching and teasing like Madonna until it went from embarrassing all the way to aggravating. And besides, with Buford carrying the plague—and Ricky queer as pink lace, so he could be positive, too—it was fucking dangerous for her. But she wouldn't stop, except when granddaddy was around."

"Veronica didn't vamp when Colonel Helides could see it?"

"Nah. She knew how to behave herself around the goose who laid the golden eggs. But everybody else? Open fucking season."

"Everybody, meaning not just the members of the band."

"You got it. Her mother drove her to granddaddy's house, Very'd sit behind the driver's side so she could run her index finger down the cheek and throat of the gate guard."

"Umberto Reyes."

"Right, right. Delgis's brother. But not just him, either. Mitch Eisen, Tranh, even that 'Plan Nine from Outer Space' David, though he'd just run away from her."

"David Helides would run. Anybody else not run?"

"You mean, like, stick their fingers in the nookie jar?"

"Take advantage of Veronica's attitude."

"Not that I ever saw, man." Lazar picked up his guitar again, reclipping the shoulder strap. "I think granddaddy wouldn't just cut off the money to somebody who did that, but cut off his balls as well. Or just have that Tranh do it while you're sleeping sometime. The Chinaman may look okay, but myself, I think he's scarier than David the Ghoul."

"Vietnamese."

"Huh?"

"Duy Tranh is Vietnamese, not Chinese."

The first chord on the guitar for a while. "Whatever."

I shook my head.

Lazar said, "That it?"

"Not quite. Any reason you can think of why someone would want to kill Veronica Held?"

"*Nada*, man. For a whole bunch of other reasons."

"Tell me."

Lazar let go of the guitar, which sagged down on its strap and then angled outward over his gut. "One, she's family to half the people at the party. Two, the rest of us get some edge, account of she asks granddaddy pretty-please to give the band money for this or that." Lazar jerked his head up toward the ceiling. "Spi may be writing crap, but it was crap that Very could put across, and she would have carried the rest of us burnouts with her. At least until some new flavor of the month got discovered by MTV or VH1."

Taking more Sprite, I thought about something else. "You said Veronica didn't turn on the floods for Colonel Helides."

"Not the sex stuff, no."

"Until his birthday party."

"Hey, man. You don't have to tell me. I was there."

I watched him a minute. "Why would Veronica do that in front of her grandfather?"

"Beats me, unless it was the coke. All's I can say is, she just about killed our fucking goose."

"Meaning?"

"The old man looked like he was gonna have another stroke, maybe the big one. And Very pissed off our money supply before we could boogie without him."

"So some people would have had a reason to kill her."

"Some people were madder than shit at her, but we figured she could kiss and make up with her grandpa."

I watched Lazar a little longer. "Last topic. Where were you after Veronica ran out of that living room?"

"At the party, you talking?"

"Yes."

Another shrug. "I figured the old man would hit the roof, and he fucking started to, so I split."

"You left the house?"

"Nah. Just figured to put a little distance between us, like help the guy forget he was paying for my room and board over here so he wouldn't decide to cut us all off for what Very pulled on him with the lap-dance."

"What kind of distance?"

More stroking of the cheek scar. "Just drifted around the place. It's got kind of a flow-through pattern to it. Ended up with Delgis in the kitchen. At least for a little while." The leer came back to Lazar's voice and features. "Though she might remember it as longer, the good time I was showing her in there."

I rose from the folding chair and ducked under the overhead mike. "Thanks for your help, Gordo."

"Hey, you're welcome, man. And feel free, you want to tell any of the tour stories, especially that Minot one."

"About the frogs."

"Not frogs, man. Toads." Gordo Lazar seemed indignant. "Toads are particular. Frogs, they'll fuck anybody."

"Who'll fuck anybody?"

A man's voice from the door to the studio, slight Southern accent. When I turned, I saw one of the others from the Skipper's birthday video. Ricky Queen wore orange shorts and a green tank top, his body still young enough to be toned without having to work at it. The left ear bore three rings through the cartilage, the right ear two, and the left nostril one. Queen's hair sprouted from his head, the roots dark brown, the mid-growth platinum, the tips the same orange as his shorts. He had a wide smile, with a single gold tooth in the bottom front.

Gordo Lazar said, "This here is John Cuddy, Rick. He's the man we got to talk to." Lazar set down his guitar and started walking empty-handed toward the door. "I'm still hungry, so you both can stay here, you want."

I said, "Gordo?"

He stopped. "Yeah?"

"I'd feel a lot better about Delgis having made me lunch if you could carry our tray back to her."

Lazar seemed to weigh something, then walked over, picked up the tray, and let Queen open the door for him.

As the door closed again, the drummer crossed his arms

and leaned casually against the wall. "That was pretty good, you know?"

"What was?"

The wide smile as he walked toward me. "Don't try to bullshit the kid, okay? I ask a cavebear like Gordo to do something domestic for a woman, he'd bite my head off. You ask it as a favor, man-to-man, and he does it." Queen extended his hand. "I'm too young to hire lawyers and stuff, dude, but I think I'm gonna have to be a little careful around you."

We shook hands, him holding on a bit longer than I would have. "Mr. Queen."

He let go of my hand. "I prefer 'Ricky,' but Gordo has some trouble with that."

"Why?"

Queen moved over to the drum set, ran his hand lightly along the paired cymbals. "Makes him feel less like he's working with a gay man in the group, he calls me by a more masculine name." Queen turned toward me. "Especially given my last one."

"You were born with it?"

"I was. In a part of Alabama where they didn't get the irony. But my family was proud of their name, and I couldn't see changing it, especially with the crossover to Freddie Mercury in the band Queen."

I said, "Mercury died not too long ago, right?"

Queen looked at me differently. "One of the many taken by the Epidemic." A pause. "I guess you aren't always quite the diplomat, are you?"

"Because?"

Queen didn't reply right away, instead easing gracefully down onto the little stool in the middle of the drums. "John, I'm guessing you have to know by now that Buford Biggs is a person with AIDS."

"So he told me."

A nod. "Well, somebody grows up gay in the South like me, he develops pretty good antennae, but I don't feel any homophobic vibes right now. So, what are you trying to do, just get a rise out of me?"

I sat back in my folding chair. "What I'm try to do is find out who killed Veronica Held and why."

Queen smiled, but without the teeth. "I don't know the 'who,' dude, but I maybe can help with the 'why.'"

"I'm listening."

"After Very stomped out of the birthday party, it must've been almost an hour till Tranh's yelling brought us all to the pool."

"I heard you got there first."

The smile never wavered. "I'm the youngest, John, and the fleetest of foot." Queen ran a finger lightly along the rim of a drum this time. "Ever since, though, I've been thinking about—what do you call it, motive?"

"Motive will do."

"Very was a hot young thing." He looked up. "You meet Spi yet?"

"Yes."

"Then with Buford and Gordo, you've seen everybody in the band. Tell me what you think of our lineup."

I thought back to Biggs praising Mitch Eisen's "casting." I said, "A little of this and a little of that."

The wide smile. "Pretty good, dude. We had Spi as the bad-boy/lead-guitar, Gordo as the paunchy-raunchy bass player, Buford for lightning-keyboard/racial-mix, and me as the pretty boy, appeal to most of the young girls and some of the young boys. But we had Very for the rest of the demographics."

"Explain that to me."

"Remember when I came in the room just before, and Gordo was telling you about somebody fucking everybody?"

"Frogs."

The smile went crooked. "What?"

"Never mind. Go on with what you were about to say."

Queen paused, then shook his head. "Very, she was what everybody wanted to fuck."

"I saw a video of her, but I just don't get that."

"Maybe you're too virtuous, John." Queen stopped smiling altogether. "Okay, let me spell it out for you. Music today is all demographics, like I mentioned before. You got the reasons I just gave why some old rock fans—and blacks, whatever—might not channel-surf past a video station, they saw us on it. But Very was the . . . the wild card, like. She appealed to everybody else." Queen leaned forward on his stool. "You got your junior high boys, want to get into her pants. You got your senior high boys, want the same with a younger chick they figure will look up to them. You got your junior high girls, want to look like somebody the senior high boys want to get into the pants of. You got your pedophiles, want to drool over any little scorcher. Finally, you got your thirty-something daddies, married to their beastoid breeders but fantasizing about what it'd be like to bang the baby-sitter."

"I can't argue with you, Ricky. I just don't see it."

"Sure you do, John. It's like with some men, they feel those homosexual urges, but they can't come out of the closet. Doesn't mean they don't take a peek around the door, though."

I wondered if that was payback for my question about Freddie Mercury earlier. "So, you think Veronica was killed because of her sexuality?"

"Because of what she was showing, and maybe because she wasn't sharing."

A prostitute from a prior case once said something like that to me. "So you don't think Veronica was sexually active."

"I'm probably the one guy at that party who wasn't in a

position to care." Queen looked at me. "Very was a pain in the ass, dude. A prima donna who knew she was the center of some people's universe. Her daddy's, on account of the band's comeback. Her granddaddy's, on account of after his stroke, I don't think he had much else going for him. Kalil . . ."

Queen stopped.

"Go on," I said.

He shook his head. "Very wasn't growing up normal. I mean, your father's a washed-up rocker and your mom's 'guided' by a 'spiritual advisor,' you probably can't be normal anyway."

"Wait a minute. Jeanette Held was seeing Malinda Dujong before Veronica's death?"

Queen looked surprised. "Yeah, dude. For, I don't know, long as I've been around here."

I filed that. "You were saying about Veronica and a normal childhood?"

"I know what it's like, not having exactly what folks back home would call a 'normal' one myself, and I felt kind of sorry for her, some ways."

"Like what, Ricky?"

Queen blew out a breath. "Like the way she got cut off from the kids she used to go to school with. Very had to take, like, tutoring for the state to buy her not going to regular classes anymore."

"Tutoring by Duy Tranh."

"Yeah, dude. And her uncle some, too."

"Her uncle David?"

"A sick puppy, but the guy's supposed to know computers inside and out. Flowers, too, I think."

"Any trouble with either one of them?"

"You mean, like Very telling me stories?"

"Yes."

"Not that she ever said."

"Did you tutor her at all?"

"No," a little quickly, then Queen backpedaled. "More like . . . counseling, maybe?"

"How do you mean?"

"Well, Very knew I was gay, so maybe she figured I was safe enough to ask. Or that I'd just know more about them, given the Epidemic and all."

"Knew more about what, Ricky?"

"Condoms."

"Veronica asked you about using condoms?"

"Which ones were the best." Queen grew serious. "Look, John. Put yourself in her position for a minute. Very had her world—at least the heterosexual part of it—by the balls, and she knew it. But Very also sensed she had to, like, stay above it, she wanted to keep her leverage over the others."

Mitch Eisen's term. "Veronica could advertise sex, but not engage in it?"

"Kind of. Plus, even though she was a hellion, Very was still just thirteen, and somewhere inside her, she was understandably scared of it."

"Of sex, now?"

"That's my take, anyway."

"Ricky, she ever ask you about drugs?"

"The cocaine the cops found inside her?"

I paused. "The Medical Examiner and the lab, actually."

"Ugh. *Not* a pretty picture, dude."

"Well, did she?"

"Ask me about drugs? No, but then, she had her father's generation as the experts there."

I turned over what Queen had told me. "When did Veronica ask you about condoms?"

No smile at all now. "About a week before somebody killed her."

"Who?"

Queen spread his hands, the helpless gesture. "Like I said, John, I don't know. Very appealed to a real wide demographic."

I thought back to something else he'd said. Or at least had started to. "The demographic include Kalil Biggs?"

Cautious now. "They used to go to school together."

"Veronica and Kalil?"

"Yeah," said Queen.

"I haven't met him yet, but somehow I had the feeling Kalil was older."

"About fifteen, I think, but his stutter—or 'stammer,' I don't know if they're the same thing—kept him back a couple grades at some point."

"So they were in classes together, too?"

"Until Spi started grooming Very for the comeback."

I could ask both of the Biggs about that. "Ricky, what made *you* want to be part of this comeback?"

"Me?"

"Yeah."

A little defensive now. "I told you, dude. The demographics." He ran a hand through his hair. "That neo-modern, surfer boy look."

"That explains why Mitch Eisen and Spi Held might want you in the band. Why did you decide to accept?"

Queen turned thoughtful. "Buford said they could use me."

"Biggs was the one who asked you?"

"Not directly. When Spi decided to try a comeback, he wanted all the original members, except they couldn't get this Tommy O'Dell, of course."

I nodded.

Queen blew out another breath. "So, they needed a new drummer, and Buford told them I was good."

"You and Biggs had played together before?"

"Some." A hesitation. "Back when I was getting started—five, six years ago? Buford got me a couple gigs with local bands he was part of in some of the clubs down here." Another hesitation. "Places that might not have hired somebody who was gay."

"You felt you owed Biggs something?"

"That wasn't the only reason I said I'd come in."

"But you're—what, half the age of the rest of the guys?"

"You see it all the time in jazz or blues bands, dude."

"And in rock bands?"

A shrug. "No, not so often. In fact, sometimes it's like I'm that young chick in *The Big Chill.*"

"Sorry?"

"The movie about you 'baby boomers' grown up. Sometimes I feel like the chick in that flick, sitting around the boomers, not getting most of what they're talking about because she was too young to remember it herself."

"And that doesn't bother you?"

"Most people my age are into alternative music, not the classic-rock stuff. But that's what gets the airtime."

"The classic rock."

"Yeah. Oh, you have some of the alternative stations getting more important for the college kids. Every kind of music filters down eventually, becomes 'traditional.' But I grew up hearing classic rock. And besides, Spiral looked like a nice springboard for me."

"How?"

"Hey, dude, I try putting together my own group, or hook up with one's just starting out, who am I? But, if I did a CD and national tour with Spiral, then I'm the drummer in the videos and the news clips, maybe even get my photo on the CD jacket itself."

"And will all that still happen?"

Queen stopped. "You mean with Very dead?"

"That's what I mean."

"It'll be tough, dude. I mean, outside of some TV stuff in Miami, she didn't really do that much performing yet. Just a couple of the local clubs, and because she was underage, they had to do some kind of juke-and-jive to keep their liquor licenses."

"I can understand the license problem, but I don't get your point."

"There wasn't really a 'Very cult' yet, with fan clubs and T-shirts, its own Website. You know?"

"I still don't follow."

Queen began speaking more slowly. "John, because she wasn't really big yet, I don't know if Mitch and Spi can put over her death as something to rally fans around. Like a Serena kind of thing."

Another version of Eisen's "spin" speech. "So with Veronica no longer in the band as a new star, Spiral might not have any comeback at all."

"That's what I been trying to tell you, dude."

I thought about it. "Would anybody benefit from that?"

"Not us guys in the band," said Ricky Queen. "Though I'm guessing someone wouldn't be sorry to see her granddaddy stop throwing good money after bad."

NINE

Walking down the corridor from Spiral's studio, I could hear dishes clattering in the Helds' kitchen, followed by the whispery sound of a sliding glass door opening. The voice of Delgis Reyes said, "Kalil, you hungry?"

I didn't hear any reply.

When I reached the kitchen doorway, I saw Buford Biggs closing the glass panel, an African-American boy standing in front of him, eyes down toward the white-tiled floor. Because Kalil had been working the camera, I hadn't seen him on the birthday-party video. He was about five feet tall and pudgy, with full cheeks and short hair under a reversed baseball cap. His clothes consisted of a Miami Heat T-shirt, baggy rayon shorts that hung past his knees, and this year's version of Air Jordans.

When Buford Biggs turned from the doorway, he took a step toward Delgis Reyes and Gordo Lazar, both of whom were sitting on stools at the center island, Lazar eating again. Then Biggs saw me and stopped.

"You still here?"

As Kalil's eyes came up from the floor, I said, "Haven't talked to everybody I need to."

The boy looked at me like a frightened fawn, then back down to the white tiles again.

His father said, "You meaning my son?"

"Among others."

Biggs weighed something, then said, "I want to be there."

Not worth the battle. "All right. How about the patio again, so you can have a cigarette."

A snort. "Don't smoke around my boy, babe, but the patio be okay." Biggs paused. "Kalil, this man, he need to ask you some questions."

A tiny nod, the face still examining the floor.

"But I be with you, the whole time."

Another tiny nod.

Buford Biggs said, "Let's go."

His son followed him back outside. As I passed Gordo Lazar, he said, "Go easy on the kid, huh?"

It surprised me a little, and I didn't say anything back.

When I reached the patio, Biggs was pulling a third

chair over to the pair we'd used earlier near the hummingbird feeder. He pointed to one for Kalil, then sat himself to
his son's right. I rearranged the last chair to Kalil's left, as
much to keep my own left eye on his father as to be close to
the person who I hoped would answer my questions.

Kalil's sneakers didn't quite settle flat on the tiles, the
balls of his feet touching but the heels jigging up and down
to no apparent rhythm. His thick fingers worried each
other in his lap as he looked down at them.

I said, "Kalil, do you know who I am?"

The tiny nod.

I looked first to Biggs, then back to his son. "Tell me?"

Kalil glanced up at me, then down again. "T-t-tell you
what?"

I could see the neck cords bulge as he clamped his jaw
so hard, the teeth clashed.

Biggs said, "Kalil, he have a blockage on his 't's.'"

Different tack. "Does your speech specialist help you
with those?"

Another nod.

"Tell me how."

A couple of deep breaths before, "She has me say my
name, real slow. Then for fluency we do different inflec-
tions on words and other speech p-p-patterns."

Biggs said, "He have trouble with his 'p's,' too."

"What else does your specialist do?"

Kalil took another deep breath. "She says there's almost
t-t-two and a half million of us in America who stammer.
That people like Marilyn Monroe and this English guy
Winston Churchill did, too, and they learned how t-t-to
deal with it." A near-smile. "She says I'm lucky, on account
of I just got blockages on p-p-particular syllables."

Shy and awkward he might be, but bright. "Kalil, I know
this isn't pleasant for you. However, Mr. Helides hired me

to try and find out what happened the day of the birthday party, and I need your help for that."

The tiny nod again.

I waited a moment, then said, "But I also need you to tell me what you remember in your own words, and I'm in no rush here, so you can take your time."

Kalil looked up at me, holding the gaze longer than before. "Ask your questions."

"When did you meet Veronica?"

"Couple years ago." Deep breath. "I had p-p-problems in school, so we had some classes t-t-together even though she was younger than me. Since our daddies knew each other, she t-t-talked with—"

A hummingbird zoomed to the feeder, and Kalil jumped half out of his chair. "Damn b-b-bird."

Biggs said, "When he get scared of something, he have troubles with—"

"I'm not scared! It was just a b-b-b-b . . ."

Kalil stopped, the teeth clashing again as he clenched and looked down at his hands, twisting in his lap.

I gave him a moment before, "Did you like Veronica?"

The tiny nod.

I took a chance. "Why?"

Kalil glanced up at me briefly before returning to his lap. "She never made fun of me."

"How often did you see her?"

A shrug. "Last year a lot, account of the classes we had t-t-together."

"Every day?"

"Most school days."

"And this year?"

"Not so much, once her daddy t-t-took her out."

"To be tutored by Duy Tranh."

Another nod.

"Kalil, did Veronica like Mr. Tranh?"

"I guess."

"She ever tell you about problems with him?"

Kalil shook his head.

A different tack. "Can you tell me why you wanted to videotape the party?"

Another glance up. "My speech specialist, she thinks it's a good idea for us t-t-to do that kind of stuff."

"What kind of stuff?"

Biggs broke in. "Things like painting or photography, babe, shit that don't need no talking."

I looked over at him. "Mr. Biggs, please?"

"I pay for the speech woman to help him, I can tell you what she think."

"Yes, you can. I'd just rather hear it from Kalil, okay?"

Biggs sat back in the chair, reaching for his cigarette pack before catching himself.

I returned to Kalil. "You enjoy videotaping?"

Tiny nod.

"Have you been doing it long?"

A shrug.

"How long, Kalil?"

He looked over toward his father. "Daddy got me the camera for Christmas, when my specialist said it was a good idea."

"So, as of the time of the birthday party at Mr. Helides's house, you'd had the camera for only a few weeks?"

"I guess."

Might explain why he didn't turn on the audio at first, but I asked anyway.

Kalil shook his head. "Just forgot, with everybody running around the house."

"Where around the house?"

"Everywhere. The living room, the kitchen, the p-p-p-p . . ."

Neck and jaw.

I said, "The pool, Kalil?"

A nod.

"Did you go swimming that day?"

Another nod.

"Tell me about it?"

"We all went, mostly."

"Who didn't?"

"I don't know. Just didn't see everybody there when I was."

"Was Veronica in the pool when you were?"

Again the nod.

"Why didn't you use your camera then?"

Kalil looked up, and his father came forward in the third chair.

The son said, "What?"

"Why didn't you shoot tape of the pool part of the birth-day?"

"Camera's not supposed t-t-to get wet."

Biggs said, "I pay near fifteen hundred for that thing, babe. Damn well not gonna get it ruint."

I glanced at him, and he sat back again.

"Kalil, why did you want the other cameras turned off during the party?"

A head shake this time.

"I mean the security cameras in Mr. Helides's house."

He looked at me, then his father, then me again. "It's like I t-t-told the p-p-police."

"Told them what?"

Hesitation. "Was Very's idea."

"Veronica wanted the other cameras off?"

A double nod this time.

"Kalil, did she give you a reason?"

Just one nod now.

"What was it?"

"Very said I was supposed to have only mine."

"Only yours?"

"Only my t-t-tape of her singing, for her granddaddy."

Which was when Kalil had turned on the camera's audio. "Did Veronica tell you why?"

"She just wanted it her way. Very was like that."

Something clicked for me. "Didn't it strike you as odd?"

"I just t-t-told you. She was—"

"Odd that Veronica wouldn't want her grandfather to have a videotape of his own birthday party?"

A shrug.

Buford Biggs said, "Could of just dubbed him one, after Kalil took the original."

I looked at the father. Even though what he said was true, I didn't think it was the truth.

Back to his son. "Kalil, why didn't you keep filming the party after Veronica sang?"

"Didn't seem much sense t-t-to, everybody mad and all."

"I don't think that's it."

A stare this time, for the first time.

"I think Veronica told you to start the audio only when she began singing, and to stop the tape after she finished."

Kalil's mouth opened as his father said to me, "The hell you talking about, babe?"

"Your son didn't just forget to engage the audio part of the camera at the beginning of the party. Veronica wanted him to do it that way, so she'd be the center of attention, even on the tape of her own grandfather's birthday celebration." I turned to my right. "Kalil, that's what happened, isn't it?"

I wasn't sure what would come out of the young man's mouth until he began to wail, jumping up from the chair and running toward the sliding glass door.

"Very wanted me t-t-to have it, like the others. She was

so b-b-beautiful." Kalil couldn't get the door to move. "She d-d-didn't have t-t-to d-d-die."

He finally slid the door open, then didn't close it after running inside.

Buford Biggs stood abruptly in front of me, his hands more fists at the end of his stringy forearms. "Mother-*fuck*er, you see what you done?"

I didn't get up with him. "Did your son take any other videos of Veronica Held?"

"You can piss shit, Mr. Mother-fucker, before me or my son talk to you again."

"Mr. Biggs, where were you and Kalil after Veronica left her grandfather's living room?"

I watched Buford Biggs stalk off toward the open doorway, sliding it violently shut behind him. Then I stayed in my chair a little longer, but not to wait for the hummingbirds this time.

I'd risen about halfway from my seat toward going back inside the house when the sliding glass door opened again and Malinda Dujong stepped out onto the patio. As she slid it back into place and came toward me, I stood all the way up and paid more attention to what she was wearing: a bright, silky dress that seemed custom-tailored as it floated with her strides, the shoulders padded a little above the delicate bone structure, the hem riding just south of her knees. Dujong's calves were slim and perfectly shaped, heeled sandals on her feet. The closer she got, the more her eyes arrested me again, set deep in a face framed by lustrous black hair.

Dujong said, "Kalil and then Buford go by me inside. They are very upset."

I gestured at the chair Biggs, Sr., had been using. "Your concern for them spares me trying to find you. Sit, please."

Dujong looked at both empty chairs, then took the one I'd indicated, crossing her legs and smoothing the dress down over her knees. "You say something to them?"

"I asked Kalil questions that he and his father didn't like."

A measuring stare, the irises seeming almost as black as the pupils. "I hope I am not wrong about you, Mr. Cuddy."

"Wrong?"

"When I believe that you do not hurt innocent people intentionally."

"Innocence is a relative quality."

"Relative." A different stare. "You make fun that Buford and Kalil are father and son?"

"No. I mean that there are degrees of innocence, just like there are degrees of guilt."

"I understand now." Dujong blinked twice. "Why do you want to talk with me?"

"I'd like to find out what you know about Veronica Held's death."

"But I was not at the Colonel's birthday party."

Given the welter of people I'd seen on the video in Sergeant Lourdes Pintana's office, I hadn't noticed whether Dujong was there or not. I reached into my inside jacket pocket and took out the list of guests Justo Vega had made for me. She wasn't on it.

Without leaning forward, Dujong said, "The names of the people at the party?"

I folded the paper and slid it back into my pocket. "Are you psychic as well as a spiritual advisor?"

"Yes."

No hesitation, no hint of humor. Just quiet confidence in the answer. "Then what am I thinking now, Ms. Dujong?"

"That you do not believe I am either one."

Not exactly a stump-the-band question, though. "Jeanette Held believes otherwise."

"Because I have been able to help her." A third stare. "Perhaps I can do the same for you."

"Help me with the case?"

"No. No, I mean with your loss."

"My . . . ?"

"The person you care about so deeply who you have lost so recently."

My turn to stare. "Who told you that?"

"You did, Mr. Cuddy." Dujong waved a hand behind her. "When we are inside the living room here."

I tried to keep my voice steady. "I think I'd have remembered."

"Perhaps, though you did not use words."

"Meaning, you can read my mind, too?"

Dujong remained perfectly still, but closed her eyes. "Meaning I can sense such things. Body language, tone of voice, aura."

"Aura."

She opened the eyes, and I felt drawn into them. "Because you wish not to believe me does not mean I am wrong. You are a man who has suffered many losses, but I think only one other more . . . difficult than this new one."

I almost said, "Beth," before catching myself.

Dujong smoothed her dress again at the knees. "It is painful for you to be doing this thing for Mr. Helides. Perhaps I can make it easier."

"A minute ago you said you weren't at the party."

"That is right. However, I know some things which you might wish to know, also."

I leaned back in my chair. "Go ahead."

"I am spiritual advisor to Jeanette, but much of what we talk about is her daughter."

"Veronica."

"Yes. Jeanette for a long time was very worried about her."

I felt as though a confidence was being breached, but I wasn't the one charged with protecting it. "Worried how?"

"Many things. Jeanette does not like Veronica singing for her husband's band."

"Because?"

"Because of the way her daughter learns to . . . move her body, use her body to . . ."

"Give off an aura?"

Malinda Dujong stopped, her face perfectly neutral. "You now make fun of what I do?"

I shook my head. "A little, probably. I'm sorry."

A smile showing bright, short teeth. "A man who can apologize is a man who can learn."

"Philippine saying?"

Better smile. "Malinda saying."

Back on track with a quality-control question. "If Mrs. Held didn't like Veronica being in her father's band, why not pull her out of it?"

Dujong stopped, no more smile for me. "You already ask Jeanette this question."

"She told you."

"No. I just feel you did." The questioning stare. "Please, Mr. Cuddy, do not play games with me. There is something very dangerous here."

"Veronica's killer."

"Yes, but more than this only. Something . . . evil."

"You feel that, too?"

Dujong's face sagged, and she suddenly seemed older than the thirty or so I'd estimated. "I know about evil, Mr. Cuddy. My village in the Philippines is small but close to the ocean. My father, my mother, my brothers go to the beach for fish, for sun, for . . . life.

"But there is also death, of course. And stories of it, too. The crab-monster, who lives in a cave and kills anyone who enters it because he wants the cave all to himself. And the jungle-monster, who hangs a person by the feet from a tree and eats one part at a time, every day. But for what happens to me, there is no story, just truth."

Dujong drew in a long breath, let it partway out. "One time when I am four years old, my family go to beach for fun. My brothers find a piece of driftwood, beautiful but strange. They carry home this piece, put it next to my bed that night before they try to find a rich person or tourist to buy it. I am asleep in my bed when I feel something bite me, sting me. I slap with my hands all around, but I cannot see anything."

Dujong fixed me with those deep, black eyes. "Except the driftwood falls over and breaks into many pieces, little pieces. I did not touch it, still it falls by itself."

She began looking down now at her knees, folding her hands on them. "The next day, my brothers are mad about the driftwood, because now they cannot sell it. I am sick, I think then from their anger. I cannot eat, that next night I cannot sleep. I begin to sweat badly, to cry out in fear."

"Ms. Dujong—"

"Please. You ask about me feeling the evil. I am telling you now."

I nodded.

She took a breath, returned her words to her hands and knees. "Two days later, I am blind. I cannot see my mother's face, my own fingers. I have only the difference between day and night. My father takes me to the clinic in a village fifteen miles away. The doctor examines me, he cannot tell anything is wrong. My father brings me home. My mother sings to me, and my brothers make toys for me, but I think I feel something moving inside me."

"Moving?"

"Yes. Like a small . . . lump. It moves through my chest and belly, and up and down my arms and legs under the skin. But I am blind, and as a little girl, I curse what I do not understand."

Dujong looked at me, trying to gauge something, I thought. "You still listen to me?"

"I'm listening."

"After I am blind almost a year, one night I get up to . . . to go to bathroom outside, because I can make my way without seeing. I fall down. I think I trip on something, but no. I cannot get back up. My legs fold under me, like kind of knife." Dujong raised up on her sandaled left foot, bending her right leg double like a jackknife under her rump, leaving her sitting on the right foot. "I cry out, my mother come. Next day, my father and my brothers carry me to village with clinic again. The doctor say same thing: He cannot tell anything is wrong. We go back home, and I cannot see, I cannot walk. My family must carry me everywhere, to beach, to bathroom outside. I am like a little baby but now five years old."

I kept listening.

"Then my mother say there is a healer visiting our village for one day, and maybe he can help me. I do not believe, but the healer comes and touches me here and here." Dujong indicated her chest, stomach. "Then he touch me there and there." Upper arms, thighs. "Then he tell to my mother, he can maybe help."

Crossing her arms, Dujong shivered. "That night, the healer makes a fire and sings words in Tagalog—our language there. I remember I drink something from cup he hold to my lips. Then I begin crying out, and I cry out all night. Then I feel the healer squeezing on my leg, here." She released a hand to point above her left knee, under the dress. "The healer squeeze and squeeze, and then the evil come out."

"It 'came out'?"

"I can feel it, break out through my skin at the inside of my leg, and the evil smell terrible and my mother's voice is screaming and the healer sound scared, too. He yell at the evil, make it go away."

"Go away?"

Dujong steadied her eyes on me again. "Crawl away, on its . . . feet."

Jesus. "Ms. Dujong, I don't—"

"Healer wrap my left leg in cloth and leaves. Next day, I can see. Not perfect, but more than just light and dark. One day more, and my right leg come straight." She brought it forward now in her chair, unbending it until her sandal heel rested on the tiled patio. "Third day, my left leg come straight. One week more, and my mother take off leaves and cloth. By then I can see well enough to . . ."

Malinda Dujong inched the hem of her dress above her left knee. There was an impression—almost a brand—in the flesh. The outline of a miniature, reptilian head, with spiky horns and a wide jaw.

Unless I was Charlie Brown, looking for portraits in a summer cloud.

I raised my head back to Dujong, and she drew the dress down over her knee again.

"That, Mr. Cuddy, is how I know evil."

"Quite a story, but—"

"You do not believe."

"That I don't believe doesn't make it untrue."

A small, fleeting smile. "Then please listen to me a little more. The day of the birthday party, I am supposed to be there."

"You were invited, but didn't attend?"

"Yes. Do you wish to know why so?"

"I would."

Dujong refolded her arms across her chest. "I am in my apartment that morning when I receive a telephone call. A woman's voice I have not heard before. She is very upset. She say Jeanette Held is a good friend, that Jeanette told her about my help to her, and that she now needs help, too."

"The woman on the phone."

"Yes."

"Her name?"

"She say 'Wendy.'"

"How about a last name, too?"

"No. She does not want to tell me the rest because of her husband. I tell her I go to a party, and Wendy becomes more upset, say she must see me that afternoon, but not at her home, her husband will be there. Wendy say she try to call Jeanette, but get only the answering machine, probably because they are busy, prepare for the party."

"Wait a minute. This Wendy woman knew about the party for Nicolas Helides?"

"Yes. Which mean she sound legitimate, especially because I call Jeanette, too, that morning, but get only machine. However, Wendy also very upset, I feel that over the telephone. So I tell her yes, I can see her at a Denny's restaurant near my apartment, only she must be on time, so I can get to the end of the party. Wendy say yes, but please to wait if she not there on time, because she must wait for her husband to leave."

"If he was going to leave anyway, why not go to her house?"

"Because he maybe come back."

"Let me guess the rest. You went to the Denny's and waited, but Wendy never showed."

"That is right."

"And when you asked Jeanette about her, Jeanette never heard of her."

The small smile. "Mr. Cuddy, you are not psychic."

At first I didn't get what Dujong meant. "You never asked Jeanette Held about whether she had this friend?"

"Jeanette lose her only child to murder. She is so upset, I did not think it important."

"How about the police?"

"The police?"

"Did you tell them about this Wendy woman?"

"When I arrive at the house of Mr. Helides that day, the police and ambulance already there in the street. I ask police in uniform what is happening, he tell me to stand back. I wave to Umberto at the gate, and he come over. I ask him, and Umberto say Veronica is dead. Then he ask me, where am I? I say I supposed to meet somebody. Then police dressed in shirt and tie come over, tell Umberto they need him and who am I?"

"You get a name on this officer?"

"No," said Dujong. "But he is like a bull and not polite, hair over his collar."

Kyle Cascadden. "What did you tell this other police-man?"

"I say I am Mrs. Held's spiritual advisor. He make a face, ask if I am at party. I say not yet, I am late. He say, 'Then stay the hell away from here,' and he take Umberto with him back to the gate."

I tried to process all that. "Meaning, neither Jeanette Held nor the police know the details about why you were late getting to the party."

"That is right."

"Then why are you telling me these things?"

A clouded look came over Dujong's dark eyes. "I tell police, they make Jeanette more upset with their questions. But the one I see that day is stupid, and he cannot get right answers or use them wisely. I do not think you would hurt

Jeanette for no reason. I do not think you are stupid, either, so maybe my answers to you can help find who kill Veronica."

"How?"

"I think somebody who come to party not want me there."

"Why would they care?"

"Because, if I am there, I maybe sense something that tell me who the bad person is."

I tried to tie it together. "You think this Wendy woman was used to keep you away from the house that day so that you wouldn't pick up an aura or something from the killer?"

"Evil kill Veronica, Mr. Cuddy. She is a difficult little girl, but no one should die like that. When you know evil is your enemy, maybe you can win." Dujong rose from her chair. "I doubt it, but maybe."

As she turned for the house, I said, "If I need to reach you again?"

"I am registered at the tennis club."

"Where Cassandra Helides belongs?"

Over the shoulder with, "Yes."

Then Cornel Radescu, too, the tennis pro I had to see. "But what if you're not playing there?"

At the sliding glass door, Malinda Dujong turned and gave me one of her small smiles. "I live there, Mr. Cuddy."

When I finally made it inside the kitchen, Malinda Dujong, Gordo Lazar, and Delgis Reyes were all nowhere in sight. I went out to the corridor, climbed the spiral staircase, and knocked on the turret door.

"Not yet," came Spi Held's voice from behind the wood.

"It's John Cuddy, Mr. Held. I want to talk with you again before I go."

A pause, then, "Just a second."

I heard some footsteps and the shifting of equipment. When he opened the door, Held seemed to be alone.

"Thanks," I said, stepping across the threshold.

"I'm, uh, kind of under the fucking gun, man. Got to get this new Very tune ready so we can rehearse it toward the CD."

I stopped in the center of the room, everything except his guitar where I remembered it, still nobody else with us. "The one about your daughter?"

"Yeah. I think it's got potential."

I turned back to him. "Potential."

"To be on the album. Maybe even the title track."

"That would be special, wouldn't it?"

"Karma, even. Now, what do you need?"

"Can I sit down?"

"Uh, sure. Take that one again."

I eased into the ergonomic chair like I had all the time in the world. "You told me before that after you and your wife chased after Veronica, your daughter insulted both of you."

The Fu Manchu did a nip-up. "Told us we should fuck off, which I'd call insulting, yeah."

"And that was the last time you saw her alive."

"Right, right. I was so mad at Very, I was afraid what I'd do, so Jeanette and me went back to the living room, try to make my father feel a little better about it."

"And did he?"

"Shit, man, you probably know him better than I do. He can't tolerate any curse words, never could. He was ballistic, least as far as somebody already had a stroke can get."

"Were you worried for his health that day?"

"Huh?"

"Since your father was so angry, did you worry it might bring on another stroke?"

"No, man. I was just—the fuck's the word? *Distracted.*

Yeah, I was *distracted* by all the other shit going down."

"Like what?"

"Like what other shit?" said Held.

"Yes."

"Look, it's no secret Buford's got the AIDS, man. He pops about a jar of different pills every day, but how much longer he can do studio work, much less the steady hump of a national tour, I don't know. Gordo's always been a loose fucking cannon, and Ricky don't have a lot of brand identification yet with Spiral as a group."

"So he could walk."

"They all could."

"Especially if your father turned off the money faucet."

A darkening. "The fuck did you hear that from?"

"Was it true?"

"Hell, no. My dad was solid behind us."

"Until the birthday party."

"Why do you keep coming back to that?"

"It's when—and almost where—your daughter was killed."

"Yeah, I know. But who's going to want Very dead? That's what you don't seem to get here. She was everybody's best ticket in the rock-'n'-roll lottery, man."

"Somebody killed her, despite that."

"Yeah, well, I don't know who. Jeanette doesn't, either. So what can we tell you?"

Since he'd mentioned his wife's name, I said, "Ever heard any of your family or friends mention a woman named 'Wendy'?"

"Wen . . . ?" Held seemed to mull it over. "Doesn't ring any bells. Why do you—?"

"Just a thought. I've seen the video of Veronica at the birthday party, and another at Mitch Eisen's office."

Held looked at me. "So?"

"I was wondering if there were any other videos lying around."

"Other ones. You mean, of Very performing?"

"Or just interacting with other people."

"Oh. Shit, yeah. Jeanette's probably got a library full of them, from the time Very was a baby." A troubled look. "Don't know how they'd help you with who killed her, though."

"Anybody else have tapes of your daughter?"

"Not that I know of. Why?"

"Just another thought." I stood up. "I'll let you get back to your work."

Held reached for the guitar plugged into his computer. "That's the hardest part of all, you know."

"What is?"

"Having to be creative when you're still grieving. It's a bitch, man."

I watched Spi Held as he adjusted some settings on the keyboard and decided he was serious about that last comment.

Serious, if not sincere.

TEN

I'm sorry, sir, but I can't let you pass without one of the members telling me you're coming."

The gate guard at the tennis club wore a blue security uniform and matching ball cap. He also had the voice of a radio news anchor.

From behind the wheel of the Cavalier, I looked up at him inside the little sentry box. "My name's John Cuddy. I'm working for Nicolas Helides."

"Mr. Helides is a member, sir." The guard gestured at a telephone on the counter in front of him. "But I haven't gotten an authorization call about you."

"Could you try him now?"

"He lives off-site, sir."

"I know. Could you call his house?"

The guard nodded reluctantly, then picked up the phone. After a moment, he spoke quietly into it, nodded more comfortably, and hung up.

"Sir, you're cleared. I'm guessing this is your first time here?"

"It is."

The guard stepped out of the gate house, and I could see the name CLINTON on his uniform. "The clubhouse is this first building on the left. You can park anywhere that doesn't have another building's name on it."

I drove slowly over the cobblestoned drive, partly because of the yellow speed bumps. I passed two residential buildings on the right, the miniature jersey barriers between the parking lines reading first BROOKS and then DAVIS. The buildings were pastel peach, four stories tall, and U-shaped. Each sported an impressive mosaic twenty feet high of an individual player in tennis togs. Real people similarly dressed were walking or standing and talking, and I could see more residential structures farther along the road.

Finding an empty space with no name on its barrier, I left the Cavalier and walked toward what Clinton had called the clubhouse. A series of staccato "thwocks" resounded through the clear, dry air.

Inside the high fence I found a pool with sky-blue water but only a few sunbathers occupying the lounges. Behind them were umbrellaed patio tables and chairs, all white and all empty. Beyond the furniture stood a rectangular tiki bar with only a couple of patrons sitting on the stools.

About half a story below the patio itself, however, the eight tennis courts in sight were full, players of all ages, sizes, and skin colors pounding away at singles and doubles with a lot of concentration and energy.

As I approached what appeared to be the main entrance, a dapper older gentleman in tennis shorts, V-neck sweater, and Kangol cap was coming out.

Smiling broadly in a way that took twenty years off his age, he stuck out a hand. "Don Floyd. Can I help you?"

I shook with him, his accent Southern, his grip like a vise. "John Cuddy. I'm looking for Cornel Radescu."

"Cornel?" Floyd gazed out to the parking area. "Well, that Checker—like the old taxis?—is his car, so he's still here somewhere. In fact"—now Floyd gazed out over the courts, shading his eyes with a hand like the Indian scout in a black-and-white western—"I thought I saw him a couple—yeah. Yeah, that's him, on Three, serving into the ad court."

Following his eyes, I saw a man with a ponytail smash the ball with the loudest "thwock" sound I'd heard toward a much smaller, slighter woman. A little puff of green dust rose from the surface as the ball bounced up shoulder high on the woman, who nevertheless hit it solidly with a two-handed stroke like a baseball batter. The man was already in position for it, though, and after two more exchanges that looked pretty professional to me, he rushed to the net and dinked the ball deftly out of her reach.

Floyd and I watched the woman bow her head, hit the edge of a raised sneaker with her racquet, then walk purposefully to the net and shake hands cheerfully with the man. As they moved to a seating area shaded by an awning roof between two courts, Floyd turned back to me.

"Their match is over, John."

I said, "Should I wait for Mr. Radescu here?"

"You could try that, but Cornel lives on the other side of

the complex, so he doesn't usually come this way. You might want to catch him down there, assuming nobody else has the court now."

"Thanks, Mr. Floyd."

"Just call me 'Don.' Everybody else does."

And with another broad smile, he strolled to the tiki bar.

There were walkways between the chicken-wire fences separating the courts spread around the club. I took a slatted path toward Court Three.

As I opened the swinging wire door, the woman who'd played against Radescu was coming out, a large bag that I thought could hold four racquets slung from her shoulder. She looked even more athletic up close, with a deep tan and bright eyes.

Surveying me head to toe, she said, "He'll kill you in those shoes," then cuffed me lightly on the upper arm and went through the doorway, laughing quietly.

I stepped onto the court surface, which did seem like pulverized green dirt. Moving around the white-tape edges of the playing area, I was about ten feet from Radescu before he turned, an insulated picnic jug to his lips.

"Tough match?" I said.

He hefted the jug. "A powder drink, to restore the electrolytes."

The accent you'd hear in a Dracula movie. Radescu stood about six feet tall and maybe one-eighty, though his serving arm was half again as big as the other. He wore a yellow, placket-collared shirt and black shorts, some fingerprints of the court's green dust on the thighs. The face looked like it was chiseled from a piece of Transylvanian cliff, with a long, straight nose and dark, steady eyes peering out from under darker eyebrows. No gray in the ponytail, either.

Radescu set the jug down on a table near a chair with another tennis bag in it. "You are this John Cuddy?"

"Good guess."

Radescu smiled slightly, but made no effort to shake hands, so I didn't either.

He looked behind me, then slumped into a chair, pulling a towel from his bag and mopping his forehead and neck with it. "I see no one to take this court, so we may as well talk here, in the fresh air and shade."

"How did you know who I am?"

"Nick's man—Duy Tranh?—calls me to say a detective will talk with me."

Nick. Aside from his wife, I couldn't remember anyone ever calling the Skipper by his first name.

Radescu shrugged. "Also, Cassandra describes you." A pause. "Quite accurately. And is this how you know me, too?"

I looked back toward the patio area. "Someone pointed you out to me."

"Who?"

"Why do you want to know?"

A feigned look of surprise. "I want to thank that person for their courtesy."

I weighed it a minute, including Don Floyd's casual way of identifying Radescu for me, then said the name.

"Ah, the unofficial mayor of our little community here. Don knows everyone."

"I would have recognized you from the videotape, anyway."

"The video?"

"Of the Helides birthday party."

"Ah, yes." More towel work, this time across the eyes. "The reason you are here."

"What can you tell me about that day?"

"What do you want to know?"

"Start at the beginning."

Radescu rubbed the towel across the bridge of his nose. "The beginning of my day, or only the party itself?"

A man who'd been interrogated more than once. "How was it you were invited at all?"

The slight smile. "Before he has the stroke, Nick played here. I still give his wife lessons."

A smirk now.

"And his granddaughter, too."

The smirk faded. "Yes."

"Why?"

"Very wants to learn tennis, and I am an excellent teacher. Also, her 'grandmother' is already taking lessons with me."

No smirk this time.

"Let's focus on the party first, then Veronica."

"The party?" Radescu laid his towel on top of his tennis bag. "I drive there. Already many cars are in the driveway, so I leave mine in the street, and I am checked in through the gate guard." Something passed across Radescu's features. "Inside the house, we are eating, drinking, trying to make it seem we have a good time."

"Seem?"

A skeptical look as Radescu leaned forward in his chair. "Come on, Mr. John Cuddy, you have seen Nick, yes?"

"Yes."

"And you know him from somewhere before, because he does not hire people he does not feel sure about."

"We knew each other a long time ago."

"So." Radescu settled back a little. "You know for certainly how . . . diminished he is by the stroke. And you must know then also that it is hard to have fun around a man such as he is now."

"But you were trying."

At first the skeptical look again, then almost a mellowing.

"I tell you, I think everybody is trying. Even his son, David, the strange one. I think we know Nick probably does not have another birthday party waiting for him in the next year."

I let that go by. "So, you're all helping him celebrate."

"To celebrate, yes, as much as he can. Then Very announces she is to sing, and the young black, he has the camera, and we all are to stand around, to hear this. But when Very sings, she is strange, too, and I do not mean only the things she sings. No, it is like she performs for everyone in the room, not just her grandfather. Do you understand?"

"The autopsy revealed cocaine in her system."

Radescu frowned and tossed the towel toward his bag. "Drugs. They are poison. But perhaps that is why she performs for him only as a mask for the rest of us."

I'd gotten a little of that from the tape. "Did you see Veronica Held after she left the main room?"

"After she runs out? No. Her father and then her mother go after her. I know, if she is my daughter, I beat her to bloody for what she did." Something went across Radescu's features again, maybe a realization of how he'd just sounded. "But she is not."

"Not your daughter."

"That is right."

"Did you see her again?"

"No. No, before she is found, I leave the party."

"Why?"

"Because her singing makes it now impossible even to seem like things are fun."

"How did you come to know Veronica had been killed?"

No reply.

"Mr. Radescu?"

"Cassandra calls me that night, and then the police come here to see me."

"And ask you questions like mine."

"An angry policeman. Not very smart."

I had a pretty good idea who that would have been. "Okay, what can you tell me about Veronica herself?"

Radescu paused. "I can tell you she is coordinated and strong enough, but she probably could not become a good tennis player, and for certainly never a great one."

"Why is that?"

"Very starts too late." Radescu angled his head at a woman playing singles two courts away. She was young, but running a tall, athletic man ragged. "That blonde there? She is ranked number one woman in Florida." Radescu came back to me. "To be truly great now, they must have the racquet in their hands when they are five, six years of age."

"Why couldn't Veronica at least have been a good player?"

"She never wants to practice her shots. She wants only to be shown them in the lesson, and then play matches trying them. That is no way to become a good player."

"Then why did you continue as her instructor?"

Radescu rubbed his thumb and forefinger together. "The money, Mr. Cuddy. Nick is a rich man, and he wants his granddaughter to have the best." Now a shrug that didn't quite come off. "Also, I am Cassandra's teacher, so it is easier."

"Because they could ride over here together?"

A little discomfort again. "That is right."

"But they lived in different homes, different parts of the city."

"Very is often at her grandfather's house."

I watched Radescu carefully. "I also heard that even when she was, Cassandra wouldn't drive her over here anymore."

More discomfort. "I don't know about that."

"What happened to drive a wedge between Cassandra and Veronica over coming here to the tennis club?"

More discomfort still, then a resolution of the rocky features. "Mr. Cuddy, look around you."

"I already have."

"Again. Please."

I took in three-hundred-sixty degrees of tennis club. The buildings and flowers that reminded me of photos from the Mediterranean. The bouncing balls and bounding players, some genuine laughter wafting down from the tiki bar. A smell of the green dust in the air, but also a sense of . . .

"You feel it?" said Radescu.

I looked at him. "Feel what?"

"The peace, the security, but also the energy here." He warmed to his subject. "That is why I live at the tennis club. In Romania when I am young—five, six years of age—there are courts in my city because it is the center of the Communist-bloc oil industry. My friends and I, we make racquets from pieces of wood, and we use the balls that the oil men hit over the fences. When I am older, I am very good tennis player, and when I am older still, in my twenties, I teach tennis, and I dream of coming to America. But the Securitate—you know what this is?"

"The secret police?"

"That is right exactly. The Romania K.G.B. They keep me under their eyes, because I am making good money, and in foreign currency, which is illegal. Finally, when I am suffocating from the Communism and bureaucracy, I decide to escape."

"Defect?"

"Yes, but I am not famous, so I must be careful. I buy on the black market fake passports, and I put what remains of my foreign currency in the handle of a tennis racquet I hollow out. The passports let me go from Romania to Bulgaria, and then to Zagreb in Yugoslavia, but no further. However, a little Jewish man tells me I can cross with all the crowds at Trieste."

"Trieste, Italy?"

"Yes. All these Italians go back and forth into Yugoslavia on business each day. I can move in the big crowd with them, and then just run."

"There weren't any soldiers at the border?"

A shiver, and I realized why a gate guard might disquiet Radescu.

He said, "The Jewish man tells me they will not shoot or release their dogs, because of all the people around me." Radescu grew quieter. "But the day I get to the Yugoslav side, there are no big crowds, so I must wait until dark, and then I crawl on my belly through the grass. I crawl like I am swimming on top of the ground, you understand?"

A frame of me doing that one night outside a base-camp in Vietnam flashed across my mind. "Yes."

"I crawl and I stop and I listen, and I crawl some more. It is a full moon, but the soldiers are not watching so carefully, and the wind is right, so their dogs do not smell me. After four hours and going across a stream of water, I know I am on the Italian side, and it is the most unbelievable feeling of my life. The meadow where I am is all moonlight, and I feel like I am floating, floating out of my body. I laugh, and I cry, too, but I am free. The big Communist rocks on my shoulders fell off then, even though it takes me six months of detention camps in Italy before I can use my foreign currency to get first to Paris and then to New York. And finally, finally here to the tennis club."

Radescu then looked around us as he'd asked me to do. "That man on Court One, he was the captain of his team at Notre Dame when the Second World War is over, and he can beat most of the club members in their twenties. The woman I am playing before I talk to you, she is the top-ranked woman over forty-five in New England. And our Don Floyd, he has won two hundred singles tournaments, including the unrestricted championship of Virginia when he is forty himself. A forty-year-old, and he beat all others, regardless of age. This place attracts quality like that, and it is not just the social life and tennis play that keeps the people young. It is that they have something to look forward to in getting older, to be the youngest players in the next competition bracket of age, and reign as champions again."

Radescu picked up his towel and shook it at me. "And that is what I want, too, Mr. John Cuddy. It is what I work hard for in Romania and risk my life to come to America and find. And no one takes this away from me."

Before I could respond, a familiar voice rose stridently from the chicken-wire door. "Cornel, the fuck is taking you so long?"

I turned and saw Cassandra Helides, pouting in the opening. Several of the players on other courts stopped their games and glanced over, a couple of them looking pretty angry.

Helides began walking toward us, wearing a miniskirt-length sundress but—from the way she was jouncing—no bra underneath. Not exactly a tennis outfit.

"Cornel?"

Radescu called out, "Cassandra, please."

I guessed Helides could see my suit but not my face under the shade of the awning, because drawing even closer, she said, "You're meeting with an accountant instead of coming to my place?"

I said, "Mrs. Helides."

Now she stopped. "The guy Nick hired."

"Good to see you again, too."

Helides didn't quite stamp her foot. "What are you doing here?"

Radescu said, "Cassandra, I tell you later."

I stood up. "I can tell you now. Cornel and I were just

wondering why it was that you stopped driving Veronica over here for her tennis lessons?"

Helides glared at me. "That fucking little tramp." Then she moved the high beams over to Radescu. "The hell are you telling him about that?"

"Cassan—"

Which was as far as he got, as Helides wheeled around and strode for the wire door.

Over her shoulder, she yelled, "Fifteen minutes, Cornel, or don't bother."

It was a measurable time before the players on the other courts finished shaking their heads and resumed playing. Maybe another ten seconds after that, Radescu said, "Mr. John Cuddy, turn around."

When I did, he was holding his tennis racquet by the handle, staring at the strings.

Radescu spoke to them. "The best players on the professional tour can serve almost one-hundred-fifty miles an hour." He looked up at me. "Even now, forty-three years of age, I can reach one-hundred-ten. A tennis ball is not a baseball, but at such a speed, it feels so when it hits you."

"Sorry if I spoiled your afternoon."

Moving toward the wire door, I didn't really expect any impact between the shoulder blades, but I was still a little relieved when none came. As I went up the walkway between the court fences, I could see Don Floyd, standing at the far end.

When I was a conversational distance from him, he said, "Everything all right?"

"From my viewpoint, anyway."

Floyd nodded. "You a tennis player, John?"

"Not since the army."

"Too bad. Man like you might find this a decidedly interesting place to live."

Don Floyd treated me to one of his fountain-of-youth smiles, then ambled away in the afternoon sun's fading light.

ELEVEN

Outside the tennis club's gate, I picked up my cell phone and tapped in the number on Justo's list for Dr. Henry Forbes. After two rings, a soothing male voice identified itself as the psychiatrist. I started talking back until I realized it was an outgoing tape announcement, suggesting that the caller could leave a message, proceed to the nearest emergency room, or follow the steps that Forbes and the caller had previously discussed. When the beep finally sounded, I gave my name and got as far as "regarding David Helides" before there was a click and the soothing voice from the outgoing tape came on live.

"Mr. Cuddy, I was expecting contact sooner."

"Sooner?"

"Nicolas told me the gravity of the situation."

Doctor Forbes seemed to have trouble finishing a thought.

"Mr. Cuddy?"

I said, "When can we meet to talk about David?"

"Well, I'm rather booked for tomorrow . . ."

I decided to go with his flow. ". . . but, given the 'gravity of the situation'?"

"Of course. Where are you now?"

I looked up at the next street sign and told him.

"Fine. Head south from there until you hit Las Olas Boulevard, then turn east."

Forbes gave me the address and said I should be to him in fifteen minutes.

It was actually twelve minutes by my watch when I pulled into the parking lot next to a freestanding bungalow with a lot of fussy trim I would have called "gingerbread" if its colors had been brown and white instead of pink and lime. Leaving the Cavalier, I went up to the front door and knocked. Hearing no reply, I tried the knob. Unlocked.

Inside was a dimly lit reception area with idyllic seascapes on the wall. Thankful that the decorator hadn't let the exterior sherbet colors seep in, I didn't see anybody behind the counter or in the open doorway beyond it.

"Dr. Forbes?"

"You're early. I'll be right out."

A muffled, echoing tone to his words. Then I heard the flushing of a toilet and the surging of water into a sink.

A short, compact man came through the open doorway, shrugging into a windbreaker over flap-pocket shorts and boat mocs. Pushing sixty from the creased lines on a deeply tanned face, his hair was still that nicotine color that goes white around the ears. He smiled at me and, clearing the reception counter, shook my hand in a no-nonsense way.

"Mr. Cuddy, Henry Forbes."

"How are you?"

He glanced over his shoulder. "I'd be better if every time I got up from a sitting position, I didn't sound like a hearthful of crickets."

A practiced line—and a finished thought—so I laughed politely.

Forbes smiled more broadly. "Still, though, it's more comfortable than the head."

"The head?"

"On the boat."

I didn't bother to follow that up.

"You know," said Henry Forbes from the helm, "it's possible to take the Intracoastal most anywhere you'd want to go."

I nodded, my hair being whipped by the wind.

We'd driven from his bunglalow/office to a marina, him leading in a Mercedes sedan. Once there, he'd ushered me along a series of catwalks to his motorboat.

Now, sitting in one captain's chair, I glanced at Forbes on my right in the other. As we went south on the wide ribbon of water, restaurants and bars with raised wooden decks lined both sides of the Intracoastal, families toting cameras waving to us. Other people were gathered at the seawall docks, getting into or out of green-and-yellow gondolas that seemed to function as buses.

"Water taxis," said Forbes, playing tour guide. "Pay a flat rate, ride all day, up and down. And over there is Bahia Mar, where John D. MacDonald set the Travis McGee series."

I'd enjoyed reading the books, so I looked at the marina going by on our left. Lots of big sailboats and power vessels, their hulls bobbing almost daintily in the constant chop, some folks drinking and eating.

They didn't wave to us.

Forbes moved a lever next to the wheel, throttling down some as he had earlier to go under buttressed causeways. "There's even a monument."

"Sorry?"

"To MacDonald, at Slip F-18 where McGee's houseboat was supposedly moored."

I nodded, and Forbes goosed the engine back to cruising speed.

After a while, we slowed down again to go under another causeway. Once through the maze of pilings, though, Forbes slowed even further, then anchored, the boat tugging tight on the line until we began to swing a little, left to right. Forbes cut the engine, and it suddenly seemed unnaturally quiet, despite the other boats going by us.

"Love the pilings."

I turned toward the stern, the closest supports maybe forty feet away. "Who does?"

"Snook, Mr. Cuddy."

I just stared at him.

"Snook, a game fish. They love to drive mullet or other bait up against the pilings, then tear them to pieces. Look, some are busting right now."

The surface of the water near the supports was roiling, almost churning.

Forbes said, "My favorite part of the day."

From under the gunwale, he pulled a two-sectioned fishing pole, already strung with thick, mustard-colored line, and matched up the halves. "Fly rod, seven weight." Forbes pointed to the red and white feathered lure, maybe two inches long, at the end of some clear monofilament. "And that blood look on the fly just drives them nuts." He smiled at me. "If you'll pardon a shrink's technical term."

"Doctor, about David Helides?"

"Just one second."

Forbes flicked the rod back and forth, getting more of the thick line out from the tip each time. Then he made the line already on the water loop and roll forward, like a rodeo cowboy doing a lariat trick, and the little fly at the end of the monofilament plunked into the water almost at one of the pilings.

"Roll cast, Mr. Cuddy. Faster way to—whoa!"

A silvery fish broke water, a speck of white and red at the

corner of its jaw, then slapped back on the surface and ran deeper, the line singing off the reel mounted under the rod's grip.

"Nice snook," said Forbes. "Maybe eighteen inches."

He played the fish carefully, drawing line in with his hand rather than using the reel. A minute or so later, Forbes lifted the snook over the stern by holding the lower lip between his thumb and forefinger. The fish was both silvery and gold, with a black racing stripe the length of its side.

Forbes eased the fly out of the snook's mouth and laid the fish along a tape measure embedded in the stern gunwale. "Nineteen inches." He smiled up at me. "Great species. Hits like a blue and jumps like a tarpon, but sweet as a sea trout on your plate."

And with that, Henry Forbes pushed his prize over the side.

I said, "You don't eat what you catch?"

"There are few enough of them around anymore, I don't keep many for the table." The smile turned sheepish. "Fact is, I flycast out here mainly as a way to stay sane after a day with clients who aren't."

I took the opening. "Which brings us to David Helides?"

"Oh, David's not insane, at least not by any legal definition. No"—Forbes flicked his line out for another cast—"he's 'just' a severe depressive."

"Meaning exactly what?"

The mustard-colored line rolled again toward the pilings. "You want professional jargon or plain talk, Mr. Cuddy?"

"Plain talk would be nice."

Forbes began yanking the line toward him rhythmically, maybe six inches at a time. "All right, plain talk. David was emotionally scarred early. You knew his mother died giving birth to him?"

"Yes."

"Well, it can't have been easy for him, what with a father mostly away and his brother behaving as he did."

"Spiro leaving home, you mean?"

"Yes, but not before spilling the beans."

"About what?"

Forbes glanced at me, then restudied his line before making another roll cast. "David's brother is the one who told him about how their mother died."

Lovely. "When was this?"

"David's fourth birthday. Long before he came under my care, but I've read the notes and reports of the colleagues up north who treated him as both child and adolescent. Do you know much about the drugs prescribed for depression?"

"I've heard of Prozac."

"Yes, I suppose everybody has. Well, to stay untechnical, there are several families of antidepressant medications. All come with side effects, though varying ones. A given drug will work idiosyncratically best for a given patient, a different medication for another."

"And with David?"

"Zoloft is the only drug that's proven at all effective for him. And he's past the top of the dosage scale even for that. It does allow David to function at a very low level, but also renders him quite . . . 'lethargic' is a picturable description."

I thought back to Helides disappearing on me in the Skipper's house. "He moved pretty fast when I saw him."

Forbes jerked his head toward me like someone had set a hook in his own mouth. "Mr. Cuddy, you weren't to interview David until after speaking with me."

His voice had lost that soothing patina and grown a burr to replace it. "I haven't, Doctor. He spotted me in a corridor shortly after I arrived at the Colonel's house, then rabbited before I knew who it was."

"Rabbited." Forbes sighed. "Actually, a rather telling verb, under the circumstances. David is lethargic unless frightened, which happens rather easily. Especially by any kind of change in his normal schedule."

"And what is David's normal schedule?"

"His mornings are hardest, as with most depressives I've seen. He may lie in his bed until eleven or even noontime, inert, staring at the ceiling."

"Why?"

"Any movement is such an effort, any 'plan of action' unimaginable."

Forbes seemed to think he should take some action himself by starting the casting routine again.

I said, "What happens at noon?"

"David drags himself from bed, makes his way to the kitchen, and has for lunch what you or I might choose for breakfast on—there we go!"

Behind the boat, another snook, slightly bigger than the first, jumped and twisted in the air before crashing back to the surface.

"Twenty-two," said Forbes. "Maybe twenty-three."

I returned to him. "So David eats breakfast for lunch. Then what?"

"Back to his room for a rest."

"Rest? You just said—"

"Depressives sleep a lot." Forbes fought this fish to the stern, before losing him on a last flipping jump. "Damn! I wanted to measure that one."

"Doctor, after his siesta?"

"After . . . ? Oh, David, yes. When he gets up again, he may go to the exercise room or out to his hammock."

From my case in the Keys, I knew that last word had a

double meaning in Florida. "A hammock stretched between two trees?"

"No. No, a 'hammock' of trees themselves."

A grove, the other meaning of the word. But . . . "Where is this hammock?"

"About twelve miles west, on one of the many tracts that Nicolas owns out there."

"Wait a minute. I thought David rarely left his room, much less the house."

"That's correct, but he developed an interest in botany as a boy, something he could do by himself with no family around. Also, plants are . . . stable organisms. They don't cause changes he can't deal with."

"A plant stays put?"

"Something like that, yes."

"But how does David get to a hammock twelve miles west?"

Forbes blinked. "Why, he drives, of course."

"He drives?"

"Yes, Mr. Cuddy. Disabilities like David's are no longer grounds for denying the afflicted all the privileges the rest of us enjoy."

"You're saying David has a driver's license."

"And his own vehicle, a small pickup truck. As you can imagine, the testing process was incredibly difficult for him. But I encouraged him to persevere, and I'm proud to say he did."

"How long ago did you begin treating him?"

"Since Nicolas moved down here permanently with Cassandra."

"In years?"

"About . . . twenty? If it's important to you, I can consult my records tomorrow."

"So how old was David when you first saw him?"

"Eleven, I believe."

"And then six or seven years later, he gets a driver's—"

"Actually, Mr. Cuddy, it was only a year ago."

"When he was . . . thirty-two?"

"Yes. I had to build David up to it, slowly."

"Which suggests that he's gotten better."

Forbes shook his head. "Unfortunately, very few depressives get 'better,' in the sense I think you mean of moving toward cured. Oh, occasionally there's a miracle, but the most we can hope for in David's case is stabilization, because his father won't authorize any more electroshock therapy or opera—"

"David's had shock treatments?"

"When he was younger, but it's still a permitted form of treatment, just not one Nicolas wants anymore. Nor does the patient, for that matter."

"David's a part of the decision process."

"Of course, Mr. Cuddy. He's of legal age and not incompetent, just severely depressed. So, I do what I can for him with the combination of drugs every day and therapy twice a week."

"At your office?"

"Ah, no. I travel to the house, actually."

"Why?"

Forbes blinked again. "Why?"

"Yes. David has a license, and the pills don't keep him from driving, do they?"

"No."

"And the Isle of Athens is—what, a mile from you?"

"Less, but David can't really manage driving himself much before four, anyway."

"You don't take late afternoon appointments?"

"I do. But"—Forbes shook his fishing rod this time—"the Helides house is conveniently on the way to my marina."

I gave it a moment before saying, "I've been told David has a computer?"

"It's a way for him to interact socially without the ordeal of a face-to-face, so to speak."

The ordeal. "So he does electronic mail?"

"And visits Web pages, perhaps even commenting on some sites and seeing others comment back."

I thought I'd heard nearly enough. "Anything I should stay away from in talking with David?"

Forbes actually set his fishing rod down now. "Yes."

"What?"

He looked at me directly. "Any mention of his niece."

I wonder what must have been on my face. "Doctor, you understand that—"

"—that Nicolas wants to find out who killed his grand-daughter, yes. And that he wants you to speak with every-one at the party inside that house on the day in question."

"But I'm not supposed to mention Veronica's name?"

Forbes patted the hair on his head. "I told you before, Mr. Cuddy. David is upset by any change, and the bigger the change, the more he's upset."

"Meaning the murder of his niece really hit him."

"Especially because she was interested in computers, and her tutor, Tranh—however smart he may be—is not nearly as sophisticated with using them as someone who lives much of his life through one."

"But Spi Held told me most of his composing was done by computer."

Forbes blinked again. "And therefore?"

"Why didn't Veronica use her father as a computer teacher?"

"I'm not sure they got along all that well."

"Spi and his daughter?"

"Correct."

"But David and Veronica did?"

"With respect to the computer, Mr. Cuddy, and that's part of my point."

"Then I'm not seeing it."

A labored sigh as he reeled in his fishing line. "One of the few . . . connections between David and the 'real' world outside his house and the hammock was his contact with his niece when she came to visit her grandfather. One of the few remaining connections is his 'virtual' linkage via computer, something he and the girl sometimes did together. I would hate to have you . . . discourage David from resorting to the online world by resurrecting now-painful memories of his niece doing that with him."

"I can live without him demonstrating his computer to me, but David was at his father's birthday party, and is therefore a viable suspect in Veronica's murder."

"No." Forbes pulled the rod in half and moved to stow it back under the gunwale. "No, I don't see that."

"Why not?"

"To begin with, my patient attended that party only to please Nicolas, and just being there was a terrible strain on David. I could tell."

I thought about my private screening at Sergeant Pintana's office. While Forbes's name was on the guest list Justo had compiled for me, I couldn't remember seeing him on the videotape Kalil Biggs had shot. "You were at the party that day?"

"Yes, but I stayed with David most of the time, and after the 'singing incident,' I checked to be sure he was all right."

"Checked where?"

"With David himself, before he went back to his suite to recover."

"Recover."

"From the emotional trauma of his niece's . . . 'performance.'"

"But you didn't stay with David?"

"No, I spent time with Nicolas instead. And again after the girl's body was discovered. And that's my second point, actually."

"What is?"

"It's my understanding from Nicolas that the police believe this killing was carefully planned. As a severe depressive, David is incapable of such."

"Since he got a driver's license, tends his plants at that hammock, and lives through his computer, I think you might be wrong there."

"I'm not, Mr. Cuddy, but even if I were, it's also my understanding that his niece was sexually assaulted."

I nodded.

"Then," said Forbes, "David isn't a 'viable' suspect, as you characterize it."

"Because?"

"Mr. Cuddy, earlier I alluded to the side effects of anti-depressant drugs?"

"You did."

Forbes moved over to the dashboard. "Well, one of Zoloft's principal drawbacks is decreased sexual desire and capacity."

I focused on the adjective. "Just 'decreased.'"

"In most who take it. However, David has been on such a high dosage for so long, he's incapable of achieving an erection."

"There are devices he could have—"

"No. No, Mr. Cuddy, even if David could have found a 'device' to accomplish the penetration, he would have no sexual interest in his niece." Dr. Henry Forbes sighed. "Or in anybody else, for that matter."

TWELVE

It was nearly seven P.M. when I turned onto the Isle of Athens. Approaching the Helides gate, I saw only one television truck and a small klatch of reporters standing in the street, two sharing a cigarette. Too late for the early news, they probably were hanging around in hopes of getting something for the eleven o'clock broadcast.

I drove through them slowly as they called out sound-bite questions to me through the windows of the Cavalier. Umberto Reyes came from his little gazebo and opened the gate. When I got to the garage, I saw the pickup truck I'd noticed on my first visit snugged up against one of the bay doors.

After ringing the front bell, I waited long enough for someone to answer it that I figured whoever it would be had to have walked a long ways.

The whoever was Duy Tranh. Wearing a pinstriped shirt, khaki slacks, and a determined frown.

"Mr. Cuddy, I thought it was clear from last night that you were to use the back entrance."

"I must have forgotten."

"When Mr. Umberto Reyes called to say you were coming, that's where I went to let you in."

"I'm really sorry for your inconvenience."

My reply wasn't meant sarcastically, but I could see Tranh took it as such anyway.

Then he said, "The Colonel is anxious to speak with you."

* * *

"Lieutenant," said the garbled voice, "I believe you've met my wife, Cassandra."

"Several times, sir."

As Duy Tranh moved to the couch in the den, I watched Nicolas Helides slouching in a monogrammed, terry-cloth robe on one of the red leather chairs. His legs under the hem of the cloth looked thin, pale, and veined. Behind the chair stood Cassandra Helides in the same kind of placket shirt I'd seen on Cornel Radescu earlier at courtside. Her hands were under the Skipper's robe at the collar, kneading his neck and shoulder muscles.

She said, "Mr. Cuddy was at the tennis club today," and then leaned down to kiss the top of her husband's left ear before looking back up at me. "Did you learn anything there that surprised you?"

I wasn't liking the challenging leer on her face. "Not really."

Cassandra nodded. "I didn't think you would." She kissed her husband once more, then said, "Well, I'll leave you to business. Mr. Cuddy, feel free to come see me if you need anything else."

"Thank you."

When Cassandra Helides walked out from behind the Skipper's chair, I couldn't see she was wearing anything but the shirt, which reached a third of the way down her thighs. I didn't turn as she went by me and out the door to the corridor.

Nicolas Helides rolled his shoulders a little, as if drawing the last satisfying sensation from his wife's massage. "Cassie needs to do that, you know."

"Do what, sir?"

A tired expression began to cross his features until it got to the paralyzed side and stopped. "Lieutenant, I had a stroke, but I've no reason to think your perceptions are impaired."

I looked at Duy Tranh, who now was smiling in a bemused sort of way.

The Skipper said, "It's all right for you to find Cassie attractive. I certainly do."

"Colonel—"

"The vamping and flirting is her way of reasserting her beauty, her desirability, since I can't offer her any . . . tangible confirmation on that score anymore."

"Yes, sir."

A nod, as though we'd gotten an awkward item off his agenda. "Well, what have you found out?"

I summarized my talks with the people at the Held house.

Helides heard me out before saying, "Beyond Kalil Biggs having made more than one video of Veronica, you haven't found much."

"Just that your party guests' alibis are pretty vague."

"Which the police already established." A change in tone, even through the stroke damage to his voice. "What about Cornel Radescu?"

I glanced at Duy Tranh, but now he was studying the rug.

"Lieutenant?"

"Sorry, I—"

"Is there a reason you keep checking with Duy before answering some of my questions?"

"I don't think so, Colonel."

"Then continue your report please. To me."

"Yes, sir. I wasn't able to ask Radescu all the questions I had for him."

"Why not?"

"We were interrupted."

The tired expression again crossed half his face before, "I understand."

I waited, and he did, too.

Finally, I said, "Dr. Forbes was very insightful regarding David."

"Henry is paid well to be so. I take it you're ready to speak with my son now?"

"I am."

Nicolas Helides turned his head toward Tranh. "Duy, if you would, please?"

"Certainly, Colonel."

As Duy Tranh led me down a first-floor corridor, I said, "How was Veronica as a student?"

He stiffened in front of me, then stopped. "Ungifted. And difficult, as I already have mentioned."

"Except I don't recall your mentioning that you were tutoring her."

"Perhaps because you never asked."

Tranh began walking again.

I fell in behind him. "No problems between Veronica and you?"

"None beyond her boredom with any subject not rooted in popular music. And my frustration in trying to provide her the sort of education the Colonel afforded me."

"So you could sort of thank him, indirectly."

"As I have expressed to him many times, in both word and deed." Tranh stopped at a closed door. "This is David's suite, Mr. Cuddy."

We'd reached a part of the house near the pool. I didn't hear anything from the other side of the door.

"Are you sure he's in there?"

"Yes. I checked the kitchen when I thought I was letting you in that way. He hasn't eaten yet."

"How can you be sure?"

"I know David rather well. He operates on a very different schedule."

From the way Duy Tranh spoke that last word, he might just as well have said, "dimension."

"You are my father's detective."

I'd used the handle to push in the door after my knock brought a quavering, "It is open." The living room area was dimly lit, except for a bright snake-neck lamp over computer equipment that looked as elaborate as what I'd seen in Tranh's suite the night before. The rest of the furnishings seemed spartan at best, like a church serving a poor congregation.

And no sign of David Helides.

The same stilted voice said, "If you would not mind, please come into the bedroom."

I moved left, around a divider in the form of a tall cabinet of bookshelves. Most of the titles suggested computer manuals, and just past the divider, I saw the foot of an unmade bed. The light—from subtly recessed bulbs inside the hung ceiling—was slightly better than in the living area. Or maybe my eyes were just adjusting.

On the bed lay a figure in the fetal position, facing me. His left hand was palm-up under his right knee, his right hand palm-down atop his left knee. David Helides wore navy-blue sweatpants, the ankle bands pulled down over his toes, like a child's jammies. A sweatshirt, also navy, covered his torso, and the hood shrouded his head, as though he'd just worked out and was afraid of getting a chill despite the shaggy hair. Helides's eyes, recessed deep under his brow, were squinched closed in a face that was thirty-three going on seventy.

"I am sorry," he said, "but it is difficult for me to keep my eyes open when it is not necessary to see. Please take the computer chair. It is comfortable."

His voice still quavered, if anything more on this longest

passage from him. The tone was apersonal, like the electronic speech of a . . . computer.

I dragged the chair over to a conversational distance from Helides, then sat in it. "I appreciate your seeing me at all."

His eyes opened for just a moment, dull and listless, then closed again with a flutter that took a little longer to dissipate. "I saw you yesterday."

"Briefly."

The lips changed position, but less like a smile and more like a person trying to get comfortable, though the rest of his body stayed perfectly still. "I am sorry I ran from you, but a stranger in the house . . . a disruption is . . ."

I thought of Dr. Henry Forbes and his uncompleted sentences. "There are some questions I'd like to ask you."

"I know."

Time to test the waters. "How do you know?"

The eyelids fluttered but didn't open. "My father . . . Dr. Forbes . . ."

"I've spoken with your doctor."

A sigh, perhaps of relief. "Then you know about . . . my condition."

"Yes, but if you don't mind talking about it, I'd—"

"It is all I want to talk about. Dr. Forbes did not tell you that?"

"No, he didn't."

Another sigh, this time more of resignation. "There are many symptoms of severe, clinical depression. Lack of appetite, no enjoyment in the doing of pleasurable things, contemplation of . . . suicide. But that is nothing compared to what happens in the brain itself. I have read many people's description of it. Some call it a raging storm, others a deep fog. For me, depression is like the images of a slot machine I have seen on the Internet."

"A slot machine?"

"Yes, where the different wheels are constantly whirring past the little windows. Well, if my eyes are those windows, it is only for short bursts each day that all the lemons line up. Except for those times, when I can concentrate on something else, the depression is my sole source of identity. It is . . . me."

"Mr. Helides—"

"David, please. It is . . . easier on the mind."

I realized I hadn't introduced myself. "I'm John Cuddy, David. Use whichever name you like."

"John would be less . . . authoritarian for me."

Clinically depressed he might be, but, like Kalil Biggs, not stupid behind his disability. "You understand that I have to ask you about Veronica."

I expected a withdrawal of some kind, but instead Helides did almost smile this time. "You use her real name."

"Yes."

"Most of the others didn't. They called her by her 'stage' name."

"That's because I think of her as a real person, not a rock singer."

"I, too."

A single tear rolled from under his right eyelid and was channeled by his nose. I thought of Jeanette Held's similar reaction. Then Helides brought his left hand up quickly to whip past both closed eyes before retreating back beneath his right knee.

"David, I'm told you and Veronica used to play on the computer together."

"Yes. I am quite interested in botany, as Dr. Forbes must also have told you."

"He did."

Because of Helides's position on the bed, his head nodded laterally on the pillow. "I study the true plants of Florida."

If he wanted to talk about them, I thought it might be a good way to get him to open up. "The true plants, you say?"

"The indigenous ones. Species like the gumbo-limbo, with its grotesquely beautiful, gnarled trunks and red bark that peels like a sunburned tourist. The Caloosa Indians began using the gummy sap from the tree a millennium ago to catch birds who might land on the limbs. The sapodilla tree, with its seedy fruit the size of a baseball, like sandy candy. The torchwood tree, whose resin will burn. Those species introduced by man—like the punk tree, the pepper, the Australian pine—are forcing out the indigenous ones because these immigrants proliferate easily and grow with no need for human care."

Helides had been speaking in an increasingly stronger voice, then suddenly fell silent. When he opened his mouth again, the quaver was back. "But I bore you."

"Not at all."

"And I am just practicing 'avoidance,' as Dr. Forbes would call it."

"Avoidance?"

"Avoiding what is unpleasant to me by talking about that which I find interesting, and . . . safe."

"Let's stay with the pleasant a little longer. Veronica and you enjoyed working with your computer?"

"Yes." A gurgle that almost amounted to a laugh. "She was not very interested in botany, I must say. But I showed her how to access the Internet and the Web. I also would buy her computer games, and she would play them here, with me."

"You bought her these games?"

"My father gives me an allowance for such indulgences."

I didn't say anything right away.

Helides said it for me. "John, do not be embarrassed by

your question. Or for me. I am long past any . . . pride of independence in my life."

I took a breath. "When you and Veronica were together, did she ever talk with you about *her* life?"

His lips grew thinner. "She tried to . . . cheer me up, I think in exchange for my showing her more computer tricks."

"In exchange."

"Veronica was not a generous girl, John. She . . . bartered for what she wanted."

Same assessment as I'd gotten from others. "But did Veronica talk with you about what she was doing in her life, maybe who or what she was afraid of?"

"No." Now a vertical shake from the head on the pillow. "No, Veronica intuited that I would not be of much use to her if she told me . . . disturbing things." A pause, and the lips parted in a slight, but genuine, smile. "Which is not to say that she did not help me, John. Truly. With all my father has spent on formal 'treatments,' the allowance money that went toward those computer games probably brought me more joy than anything else. And that was because of Veronica."

Since Helides brought up the "treatments" issue, I decided to push it a little. "Dr. Forbes said you'd had electroshock therapy?"

A visible cringe, the whole body drawing more tightly into the fetal position. "Yes. . . . But even if I . . . wanted to talk with you about them, I could not. My . . . short-term memory before the . . . 'sessions' was wiped out by the current applied."

Move to safer ground. "Dr. Forbes also said you take some drugs now."

The slight smile again as Helides relaxed a bit. "I have no remaining pride on that subject, either. The Zoloft renders me impotent, and I must not mix it with alcohol or other substances."

"So you don't."

"No."

"Not even at your father's birthday party."

Another cringe and tightening of the body language. "Let us not . . . avoid anymore. Get it over with, please?"

Okay. "What can you tell me about that day?"

"It was very . . . disrupting. Many people in the house, my brother's friends, others. Dr. Forbes tried to keep me . . . at ease, but it was not possible."

"I've seen Kalil Biggs's videotape."

"Another . . . disruption."

"His doing the taping, David?"

"The noise, the unusual . . . movements. His lens . . . following me wherever I went."

I didn't recall Helides being on the tape, but then, perception is uniquely personal. "You were there when Veronica sang to your father?"

The worst cringe of all, the body on the bed seeming to spasm painfully. "It was . . . horrible."

"You didn't anticipate it, then."

"No. Oh, when we played some of the computer games, Veronica would make some . . . remarks I assume she heard from my brother or his friends." A pause. "Sexually charged remarks. But to act out like that in front of her grandfather. . . ."

"David, what did you do after Veronica ran from the room?"

"I . . . ran, too."

"Where?"

"Into the corridor, toward my suite here."

And the pool. "Did anyone see you?"

The smile again. "John, surely you asked Dr. Forbes that question?"

"I know what he remembers. How about you?"

"I remember him catching up to me in the corridor, saying something to me. Something . . . soothing, probably."

"Then what?"

"I came back here."

"Did you see Veronica?"

"Not after she left the room. I could . . . hear my brother, though."

"Hear him?"

"Veronica was behind me, running in the other direction at that moment. My brother was . . . yelling after her."

"What was he saying?"

"Foul, foul language."

"As best you can recall it?"

Helides braced himself. "My brother said, 'You little cunt, you've cut our fucking throats.'"

The room seemed awfully still. "Do you remember anything else?"

"No. I came back here, as I told you already. I closed the door to . . . cushion the fall from hearing Veronica do what she did."

"The song, you mean?"

"The song," said Helides.

"Did you hear anything from the pool area?"

The vertical shake again. "No, the . . . soundproofing in this house is quite good. Once that suite door is closed, nothing comes through."

"So you never saw Veronica again, either?"

"No. Duy Tranh came to me later, so I wouldn't stumble out into . . ."

His body quivered and drew itself more tightly.

"David, do you remember anything else?"

"Yes." The eyes fluttered open. "Yes, I do."

"What?"

His eyes stared at the wall opposite the bed. "I remember

that in a family rather . . . short on love, Veronica gave me her version of it. A love I'd never felt, not even from my own . . . mother. It may have been bartered rather than freely . . . offered, but Veronica's was love nonetheless to me." Helides closed his eyes again. "Do you remember when I talked about the . . . gumbo-limbo tree earlier?"

"The one the Native Americans used to catch birds?"

"A good listener you are, John. Yes. Well, not all the indigenous flora is quite so . . . benign."

"What do you mean?"

"There is also the poisonwood, which grows as a tree but functions as poison ivy does up north. And the Christmas berry, which is a member of what you might know as the 'nightshade family,' with lovely five-petaled white or lilac flowers but also deadly fruit."

Again, the voice got progressively stronger as Helides spoke about things botanical.

"But John, the one species I'd like to find is a manchineel. The local agricultural authorities tried to stamp them out, and I've never seen one, not even at Flamingo Gardens in Davie, though the books say it still grows in the wild. And, like the Christmas berry, it produces a deadly fruit the size of a crab apple. But better than that is its sap."

"Sticky, too?"

"No. No, the sap of the manchineel is supposed to ooze out of its trunk and branches and even leaves. And it is so caustic, those Caloosa Indians used the tree to interrogate their captives."

"Interrogate them?"

"Yes. The prisoner would be lashed to the tree with strong vines, and the sap would run onto his skin, burning the flesh off the captive's bone until the Caloosas were told the truth."

Jesus Christ.

Helides opened his eyes again, but this time they rolled around in their sockets. "That is what I would do, John, if I could find a manchineel. I'd tie the one who killed Veronica to it until he told me why, why he had to take her like that."

"David—"

"And then, after he finally told me the truth, I'd leave him there. To be . . . melted slowly by liquid fire as he yearned for even a drop of the pool water he used to kill Veronica."

Standing up, I told David Helides that I hoped he'd have better dreams than I would.

THIRTEEN

Driving back to my hotel, I was stopped at a red light when the cell phone made a deedling sound. I picked it up and looked for a RECEIVE button near the SEND one. Not seeing any, I pushed SEND just as a green arrow in the traffic signal told me I could make my left-hand turn.

"Hello?"

"John, Justo here. Did you not get my message?"

"Where?"

"At your hotel. I tried you there three times today."

"Justo, I'm sorry. Why didn't you use this cell number?"

"I did that also."

Which he could have, since I hadn't been carrying the phone on me. "What's up?"

A pause, then, "I grow weary, as I try to balance the demands of a law practice with my concerns about a certain client."

Cryptic. "Meaning, that since cellulars are insecure radios, you'd like me to call you back on a land-line?"

"Yes, as to security, but no as to calling me back. I just wanted to know if you have had any success with that client's matter, since I am to drive up there tonight to see him."

"Not much. And I'm pretty beat, too. Try me at the hotel later if you need me."

"More likely tomorrow, John."

I left my car in the hotel garage and walked through a lushly landscaped pool area to the lobby entrance. The desk clerk—who wasn't my "ally," Damon—told me I could access their voice mail system from any phone. When I held up the cell unit, she nodded and gave me the number to call and the code to enter.

In my room, I saw the red dome light flashing on top of the telephone next to the bed. After showering, I plumped up two pillows and dialed for my calls. In between the three expected messages from Justo Vega were one each from Mitch Eisen, Spiral's manager, and Malinda Dujong, Jeanette Held's "spiritual advisor." Both just said to return theirs, and since Eisen's had been the earlier, I tried him first.

"Hey, Cuddy, I'm glad you called me back. What're you doing tonight?"

"Going to bed."

"What?"

"I'm tired, Mitch."

"Tired's one thing, but eight o'clock is the shank of the fucking evening. You eat yet?"

I had to think about it. "Not since lunch at Spi Held's house."

"Yeah, he called me, said you'd been out there. Well, look, you got to have dinner, right?"

"I suppose."

"Okay, I'll pick you up at your hotel in half an hour."

"Mitch—"

"This first place, it serves great food, and we ought to be timing it about perfect."

First place. "Mitch, I'm not really up for a night on the town."

"Just dress casual, account of it's more like a seminar for you. Music appreciation, so you understand Spiral better as a band."

I didn't answer for a moment, thinking of how discouraging it had been for me to be with David Helides and most of the other people I'd interviewed that day.

"Cuddy?"

"Half an hour, Mitch. I'll be outside the lobby, downstairs. What are you driving?"

"Don't worry. You can't miss it."

I depressed the connection button, got another dial tone, and called Malinda Dujong's number. After four rings, an outgoing tape of her voice repeated the seven digits I'd just entered before a "please leave any message." I said something like "John Cuddy, returning your call," and gave her the hotel number again.

Then I went back to the bathroom to dry my hair before pulling on a short-sleeved shirt and some olive-drab slacks.

"Didn't I say you couldn't miss it?"

Changing lanes, Mitch Eisen sent his eyes back to the road. The plugs of his hair transplant stood straight up in the wind.

I said, "A fifty-eight?"

"Fifty-nine, like they used on *Route 66*, though that show was in black-and-white, so you couldn't see the colors."

From the lobby door, I'd watched the orange-and-cream

Corvette slew around the circular drive, top down. Mitch Eisen had waved for me to climb into the passenger seat of the two-door sports car.

As we swerved around a delivery truck, I said, "How long have you had it?"

"Just about a year, so it's almost time to turn it in."

"Turn it in?"

"Yeah. I rent them, I don't buy them."

I remembered Pepe telling me he could get me a flashier car before I chose the Cavalier. "That's cost-effective?"

"Hey, it's 'image-effective.' A producer or promoter sees me drive up in wheels like this, he figures I'm still a player."

Still a player. "I meant more, wouldn't you be better off buying the car?"

"Oh. Used to, in fact. Had a sixty-five Imperial Gray Ghost, a sixty-nine GTO loaded. But you lease these things, you don't feel so bad about the ding in the parking lot at the supermarket, you know?" Eisen grinned. "Of course, I still got to pay the body shop."

We turned onto Route A1A, which I remembered as the beach road. "Where's this place you're taking me?"

"Just south of Las Olas. Great food, but that's only the warm-up."

The parking lot of "Coconuts" was crowded, but Eisen found a space near some large boats docked on what looked to me like a spur of the Intracoastal. As we walked up to the restaurant, I could see it had an outside deck for drinks and dining. I wondered if Dr. Henry Forbes and I had passed it that day.

Eisen said, "Outside's nice for eating, but you can't hear as well, so we'll go inside."

The hostess led us to one of fifteen tables, arranged

cabaret style in front of a small, raised stage with three stools on it. Eisen ordered a bottle of Australian shiraz from the wine list. By the time we'd put napkins on our laps and opened the food menus, a waitress was popping the cork. After she dribbled a dollop into Eisen's glass, he sampled the wine and approved it. We'd just told her our entrées— filet mignon for him, sirloin strip for me—when somebody dimmed the room's lighting.

I looked around, didn't see any entertainment just yet.

Eisen said, "They like to draw it out." He lifted his glass, clinked it against mine. "Here's to what you got to do *not* being drawn out."

As our salads arrived, two guys moved to the end stools on stage, leaving the middle one open. Both wore beards and seemed to be guitarists, though one took a harmonica from his pocket and slapped it against his thigh a few times.

By the time we'd finished the salads, each guitarist had played and sung a couple of easy listening pieces. Occasionally, Eisen would lean over to me and say, "Remember Seals and Crofts?" or "Next to last one Jim Croce ever did."

Our entrées arrived, and Eisen refilled the wineglasses. "Kind of music we been hearing, you're wondering what the fuck we're doing here, right?"

I nodded.

He said, "Take a look around us."

I did. It had become a standing-room-only crowd. The people were all ages and races, many dressed expensively. Then a rising buzz of different voices began saying "Hey" or "How you doing?" And a tall African-American woman in her twenties with a beautiful face and ginger-colored hair weaved through the well-wishers.

Eisen touched my forearm. "The franchise."

As the woman took the stage and the middle stool, one of the guitarists said, "Give it up y'all for—"

The mounting applause drowned out the name.

Eisen leaned closer. "L-A-G-A-Y-L-I-A, capital 'L' and 'G,' pronounced 'Lah-*Gale*-yuh.'" He leaned back as the woman moved her mouth toward the microphone in front of her. "Now I'm gonna shut up, Cuddy, but once she starts, don't forget to eat your food."

After about two minutes, I knew what Eisen meant. LaGaylia could sing, yes, but the interpretations she put on the composer's notes and lyrics, the facial expressions and hand gestures—of joy or pain, love or jealousy—were extraordinary. By the end of her set, I'd seen and heard the best female vocalist of my life.

I also realized that Eisen had been right about my meal.

"You want, they can doggy-bag the rest of the steak?"

The crowd was still buzzing about LaGaylia as I lost sight of her. "I can eat it cold."

"Okay," said Mitch Eisen, "But we got two more places I want you to see before we call it a night."

As we drove down Route 1, I said, "Why haven't I ever heard of LaGaylia before?"

"You mean, she does Alanis, Mariah, even Melissa and a few more, with incredible range and fire, how come she isn't a superstar herself?"

I didn't get all his allusions. "Basically, that's my question."

"Okay, Professor Eisen's opening lesson of the night. The year LaGaylia was twenty-two, there were ninety-nine others her age with just as good a voice, face, and body. The year she was twenty-three, there were a hundred girls twenty-two, coming up behind her."

"But how can the woman I just saw not be . . . ?"

"Discovered?"

"And appreciated, I suppose."

"Well, first of all, she is appreciated. LaGaylia's a hell of a success down here. Packs them in three nights a week at Coconuts alone."

"Okay."

"Second, though, and more to your question, there's got to be that magic of luck. Something special in a song, somebody like me hearing her sing it in a local place like Coconuts, with the right connections to launch her regionally and nationwide."

"And even you haven't made that happen for her?"

A glance over at me. "Cuddy, I don't represent the lady. I know what I do best, and unfortunately, her sound isn't it."

"But Spiral's is?"

"Let you know later."

The second place Eisen brought me was decorated in dark woods and brass, elegant yet comfortable. As we took seats at the nearly full bar, he said, "Kitty Ryan started O'Hara's on Las Olas about twelve, fifteen years ago. We're in Hollywood—the name of the town, I mean. Kitty and her partner, Rich, just opened this branch, but once they're finished, there'll be a three-hundred-seat venue upstairs, big enough to attract national jazz acts."

As a bartender named Mary brought us glasses of Merlot, I looked toward the stage. A diverse group of men and women started taking their places by different instruments, including a fiddle.

I said to Eisen, "Jazz, not Irish?"

"Actually, the Pamala Stanley Band's not really jazz, even. But despite not having an Irish person in the group— they're Italian, Greek, Puerto Rican, Jewish—Kitty had them for her St. Patrick's Day party in Lauderdale last year. You'll see why in a minute."

The group began to play, and after five terrific renditions,

I hadn't heard what I'd have called the same category of material twice. Blues to rock to folk to jazz, including some riffs by a woman named Randi on the fiddle that brought down the house.

At the band break, Eisen set his empty glass next to my half-full one. "You up for another 'lesson'?"

"Only if it's on the way home."

"It is." He pulled out a tiny cellular phone. "Lemme just make a call first while you finish your drink, be sure they got the right act there."

I watched as Mitch Eisen walked out onto a fringe patio that bled into the sidewalk.

"Here, the valet makes sense," he said, exiting the Corvette at our third stop.

Inside the main entrance, a tuxedoed doorman nodded to Eisen and said, "Welcome to 'September's.'" My eyes took some time adjusting to the cavernous space, a huge stage spotlit at a distance of at least a hundred feet, six or eight musicians and singers performing bombastically on it.

Moving toward them, we passed an oval, multitiered bar with female 'tenders in black Eisenhower jackets and fishnet stockings. The ceiling rose twenty feet, with dark, rough-hewn beams and a jungle of plants trailing leafy vines. A lot of people held lit cigarettes, though, and the air was pretty thick with smoke under the kind of revolving glitter-globe I've always associated with *Saturday Night Fever*.

Just as we ordered brandies, a slim black man in a double-breasted suit moved to the microphone at center stage, and the room grew quiet, even the people on the stainless steel dance floor stopping to watch.

"He's why we're here," said Eisen into my ear.

The man began to sing, but with just murmurs of

accompaniment from a keyboard and guitar. I'd heard the song before but never thought of the tune as a hit.

Until this guy began singing it.

The precision and control he had over his voice and mannerisms was astonishing, his range at the high end enough to shatter crystal. When he finished five or six minutes later, the stage went suddenly dark, and everybody stood and applauded wildly, including waitresses and bartenders who must have heard him in the past.

I turned to Eisen. "Wow."

"Johnny Mathis and Al Jarreau, rolled into one."

Recorded music came on, a guy in the raised booth taking over from the live entertainment.

Eisen said, "You want to ask somebody to dance, go ahead."

"Not tonight, thanks."

He nodded before downing the last of his drink. "We about ready, then?"

"To go, yes."

The night's breeze felt good after all the smoke inside September's. Eisen drove the Corvette carefully, constantly checking his speed and slowing down for significant stretches on the fairly empty streets.

I said, "Worried about a ticket?"

He didn't glance over. "Hot car like this, the cops expect you to be going over the limit. And after a brandy, you can get stuck by the Breathalyzer even if your blood's still fine. So, I don't give them any excuse to stop me."

"What's the excuse for where we've been tonight?"

Eisen did glance over this time. "What do you mean?"

"Those bars, and your 'lessons' on music."

His eyes went back to the road. "Cuddy, what did you see and hear?"

"Three different kinds of entertainment."

"Describe them."

"Why?"

"Indulge me."

I said, "Female vocalist with accompaniment, versatile band with fiddler, show band with a male lead singer."

"Okay, that's objective. How about subjective?"

I tried to capture what I'd felt. "People with talent, enjoying themselves."

"That's it. On the fucking button. Everybody on those stages was talented, and the better performers brought out the best in the rest. Made them play up to the level of the most talented person on the stage."

"Your point?"

"My point," said Eisen, "is that those people are gonna be talented, and perform like that, no matter what's hot on the CHR stations."

"The top-40 ones."

"Like I told you in my office. All the performers you saw tonight, they're gonna be fine, regardless of which way the fickle fucking wind blows."

I thought I saw it. "But Spiral won't be."

A nod, sad in its certainty. "That's right, too. Spi and the boys, they're has-beens, a garage band that just happened to have the right sound for a couple of years, and an echo of the right sound for a couple more. Except maybe for Ricky, and even he has just the talent, not the instinct."

"The instinct?"

"It's like an animal thing. The desire to climb the ladder of success with a fucking knife between your teeth."

"I thought I saw some of that when I spoke with Spi Held."

"No." A shake of the head, even sadder than the nod had been. "No, what you saw in Spi is desperation. The guy was on top once, and that's a hell of a sweet taste to have in your mouth, Cuddy. Only problem is, it doesn't last very long. And when that sweet taste works its way from your mouth to your gut, it starts rotting down there. Makes you do things you wouldn't ordinarily."

Eisen turned into the drive for my hotel. Instead of using the circular spur servicing the main entrance, though, he went past the pool area and came to a stop at the entrance to the parking garage.

I shifted sidesaddle in my seat to face him. "There a reason we're back here?"

"Yeah. I don't want some fucking bellhop hearing me ask you questions with names attached to them."

"Like what?"

Eisen squeezed the steering wheel of his car like an exercise machine. "Twenty, twenty-five years ago, I managed a mixed bag of fucking kids with more energy than talent, and more talent than brains. You saw for yourself how fucked up they all are, and believe me, Tommy O'Dell was even more fucked up than the ones who lived through it."

"Through what?"

"The rock-star scene, with all it does to you for the little it does for you. But there's one thing it does real well, Cuddy, and that's produce money. Fuck, you'd think it shits the stuff, the way the green rolls in."

I thought back to Gordo Lazar's description of Eisen and Held, on that "comforter of cash" in the bedroom of their tour bus. "But that was then."

"And this is now. Or it could have been, Very didn't piss somebody off enough to snuff her."

I stared at Eisen. "If you have a point, Mitch, I'm not seeing it."

He returned my stare, the eyes hard. "There's a possibility, a faint fucking thread of a chance, that I can get that mixed bag of fuckheads up and running again enough to make some real money out of all this."

"You said as much in your office."

"The right spin, yeah. But that'd take a lot of my time for no real return unless that thread comes through." Eisen's eyes grew harder. "And even that fucking thread gets cut, the money train don't stop at the station anymore."

"Colonel Helides backing the band."

"Right. So here's what I figure. Very's killed by somebody in the band, we're fucked with the Colonel. He's never gonna keep writing checks'll remind him of what one of them did."

"Go on."

"But, I figure that if somebody else did his granddaughter, then maybe, just maybe, the money train rolls on, kind of a sympathy vote, you might say."

I willed the words to my lips. "A memorial almost."

"Exact-a-mundo. Like a fucking memorial to the dead kid." The eyes grew even harder still, the hair plugs marching down his forehead. "So, what I want to know is, you getting any vibes on this thing?"

"Vibes."

"You know. Feelings, hunches, whatever the fuck you call them."

"About who actually killed Veronica Held."

Now the eyes widened. "Of course about who fucking killed her."

I decided to use Eisen before he used me. "I think Spi Held cared more about his comeback than his offspring."

"No question there."

"I also think for Buford Biggs, it's the reverse."

"Agreed again. Once Buford found out he had the plague, Kalil's been about the only thing he talks about."

"What was Kalil's relationship to Veronica?"

That stopped Eisen for a moment. "Relationship? You

mean, would I bet on whether those two jailbaits were fucking each other?"

I bit back what I wanted to say. "Start there."

Eisen thought a moment more. "Not unless it was Very's
idea."

"Because?"

"Because Kalil fucking worshipped the ground she
mashed him into."

"Mashed?"

"The little vixen used people, Cuddy. Like I told you,
and like probably everybody but her mommy told you,
too. Any time I saw them together, Very made Kalil her
gofer. Or her whipping boy. She'd do jokes on his stutter
thing."

"Kalil said she didn't."

"Maybe not to his face, but let him go to the kitchen, get
her a soda, and Very'd be saying, 'I j-j-just love Dr P-p-pep-
per.'"

"Are you telling me Kalil was aware of that?"

"Buford sure was. I heard him lay into Spi once about it.
'Can't you teach your fucking child some manners,' etc., etc."

"And?"

"And nothing. Spi couldn't control his daughter any
more than . . ."

"Any more than what, Mitch?"

"Any more than anybody else. She had a mind of her
own, the little bitch."

I waited a minute before saying, "How about a reason why
Gordo Lazar or Ricky Queen would want to harm her?"

"Maybe just for being a pain in the ass, but I don't see
either of them getting that passionate about it." A grunted
laugh. "Especially Ricky, for obvious reasons."

"His sexual orientation?"

"If you like to call it that." Eisen suddenly checked his

watch. "Look, it's getting late, and I gotta be up and at 'em early tomorrow. So, what's your take?"

"Beyond the things we've talked about, I haven't gotten any 'vibes' yet."

Mitch Eisen nodded, but not sadly now. "Let me know if you do, huh? Be a bonus in it for you."

"Bonus?"

"Yeah. I don't want to waste any more of my time on those fuckheads if one of them got terminally stupid."

After getting out of the car, I watched Eisen drive away, his shifting of gears winding out into the quiet night air. As I began to cut across the mini-jungle surrounding the pool area, my mind started heading toward the dream of Nancy I might have again. And dreaded having.

When I got nearer the pool, the hotel lights danced off the water like a dozen setting suns, and a couple of geckos skittered across my path. Then I heard a skittering noise behind me, too.

It could have been one of the geckos' cousins, if that side of the family weighed in at two hundred and change.

I wheeled around, the blade in the guy's right hand glinting from the lights reflecting off the water. I went back a step with my left forearm up to protect the throat and eyes as my right hand stayed flat and belt-high to shield the belly and chest. But he'd already slashed across the top, my left forearm feeling wet just a second after the branding-iron sensation shot to my brain.

The guy strode in closer, comfortable with the buck knife. "This is for Sunday, fucker."

An accent like Detective Kyle Cascadden's, though I didn't have time to think much about it.

Now the guy came up from under, for the heart or a lung. Not trusting my left hand for gripping, I pivoted on my left foot, parrying the thrust of his arm with my right hand. Then I kicked out with my right foot at his right knee, getting part—but not all—of the joint as my plant foot slid on the pool tiles like a field-goal kicker's on a slick turf. I went down and heard more than felt my head hit the corner of a lounge chair, the stars rising up behind my eyes.

I thought he'd finish me until I registered the whooshing sound of his blade going by, where my throat would have been if I hadn't slipped. I kicked up this time, catching his elbow and hearing a cracking sound before he roared in pain. The buck knife clattered off the tiles to the right of me.

Shaking my head to clear my vision, I saw a blurry figure hobbling toward the parking garage. He was favoring his right leg and cradling his right arm.

Then, from a middle distance, I heard him yell, "Fucker, next time I won't stop . . . to see your eyes before I do you."

Starting to get up, I found my feet wouldn't work quite right, and my head spun no matter how hard I shook it. There was quite a lot of my blood seeping through—hell, pouring through the slash wound in my left arm, and I realized that's what had made the lip of the pool so slippery.

A vehicle I couldn't see through the bushes peeled rubber coming out of the garage and up the drive toward the road. My feet were still flopping a little at the ends of my ankles when I heard the sound of a heavy door by the hotel building and some shouts followed by running footsteps and more shouts.

I closed my eyes, tried to picture the guy. White, rough features, solid build. Oh yeah, and a tattoo on the forearm of his knife hand. Not a Marine Corps one, though. This was of a spider.

Some people were over me now, at least one gagging as another yelled to get a towel or something, for crissake. A third person from nearer the hotel said they'd already called 911.

I'd been hurt before, and I didn't think I was in shock. In fact, I was sure of it, right up till the moment I passed out.

FOURTEEN

As Nancy sank deeper and deeper, I dived into the water after her. I thought my clothes would weigh me down, but instead they buoyed me up. Then I realized I was wearing a life vest, which I couldn't seem to make my fingers unbuckle. When I finally got the thing off, I took a huge breath and started kicking for the bottom.

The salt water burned my eyes, and all I could see was blue-black shimmering, some tiny organisms drifting past my face. Then I spotted Nancy. Or her hair, at least, still billowing up but still out of reach as well.

Locking my knees, I kicked even harder, both legs scissoring from the hips as I extended my fingers toward the waving strands of—

Which was when somebody dropped a garbage can lid next to me.

The other guy in my hospital room looked over, sheepish in the dull glow of the EXIT sign above our door. "Sorry, pal. Bedpan slipped right outta my hands."

I think I said something, then lay my head back against the softest pillow God had ever helped the hand of man to fashion.

* * *

"I don't think it was shock," said the doctor with a Creole accent overlaid with some French, flipping through my chart at the side of the bed.

"Neither did I before I blacked out."

She frowned, creating bittersweet chocolate lines in a milk chocolate complexion. "Mild concussion, more likely. Here," her finger ran across a page, 'Patient says that he fell and struck the back of his head.'"

I still felt a little ache there. "Yeah, but just on a lounge chair."

"Mr. Cuddy from"—the doctor glanced back at the chart—"Boston, you are almost six feet, three inches tall. Whether we are in your Massachusetts, my Haiti, or our Florida, that is a long way for your head to gather momentum before striking anything." She put the chart back on its hook at the foot of my bed. "The reason I admitted you after Emergency finished its work."

I looked down at my left forearm. The flesh under the white gauze sent a muffled throbbing all the way to my brain. "How long have I been here?"

"About nine hours."

Making it sometime Thursday morning. "How long have you been here?"

A tired smile. "It is less that and more how much longer I will be here." Then back to her immediate business. "You may have some short-term memory loss or confusion about the last forty-eight hours. Other memories may fade in and out. Simply work through all this without worrying about it. There will be two prescriptions waiting for you at the Discharge Desk, both regarding your arm. One will be for an antibiotic; please take it as directed until the pills are exhausted. The other will be a painkiller, to be used at your discretion within the limits on the prescription itself. Please don't engage in any strenuous activity for a week.

After that time, you should come back to us or visit your physician in Boston to have the sutures removed."

"How many stitches did it take?"

Another tired smile. "Thirty-six."

I looked down to my left again. "Seems like a lot."

"You were lucky a plastic surgeon was available. A first-year resident would have used about twelve, and your forearm would thereafter resemble a railroad track."

There was something she said before that. . . . Right. "You mentioned the Discharge Desk. When can I get out of here?"

Her smile disappeared. "As soon as the police have finished with you."

Detective Kyle Cascadden actually held the door for Sergeant Lourdes Pintana. Both came to the side of my bed.

Pintana said, "I hope you are comfortable."

"If only I could afford the accommodations."

She grinned without showing any teeth. "I am sure Mr. Nicolas Helides will pay your bill."

Cascadden wore another short-sleeved shirt, the Marine tatt' on its side to me as he pointed toward my bed. "Heard you brought your arm to a knife fight, Beantown."

I said, "The expression is, 'bringing a knife to a gun fight.'"

He stopped. "You were carrying, you'd have a lot more to worry about than a couple stitches."

"At least he didn't jump me in my hotel room."

Cascadden froze, Pintana looking at me strangely, as though knowing she'd missed something.

I said, "Then my blood would have wrecked the carpeting."

Pintana flicked her wrist toward my bandaged arm. "What happened?"

"I didn't give any statement?"

She paused. "The patrol officer who rode with you in the ambulance said you didn't wake up."

"Did this officer also recover the buck knife from the scene?"

"Sí. It is being checked at the lab now." Different tone of voice. "Tell us what happened."

"Mitch Eisen took me—"

"That manager fella?" said Cascadden.

"Yes. He drove us from my hotel to three bars for some food and music."

"And booze," from Cascadden again, but not as a question.

Pintana said, "Kyle?"

Cascadden folded his arms across his chest and stood down a little.

I talked to the sergeant. "After the third place, he brought me back here."

"Here?" said Pintana.

I shook my head. "Sorry. I mean the hotel."

She canted her own head, so much like one of Nancy's mannerisms that . . .

"Mr. Cuddy?" said Pintana, now a look of concern in the amber eyes.

I took a breath. "The doctor said I probably have a mild concussion."

"Handy," said Cascadden, but a glance from Pintana stopped him there.

"All right." She shifted her feet. "I get that Mr. Eisen drives you back to your hotel, but why were you by the pool at that time of night?"

"He dropped me at the garage."

Pintana closed her eyes a moment, as though picturing something, then opened them again. "Why didn't he drive up to the lobby entrance?"

"We talked in his car for a bit."

"What about?"

"The band."

"Huh?" said Cascadden.

"Spiral. He's worried about his clients."

Pintana watched me. "So you get out of Mr. Eisen's car . . ."

". . . and I start walking through the pool area toward the hotel. I hear a noise behind me and turn just in time to take the first try on my arm."

"Good reflexes," she said.

"They used to be better."

A slow nod from her. "Go on."

I explained about my kicking the guy and hitting my head.

Pintana said, "So we are looking for a man with possibly a hyperextended knee and/or elbow. Can you describe him any further?"

"White, a little shorter than I am, solid build, rough features."

"Big help, Beantown," said Cascadden.

"Southern accent."

He said, "You mean 'redneck,' you fucking—"

"Kyle?"

Cascadden shut up.

Pintana sighed. "That it, Mr. Cuddy?"

"Except for his prints on the knife. Oh, and the tattoo."

Both of them perked up.

Pintana said, "What kind and where?"

"Some kind of spider, on the right forearm."

Cascadden's mouth opened as he looked to Pintana, but she stayed with me.

"Mr. Cuddy, did this man say anything to you?"

Christ, the concussion at work. "Yes, but it didn't make any sense."

Pintana seemed to rein herself back. "What did he say?"

"'This is for Sunday.'"

Now Pintana did look at Cascadden.

I said, "I was still in Boston then."

Sergeant Lourdes Pintana came back to me. "Mr. Cuddy, I think you'd better get dressed."

I stared at the array of ten mug shots on my chair's side of Pintana's desk in the Homicide Unit. All were white males, seemingly the right build, so much as you could tell from the biceps on up.

"Your assailant among these men?" asked the sergeant from her chair.

I studied them slowly, making sure.

Behind me, Cascadden said, "Come on, Beantown."

I ignored him, going back and forth between two of the photos.

"Take your time, Mr. Cuddy," said Pintana, rather pointedly.

Focusing on the third mug shot in the array, I said, "This is him."

Pintana spoke slowly. "Please pick up the one you are identifying."

I did.

Cascadden laughed behind me.

I said, "What's so funny?"

Pintana extended her hand, and I gave her the photo.

She laid it on her desk. "This man is named Ford Walton."

I shook my head. "Means nothing to me."

Pintana said, "Approximately eleven days ago, a female prostitute, last name Moran, was slashed to death with a knife very much like the one used to attack you."

I remembered Cascadden saying something about another murder the first time I'd met them. "Meaning, right around the time that Veronica Held died?"

Pintana nodded. "Within ten hours or so. Moran's body was left in a cheap hotel room with the air-conditioning on high."

"Fuzzing any determination regarding her time of death."

"Yes," said Pintana. "But there are two further points about the case."

Cascadden cut in. "First is, old Ford was the whore's sometime boyfriend."

Pintana let him finish before saying, "The other is that Moran spelled her street name 'S-U-N-D-Y.'"

Half an hour later, I was still sitting in the same chair—looking down at the bandaged part of my left arm and giving serious thought to trying one of the Haitian doctor's painkillers—when Cascadden came back into the room.

He handed a folder to Pintana, who opened it, read something, then looked up at him. Cascadden nodded to her.

She turned to me. "The prints on the knife used to attack you belong to Ford Walton."

Cascadden said, "Blood work's gonna take longer, Beantown, account of so much was yours."

I watched Pintana. "Meaning, the lab's checking the knife for this Sundy Moran's blood?"

"Yes."

"Walton would have to be pretty stupid to keep a knife used in a killing."

"Old Ford ain't never been no brain trust."

I looked up at Cascadden. "You know him?"

"Went to high school with the fucker. Back when we

had just Stranahan for us and Old Dillard for the nig . . . blacks."

I kept looking at Cascadden. Could he be that stupid, to roust me himself, fail, and then get somebody he admitted knowing to—

"Mr. Cuddy?" said Pintana.

"Sorry. That concussion again."

She nodded, but not like she was convinced. "I'd like to know what connection you had to Sundy Moran."

"None that I know of."

"From what you said earlier, Ford Walton appears to think otherwise."

"Sergeant, Moran was dead over a week before I was even in your state, and I'm sure I'd never seen Walton before last night." I thought of something. "After Moran's body was found, you must have looked for her boyfriend."

"And found him, Beantown," said Cascadden, proudly.

Pintana glared at him.

I waited for her to look back toward me. "But not the knife in question."

Cascadden seemed to have decided he'd said enough.

The sergeant drummed her nails on the desktop. "Ford Walton likes to use knives, Mr. Cuddy."

"I could tell."

She didn't nod. "But he had an alibi for the time period that Sundy Moran must have been killed."

"What kind of alibi?"

Kyle Cascadden changed his mind. "Old Ford was shacked up with the whore's mother. Now, can you beat that?"

From the passenger's seat of the unmarked sedan, I said, "How many cases has Cascadden blown for you?"

Sergeant Lourdes Pintana shook her head. "I thought we already had this conversation."

"Seems timely again."

We turned north on an avenue toward my hotel. "I told you, Mr. Cuddy. Kyle was a hero here, from the gridiron for his school to the streets for our department. He gets cut some slack for that."

"The department ever cut you any slack?"

Pintana glanced over, frowning. "For what?"

"There's only one woman in the Boston Homicide unit, and she doesn't command it."

Frown became grimace. "Meaning, how did a '*cubana* chick' get to the top?"

"Meaning, how did an immigrant woman in a man's profession end up doing so well so young?"

Pintana seemed to relax a little. "I worked hard, got my degree in criminal justice, then a master's. Scored the highest on every test the department gave." Almost a smile. "As a detective in Homicide, I also cleared most of my cases, which mattered a little more."

"Still, there had to be barriers."

Another glance, but kind of quizzical this time. "Your people are from Ireland originally?"

"Yes."

"And you're which generation?"

"The second born here."

"Maybe that explains it."

"Explains what?"

"How you could have forgotten what it takes to get ahead in this country."

My turn to look at her. "I'll try to remember that in the future."

Almost a smile again. "Even through the . . . concussion?"

I smiled for real. "That supposedly affects just short-term stuff."

I felt a tingle at the back of my head. Something that wouldn't quite . . .

"Mr. Cuddy?"

"Sorry."

"Before you banged your head, did you space out like that?"

I stared at her, the expression so like Nancy's, even the head canted the . . .

Pintana glanced at me again. "You all right?"

"No, but at least I know why."

A pause before, "You enjoy the barhopping with Mitch Eisen?"

"Yes," I said, surprising myself before I realized it was true.

"Where did he take you?"

I named the places.

"Which O'Hara's?"

"The new operation in Hollywood."

"You should go to the one on Las Olas, too."

"I'll make a note of it."

"They're having a great jazz group tonight, as a matter of fact." We pulled into my hotel complex, Pintana taking the circular drive to the main entrance. She said, "Sax and guitar. I was planning on getting there around ten, myself."

"Sergeant—"

"If you stop by, fine. If not, fine, too."

"Sergeant, there have been only two women in my life. Both died young, one two weeks ago."

Lourdes Pintana leveled those amber eyes on me. "I think you're getting ahead of yourself," she said, flicking her wrist at my passenger's side door.

Upstairs, I lifted the not-so-new-day's *Sun-Sentinel* in its plastic bag off the room handle and went inside.

Everything looked undisturbed, including the photo of Nancy and me on the bureau.

I stripped and took a shower, being careful to keep my bandaged arm above the stream of water. After wrapping a towel around my waist, I downed one of the painkillers, then walked to the bedside phone. The little dome light said I'd had callers, but I dialed room service first, since I hadn't eaten since the prior night's dinner at Coconuts. After ordering a sandwich plate, I checked my voice mail, finding three messages in my electronic box.

Duy Tranh with, "Please call me regarding a certain hospital bill."

Justo Vega with, "John, I am in Miami, but the people at the hospital said you had been discharged, and I did not want to drive a fool's errand up there. Please return my call to say how you feel and if you are in need of Pepe or me."

Mitch Eisen with, "Don't forget what I said last night."

I felt vaguely disappointed, but whatever it was wouldn't come consciously to mind. Depressing the plunger, I returned the calls in the order they appeared, getting an outgoing announcement for Tranh and a secretary for Justo. After leaving messages with both, I tried Eisen's number.

"M. Eisen, Limited, please hold."

A poorly disguised version of his voice, then a click. After three minutes, "Mitch Eisen."

"Mitch, John Cuddy."

"You found out something?"

"Not exactly."

A hesitation. "Then why are you calling me?"

"I'm returning yours, Mitch."

"Yeah, but all I said was don't forget to tell me if you had anything about the band being on or off the hook."

"And I don't."

Another hesitation. "Hey, Cuddy, you okay?"

"No. After you dropped me off last night, somebody tried to stick a knife in me."

"What?"

"In the pool garden. Which I had to cross because you let me out by the garage."

A third hesitation, much longer than the first two. "The fuck are you implying here?"

"When we were leaving O'Hara's, you made a call."

"Yeah. To be sure that the right group was playing at September's."

"You sure that was the only one you made, Mitch?"

"Who the fuck else would I call?"

"How about a guy named Ford Walton?"

"Sounds like somebody off that stupid TV show with 'John-boy' and—"

"How about Sundy Moran, then?"

A short hesitation, and a different tone. "Cuddy, I got work to do. I'm sorry about your mugging or whatever, but hey, Lauderdale's not exactly Small-town America, you know?"

"I'm learning, Mitch. I'm learning."

Room service brought my sandwich plate, and I ate it with one of the antibiotics because the label read TAKE WITH FOOD. Then I went through the White Pages in the room. Lots of "Morans" listed, but no "Sundy." I called directory assistance, but without a town or city, they couldn't help me. Hanging up, I had a thought and picked up the phone again.

"Mo Katzen," said the gruff voice on the other end of the long-distance line. "What are you bothering me about?"

I pictured the old reporter, sitting behind his desk at the Boston *Herald*, an even older typewriter still squatting where a computer should be. "Mo, it's John Cuddy, calling from Florida."

"Florida?" I could hear him roll something—probably an unlit cigar—from one corner of his mouth to the other. "What are . . . oh. You down there kind of . . ."

He'd been at Nancy's memorial service. "Kind of, Mo. Listen, I need a favor."

Usually, it would be ten minutes of pulling teeth to get him to the point of helping. This time, he just said, "Name it."

"You know any reporters on a paper down here called the *Sun-Sentinel?*"

A moment before, "That's the big one north of Miami, right?"

"Right, Mo."

"Yeah. Miami's got a *Herald*, too, though I don't know who owns them. If it's our—"

"Mo?"

"Yeah?"

"I'm in kind of a hurry here."

"Oh, sure, John, sure. Let me see, let me . . . Yeah. Good gal, too, as a matter of fact. Missouri by way of New England, but I'm ninety percent sure she's at your paper there. Let me spell her name for you, though, 'cause it's different."

I didn't ask Mo Katzen different from what, though I did suggest to him what he might tell her about me.

If the Fort Lauderdale police department would remind you of a resort hotel, the *Sun-Sentinel's* building looked like it belonged to a law firm. A large and prosperous one.

At the security desk in the palatial lobby downstairs, I asked for Oline Christie. I was given a clip-on pass and told to go to the tenth floor. When the elevator doors opened there, the law-firm image got reinforced by a wide, internal stairway and plush carpeting, the walls full of dramatic photos.

The image was reduced some by the second security desk just in front of the stairway. I mentioned the name of Mo's friend again, but this guard suggested I wait a minute, because the reporter had just called about me.

"Mo Katzen seems to think highly of you."

Soft, Southwestern inflection. I said, "We've known each other a long time."

Oline Christie sat in the swivel chair, her back to the computer monitor on her desk in the cubicle. Brown hair, blue eyes, and just to the smart side of pretty.

"Quite a bandage," she said.

"You know how doctors are these days. Overkill."

"Uh-huh." Christie's expression never changed. "So, what can I do for you, Mr. Cuddy?"

"How about 'John'?"

"Fine. I'm Ah-*leen*."

"I've been hired to do a confidential investigation for someone down here. The name 'Sundy Moran' came up, and I was wondering if you knew anything about her."

"Sundy Moran. The woman who was killed in that motel room?"

"Yes."

Christie's face grew a little smarter. "Right around the time the Held girl was drowned."

"I believe so."

Christie leaned forward in her chair. "John, we don't go any further without leveling with each other."

I didn't say anything at first, assessing if I could trust her eyes and Mo's recommendation. Then I decided I didn't really have a choice.

"Oline, I need some help here, but it can't get printed, at least not yet."

"That's a start."

"A start?"

"Toward leveling." Christie leaned back in her chair, swaying slightly. "I was off the day of that bizarro birthday party at the Helides house, so somebody else got to be lead reporter on the killing there. That doesn't mean I haven't followed the story, though, and you look a hell of a lot like the man seen going through their security gate a few days ago."

"I was."

"So," said Christie, drawing out the word, "what's the connection between Veronica Held and Sundy Moran?"

I described my being attacked the night before, including what Ford Walton had said to me then and what the police told me that morning.

Christie swayed a little more in her chair. "The Moran woman's death received kind of short shrift, what with all the attention on the Held murder. But a week or so later, I persuaded my editor to let me do a piece on Moran's mother, Donna. It turned out kind of kinky, because of the boyfriend aspect."

"Walton being with both the women."

"Right. So my story got cut down to family-size, you might say."

"Family-size?"

"The right 'graphs—paragraphs—for a family-type newspaper."

"I see."

"Maybe you'd rather see the original?"

"Of your story?"

Christie swung her chair around and started clacking away on the computer's keyboard. "Won't take long . . . there."

I read about half of the first column on the screen before closing my eyes. Christie's slant featured mother more than daughter. Donna Moran had been born poor thirty-seven years before and gotten pregnant at sixteen, father never identified. Sundy arrived eight months later—four weeks premature—and took her mother's last name. It was a struggle from the beginning, the unwed mother's own parents disowning their daughter and her child. Donna worked as a waitress in a roadhouse and tried "the best I could, but us living in a hole like this here trailer park, with not even a telephone, what kind of chance did my Sundy have? I'll tell you: Same as me, meaning none."

I read the rest of the story. Sundy found her way out of the trailer park and into booze, drugs, and prostitution, mother trying to get daughter "back on the right track afore it was too late." Ford Walton "declined to be interviewed," but there was an allusion to his "lengthy" criminal record. And a depressing passage on how Walton and Donna Moran spent the time during which Sundy was killed.

Christie put her finger on the paragraph I was reading. "That's the one that got my story truncated."

Without believing in censorship, I could see why. "Too bad you don't work for one of the tabloids on the checkout line."

"Wouldn't have flown there, either. No star quality to the victims." Christie looked up at me. "Any help?"

The second paragraph had contained the town and road for the trailer park where Donna Moran lived. "Yes, Oline. Thanks."

Christie turned from her screen. "John, you find a connection between these killings, you owe me the first call, right?"

"So long as my client agrees."

Oline Christie smiled, smart yielding to pretty. "Mo Katzen said you were a little *too* trustworthy."

FIFTEEN

The drive west took longer than it looked on the rent-a-car map. I went through a run-down section of Fort Lauderdale, then different communities with the word "Lauderdale" also in their names. The character of the land grew increasingly rural after about ten miles, the acreage more undeveloped than farmed, with hammocks of trees and meadows of tall grass. The land was flat and hot and desolate enough to pass for the African veldt, even a few vultures making slow circles overhead.

Twenty minutes later, I hit the town where Donna Moran lived. After three or four intersections, I turned north onto a marked but unpaved road. There were shacks and sheds alongside it, chickens strutting and pecking in the gravel at the shoulders. The entrance to the trailer park came up on my left.

The driveway was pure dust, a cloud of it kicking up so thick behind me that I couldn't see anything through the rearview mirror. The windshield showed an old man wearing a farmer's straw hat and blue overalls, sitting outside one of the closest trailers.

I set the brake and got out of the Cavalier, leaving my suit coat in it. "Morning."

He looked up at me, took a pull on the pipe in his left hand. When I got closer to him, I could see he ranged closer to forty than sixty. His lawn chair was rusty, the cross-straps of the seat frayed at the frame. He also gave off an odor that came less from smoking and more from not bathing.

The man still hadn't said anything.

I stopped three feet in front of him. "I'm looking for Donna Moran."

Just a stare, the corners of his mouth turned up around the stem of his pipe. Then, "Got yourself a hell of a bandage there."

"Thanks."

"You got a badge, too?"

"I'm not police."

"Didn't think so. Would of led with it."

"I'd just like to see Ms. Moran."

"Just . . . 'see' her, eh?"

A lewd edge on his words. "Talk with her," I said.

"You don't got yourself no badge, I don't got to talk with you."

He made no effort to get up, though.

I reached behind me for my wallet. "I do have some money."

"Thought you might."

I extended a ten to him.

He just stared at it. "Man starts with a ten, he'll likely go twenty."

"Or just drive up to another trailer, and start with a five."

He blinked first. Taking the ten and stuffing it down inside the overalls, he waved the pipe back where I'd come from. "Donna's to work."

The roadhouse from Oline Christie's article. "How do I get there?"

"South to the state route, west to the filling station, then north on a dirt and marl stretch."

"Name of the place?"

"We call it 'Billy's,' but it don't have no sign says that."

"Then how will I know it?"

An open grin, four stained and staggered teeth showing.

"You follow my directions, and see something ain't a tree, it's Billy's."

The word "ramshackle" in the next edition of Webster's ought to have a picture of Billy's next to it. The wood was splintered and weathered to a dozen different shades of gray, one neon sign for BUD lit, another for COORS not. There were a half-dozen vehicles in the parking area, splattered mud on bumpers, fenders, and doors. Most were pickups, a few others older American cars rusted through and roped or taped together. Putting my jacket back on, I walked on the ridges of ruts to what seemed to be the entrance.

The door pushed open, no air-conditioning blast hitting me as I stepped into the place. It was dark, the atmosphere piss-warm and sour. A female singer warbled some country-and-western tune from the tinny jukebox. A square bar occupied the right side of the big room, clusters of empty tables and chairs the left around the perimeter of a dance floor laid with scuffed lineoleum.

Most of the patrons I could see sat alone on stools at the bar. All were male, many smoking over long-neck beer bottles. Beyond them, two more guys cued sticks at a pool table. One wore a Peterbilt ballcap, the other a bandanna tied at his hairline. Both watched me.

Inside the bar enclosure, a woman looked up at a television set. From what I could see, the program was a Jerry Springer knock-off, but she had the audio low enough that I couldn't hear it. I wasn't sure the woman could either.

She turned toward me as I moved to the bar. Her hair was lifeless, piled up under a scrungie to form a topknot ponytail. Heavy breasts stressed a faded Miami Dolphins jersey with a player number on it, stained jeans below. Her face was more faded than her shirt, not so much in color as animation, and a cigarette smoldered between the index and middle fingers of her right hand.

When I reached the bar itself, she gave a hiccupy laugh. "A suit in Billy's. Somebody get the camera."

"Donna Moran?"

She shifted her stance behind the bar, almost defensively. "Who wants to know?"

"My name's John Cuddy. I wonder if—"

"That boy giving you trouble, Donna?"

I looked over to the pool table, the Peterbilt guy with his mouth still open, the Bandanna just kind of grinning.

Moran said, "Not yet, Luke. But I'll be sure to let you know."

One corner of the bar was empty except for an oversized wipe-towel. "Could we talk over here, Ms. Moran?"

"'Ms.' Moran?" she said with another hiccupped laugh. "Boy, why do I think you don't got no idea who I am?"

There was a glimmer from her face then, the eyes kind of flirty as she moved to the inside of my corner, scraping an ashtray along the bar with her. I sat on the closest stool.

Moran said, "A drink, or you on duty?"

The impression I create. "Budweiser would be fine."

Putting her cigarette in one of the notches of the ashtray, Moran reached below the bar. She brought out a brown bottle with some ice still clinging to it and used a bar-mounted opener to pop the top. "Two."

I put a five-dollar bill on the gouged wood in front of me. Moran set the bottle beside it.

"All right, Suit, what do you want?"

"I'd like to talk with you about your daughter."

"My . . ." The face became troubled again, and her eyes went away for a moment. "Why? Ain't nobody but one girl reporter cared about Sundy when she got killed."

The jukebox began playing a new song, still that country twang to the now-male singer's voice. "I have a feeling your daughter's death might be connected with a case I'm working."

"Yeah, well, might have been nice if y'all came around about Sundy's case."

"Nobody from Homicide visited you?"

"Oh, they 'visited,' all right. Some asshole with a Marine bird burnt into his arm. But you been poor most of your life, you can tell when the police are just going through the motions. All he really cared about was could I alibi Ford, and"—the eyes went away again—"may the Good Lord send me to hell and back, I could."

"You and Mr. Walton were together."

The eyes returned. "You're a polite man, Mr. . . . ?"

"Cuddy, John Cuddy. And I'm not police."

"I don't—sorry."

Moran reached a palm up to blot her tears. The cigarette in her ashtray was mostly gone, and she moved away to get the pack.

"Hey, Donna," said Luke of the Peterbilt, "that boy making you cry?"

"Got smoke in my eyes," Moran replied. "And mind your damn game afore Hack runs the table on you."

That got a barnyard sound from Hack of the Bandanna.

Moran came back to me, lighting up. "All right, Mr. John Polite, what do you want to know?"

I decided to save my Ford Walton questions for last. "Can you tell me something about your daughter as a person?"

"As a person?" A cloud of smoke came out with her words. "Well, Sundy couldn't learn from the lessons of others."

"Others like you?"

The smoke stopped, then came out more diffused. "For instance."

"Which lessons did you try to teach her?"

Moran hardened, pointing the burning end of the cigarette at me. "And I thought you was polite."

"You said it."

"Yeah, well, ain't but one person I talked to about Sundy dying, so I'm guessing that reporter girl is who put you on to me."

I took a calculated risk. "Just by reading her story in the *Sun-Sentinel*, combined with what the police told me."

More hardening. "Why you really come out here?"

"Ms. Moran, if I can find a connection between my case and your daughter's, I might be able to solve both of them."

Now skeptical, the eyes closed to slits as she inhaled more tar and nicotine. "Find out who killed my Sundy?"

"I hope so."

Moran seemed to study me, then quickly blew out the smoke she'd been holding and set the cigarette down in the ashtray next to its dead mate. "Ask your questions, then. Straight out."

Taking Moran at her word, I said, "You know of anybody who'd want to kill your daughter?"

"Lord, I've been thinking on nothing else. But aside from"—Moran leaned toward me, dropping her voice—"maybe one of her customers, I can't."

"Any one in particular?"

"Sundy didn't never talk names, just 'this tall fella' or 'this short fella.' And she said most of them weren't so much bad as lonely."

"Hey, Boy," yelled Luke from the pool table, "you jew Donna down to twenty dollars, Hack and me'll go halves with you."

Another barnyard sound from the Bandanna.

Moran barely bothered to turn. "Yeah, Luke, and Hack can hold your damn cue for you, too, so it don't keep slipping out."

Nervous laughter from around the bar, reinforcing my impression that Luke in the Peterbilt cap was cock of this particular roost.

I said, "Ms. Moran?"

She turned back to me. "Yeah?"

"If there'd be a better time . . . ?"

A shake of her head, dislodging some strands of hair from the scrungie. "Ain't no good time for this kind of talk, so let's finish it."

"How about anybody not a customer?"

"What, who'd want to kill Sundy?"

"Yes."

Moran picked up her cigarette. "No. Ford Walton on the worst drunk of his life, maybe, but, like you said, he was with me."

"The whole time?"

Her eyes went to slits again. "Mr. John Polite, let me draw you a picture, all right? Ford and me was in my bed or within sight of it for all of that Sunday into Monday, and he was gone maybe half an hour when the sheriff's car come into the park, telling me they'd found my Sundy over to Lauderdale an hour before that. So, no way—"

A song burst from the jukebox, thunderously loud. Another female vocalist this time, yowling something about satin sheets and satin pillows.

I glanced over to the machine. Luke and Hack were leaning on their cues, grinning so widely their mouths nearly formed a single smile.

Luke tipped back the Peterbilt and yelled, "Hey, Donna. I got some satin sheets back of my truck. What do you say?"

This time Moran wheeled on him, screaming. "I say if you'd washed them after you flogged your three-inch dog all over them during your one good hard-on a month, you might find they're just cheap shit, like you."

I glanced behind me, to make sure nobody else had come in that I might have to worry about.

Luke was still grinning, but differently, and Hack didn't seem happy at all.

Looking down at the floor, Luke pawed it a little with the toe of a workboot. Then he started walking toward the bar, Hack in tow.

And both still with their pool cues.

Glancing down at my long-necked bottle, I said to Moran's back, "What've you got behind there?"

Over her shoulder with, "Just a bitty little billy club."

"That's it?"

"Why the place is called 'Billy's' to start with."

Passing on my Bud bottle, I got off the stool, slipping the oversized towel from the bar so Peterbilt and Bandanna couldn't see it.

"Boy," said Luke, his upper teeth showing, "don't you be going nowhere, now. Cause you're next, even with that bandage peeking out under your sleeve."

As Hack grew back his grin, I said, "I've still got a lot to do today. Could you maybe take me first?"

Luke and Hack both lost their grins, exchanged a quick glance.

I said, "After all, if I bolt out that door, you'd have to start running, too, unless you wanted everybody here to tell a story on you."

"What kind of story?" said Luke.

"That you both ran yourselves ragged after this poor jerk in a suit while Ms. Moran called the Sheriff's Office."

Luke sneered at me. "One, 'Ms. Moran' ain't gonna call no Sheriff's Office. And two, ain't no way somebody as old as you gonna outrun me and Hack."

"I did the Boston Marathon not so long ago, my friend. Up hill and down dale for twenty-six miles without stopping."

Hack squinted, like a man in deep denial.

Luke kept his sneer. "Then maybe we shorten your legs some, make it a fairer race for us."

"Anytime you're ready."

I was hoping neither of them had been in the service, because drills with bayonets or even riot batons would have made two-on-one pretty untenable for me. But I was lucky: They'd watched more baseball games than training films.

Luke dropped his hands to the tapered part of the cue and took the first swing, a right-handed batter going level for a line drive. I got the towel stretched between my hands and up, the wet cloth absorbing most of the momentum at the sweet spot of the cue, but drawing Luke off balance with its give. Then I dropped my left elbow quickly, catching the thick end of the cue under my left armpit. I yanked before Luke did, and his hands slipped off the tapered end as he stumbled backward.

Hack came forward like a man intent on splitting a chunk of wood with a maul. While his arms were still rising on the upswing, I drove the tapered end of Luke's cue into Hack's belly until I thought it touched his spine.

He went down, first coughing, then vomiting. Luke flexed his arms and clenched his fists, dancing around like he wanted me to come after him in a "fair" fight.

Holding the cue like a quarterstaff, I took two steps toward him, and he dropped back three. I advanced one more, he retreated three more.

I said, "Appears we've reached an understanding." I looked over to the bar. "Ms. Moran, thanks for your help."

As I moved to the door, the jukebox was signing off on the satin-sheets tune, making Hack a little more audible as he waited for his internal organs to realign themselves.

I leaned the cue upright against the wall and spoke into

the relative quiet. "Never cared much for country and western."

"Me, neither," said Donna Moran, though I didn't see her smiling about it.

There was something else I didn't see, at least not until I'd gotten back in the Cavalier and went to make a turn.

"You do know, Mr. Cuddy, that I am not here twenty-four hours a day to care for you?"

"Why I called ahead to be sure, Doctor."

"We both know you did not." The nice Haitian woman with the French/Creole accent smiled more wisely than tiredly. "Now, hold still while I see how many sutures are . . . ugh. What strenuous thing did you do that tore open so many of these?"

"Pool."

"Then the dressings would be wet, not the sutures torn."

"It wasn't a swimming pool, Doctor. I was playing pool."

She frowned. "And you did this pushing a little ball with a stick?"

"My opponents didn't like the way I kept score."

The doctor began threading a needle. "Perhaps if you watch what I am about to do, you will next time choose a different game."

"I've already made that decision, thanks."

The tired smile reappeared, joined by the concentration a professional brings to bear on what must be a tiresome task.

I drove back to my hotel to drop off the bloodied jacket. Carrying it folded over my arm as I crossed the lobby, my clerk friend Damon called out from the desk.

"Mr. Cuddy, I have something for you."

When I walked over to him, he caught a better look at my jacket. "Oh, God! You're hurt again?"

"I'm fine, Damon. What've you got?"

He handed me a simple number-10 business envelope, sealed but with no markings other than "Cuddy, J." scribbled on the back.

"Who left this?"

"I don't know," said Damon, still eyeing my stained sleeve. "I was registering a guest, and that just kind of plopped on the counter. A man said, 'For John Cuddy,' so I wrote your name on it."

"You wrote?"

Damon nodded as his phone began to ring.

I said, "What did the man look like?"

"Sorry, never looked up from helping the guest."

Damon lifted his receiver, and I used a nearby letter opener to slit the envelope. A single sheet of copy paper came out, creased in threes.

When I unfolded it, there were differently sized letters cut from newspaper headlines or magazine advertisements, pasted on the page like an old-fashioned ransom note. Only the message was a little different:

AsK The bAnD
abOuT SuNDy MoRAn

Hanging up his phone, Damon said, "Is everything all right, Mr. Cuddy?"

"I doubt it."

Up in my room, the phone-message dome was blinking. When I dialed for voice mail, the electronic announcer said I had one new call, which turned out to be Duy Tranh, returning mine about the hospital bill and specifying curtly when he'd be available for me to reach him. I felt that tingling in the back of my head again, but what was causing it just wouldn't come to mind. Then again, the doctor had told me that my memories might fade in and out, so I pressed the buttons for Tranh's number.

"Hello?"

"Mr. Tranh, John Cuddy."

"You have been remiss in—"

"That hospital bill. You got called by the credit card company about a charge on the one you'd given me, right?"

No reply.

I said, "Thanks for your concern. I'd like to see the Colonel sometime soon."

"One hour," said Tranh, hanging up on me before I could disagree with him.

Nicolas Helides was sitting in the stern of the big sailboat moored behind his house. A gangplank went from its deck to the dock, probably to allow him to get on and off using the aluminum brace. He faced toward the Intracoastal and away from the glass wall to the internal portion of the pool. Where Duy Tranh had found his granddaughter.

As I reached the bottom of the gangplank, I could see the Skipper was alone, a blanket over his legs, the brace leaning against a seat cushion in the cockpit. A white motor yacht at least a hundred feet long cruised by slowly, with—and I had to look twice—a helicopter on its uppermost deck.

I thought Helides was focused only on the passing yacht before he said, "Lieutenant, that's fifteen million of materiel going by, not counting the whirlybird."

I stopped. "You recognize my footsteps?"

The good hand rose from his lap, a portable phone in it. "Umberto called me from the gate." A change of tone as the hand came down again, the wake from the yacht rocking his sailboat like a child's cradle. "I understand from

Duy that you had some sort of . . . medical problem."

I climbed the gangplank. "You might want to hear about the cause of it."

He looked at my bandaged arm as I sat in the cockpit across from him. "Please."

I summarized my barhopping with Mitch Eisen, being jumped by Ford Walton outside the hotel, and my visit to the Homicide Unit after the hospital stay.

The Skipper said, "And what have you found out about this . . . prostitute?"

I described my trip to the trailer park and roadhouse.

Helides actually smiled. The half of his mouth that the stroke didn't prevent from smiling. "A bar brawl. Like the old days, eh?"

I thought back to Saigon, the dozens of times I watched my MPs—our MPs—crawl on their hands and knees into bars. Inside, combat troops from the bush on two-day passes did their best to drink a month's worth of booze and forget what they'd just been through and would be going through again. Forget by starting a free-for-all fistfight with whomever supposedly slighted them, any opponents having roughly the same attitudes.

The MPs would crawl into the bars because the safest way to break up a brawl was to sneak up below the revelers' line of sight and whack them behind the knees with a nightstick, causing the muscles back there to spasm so badly that nobody could get to their feet for fifteen minutes, by which time the desire—the raw *need*—to swing on somebody would have—

"Lieutenant?"

The concussion, or just me since Nancy? "Sorry, sir."

The Skipper searched my eyes. "I really appreciate what you're trying to do for me."

"Glad to be here, Colonel."

And I knew that I was. At least by comparison.

He looked back at the Intracoastal, a parade of small fishing boats going by now. "You remember my penchant for sailing?"

"Yes, sir."

"This is a forty-eight-foot sloop, custom-built for me but modeled after one of Phil Rhodes's Carinas. Cassie and I used to take this fine craft out into the ocean and sail her two-handed to Bimini. We'd hire a guide there, fish the reefs and the flats, then sail back. Idyllic."

I waited.

"Now, Cassie doesn't care much for sailing anymore. And while Duy is perfectly competent as crew for the rigging and manning of sheets, it has to be a pretty calm day for me to be able to take the helm for more than an hour at a time. And a 'pretty calm' day rather defeats the purpose of going out under sail in the first place."

I waited some more.

Nicolas Helides drew in a deep, deep breath, then let it out slowly, the ruined side of his face making his right upper lip flutter a bit. "Lieutenant, what possible connection could exist between Veronica's death and the murder of this prostitute?"

I didn't mention the note I'd gotten at the hotel. "I'm going to be spending the rest of today trying to find out, sir."

A nod. "Could you also check in with Duy? I'm not sure we've covered everything he needed to speak with you about."

Tranh was in his suite, sitting at the computer but turned toward the door as I opened it following his "Come."

Dressed in a burgundy, short-sleeved safari shirt and contrasting khaki pants, his solemn eyes and sharp features walked me into the living room area. As I sat in the single armchair, my own eyes went up to his wall of knives. Most were more ornate than the one Ford Walton had tried to use on me, and I didn't see any empty spaces.

Tranh stayed seated, but swiveled more to face me squarely. "Mr. Cuddy, you and I really must reach an understanding."

I thought back to what I'd said to Luke as he backed off at the roadhouse that morning. Still a form of brawling with Tranh, just more civilized.

"Mr. Tranh, I think we understand each other just fine. You don't like me, and I don't like you."

A pause, his features softening slightly. "And yet, we are both devoted to the Colonel. Does that not strike you as . . . odd?"

"Odd because we're so different?"

"From each other, or from his real sons?"

Tranh's insight did strike a chord in me, but I said, "Justo Vega is devoted to him, too. Just a matter of individual choice."

"Or character, perhaps?"

"Perhaps." I wanted off the topic. "Colonel Helides asked me to check in with you."

A slight smile. "Which is the only reason you would have?"

"Probably."

"Very well, Mr. Cuddy. If we cannot be friends, let us at least be forthcoming." He glanced down at my bandaged arm. "What caused you to be hospitalized this morning?"

"Last night, actually."

"Last night," very evenly.

"I've already told the Colonel outside."

Tranh frowned. "I could have been there, as I was in the library on your first visit here. You know he would have permitted it."

"I know the Colonel had a phone in his lap just now. He could have called you to join us, but he didn't."

Tranh watched me, but something was moving behind his eyes. Finally he said, "Your point?"

"Think about it, Mr. Tranh. It'll come to you."

Closing the door to his suite, I caught a flash of motion at the end of the corridor where it intersected with a crossing one. This time I knew to use a name. "David, wait. Please."

Again, I didn't hear footsteps going away or coming back, but his shaggy head peered around the corner timidly, like a deer ready to bound away at the slightest threatening movement.

I said, "Can I talk with you, just for a minute?"

Helides moved his lips before speaking. "It is time for me . . . to eat, John."

I took the remembering of my name as an encouraging sign. "I'm a little hungry, too, and I just need the answers to a few questions. Please, David?"

The hollowed eyes looked down and then around and behind him. "In the kitchen."

"This time of day here . . . is not so bad."

"Why?"

"No one else eats now, so all is . . . quiet. Orderly."

In the same navy-blue sweatshirt and pants I'd seen him wearing in bed, David Helides picked black shavings— olives, I thought—from his pizza. He'd nuked a slice for each of us, every step of the process from refrigerator to plate to microwave executed excruciatingly slowly. To help, I'd poured us both glasses of Coke over ice, and now we sat at the center island of a room laid out exactly like the kitchen in his brother's house.

Helides had gotten most of the shavings off his slice of

pizza. "Duy Tranh knows I do not like olives, but he . . . gets them anyway."

"They're not my favorite, either."

Helides looked from his meal to my bandage. "Your . . . arm."

A potential "disruption" for him. "Just a little cut. Nothing to worry about."

A nod, but wary.

"David, would it be easier for you to eat first, or to eat as I ask my questions?"

"I do not know." He looked up now, almost smiled. "I do not usually eat with anyone . . . who talks with me."

I paused. "As we eat, then."

Helides moved his mouth close to his plate and bit into his pizza.

Before doing the same, I said, "David, last night I asked you if Veronica ever spoke about her life."

Chewing, he squinched his eyes shut. "I thought we were finished with . . . those questions?"

"I have some more, but only a few."

A nod as Helides swallowed.

"I'm going to say some names, then you tell me if Veronica ever mentioned them to you."

Another nod as he opened his eyes and tore off another piece of pizza.

"The first one is Ford Walton."

No reaction as Helides opened his mouth. "'Ford' like the . . . car?"

"Yes."

His head shook.

I said, "Veronica never mentioned him?"

"Never," around his food.

"How about Sundy Moran?"

Helides swallowed again. "'Sunday' like 'Monday'?"

"Not the way it's spelled, but anything like that name?"

A slower shake of the head. "No."

I tried my pizza and washed it down with some soda.

Helides bit another hunk off his slice, causing me to notice something.

"You don't like Coke?" I said.

He blinked. "The ice would give me a . . . chill."

Helides shivered.

I said, "Let me pour it out, get—"

"No!" Then an intake of breath. "No, my father does not like . . . waste." Another almost-smile. "And the ice will be gone soon." Even the almost-smile disappeared. "Like Veronica, gone . . . forever."

David Helides raised the slice all the way to his mouth, getting the food safely in despite squinching his eyes shut again.

SIXTEEN

Driving down the driveway, I could see Umberto Reyes coming out of his gazebo to open the gate for me. Instead of continuing through and onto the street, though, I stopped and got out of the Cavalier.

Because something I hadn't thought of before occurred to me.

"You need help?" said Reyes, looking down at my bandage.

"Yes, Berto. The first time I was here, you said you'd logged in all the people who came to the Colonel's birthday party that day."

"Yeah, but the police took the page and never gave me back a copy."

"How about for the days since?"

"Since the party?"

"Yes."

Reyes said, "Sure. They're in here."

I followed him toward the little structure, though he just reached in and came out with a blue looseleaf notebook. "What dates you want?"

"Start with yesterday and today."

He flipped a page. "Yesterday, Wednesday the twenty-first."

Reyes held it open for me. No mention of Duy Tranh leaving the house or coming back to it. "And today?"

Reyes turned the page. "Thursday."

No entry for Tranh again, much less one for around the time Damon noticed the envelope for me on his hotel's registration desk. In fact . . . I flipped back to Wednesday's page, then glanced up toward the garages. "Is Mrs. Helides home?"

"No."

I looked at Reyes. "Then how come you didn't log her out?"

He skewed his head. "I never do."

"Why, Berto?"

"All the Colonel wants is a list of people who come here, so that we can trace them if something turns up missing in the house or something else bad happens."

"So?"

"So I don't log Mrs. Helides in and out. Or call the Colonel about her, either."

"Because . . . ?"

Reyes's head skewed even more. "She lives here."

I looked at him a bit longer before saying, "Thanks, Berto."

* * *

It took me a while to drive northwest to the Held house. When I got there, only one car was in the driveway, none on the street.

Instead of walking around to the pool area, I went up to the front door with its spiral handles and rang the bell. After a moment, the door opened, Jeanette Held standing listlessly behind it. Bowie first wagged his tail, then began growling at me over the sill.

I felt that tingle in the back of my head again. "Jeanette, I'm sorry to—"

"Bother me?" No smile, no frown. "Doesn't seem to stop you, though, does it?"

"I'd like to see your husband."

"Spi's not here."

"Do you know when he'll be back?"

A slow movement of her head. "Not for a long time."

The way she enunciated the words, Jeanette Held might have been talking hours or years.

I said, "Do you know where I might find him?"

"Yeah."

I waited.

She exhaled. "The band's doing a sound check at this club in Lauderdale."

"Which club is that?"

"I don't remember the name, but Spi said it was on southwest Second."

"Street or avenue?"

"You know that much about the city, you'll find it."

As she began to close the door, I said, "Jeanette, are you all right?"

"No," a little energy working its way past the surface. "No, as a matter of fact, I'm pretty shitty. My daughter's dead, and the one person I thought could maybe carry me through that never showed up today."

"Malinda Dujong," I said, the tingle in my head turning into a penny and dropping through its slot as Jeanette Held closed her door.

Dujong hadn't returned my call back to her, which I thought explained why I'd felt the tingle checking my voice mail at the hotel. I figured the concussion explained why I'd forgotten to try her a second time.

On the other hand, she was the one who wanted to reach me.

Driving toward the southwest part of Fort Lauderdale, I picked up my cell phone and got Dujong's number at the tennis club from directory assistance. After I dialed and heard a ring, though, all I got was her same outgoing tape announcement. I left another message, giving both my hotel and portable numbers again.

Pushing the END button, I set the phone on the seat beside me. I might not be able to locate Malinda Dujong, but I thought I could find the people in Spiral.

Who supposedly knew something about "SuNDy MoRAn."

On a rough day, I finally got some luck. There were rows of bars and restaurants a couple of blocks west of the railroad tracks on S.W. 2nd Street. Since it was only late afternoon, I found a space in front of a place trying very hard to look like an authentic English pub. I went inside, the place more a spot for sedentary drinking than live music. A barmaid smiled at me, an impressive selection of labeled tap handles mounted on the wall behind her.

"What might I get you, luv?"

Even an English accent. "Any idea where a rock band would be doing its sound check on this street?"

She looked toward the door I'd come in through. "Lots

of us have live music at night, but when I took my cigarette break a while ago, some guys were yelling inside Dicey Riley's across the street."

"Yelling or playing?"

A wry smile. "More of the first than the second, I'm afraid."

There was a large bar catercorner from the English pub. Halfway through the intersection, I could hear what the barmaid had meant.

"Jesus fuck, Buford, that's the second time you came in late on that—"

Spi Held.

"Wasn't late, babe. You got to listen for the—"

Biggs.

"I know late from right, man." Held again. "And late is—"

As I drew even with the open doorway, Ricky Queen said, "Dudes, we got only another hour before—"

Held's voice cracked as he nearly screamed his words. "We got all the fucking time we need to get this shit right!"

It was dark and smoky inside the bar, which seemed to reach deep beyond a ramp wide enough for a platoon to march up it three abreast. The performance area lay to the right, a man I at first didn't recognize standing with his back to me, black hair cascading onto his shoulders in almost lush waves.

Gordo Lazar was facing me. "Spi, we got company."

The man with all the hair turned around abruptly. Held himself, wearing a rug that blew past toupee all the way to wig.

"The fuck do you want?" he said to me.

"Hey," came an unfamiliar voice out of the darkness. "If you're gonna talk with your lawyer or whatever, I'm gonna—"

Held wheeled around toward the voice, an index finger

swiping viciously under his nose. "The fuck kind of house-man are you?"

"The boss said you guys were supposed to be profes-sionals—"

"—sup-*posed* to be?—"

"—from the old days. Well, I run this control board seven nights a week, and this is the longest I've ever seen a sound check—"

"Go fuck yourself!" from Held.

"Okay," said the voice in back. "I'll tell the boss you're gonna wing it tonight."

Footfalls sounded hollow in the nearly empty place.

"Christ, babe," said Buford Biggs to Held in a mollifying tone.

Now Held wheeled on him. "We don't need a house-man doesn't stick with his job."

Queen came out from behind his drums. "Like I told you coming in here, I know the dude. Let me talk to him."

I said, "First I'd like to talk with all of you."

Spi Held wheeled on me, now, like the villain in a car-toon. "This is more important."

"Not to the man paying the freight."

Held opened and closed his mouth twice, but no words came out. Then he sniffled.

Ricky Queen said, "How about if we break for ten, Spi? I go talk to the houseman, you guys talk with the detective here, and when I come back, he's still got questions, I'll handle him myself?" Queen looked over to me, a little grin toying with the corners of his mouth. "I think I can handle Mr. Detective until he's . . . satisfied."

Held never turned to look at his drummer. "Yeah. Yeah, good idea, Rick. We could use a break."

"Amen to that," said Buford Biggs, lifting his hands from the keyboard in front of him.

* * *

We sat at a square table on the fringe of sunlight spilling through the door to the outside world. Spi Held was across from me, Biggs to my right and Lazar to my left.

Held said, "Okay, ten minutes."

I decided to lead with the bomb. "Sundy Moran."

Gordo Lazar flinched, then looked over at Buford Biggs, who tried very hard to be casual. Spi Held glanced in a confused way at Lazar first, then Biggs.

"What the fuck is a Sunday Moran?" said the leader of the band.

I watched Lazar before answering. "Not 'Sunday,' but S-U-N-D-Y. A woman's name."

The bass guitarist furrowed his brow. "Actually, it started out as 'Sunday.'"

Held joined me in looking at Lazar, who made a point of not looking at Biggs anymore.

I said, "Let's hear it."

Gordo Lazar ran a hand over his shaved head, then stroked a scar on his right cheek. "It was back when we were touring, man. The original Spiral. We did a gig down here — Miami somewhere, I don't know, they kind of blended together." Lazar inhaled and exhaled. "Anyway, this one chick was standing near the stage, flashing Tommy."

"Flashing?" I said.

"Yeah." Lazar realized I didn't get it. "You remember 'streaking,' right?"

"Somebody running naked through a crowd."

He nodded. "Or when that guy did it at the Oscars, and the television camera just missed bringing his dick into fifty million living rooms." Lazar's eyes went down toward the tabletop. "Well, flashing was when a braless chick flipped up her shirt, flashing tittie."

"And this woman did that to Tommy O'Dell?"

"Her and dozens of others. Man, Tommy had the magic. But this one, she had a set could poke your eyes out, and so he had one of the roadies tap her to come backstage afterwards."

Spi Held swiped under his nose again. "The fuck does this have to do with Very getting killed?"

"Be patient," I said. "We might be about to hear."

Lazar glanced up at me, then back down again. "Before you know it, Tommy's planking this chick in the bed on our bus."

Held sniffled twice. "The fuck was I?"

Biggs pointed to his own nose. "Riding Snow White's trail, babe."

Held looked at his keyboardist, but didn't say anything.

I stayed with Lazar. "Go on."

He worried his scar some more. "Well, a while later, this chick writes to Tommy. Claims she's pregnant, and that it had to be him. He hands me the letter and says, 'What do you think?' Well, there's like details in there about the concert, songs we played and all. So I read what she wrote and said to him, 'She claims it was on a Sunday, why don't you call her kid that?' And Tommy laughed and said that's what he'd tell the chick to do."

Donna Moran, the woman who didn't like country music, apparently felt different about rock. I tried to picture her as a young groupie. Couldn't. "Is that it?"

Lazar glanced up to Biggs, then Held. "Spi, you said we're supposed to level with this guy, right?"

"Right," said Held, without much conviction. "But I still don't see shit about what this has to do with Very."

Lazar went back to Biggs. "You want to tell him the rest?"

The keyboardist obviously wasn't relishing the opportunity. "What 'rest,' babe?"

"At Spi's dad's place, man."

I said to Biggs, "You know what he means?"

"Not me."

"Christ, Buford." Lazar looked at Held. "It was months ago, when we were at your father's house about him maybe bankrolling the comeback."

"Wait a minute. Yeah." Held sniffled some more but also sounded far, far away. "Yeah, I remember that."

Lazar said, "We're all sitting around in that big living room, where the birthday party was. Very, Tranh, even Cassandra. And your father's not too happy about Very being in the band, especially using that name, 'Very,' and we all start talking about the really weird ones from the old days, like Frank Zappa's kid 'Moonbeam' and somebody from TV being 'Seagull.' And then I said 'Don't forget Tommy's Sundy, too.'"

Lazar pronounced it without the "a." I leaned toward him. "How did you know it was shortened like that?"

He stared across the table this time. "Buford, your lead."

Biggs gave him a sour smile.

Spi Held said, "Come on, tell the man."

Biggs turned his head toward me. "After Very convince her granddaddy that she really, *really* want him to make the comeback happen, we all start drifting out into that big corridor towards the front door. I pull Gordo aside, say he shouldn't be bringing up Tommy's kid, account of I heard she use the street name 'Sundy' when she on the stroll."

"Meaning working as a prostitute."

"Yeah, babe. We want Spi's daddy to back us, don't need him having no thoughts about his granddaughter turning whore just 'cause she be using a funny kind of name."

I thought about it. "How'd you know about Sundy Moran being a prostitute?"

Biggs shrugged. "You hear things, that's all."

"But how did you connect the 'Sunday' name from that letter O'Dell received twenty years ago to a prostitute around here these days?"

He looked uncomfortable, the stringy black hands worrying each other on the table in front of him. "Used to see the girls during my bad times, maybe where I got the H.I.V. even. I met this Sundy once or twice. Never spent any money on her, though."

I wasn't sure I believed that last part. "When you and Lazar here were in the corridor at the Colonel's house, could anybody have overheard your conversation?"

Biggs said, "What, about Tommy's kid being this whore?"

"Yes."

"Not unless the walls have ears, babe. Why you think I be pulling Gordo aside, give him the hush?"

I let my gaze go around the table. "Anything else about Sundy Moran that any of you remember?"

Spi Held opened his mouth, then closed it again, kind of his reaction fifteen minutes earlier.

I said, "Let's have it."

He sniffled and shook his head. "Man, this is like decades ago. I'm not even sure it was the same chick."

"What was?"

Held shook his head once more, but said, "Just before he died, Tommy's ranting and raving about a lot of shit. He was way too heavy into the junk, and it made him act moto-weird."

"Weird in what way?"

Held opened his hands. "Tommy was giving me this tap dance about how some chick made him a daddy, that he wanted to be sure his kid was taken care of."

"What did you do about it?"

"Told him to go see Mitch."

"Your manager?"

"Yeah," said Spi Held. "I figured it'd ease Tommy's troubled mind, you know?"

I looked around the table again. "What did it do to your minds when Sundy Moran turned up dead?"

"Say what?" from Biggs.

"Dead?" from Held.

"Aw, shit," from Lazar. "Tommy's luck's still the same."

To me, Biggs said, "Wait a minute, babe. When did this girl get herself dead?"

"Within ten hours of Veronica's being killed. And Moran had help, too."

Biggs seemed to be trying to process something. Lazar just stroked his facial scars.

Held said, "How come we didn't know about it?"

"Your daughter's death pretty much pushed everything else off the news, right?"

"Yeah, but . . . Tommy's kid?"

Biggs nodded. "Make sense, though. Nobody outside us knew Tommy her daddy, and probably that never been proved nowhere, or Mitch would of told us. So, one more hooker gets herself offed, not likely the police gonna talk with the grieving family of a thirteen-year-old about it. Right, babe?"

In a very level voice, I said, "You've explained it better than I could."

Now even Spi Held seemed to be putting the pieces together. "Hold on, hold on. Man, you telling me that the same maniac who drowned my Very stabbed this hooker, too?"

I saw Biggs's eyes flicker to Held, then to me. Lazar was just shrugging.

I said, "Spi?"

"Yeah?"

"How did you know the Moran woman was killed with a knife?"

Biggs closed his eyes now.

Spi looked from one of us to the other before settling back on me. "Isn't that how they always get it?"

"Always?" I said.

"Yeah." Spi Held became almost enthusiastic. "You know, the phallic thing?"

The four of us were rising from the table when Ricky Queen came out of the shadows at the back of the club.

"Party breaking up?" he said.

Spi Held swiped under his nose. "You straighten out that fucking houseman?"

Queen winced a little. "We're cool with the dude again, but let's keep it that way, huh?"

Held looked around. "Where's he hiding?"

"Had to bug for a minute. Be right back."

"Fucking wanna-bes, don't got no sense of professionalism." Held sniffled again. "Look, I gotta hit the head, anyway, so we're back on in five, got it?"

Mumbled response from Gordo Lazar, Buford Biggs saying, "Don't forget, I'm picking up Kalil in half an hour."

"This numbnuts houseman ain't got his shit together by then, I'll be drowning him in a toilet, anyway."

An awkward pause as Spi Held lumbered off toward a rest room sign, he apparently the only one unaware of how awful his remark sounded less than two weeks after his daughter's death and barely two minutes after being reminded of it.

Walking toward the street door, I felt a tug on my good arm, and Ricky Queen fell in beside me as I hit the sunshine.

He turned his face to the sky like a convict in the exercise yard. "Man, feels good to be out in the fresh air, huh?"

"It does that."

"I don't mind the gigs at night so much, even the ones that stretch to dawn, because that way, you get to see the sun come up over the beach," Queen gesturing toward the east and an ocean I guessed to be a good mile or two away.

I said, "You walking me to my car?"

"Kind of." He glanced at my bad arm. "Any of those old druggies even notice you were hurt?"

"Not that they mentioned."

Queen brought his face toward mine, the platinum and orange hair looking even more bizarre in natural light. "Before you said that the guy paying the freight wants us to cooperate."

"Colonel Helides."

"Right. Our angel on this comeback thing." Now Queen looked down at his sneakers. "Well, I think the old guy's had it pretty tough, but he's been good to me, and good to Buford, looking past my being gay and Buford being full-blown."

With AIDS. "The kind of man the Colonel's always been."

Queen nodded, then squinted. "After I finished with the houseman, I came back, heard part of what you guys were talking about."

"What part?"

"You asking about this hooker named Sundy, and Spi saying how he couldn't see what one had to do with the other."

Uh-oh. "And you can?"

"Can what?"

"See a connection between the deaths."

"Between the deaths, no way. I'm a clean gene on that

score. No, I meant more between the girls themselves."

I stopped at the curb, my car diagonally across the intersection. "Sundy Moran and Veronica Held."

"Yeah." A quick glance around, but nobody was in earshot or even coming out the entrance to Dicey Riley's behind him. "Something Very said once when Spi was pissing her—and the rest of us—off with one of his tantrums."

"Like I saw today?"

"Dude, what you saw inside there was mild crankiness. Spi gets the wrong powder up his nose, and he goes ballistic."

"I'm listening."

"All right. Like I said, this one time, we're rehearsing and Spi wants the chord one way, but Very thinks the harmony should be hers, so she's the center of attention, you know?"

I thought about my impression watching the videotape of her performing at the party. "I'm following you."

"Okay, then. Follow this: After they explode at each other, the fighters retire to their corners. Very, though, comes over to me before we get started again, and she says, 'Like he never experimented in the seventies.'"

"Experimented?"

"Yeah. The song had to do with a black chick and a white dude, getting it on in a tough club. Would have made an awesome video, too, if the actor/dancers—"

"*Would* have made?"

"Spi killed the song, said we weren't going to do it. And Very's asking me, 'What's wrong with a little vanilla and chocolate together?'"

An image of Kalil Biggs crossed my mind. "Anything else?"

"Yeah, the weirdest part. To me, anyway. Very says, 'Ricky, you ever do girls?' And I knew she meant the dirty, so I told her, 'Sorry, hon, not my taste.' And Very goes, 'Well, I think

I'd like to experiment a little more than just vanilla and chocolate. Maybe a sundae, even.'"

I stared at him.

Queen said, "At the time, I thought she was just pushing the ice-cream metaphor, the way a songwriter might, you know? Now, though, I'm not so—"

"Rick!" Spi Held's head curved around the doorjamb of the bar, the lush but silly wig still in place. "Will you get the fuck back here before we lose Buford to his chauffeur service?"

"Right there, Spi." Then Queen turned again to me. "You ever . . . experiment, John?"

"No."

"You decide to enter the laboratory, keep me in mind, huh?"

And with that, Ricky Queen walked back toward the entrance of Dicey Riley's, rolling his buns under what I now noticed were pretty tight jeans.

Figuring I wouldn't have long to wait, I got behind the wheel of my Cavalier.

About twenty minutes later, Buford Biggs hurried out of the bar and sprinted to an old Pontiac Bonneville I'd seen at Spi Held's house the day before. He fumbled some with his keys at the lock, which gave me the chance to leave my car and walk over to him.

Glancing at me, Biggs scowled. "Don't got no more time for you now."

"And I understand why, so I'll ride shotgun a while."

The lines on his collapsing face grew deeper. "Say what?"

"I'll come with you, and we can talk on the way to picking up Kalil."

"How about if I don't want you in my car?"

"Then I follow you in mine, and eventually we talk, or I

tell Colonel Helides he can write one less check this month."

"You'd do that?"

"Reluctantly."

Biggs gave a look harder than his scowl, trying to back me down. Then he gave it up. "Yeah, you would, babe." Biggs opened his door. "Go around, I let you in."

Once we were settled, he started up and drove east on Second Street. We had two cars ahead of us when the railroad gate came down.

"Shit-mother-shit!"

Biggs craned his neck around, but there were three or four cars behind us, with nowhere to back up or turn around.

"Mother-*fuck*-er. You let me alone, I'm way past here by now."

"Maybe, maybe not." I stopped for a moment. "Just how much cocaine is Spi Held using?"

Biggs watched the train roar by, mostly flatbeds with road equipment lashed to them.

"Mr. Biggs?"

"You got me by the shorts, you might's well call me Buford, like any other white mother'."

"How much is Held snorting?"

"Don't know." A slap at the steering wheel. "He always done some, but it was under control, 'less the man start mixing and matching."

"With other drugs."

"Booze, more likely."

I thought back to Jeanette Held telling me about her husband's twin addictions. "And is he mixing cocaine with alcohol now?"

Biggs glanced at me once, then back to the seemingly endless line of railroad cars. "Like he think to make cement from them."

"How's it affecting the band?"

"How you think? Man's switching to a different arrangement every fucking day, trying to polish cowshit so it look like leather."

"His new songs are no good."

"Tunes are mediocre, babe, mediocre at best. It the lyrics that really fuck the duck, though."

"What Tommy O'Dell and Veronica used to help him with."

"Them mostly. But even then, the sound—Spiral's sound—it yesterday's bread, babe."

"Stale?"

"You had the choice, you buy fresh."

"What'll happen tonight?"

"At the gig? We get the houseman turn the speakers for the audience up so high, they fucking chests be bruised. If it just college kids and drunk enough, they'll go 'awesome' and 'way cool,' and we get a nice blurb on the radio about how we play this surprise—call it 'impromptu'—little concert for them, give a taste of what's to come on our new CD. But if anybody be there know shit from Shinola and carry a pad and pen, print review gonna make us look like a garage band again, the critic stay long enough to see how bad we really are."

"That why Mitch Eisen wasn't back there?"

"Mitch? Fifty-fifty he won't even be at the club tonight when we play. Shit, babe, he just promoting us for some bucks. Man's not exactly a fan of our music." This time, Biggs struck the top of the steering wheel with the heel of his right hand. "Didn't know they allow to run trains this fucking long."

I said, "Let's make the transition from music to video."

Biggs stiffened, but just kept watching the parade through his windshield.

"Buford, I need to know about Kalil's other videotapes."

"Why," clearing his throat, "so you can turn him in to the police, put him away somewhere?"

I gave it a beat. "You've seen the tapes?"

Half a glance toward me. "I seen them. Garbage."

"The tapes?"

Biggs turned his head more toward me, the muscles on his neck stark against the sagging skin. "The tapes was garbage, and that's where I throwed them."

"When?"

"Right after that little bitch tease me about how my son got the stutter with his hands like he do with his mouth."

I tried to phrase the next question very carefully. "So, before Veronica was killed?"

"Of course before she killed. How she gonna tease me about Kalil, she dead already?"

"Tell me what happened?"

Biggs went back to the train. "We was at Spi's crib, just finishing up trying to salvage one of his cowshit songs. I go out on the patio there—by the pool, where you and me sat—for a smoke, and Very sashays on over through those glass doors, sets her tight little ass down across from me."

Biggs had trouble with the rest. "She say to me, 'How come Kalil want me to do the strip for him, but not the tease?' I say to the child, 'You too young for that shit, both of you. Stay the hell away from my son.' And Very say, 'Kalil's not so young, and I like some variety in my experiences.' I say, 'Just stay away from tempting him,' and she say, 'He can have me anytime he want, on television.'"

Biggs swallowed hard. "I like to swat that little bitch hard enough to send her into the wall, but I thought about what she say, and later on I ask Kalil what Very mean by 'television.' And he bring out these videos he shoot."

"I know this isn't easy for you, Buford, but it might help me if you could describe—"

"I ain't gonna describe nothing. There was three tapes, and I burned them. But I tell you this. You seen the video Kalil do of Very singing for her grandfather at his party?"

"The police screened it for me."

"Yeah, well, you picture the same kind of song and her in the same kind of outfit. Only now it just Kalil in the room, and Very not in her outfit very long." Biggs blew out a breath. "The little bitch was right about one thing. Kalil, he so excited, that camera musta been jumping on his shoulder, account of the way Very look on that tape."

"The way she looked?"

"Like it was her and not her daddy Spi bouncing around the room from the nose candy."

I thought again about the autopsy report. The train's caboose finally whooshed by, and even the bells and whistles from the crossing gate couldn't dent the silence I felt sitting next to Buford Biggs before getting out of his car.

Driving to the tennis club, I used the cellular phone to check my voice mail at the hotel. Nothing from Malinda Dujong, but Mitch Eisen was on it, asking me to call him as soon as possible.

After dialing, I heard a few clicks before "Mitch Eisen."

"Mitch, John Cuddy."

"Hey, how's the boy detective?"

"In need of a few more answers."

"Well, I might have them, and you're lucky."

"Lucky?"

"I forwarded my office phone to my cellular, because I didn't want to be out of touch riding to the beach. Where are you right now?"

I told him.

"Perfect. Just go down to Las Olas and take it east to the beach. Park wherever you can."

"And you'll be?"

"In the place on the oceanside corner, second floor," said Mitch Eisen. "Can't miss it, in both senses of the expression."

At street level, a sign read THE ELBO ROOM. An open-walled bar was packed, mostly by older males acting like college kids. The steps leading to the second floor felt sticky enough to have been slopped with leftover beer. Reaching the upper bar, I couldn't see much change in the clientele. But a live band was playing surfer music from the sixties, many people chanting the well-worn lyrics. Altogether, it was just about quiet enough to hear a bomb drop.

From the railing overlooking the beach road, Mitch Eisen waved to me. I slalomed around clumps of swaying party animals, Eisen glancing at the bandage on my arm when I reached him.

"That from the mugging thing?" he shouted over the din.

"Primarily."

"Well, I hope you're feeling better." He motioned with his hand in an encompassing way. "So, what do you think?"

"Of what?"

"The Elbo Room. This is it, man. When Lauderdale was the Mecca of Spring Break, where you're standing now was the holiest of mosques."

I noticed Eisen had most of a beer left in a plastic cup. Leaning into him, I said, "Can we find someplace quieter?"

He seemed shocked. "But the view of history . . ." The hand now went out toward the palm trees and a white, two-foot-square wave wall separating the sidewalk from the sandy beach. "Remember *Where the Boys Are?*"

I made a hitchhiking gesture toward the stairs I'd just

used. Shaking his head, Eisen drained maybe half the beer remaining in his cup and waved a theatrical farewell to the crowd, though I didn't notice anybody waving back to him.

When we were on the sidewalk, he said, "There are some great new places just opened last year. Sloppy Joe's, that Hemingway bar from Key West. Howl at the Moon, which is a franchise operation, but—"

"Mitch, how about we just sit on the wave wall over there, talk about some things?"

"Sure," said Eisen. "I've always been a people-watcher."

After crossing A1A, we found a spot fifty feet from our nearest neighbors, so nobody could eavesdrop on us. I brushed off the top of the wall and sat facing the ocean, my shoes in the sand.

Eisen eased himself down to my left, facing the street but even enough with me that a single bullet could have gone through all four of our ears. "I don't know about your choice of viewing there, John. Kind of late for bikinis on the beach."

"After the day I've had, I find it peaceful."

Eisen frowned, his hair plugs inching downward. "Things okay?"

"No, but I don't need to tell you most of it."

"Hey, I'm happy to hear what you got to say. Like I mentioned last night, it'd be good for me to stay ahead of the media curve on this."

"Investment-wise."

"Every-wise. What have you got?"

"Sundy Moran's connection to Spiral."

Eisen made a clucking noise in his mouth. "Shit."

"I'm glad to see you're mourning her, too."

"Frankly, I was kind of hoping that'd slide on through."

"Her murder?"

"No. Any whiff that she was tied into the band." Eisen turned sidesaddle to me, his left leg now bent at the knee but resting flat on top of the wall. "Look, Cuddy. One death from an overdose twenty years ago, that was to be expected, the times and all. A current death of the little girl singer who's gonna bring an old band back from the grave, that's like . . . cachet, we can handle the spin right."

"I heard enough of this angle back in your office."

"Yeah, but you're adding a new ingredient. We got to go for damage control here, and I can't afford another leak in the good ship Spiral."

"Which Sundy Moran's connection with the band would spring."

"Exact-o-mundo."

"She came to you, didn't she?"

Mitch Eisen could have been one of those modern statues cast from bronze and placed in casual positions on park benches. I'm not sure even his lips moved with "Came to me?"

"When Tommy O'Dell was on the way out, didn't you meet with Donna Moran, the mother?"

"The mother?" Eisen seemed to relax. "Yeah, yeah. The mother. She claimed Tommy was the father of her little bundle of joy."

"Some of the other band members might be able to back her on that."

"Hey, John, you gotta remember the times. Nobody ever heard of sexual harassment or date rape. Shit, you worried about statutory rape—account of a lot of these chicks looked legal—and maybe whether you'd get a case of lice or crabs."

"But not a paternity suit."

"Look, this Donna Moran comes to see me, belly like it oughta be carried in a wheelbarrow. Says she's pregnant by Tommy, and I'm the manager, and what are we going to do about it?"

"We?"

"The band, Spiral. I told her we'd pay for an abortion—
God bless *Roe versus Wade*—but Moran says no, she wants
the kid but we should pony up for supporting it. I tell her
no way, and eventually she sees our side of things."

"And what, just goes away?"

"Has the kid, gives it her own name, turns out. Never
bothers us again." Eisen leaned toward me. "Frankly, I'm
surprised she didn't shoot her mouth off about it to the cops
or the media once Very turned up dead."

The cops. "The police don't know Sundy Moran was
Tommy O'Dell's daughter?"

Eisen cringed. "Man, you keep saying that, don't make
it so. Girl's gonna flash her boobies at some strung-out guy
on stage she don't know from a serial killer, how many
other dicks you figure blazed the trail for Tommy's?"

I kept my temper. "Aside from coincidence, any possible
connection between the killings of Veronica Held and
Sundy Moran?"

"Hell, no. I read the paper and see the little piece about
the Moran girl, all I can imagine is some high-school
friend of the mother thinking, 'Wait a minute, maybe I can
get my fifteen minutes on Montel or Leeza, blow the whistle on who Donna thinks the daddy was.' But that never
happened, so I'm guessing the mother didn't tell anybody
about Tommy."

"Did Sundy Moran ever know?"

"That Tommy was—*might* have been—her father? Beats
me. She sure never came around to my office with her hand
out, anyway."

I thought back to something Buford Biggs had told me
the day before. "Even if Sundy had shown up on your
doorstep, though, Tommy O'Dell really didn't have any
estate to leave her, right?"

"Right," a little too quickly.

"And that's because all his composer royalties—"

"Lyricist royalties, actually."

"All his royalties from Spiral's music devolved under his will to you."

Eisen swung back around, facing the street again. "That was the deal we had. My original venture capital, their unrealized potential."

"Which got 'realized.'"

"Yeah, but only because of me." Eisen began flaring. "What those fuckheads had before I took them on was pie-in-the sky, over-the-rainbow royalties."

Then he hung his head. "You see this little strip?"

I swung my legs around to the sidewalk. Eisen was studying a snaking tube embedded in the wave wall. Something within or behind the tube made it glow pink, then blue, then green, then—

"It's a nice touch," he said. "You drive north on A1A here at night, you can watch the little strips in the wall change color as you go by. I don't know how the city does it, but it's a nice trick."

Mitch Eisen looked up at me now, his eager eyes seeming to belong more in a child's face. "Like you're really getting near the end of the rainbow, even."

SEVENTEEN

A guard—named Lenny this time—said, "Ms. Dujong doesn't answer, sir."

Through the Cavalier's open window, I looked up at him in the sentry box of the tennis club. Fiftyish, solid. "No answer at all, or just her telephone tape?"

He thought about it, maybe whether or not he should tell me. "Her machine."

Same as I'd drawn when I tried to call her. "How about Cornel Radescu?"

Lenny said, "I know for a fact he's playing a featured match on Court One right now."

"Can you interrupt him?"

"No, sir."

"Okay. Let's go with Cassandra Helides."

Lenny picked up the phone again. After a minute, he said, "Sorry, no answer period."

I was beginning to feel a little stupid. "And there's no way you can let me in without somebody vouching for me?"

"Correct, sir."

"But I came in yesterday when Clinton was on duty."

"Someone has to authorize a visitor for each day, and your name's not in my book for this shift."

I didn't want to call Duy Tranh. "Could you try Don Floyd?"

Lenny perked up. "Mr. Floyd? Of course."

A few seconds after he punched in a number, I could see Lenny's lips moving against the receiver before he nodded and hung up.

I said, "You reached him?"

"Yessir. Mr. Floyd thinks seeing you again might prove to be . . . interesting."

Lenny gave me simple directions to the right building before raising the gate.

"You're sort of lucky to catch me, John." Don Floyd tilted his head behind him. "I was about to walk over to Court One, watch an acquaintance of yours play some."

Floyd was dressed in another tennis outfit, and even the

same Kangol cap, I thought, but the sweater vest of the day was a lemon yellow. "I appreciate your vouching for me."

"With Lenny at the gate? The visitor procedure's a necessary precaution, but I remembered how you kind of stirred things up last time, so I figured you might be worth a second look."

The wide smile that made him seem twenty years younger, but he dropped it when he looked down at my bandage. "What happened to your arm?"

"Just a cut." I lowered my voice. "Actually, Don, I'm a little worried about someone else."

"Who?"

"A resident here, Malinda Dujong."

"Malinda? Fine woman, and a wonderful player. Won a couple of tournaments till she started spending more time on that spiritual advising she does."

I explained about Dujong trying to reach me, then not returning my calls.

Floyd ruminated. "Well, now that you mention it, I haven't seen her around the courts for a few days, and that's a mite odd for the lady, even with all her advising lately." He looked at me squarely. "Come on."

We walked to one of the Mediterranean-style buildings, Floyd going up to a first-floor door and knocking. He put his ear to the wood, shook his head and knocked harder.

"Nothing?" I said.

Floyd looked at me, then walked over to the next door. His knock was answered this time, though I couldn't see by whom.

"Why, Don," said a very pleasant female voice through the open doorway.

"Shirley, how you doing?"

"Just fine. And you?"

"Couldn't be better."

"What brings you visiting?"

"Gentleman here's been trying to get hold of your neighbor, Malinda. You seen her these last few days?"

The door opened wider, and an attractive woman in her sixties smiled out at me.

"John Cuddy," I said.

"Shirley Nole." Her face darkened. "You know, Me Sue asked me that same question just this morning."

I wasn't sure I got the name. "Me Sue?"

"Another player here, from Korea. She spells it 'M-I S-O-O.'"

Floyd said, "Did Mi Soo tell you why, Shirley?"

"I guess she had a game scheduled with Malinda for ten, but Malinda never showed up."

Now Floyd darkened, too. "That's not like her, would you say?"

"No, not at all." Nole looked from Floyd to me and back again. "I have a key to Malinda's door, for deliveries or watering her plants if she's traveling."

I said, "Ms. Dujong ask you to water the plants recently?"

A pause. "No. No, she hasn't."

Don Floyd let out a breath. "Shirley, I think maybe we should use that key of yours."

Nole disappeared briefly, then came through her doorway, key in hand. We walked over to Dujong's, Nole knocking and calling out "Malinda" twice before sliding the key into the lock.

As she pushed the door open, I braced myself for that sickly sweet odor of decaying flesh, but all that greeted us was heat and stuffiness.

I touched Nole on the arm. "Maybe I should go in first."

She turned sideways and let me pass.

I entered a foyer, kitchen to the right, living and dining areas in front of me. No sign of a struggle or even a search.

In fact, everything was orderly to the point of immaculate, though the air felt as though the windows had been sealed for a year.

Behind me, Nole said, "Malinda likes it warm in here, but not this warm."

I walked by a closed closet door on the long wall to the left, tennis trophies dominating an adjacent entertainment center. Most of the other decorations were exotic, including some beaded, pendant talismans, I assumed from the Philippines.

I turned around. "Can we check the bedroom?"

Nole nodded, gesturing to the left.

Just past the trophy shelf, a doorway stood open. The furnishings were very feminine. Bed made, plush comforter on top. Again, nothing out of the ordinary.

"Bathroom?"

"Master bath is that way," said Nole.

I walked into the alcove for sink and mirror, separate shower beyond. Big enough for two people, with frosted glass doors so you couldn't see into it.

I moved over to the handle, hearing Floyd and Nole coming up behind me. I slid open the door.

Nothing.

I leaned in to touch tile and soap, then checked the towel on a brass hatrack. All dry as a bone.

I looked at Nole. "You said master bath?"

"Excuse me?"

"You said 'master bath' before. Does that mean there's another?"

"Oh. Yes, back this way."

She led us to what I'd taken for a closet, but the door opened onto a separate suite with bath to the right and bedroom to the left. The bed was stripped, the bathroom feeling sterile.

I asked, "Ms. Dujong doesn't use this part?"

Floyd said, "These two-bedroom units were designed so that owners could rent out a section during our high season."

"Does she do that?"

"Not for a while," said Nole. "At least, I think I'd have noticed."

The feeling in the air backed her up.

Don Floyd stared at me. "So, John, what do you think?"

I moved past them and into the living room. "Ms. Nole—"

"Oh, Shirley, please."

"Shirley, where are these plants you water?"

"Out there, on the porch."

I crossed the living room to draperies on a pull cord. I drew them open. Beyond the sliding glass door, a six-by-twelve, screened porch contained eight or ten large plants in colorful pots.

Unfortunately, the pots were a lot more colorful than the plants.

"Oh, no," said Nole. "They're dying."

Several looked okay, but most were drooping or worse.

As Nole went toward the kitchen, I said, "Shirley, how long would it take for these to get like this?"

Over the sound of running water, she said, "The southern exposure really bakes plants, though it also helps them grow faster. Malinda's always had me come in every morning."

I'd seen Dujong late on the afternoon before, at Spi Held's house. "Could they get this way within twenty-four hours?"

"Maybe, but I don't know for sure."

Floyd said quietly, "I don't like what I'm feeling, John."

I nodded.

Nole came out with a plastic can, sticking its snout under leaves and sprouts. "But I can tell you that Malinda would never have left these long enough for them to get so parched without asking me to tend them."

"Anybody else she might have contacted?"

"Mi Soo, but like I said, she hadn't heard from Malinda either."

I could see an answering machine on a lower shelf of the entertainment center. "Maybe we could listen to Ms. Dujong's tape messages."

Floyd and Nole exchanged troubled glances. She said, "Her telephone calls, you mean?"

"Yes."

Floyd shook his head. "That'd feel mighty like intruding on Malinda's privacy."

Shirley Nole nodded, and I guessed I couldn't blame either of them.

Don Floyd said, "What else do you think we should do, John?"

Only one more thing. "What kind of car does Ms. Dujong drive?"

The three of us walked separately over the entire parking area, but nobody could find Dujong's yellow Toyota Celica. When we met back at her building, I told Floyd and Nole that I'd call the police, but not to expect much of a response, given the absence of evidence that anything suspicious had happened to her. As they thanked me for my concern, there was a loud cheer and some sustained applause from near the clubhouse.

Floyd looked in that direction. "Well, somebody seems to have won their match."

I said, "The one with Cornel Radescu in it?"

"Timing's about right."

"I'd like to talk to him again."

Don Floyd smiled. "And I'd like to see that, but I'm

afraid I'll have to take a rain check. My bride and I scheduled an early supper." He stuck out his hand. "You need anything, John, you call me, hear?"

I thanked him and Shirley Nole both, then started walking toward the clubhouse.

There were about twenty people in the patio area between the pool and the tiki bar, but I spotted her right away. She stood behind him at one of the umbrellaed tables, kneading his neck muscles the way I'd seen her do once before.

Though it'd been for her husband then.

From ten feet away, I said, "Mrs. Helides."

Both of them looked up at me. Cornel Radescu, shirtless, opened his mouth, but his masseuse beat him to the punch.

"We ought to charge you for a membership. You're here as much as I am."

"I doubt it."

There was a chair across from Radescu, and I sank into it.

From under his dark brow, he looked at my bandaged arm but just said, "Why have you come back to this place?"

"Couple of reasons. Let's start with Malinda Dujong."

"Malinda?" said Helides.

"Yes. Either of you seen her recently?"

Radescu looked confused, Helides just vacant.

He gestured toward Dujong's building. "She lives over there, on the ground—"

"We've checked. No sign of her, and some indications that she hasn't been in her unit for a while."

Radescu put on a wary expression. "If already you know this, why do you ask us?"

"Originally I thought the killing of Veronica Held was an isolated incident. Now I'm not so sure."

Helides stopped the massage and came out from behind Radescu. "Malinda was just giving Jeanette 'spiritual guidance' or something."

"Partly because of Veronica's death."

"Yes," said Radescu. "But Malinda was not even there at the party that day."

"So she told me." I looked up at Helides. "Do you know why?"

"Why what?" she said.

"Why Ms. Dujong wasn't at your husband's house."

Helides nearly stamped her foot. "It's my house, too, Mister."

"But do you—"

"No!" barked Helides.

I noticed six or seven people turn to stare at us. "Ms. Dujong told me she'd received a call to meet someone, supposedly referred to her by Jeanette Held."

Radescu said, "What difference does it make, the reason Malinda was not at the party?"

"It was a woman's voice on the phone."

"Okay," said Helides. "Maybe I'm stupid, but I don't get what you're talking about."

I waited a beat. "Did you make that call?"

"Me?"

"Yes."

Fists to hips now. "Why would I need a 'spiritual advisor'?"

"Wait a minute," said Radescu, coming forward in the chair, muscles bunching. "Are you saying somebody kept Malinda from the party on purpose, and now has done something to her?"

"Pretty good summary."

Helides looked to him, then back at me, the expression on her face like a kid accused of stealing a piece of somebody else's candy. "Well, I sure as hell didn't have anything to do with it. Why would I?"

Time to test the waters. "Sundy Moran."

They exchanged looks again, but it was back to confused and vacant, respectively.

"What is this, a name?" said Radescu.

"Of a young woman killed within hours of Veronica Held."

Helides said, "Never heard of her."

Radescu worried his hands atop the patio table. "Why do you tell us about this thing?"

"Sundy Moran was probably the daughter of Tommy O'Dell."

The tennis pro shook his head, now more exasperated than confused. "Another name I do not know about, or care about."

Helides glanced at him. "He was Spi's drummer."

Radescu said, "What?"

"In the original band." She came back to me. "He wasted himself with drugs."

Her certainty stopped me. "I thought that was long before you knew even the Colonel?"

"It was, but I've heard the guys talk about him. Only, what the fuck does somebody dead twenty years have to do with Very or this Moran girl?"

"Actually I was hoping you two could help me with that."

Helides glared at me as Radescu drew back in his chair, arms folding across his bare chest.

She said, "What's that supposed to mean?"

"You used to drive Veronica here for tennis lessons with her"—I glanced at Radescu—"teacher, right?"

Now Helides crossed her arms, too. "So?"

"So then you stopped, and Delgis Reyes had to do it. I'm wondering why?"

"Because that's the little wetback's job."

I bored through the slur. "But there must be a reason why you decided to stop bringing her to see your mutual instructor."

"Okay, mister." Helides raised her voice again, and other conversations around us halted abruptly. "You think Cornel was hitting on our poor little Very, right?"

Radescu shuddered. "Cassie, please don't—"

"Well," she continued, a few decibels louder. "Let me tell you, that wasn't it."

I said, "Veronica was hitting on him."

Helides actually smiled, but cruelly. "No, mister know-it-all." Then she leaned down, nearly hissing out her words. "The little bitch started hitting on *me*."

I didn't say anything.

"That's right." Helides straightened up again. "I was driving her here one day for a lesson with Cornel, and Very moves her hand over to my thigh. Then she starts walking her fingers toward the secret garden."

I could hear people at the tables around us speaking in low tones as they pushed back their chairs. "Mrs. Helides—"

"No fair, mister. You asked for it, now you're gonna hear it. The little bitch says, 'If that feels good, you want to do it to me?' And I slap her hand away, tell her what an incredible cunt she is, and she clouts me—*me*—across the face. Well, I'm halfway to punching her lights out when I decided instead to do a U-ey and take her back to granddaddy, let him know what his little angel tried on step-grandmummy."

"You told the Colonel that Veronica—"

"No, of course not. It would've fucking killed the poor old guy." Cassandra Helides rocked her head side to side like a clown making a discovery in center ring at the circus. "But that, mister, is how come I stopped driving precious little Very to her tennis lessons."

Radescu said, "Cassie, I do not think we should say anything more to this man, no matter what your husband told you about cooperation."

"Fine," replied Helides quickly. "I'm even sick of looking at him."

I got up from my chair. "The police may be by about Malinda Dujong. I hope you have a better story for them."

"We don't need any story," said Radescu, standing also. "And you better remember the last thing I told you on the tennis court."

His threat about nobody taking away what he'd worked so hard to acquire. "Actually, that reminds me. Who won today's match?"

Cassandra Helides moved toward Radescu. "Cornel, six-three, six-one." She slipped her arm around his, like links in a chain. "And to the victor belongs the spoiled."

I almost corrected her before realizing she was right.

Outside the gate of the tennis club, I called the direct cellular number on Sergeant Lourdes Pintana's business card. When her voice mail kicked in anyway, I left a message about Malinda Dujong trying to reach me and what I'd seen with Don Floyd and Shirley Nole in the apartment. After clicking off, I tried to think of someone else to see before going to the Skipper's house and telling him—and possibly Justo Vega—about Sundy Moran.

Just one name came to mind. Directory assistance gave me the telephone number, but a man answering told me the woman I wanted was home sick.

This time I drove in slowly enough that the dust cloud stayed below window level on the Cavalier. I brought it to a stop near the man in the straw hat and overalls, lighting his pipe.

When I opened my door, he spat in the other direction

before saying, "Information booth's still open, but this late in the day, I'm on overtime rates."

I took a five from my wallet anyway. "As a repeat customer, I'm entitled to a discount."

He looked at the bill disdainfully, then reached out and took it. "Reckon I'll have to charge the next one double."

"Her trailer?" I said.

He used the stem of his pipe as a pointer. "Four down on the right, puke-green siding."

"Thanks."

"Don't be too hasty."

I got back in the car and drove. My guide was dead-on about the color of Donna Moran's trailer. I had thoughts about whether Ford Walton might be in there as well, but only one vehicle slouched in front of it, and I couldn't remember if the multiprimered Dodge was one of the many clunkers I'd seen outside Billy's the day before.

Cement blocks created a stoop leading to an aluminum door. I knocked on it.

"Go away," came more through an open window than from behind the door, but it was her voice.

"John Cuddy, Ms. Moran. Yesterday at Billy's?"

Now the sound of bedsprings and heaving weight. I could hear someone pad to the door, then had to step down as it swung open at me.

"Jesus," I said.

Donna Moran looked out through the one eye that wasn't swollen shut. The closed eye and both cheeks were that purplish yellow of a recent beating.

She coughed. "Got you to thank for this."

"Luke and Hack?"

"They kept drinking after you showed them up, but they didn't have you to take it out on."

"Ms. Moran, I'm sorry."

"Just like a man. You're always sorry afterwards." Now the open eye grew almost curious. "Wait a minute. How'd you know they whaled on me?"

"I didn't."

"Then why're you here?"

"I want to ask you some more questions."

Her face showed a different kind of pain. "Not about Sundy."

"Only indirectly."

"What?"

"Tommy O'Dell."

The eye went dull. "Why can't you just leave me alone?"

"Because somebody else has maybe disappeared." I decided to take a leap of faith. "And she was trying to help me."

Moran hung her head. "For such a polite man, you don't seem to be much luck for the women around you."

An image of Nancy's hair in my nightmares skipped across my mind. "That's a fact."

Moran lifted her head, the face trying to form a new expression before the pain overcame it. "All right. Might's well come set with me."

The air inside the trailer was stifling, filled with that stale pong of long-smoked tobacco, even though every window I could see stood open. A torn sheet in a daisy print acted as a slipcover for the sofa, some unwashed mugs and dishes next to the sink. The hatchlike door to a closet or bathroom was closed, but through an open doorway at the end of the trailer, I could see the foot of a bed, the covers mussed.

Moran said, "Kind of like that bus."

I looked at her.

She slumped into the sofa, the slipcover pulling down off the top. "When I met Tommy. You know about me and him, somebody must've told you how the band got its girls."

"I've heard about the bus."

Moran sighed. "Well, I got to say, it looked a lot more glamorous at the time." The laugh like a hiccup. "Probably about the same size as this place, though. Haven't exactly moved up in the world, have I?"

"When we talked at the bar, why didn't you tell me that Tommy O'Dell was Sundy's father?"

A shrug that pain stopped like a freeze-frame. "Didn't seem to matter much."

"That the daughters of two members of the same band were killed within hours of each other?"

"That Held girl, you mean?"

I made my voice stay patient. "Yes."

The good eye closed. "Mr. John Polite, they were gonna make her a rock star, right?"

"Right."

"Well, my Sundy was—Lord forgive me—a streetwalker. Just what do you think those two could've had in common?"

"I was hoping you might know."

The eye opened again. "Tommy and me, that was over twenty years ago. After I missed my . . . after I realized I was pregnant, and that it had to be him, I went to their manager person, Mr. . . . ?"

"Eisen?"

"Mr. Eisen, yeah. He told me Spiral got . . . bombarded. That was the word he used. Mr. Eisen said they got bombarded by . . . 'sluts' like me all the time. I didn't go away, he'd call the police. I tried to sue them, they'd stand together, say none of them ever seen me afore. And after the band stonewalled it, this Mr. Eisen said probably the social services would take my baby away from a slut didn't know who the father of her child really was."

"What did you do then?"

"I shut up and had Sundy." A moment of serenity came over Moran. "I named her after the day Tommy and I . . . met, only not quite, account of it was the Sabbath, and it didn't seem right to spell her name out the same way." The moment passed. "I'd gotten more religious by then, carrying Sundy around in my body like the Virgin Mary must have Him."

"Did you ever see Tommy O'Dell again?"

Another sigh. "On the TV."

"And after he died?"

"Oh, I went back to that Mr. Eisen, said now that I can't hurt Tommy no more, could the band maybe do something for my baby? Mr. Eisen told me they couldn't, that any money Tommy had coming to him was all tied up in legal things. And that now Tommy was dead and buried, I'd never be able to prove he was Sundy's daddy any which way."

Eisen had concocted a more sugar-coated version for me that amounted to the same thing. "Ms. Moran, anything else you can think of?"

A hand went to her forehead. "Sundy was always carrying on about how she was gonna travel all over the country. Travel in style."

"Maybe with a . . . rock band?"

"But that's what don't make no sense. I never did tell my girl who fathered her. And if Sundy somehow got connected up with this Held child, why wouldn't my daughter have told me? And why would somebody kill the both of them when somebody else like you might find it out?"

I thought about Cassandra Helides that afternoon. "I'm sorry to ask you this question, but it may be important."

The hand stayed on her forehead. "Please just let it be the last one, all right?"

"Ms. Moran, there's some reason to believe that Veronica Held was interested in experimenting with sex."

The hiccup laugh. "She should have asked me about it first."

"Maybe with . . . a woman older than she was."

The hand came down, the face tightened from more kinds of pain than I could imagine. "You're saying she . . . That my Sundy and this little girl . . . ?"

"Did your daughter ever tell you any—"

"No!"

The only thing louder than Donna Moran's answer was the shattering sound from outside her trailer.

EIGHTEEN

A second shattering sound reached me before I got to the window next to the door. The Cavalier's two headlights were smashed, glass and plastic and tin on the ground in front of its bumper. Luke, the guy in the Peterbilt ballcap, was moving around to the rear of my car, Hack wearing his bandanna and doing his barnyard laugh. Luke had an aluminum bat over his shoulder, receiving compliments on the quality of his swings from my guide in the straw hat and overalls, standing off to the side, his pipe in a corner of his mouth.

No firearms in sight, though.

I turned away from the window. "Ms. Moran?"

"Luke and Hack, right?"

I heard what I guessed to be one of my taillights. "Do they carry handguns?"

"Never known them to."

I glanced around. "There another way out of here?"

* * *

Coming around from the back of the trailer, I saw Hack's bandanna first, his face turned toward the door I'd entered by. Sticking up from a back pocket of his jeans was a wrench the size of a camp hatchet.

Crouched low, I was on him just as my guide yelled, "Behind you!"

Hack turned obligingly into the heel of my right hand, his nose going flat as I felt the cartilage collapse on itself. There was a torrent of blood and snot running down his shirt as he sank to his knees, both hands going up to his face, what was coming out of his mouth not identifiable as words.

I stepped past him and yanked the wrench out of his jeans pocket. Holding it by the handle, I felt the head of the tool dowsing toward the ground.

Luke had the bat off his shoulder now, as though he were in a hitter's stance at the plate but advancing on the pitcher's mound.

I said, "That was for what you two did to Donna Moran."

"Boy, I'm gonna take your head clean off your shoulders."

"He can do it, too," my guide offered around the pipe stem. "Luke led the county in home runs, his senior year at the high school."

I let Babe Ruth get to within ten feet of me before saying, "You ever see *The Last of the Mohicans*, Luke?"

He stopped his advance. "The what?"

Which is when I brought the wrench back behind my neck and let it fly like a tomahawk.

Luke's reflexes were still pretty good, but he probably— instinctively—thought I'd be aiming at his head, so he tried to duck under my chin music. I'd hoped for his chest, though, to knock him enough off balance that I could get inside the bat before he could swing it. The combination of his reaction and my target made his left cheekbone the bull's-eye.

There was a sickening thud, and Luke folded like a crash-test dummy.

My guide said, "Waste of the man's ten dollars."

Stepping past Luke this time, I spoke over the sound of Hack groaning and rolling in the dirt behind me. "You called him."

A hand reached into the overalls. I tensed, but all that came out was a cell phone.

"Great invention," said my guide. "Call cost a buck, but that's still ninety percent profit on my time."

I bent down, picked up Luke's bat. My guide's pipe fell from his mouth to a spot between his feet.

"Hold on there," he said. "I wasn't hurting you none."

"These two tried beating me up in that roadhouse, and when they fumbled the ball, they attacked Donna Moran instead."

"Maybe so, but I'm no part of that."

"You told me about the roadhouse."

"Only because you asked. And paid for it."

He was right there.

"So," said my guide. "Why don't we just leave things where they be?"

"Not quite." I moved forward, he moved back the same distance. Then I looked down at the ground.

"Aw, no. That was my daddy's pipe."

"Your phone, then."

"My . . ." He glanced at the thing still in his hand. "But this here cost me—"

"Your pipe, your phone, or your hand."

He dropped the cellular and backed up.

After finishing with it, I said, "Take Hack and Luke to a hospital. One's got a broken nose, the other at least a fractured cheekbone. And if either of them, or anybody else, touches Donna Moran again, simple medical attention won't be enough. We clear on that?"

"Clear," whispered my guide.

"I didn't hear you."

"Clear," he said, with some effort.

"I truly hope so."

My adrenaline surge abated enough in the car for me to think ahead again. Using my own cellular phone, I called the hotel for voice-mail messages. The first was from Justo Vega, saying he would meet me at the Skipper's house by six for dinner. The second, via Duy Tranh, conveyed the same information, though his tone suggested he viewed the invitation as more an order. The third was from Sergeant Lourdes Pintana, saying another matter kept her at a crime scene but that she'd meet me to talk about Malinda Dujong "at ten as we agreed."

After hanging up, I tried Dujong's number at the tennis club, though without much hope. When I got only her outgoing tape, I clicked off the cell phone.

The same woman who'd helped me the last time was behind the rent-a-car counter at my hotel. When she saw me walking up, the back of her right hand went to her mouth.

"Sir, are you all right?"

How could she . . . ? "What do you mean?"

She spoke the next words very slowly. "Your shirt."

I looked down. Hack's blood had spattered on me in a blotchy, polka-dot pattern.

I looked back to the woman behind the counter. "Guess I'll be needing another one."

A very guarded expression on her face as she nodded.

I trotted out some kind of smile. "I'm afraid I'll be needing another car, too."

* * *

After five forms in triplicate, followed by a shower and change of clothes, I was behind the wheel of a red Olds Achieva. When I got to the Skipper's house, Pepe was talking with Umberto Reyes outside the little gazebo.

"Hey," said Pepe as Reyes opened the gate for me. "What happen to you Chevy?"

I pulled up even with him and braked. "Batting practice."

Pepe nodded, as though my explanation made perfect sense when it came to rental vehicles. "This look like a better car for you, anyways."

As Reyes closed the gate behind us, I said to Pepe, "Justo already inside?"

Another nod. "Mr. Vega and me, we got here maybe ten minutes ago."

"Do you know who else is in there?"

Now a grin. "How you say it, the usual suspects?"

Based on the number of cars parked near the garage bays, I could see Pepe was close to right. Leaving the Olds next to Cassandra Helides's Porsche, I could also see they were the identical shade of red, though I doubted the Bavarian company's promo literature would agree on that.

When I knocked at the back door, Duy Tranh came to it, wearing a very tight smile on his face.

Through the screening, he said, "You do this intentionally."

"Do what?"

"Come to a different entrance of the house each time."

I reached up for the handle on the massive door. "Why would I?"

"To disturb my composure." The smile went from tight to defiant as he raised his hand. "You will not succeed in such an endeavor, Mr. Cuddy."

"Frankly, I hadn't realized I was trying."

But I did let him open the door for me.

"Forgive us, Lieutenant, but my medications require me to eat at the same time each evening."

The salad course had already been served, though most of the people around the elliptical dining table were less than halfway through it. Nicolas Helides sat at one end, his wife Cassandra opposite him, a good twenty feet away. On the near long side were Justo, Mitch Eisen, and two empty chairs, a tented napkin still at one of the place settings. On the far long side were all four members of Spiral, which surprised me. I didn't see David Helides, which didn't surprise me.

I took the chair with the tented napkin as Duy Tranh slid silently into his on my left. If pecking order mattered, Justo was closest to the Skipper, with me next and even the band's manager before the trusted almost-son.

Our host raised a glass that appeared to be just water. "A second toast, to the success of Spiral in its public appearance tonight."

Which explained why the band members were there.

The meal might have been intended as a banquet, but the pace and conversation resembled more a wake. Any small talk was forced, the only exceptions being Justo asking polite, softball questions of Spi Held, Mitch Eisen answering most of them too elaborately in what seemed an effort to fill the voids of air and time. Cassandra Helides drank wine as though it were Gatorade during the third set under a blazing sun. Delgis Reyes served the courses; each time she got to me, Veronica Held's former au pair wouldn't meet my eyes.

As the last dessert forks clattered against empty dishes that had held slices of rum cake, the Skipper turned to his right and said to the band, "Well, I believe you all need to go. Can't be late for your big evening."

It was painful to hear, maybe because he sounded like
an emotionally distant man speaking to a twelve-year-old
son home for the weekend from boarding school.

Spi Held stared at his father, his eyes milky. "Thanks."
He stood. "Dad."

Buford Biggs, Gordo Lazar, and Ricky Queen all got up
like a drill team, mumbling softly in appreciation as well.
Mitch Eisen took the trouble to approach the Colonel and
shake hands. After the five of them trooped out, the table
seemed unbalanced, and not just because there were four
empty chairs along the far side of it.

Nicolas Helides looked at his wife. "Cassandra, I'll be
needing to speak with these gentlemen for a while."

"You're excused," she said, slurring the last syllable.

Then the Skipper's eyes went past mine to Tranh. "Duy,
we'll be in the library, should you need me."

I didn't turn, but the air leaving the lungs of the man to
my left sounded like a death rattle.

"Brandy, Lieutenant?"

Justo said, "No, thank you."

Nicolas Helides looked at me, inclining his head toward
the decanter on the sideboard between two tall shelves of
books. I shook my head in return.

The Skipper settled deeper in his chair. "Could I have
your report?"

I told him about Malinda Dujong and what I'd learned
of Sundy Moran from her mother and Mitch Eisen. I didn't
mention how Cassandra Helides had described Veronica's
behavior on their last drive to the tennis club or what Ricky
Queen had implied outside Dicey Riley's regarding
Veronica's "experimental" attitude. I finished with the incident involving Luke and Hack at the trailer park.

A glimmer came into Helides's eyes. The same one I'd

seen after describing the bar brawl of the day before.

Which is when it hit me. The man was living vicari-
ously, feeling capable again through hearing about an
investigation involving violence. And a part of me—deep
inside—withered a little.

Justo said, "John, you have not yet spoken with the
police about the disappearance of the Dujong woman?"

"I'm supposed to meet with one of the homicide investigators tonight at ten."

The Skipper frowned. "Pity."

"I'm sorry, sir?"

"You'll miss the band's re-debut."

A smile that for a moment made me think Helides had
become senile.

Justo filled the gap. "Anything else, John?"

I refocused. "Colonel, it seems pretty clear to me that
you've cut Duy Tranh out of the loop."

No smile now. "I imagine it's pretty clear to him as
well."

"Can I ask what made you change your mind?"

The Skipper's left hand went to the brace leaning against
his chair, the fingers almost caressing its metal. "Since my
stroke, I have relied on Duy to be my effective . . . self.
Financially, administratively, totally."

Helides stopped. I waited.

The Skipper's hand came back into his lap. "However, he
was the person who found Veronica's body. And what I've
heard from you so far about this Sundy Moran seems a
remarkable coincidence, but not tied by evidence to anything approaching a motive—even an irrational explanation—of why anyone else would want to kill my grandchild."

Very quietly, I said, "Colonel, could Veronica's death
have been related to the way she acted at your party?"

The face flushed, the eyes squeezed shut, and for a

moment Helides's features could have been an older version of his son David's. Then the moment passed, and the eyes of the man I'd served under in Saigon were piercing me again across thirty years. "Find out, Lieutenant. Find out."

After Justo and I went through the back door, there were only a few cars remaining by the garage, and the red Porsche wasn't one of them.

I said, "Cassandra Helides shouldn't be driving after what she drank at dinner."

"I am afraid the Skipper has long ago given up any hope of affecting her decisions."

We reached my Olds, and I could see Pepe walking toward us from the security gazebo.

"Justo," I said. "A difficult question?"

He read my face, and then held up his hand in a stop-sign gesture. Pepe turned and began walking back toward the gate.

I leaned against the driver's door of the Achieva. "What happens when the Colonel dies?"

"Financially, you mean?"

"Start there."

Justo hesitated. "I did not prepare the estate plan for him, but I have read it at his request. Why do you ask, John?"

"I'm trying to think of any reason for Veronica Held behaving the way she did in front of her grandfather at that party when everyone's told me she had a knack—and a willingness—to push the right buttons to get what she wanted from people."

"You think perhaps she did it to . . . please someone else?"

"Or maybe that somebody else told her it would work on the Colonel."

A shake of the head this time. "I do not see how."

"Work the wrong way, maybe."

Now a slow nod. "To upset the Skipper."

"Maybe even push him over the edge, healthwise but apparently naturally."

"*Dios mio*, John. You think someone used Veronica in an attempt to kill her grandfather?"

"And when it didn't happen right then . . ."

". . . Veronica would have to be silenced before she could tell the Skipper whose idea that song was."

We both let it lay there a minute.

Finally Justo said, "The estate plan, though detailed, is really quite simple in structure. But first you must know that Cassandra signed an antenuptial agreement. Upon divorce, separation, etc., she receives a lump-sum payment of only half a million dollars."

"Only."

Justo nearly smiled. "From her perspective, today that would work out to less than thirty thousand dollars for each year of marriage."

"During most of which the Colonel was hale and hearty."

"That is correct, John."

"But if he died before a separation or divorce?"

"Then the antenuptial agreement yields to the estate plan, and Cassandra receives one-half of the estate."

"Amounting to . . . ?"

". . . seven million, give or take."

God. "And the rest of it?"

"Another million to various charities, three in trust to care for David in perpetuity, and the remaining three in trust for Veronica."

"With a provision for his granddaughter predeceasing him?"

Another nod, slower than the first. "Her three million to Spi Held, though again in trust, so he could not squander the inheritance."

I turned it over. "There a reason you didn't tell me that last part before?"

"John, you only just now asked—"

"I mean without my asking you."

Justo stiffened, then his shoulders sagged in a relenting way. "My client's wishes."

"Go on."

"He did not want to believe that the reformed Prodigal Son could have wanted his own daughter dead."

"And so the Skipper told you not to say anything about a three-million-dollar motive for the girl's father?"

"But that is where you are wrong, John. Spi Held wanted nothing more than to see his band be a success again, and he knew Veronica functioned as the linchpin of that hope. Not just the hope of money, either. A hope more strongly, I think, of the ego, to be on top of his music's heap once again."

"Dreams of fame and fortune trump a motive for fortune only."

"Exactly."

"Justo?"

"Yes."

"Have you heard Spiral play lately?"

Another stiffening at the shoulders, but a slow shake of the head, too.

I got to O'Hara's on Las Olas by 9:45 P.M. As I went through the front door, an African-American bouncer at least six-seven and two-sixty greeted me warmly. Rabid applause was just dying around the red-bricked room, which looked like a cozier version of the Hollywood operation Mitch Eisen and I had visited the night before. On the small stage, a compact guy about thirty with curly, Prince Valiant–length hair was shaking out a soprano sax the color of mercury, a much taller and broader guy around the same age nodding thanks to the nearly S.R.O. house while he turned the little tuning pegs at the top of his guitar. A second guitarist and a drummer rounded out the group.

The small square bar inside the entrance was full, but I saw two empty stools on the left side of a larger oval bar in the middle of the room. As I got there and took the closest seat, a barkeep cleared the empty glasses of the recently departed and swabbed the drink rings with a towel.

"What'll you have?"

I didn't see any draught pulls. "No taps?"

He pointed to a shelf of sample bottles above him. "All of those, and Harp as well."

"A Harp, please."

As he said, "You got it," I missed the name of the next piece, which the saxophonist also announced could be found on "our latest CD." There was a swelling of applause before the first chord, and the song turned out to have a salsalike beat, the sax establishing as pretty a melody as I'd heard in years.

The bartender set the bottle of Harp on a coaster in front of me. "Glass?"

"No, thanks."

As he turned away, I felt a hand rest lightly on my left shoulder and whiffed a little perfume mixed with that distinctive tang of female perspiration.

Sergeant Lourdes Pintana leaned into my ear to say, "How much have I missed?"

I watched her fold onto the stool next to mine and arrange a tote-sized handbag between her feet, the strap around one ankle. She wore a lime-green blazer and pale-yellow skirt, the hem riding eight inches above her knees.

I leaned toward Pintana, but not as closely as she had to me. "Just got here myself."

The bartender automatically brought over a clear, carbonated drink with a straw. She nodded to him, then glanced at the guitarist before leaning into my ear again. "His name is Mark Vee. Enjoy."

We sat in silence as Vee contributed three minutes or so of virtuoso lead before yielding back to the sax. Pintana and I joined in the applause, the guitarist grinning shyly.

Pintana leaned into me again, this time her lips actually brushing the hair over my ear. "He's from Chile." She reached for some purple bookmarks on the bar to her left, putting one in front of me and pointing to a photo and caption under it. "The sax man's Joe Sha-shaty, Lebanese heritage. And this is a list of the other places they'll be playing this month."

I watched her lips close on the straw sticking up from her glass.

When the piece ended, there was an ovation of applause, whistling, and cheering. Then Sha-shaty announced they'd be taking a short break and reminded us to be good to the bartenders and waitresses.

As the crowd quieted, some getting up to leave, Pintana leaned into me again. "They're as good as you'll hear live."

I looked at her.

"What's the matter?" she said, leaning back now.

"When you asked me here this morning, I told you about what happened to me."

A neutral expression. "The women in your life."

"Who *were* in my life. I'm not claiming sexual harassment, but you don't have to blare into my ear for me to understand your words."

A mask came down over Pintana's features. "Remember I told you about Kyle taking a bullet for me?"

"Yes."

"Before I put the shooter down, he capped off another round about two feet from the right side of my head."

"Got you." I closed my eyes. "Sorry."

"Thirty percent hearing loss in this ear. So I sometimes overcompensate, especially with background noise like—"

Opening my eyes, I turned toward her. "I said I was sorry."

Pintana hardened the mask, then let it slide off like a gossamer veil. "You would be a hard man to love, and an impossible one to leave."

I picked up my Harp. "Now's who's getting ahead of themselves?"

She dipped toward her drink instead of raising it, the lips once again on the straw before she straightened again. "You called me."

"About Malinda Dujong."

"I'm waiting."

I told Pintana about Dujong's message on my voice mail at the hotel and what I learned from visiting the tennis club, including not listening to Dujong's own tape machine.

"Department policy says forty-eight hours before we classify it a missing person."

"Hasn't been that long yet."

"And might never be. All I've heard so far is she makes one call to you, blows off a tennis game, and forgets to water some plants."

It was a way to see it. "When I spoke with Dujong yesterday afternoon at Spi Held's house, she told me something she said didn't come up when Cascadden interviewed her."

Pintana dipped to take another—but now very casual— sip of her drink. "What?"

"That someone calling herself 'Wendy' lured Dujong away from attending the Helides birthday party."

A look of genuine interest this time. "Lured her how?"

I went through it.

"So," said Pintana, "we add this mystery woman Wendy, and we still don't have anything that authorizes me to violate the privacy of a maybe-missing citizen's tape messages."

"So maybe we do it without authorization."

Her eyes went toward the front entrance. "Let me find a pay phone first."

I watched Pintana as she did a ninety-degree turn away from me. Sliding the strap of her totebag over a shoulder, she went back toward the rest room signs. Just as I lost her in the crowd, I felt that tingle of not remembering something important. Then I felt something else.

The weight of hands substantially heavier than Pintana's landing on each of my shoulders.

NINETEEN

Sitting in the backseat of a Ford Crown Vic cruiser with the bigger of two patrol officers, I remembered what the tingle had been trying to tell me.

I said, "You have a cell phone."

Sergeant Lourdes Pintana turned around in the front passenger's seat, speaking through cage wire at the edge of a Plexiglas divider. "What?"

"You have a cellular, so you didn't have to look for a pay phone."

From behind the wheel, the smaller patrol officer laughed. "You sure this guy's smart enough to—"

"Not another word," said Pintana to him, and the four of us rode mute the rest of the way to 1300 West Broward Boulevard.

"Glad to see you back, Beantown."

"Glad to be back."

Standing against the wall of Pintana's office in the Homicide Unit, Detective Kyle Cascadden probably would have rubbed his hands together with glee but for the light-brown folder swaddled against his chest. "You won't be glad for long, especially once—"

"Kyle?" said Pintana, sinking into the chair behind her desk.

"All right, all right."

I took the seat across from her again, the two uniforms having left us at the reception counter on the second floor.

She said to me, "You have any idea why you're here?"

Figuring that nobody from the trailer park would be likely to contact the Lauderdale police, I shook my head.

"Kyle?" said Pintana again, but with a different inflection.

Cascadden came toward my chair, brandishing the file like a blackjack. Instead of hitting me with it, he slipped out an eight-by-ten photo, slapping the glossy on the desk in front of me the way an aggressive kid might play the game of "Go Fish."

I looked down at the photo, a head and shoulders shot of a man bare from the breastplate upward. You didn't need to see the tattoo of a spider to know it was Ford Walton, and you didn't need to have seen many dead bodies to know this was another one.

I looked back up at Cascadden.

"Well?" he said.

"I'll take a dozen wallet-sized."

He raised the Semper Fi forearm as though he was going to backhand me.

"Kyle!" from Pintana, and Cascadden dropped the pose before stepping back stiffly to his place at the wall.

I said, "Where was Walton killed?"

Pintana put a forefinger to her gleaming, even teeth. "Found him in an alley, warehouse district off Andrews Avenue. But, from postmortem lividity, the M.E. figures he was just dumped there."

Cascadden clearly didn't like the way his commander was sharing information with his prime suspect.

"How about cause of death?" I said.

"Another knife, back of the neck this time."

"You mean through the spinal cord?"

Cascadden said, "Just like they teach you in the Corps."

I looked at him. "I was Army."

"Don't matter, Beantown. That's where you could've learnt it."

Back to Pintana. "You wouldn't be telling me all this if you seriously liked me as the killer."

She tapped the forefinger's nail against her teeth. "We think it's kind of odd that a man supposedly attacks you with a knife after his girlfriend dies by one and then he ends up dead from one himself."

"But three different methods."

"Huh?" said Cascadden.

"Of using a knife. You told me Sundy Moran was slashed."

Pintana barely moved her lips. "Repeatedly."

"Well, when Walton came after me at the hotel pool, he used the slash move only as a feint. The rest of it was pure street fighter, up from under."

Cascadden grinned. "Maybe old Ford reckoned you'd be more trouble than a ninety-eight-pound whore."

Pintana blinked, but kept the lids down for longer than the level of light in the room required. "And Walton himself was killed by somebody who knew where to stick a man from behind."

"Or by somebody who wanted to give you that impression."

More tapping of her forefinger. "Let's hear it."

I came forward in the chair, resting my elbows on my knees. "There's no reason Ford Walton would attack me last night saying it was 'for Sundy.' I didn't know him from Adam, or him me. And I wasn't even in Florida when she was killed."

Cascadden said, "Lourdes, I—," but stopped when Pintana shook her head.

I stayed with her. "On the other hand, whoever did slash Moran maybe knew something about her life, and therefore could have known Walton, too."

"Or at least that he was Moran's lover."

Cascadden grunted. "Seems old Ford was rutting through the whole goddamned fam—"

"Kyle," said Pintana, in her "knock-it-off" tone.

I didn't bother to glance at him. "And our killer also could have known Walton liked to use a knife, and might even be blamed for both deaths."

Cascadden looked genuinely confused. "Both?"

I said, "Sundy Moran's and mine."

He didn't seem to appreciate my help.

Pintana said, "We got back the lab results on the residue from that knife you say Walton used on you."

"Moran's blood, too?"

"Don't worry, Beantown. You can't get AIDS from a goddamned blade."

Neither Pintana nor I bothered with Cascadden now. She said, "Moran's blood, too."

"So whoever killed her went to the trouble of keeping the murder weapon . . ."

". . . to plant on somebody else, let us close the case."

I worked it through the other things I'd found out. "I think I know who played the role of prospective client in that telephone call Malinda Dujong received."

Cascadden said, "What call?"

I stayed with the sergeant. "'Sundy' is a contraction of Sunday."

Pintana's eyes widened. "And 'Wendy' of Wednesday."

"Contractions?" said Cascadden.

I leaned back in my chair. "And after Sundy Moran did that little favor for someone, the person killed her, and then used Walton, figuring he'd be mad enough to take out whoever the real killer said had slashed his girlfriend."

"What call and what contractions?" said Cascadden again.

Pintana let her hand fall to the desktop. "Which meant Walton had to be killed—"

"—whether he finished me or not, because Walton could somehow link Moran's killer to her and me both."

Cascadden came off his wall now. "The hell are you two talking about?"

Pintana said, "Then why didn't our killer take out Walton right away?"

"Because maybe Walton couldn't link Moran's killer to her until the killer approached Walton to knife me."

Cascadden said, "Beantown, if you don't fucking answer my—"

"Kyle, shut up or get out."

Pintana didn't say it very loudly, but the edge in her voice would have cut cold steel.

Cascadden turned red as a beet just before stomping from the room and slamming the door behind him.

I looked back at Lourdes Pintana.

She said, "I think maybe we should go hear Malinda Dujong's telephone tape messages now."

From the shadow of her front door, Shirley Nole shaded bleary eyes with a hand.

I said, "We're sorry to bother you, Shirley, but this is Sergeant Pintana from the Fort Lauderdale Police, and she needs your key to Ms. Dujong's unit."

Nole drew in a breath. "Is Malinda . . . okay?"

Pintana said, "We don't know."

Head bowed, Nole said, "Just a second, please."

Everything looked the same as it had early that afternoon, except that the plants on Dujong's porch seemed to be faring a little better.

Nole had left us in favor of sleeping. Pintana said to me, "All right, where's this tape machine?"

I started walking toward the entertainment center. "Over here."

Pintana joined me, taking a pen and notepad from her big handbag. "Push PLAY."

I did.

There were about twenty messages. I didn't pay much attention to the specifics on any of them, though Pintana looked up at me each time my voice came over the tiny speaker. Jeanette Held accounted for half a dozen herself, each time sounding a little more frenzied. Another woman—Mi Soo, Dujong's tennis opponent—called twice, once about being stood up for the match, a second time concerned about whether "you maybe sick or something." Others were names and voices I didn't recognize, but the nature of all was pretty consistent: Malinda, where are you?

I waited until after the last message before saying, "I really don't like this."

Pintana pointed toward the machine. "Anything on there you want to tell me about?"

"Nothing you haven't already heard."

She put away her pad and pen. "Leave the tape as is. I'll get a forensics team over here, although"—Pintana glanced around the living and dining areas—"nothing looks wrong to me."

"And Dujong's car is gone, too, so given the security you saw at the gate, I'm guessing our friend waited until she was somewhere outside the club, where his taking her wouldn't be noticed."

"His?"

"I don't see any of the women I've met so far being this . . ."

"Elaborate?" said Pintana.

"As good a label as any."

"But still no idea on who might have taken Ms. Dujong?"

"Or where, for that matter."

Lourdes Pintana started for the door. "After we give back this key, I'll drive you to O'Hara's."

"I'm not much in the mood for music anymore."

A shake of her head, the honey-colored hair whisking her shoulders. "Maybe you really do have that concussion."

"Sorry?"

"I meant that I'd give you a lift so you could pick up your car."

"Oh."

Pintana pulled her unmarked sedan into the open space in front of my Achieva on Las Olas Boulevard. "The least I could do."

"After setting me up in there?"

I thought she'd keep her eyes forward until I got out, but

her head turned to me now. "I didn't intend it as a setup originally."

"Just after you found Ford Walton's body."

Pintana turned back to her windshield. "A suggestion?"

"What?"

"Get somebody to teach you how to recognize a compliment."

I closed my eyes, realized how tired I was. "Under other circumstances, I might be able to learn it from you."

Lourdes Pintana's voice said, "God didn't give me that kind of patience."

TWENTY

I woke up Friday morning at five-thirty, as though my body was punishing itself. Lying under and on the sheets made clammy by my own sweat and the hotel room's recycled air, I had a strobe memory of the dream I'd been having.

The churning sea again, the body sinking through the water below me, the dark hair billowing upward. But this time, when I finally dived down far enough to grasp the hair, the face that tipped upward belonged not to Nancy, but Malinda Dujong.

Which at least gave me a reason to get out of my bed and on with the day.

The fleet of parked cars had returned to Spi and Jeanette Held's house. When I pressed the button at the front door, though, no one came to answer it, despite the song chords chiming inside.

After two more tries, I walked around the side of the

house to see if I could raise anyone at the sliding glass doors to the kitchen. Once I came in sight of the pool, though, I spotted Buford Biggs, apparently asleep on a lounge chair. He wore a sweatshirt and sweatpants, reminding me of David Helides.

Except for being out in the morning air.

As my shoes hit the tiles of the pool apron, Biggs opened his eyes. When I reached him, he closed them again, a sour smile curdling his lips.

"Didn't see you at the slaughter last night, babe."

I said, "The slaughter?"

"Our gig at that place you caught us doing the sound check."

There was a patio chair close enough that I didn't have to move it. Sitting down, I said, "Things didn't go well."

"'Well'? Babe, thirty years ago, we would of got lynched, white boys included."

"What happened?"

"What didn't?" The eyes moved under his closed lids, like a dog dreaming fitfully. "Even after Ricky talk with the houseman, the mikes and the P.A. system for the audience still all fucked up. And it didn't help none that Spi figured he needed a toot on the drive over, Gordo not letting any of the lines go to waste." Biggs moved his head slowly, left-right-left. "The groups that come back, they don't do that nose shit no more. Their drug of choice be golf now." His head stopped moving. "And then Spi start ragging on the crowd, chase most of them out before we could do a second set."

"That go any better?"

"Some, but not enough." A sigh. "Problem wasn't just the P.A. and how we sound coming over it, though. Or even Spi and Gordo cruising the ozone. Uh-unh. Problem is, the new songs just plain suck, and ain't no sound system or musicians in the fucking world gonna save bad material."

"You sound pretty philosophical about it."

Biggs opened his eyes. "Philosophical?"

"For a man who told me how much he needed the money from Spiral making this effort."

"My best hope." The eyes grew troubled. "And Kalil's. But when hope die, you better off digging the grave soon's you can, and move on."

"To what?"

Buford Biggs closed his eyes again. "Remain to be seen, babe. That remain to be seen."

The sliding glass doors were unlocked, and inside the kitchen, things were quiet enough to hear a clock ticking. It felt as though the rest of the house's occupants were sleeping off the bad night before.

As I walked into the hall, I heard a cough from the direction of the living room. A sound I thought might belong to the person I'd come to see.

When I got to that open doorway, Jeanette Held was lying on the couch. She wore an oversized T-shirt with a Mickey Mouse pattern on it. From the way the bottom of the shirt clung to her, I didn't think she had anything on underneath.

Bowie, lying on the floor near her, growled as I said, "Jeanette?"

She started, then sat halfway up, thinking after a moment to tug the T-shirt farther down her legs. "What do you want?"

"I'm sorry to bother you, especially after hearing how badly things went at the club last night."

"Yeah," she said, swinging her feet down onto the floor and rubbing her eyes like a cranky child. "That's what I heard, too. But not before three in the morning."

"You weren't there?"

"What, at the big 'comeback' show? No, I couldn't see the point." Held left her eyes alone, raking at her reddish-blond hair with the left hand. "You haven't been around here enough to get a sense of just how shitty Spi's new stuff is. Believe me, I have. But even if I'd never heard a note or a word, Spi was happy to let me know how everything that went wrong last night was because of the 'fucking asshole on the control board,' or the 'fucking college pricks don't know what the Beach Boys and Beatles did for the music,' and so on till I couldn't stand him anymore."

"So you came down here to sleep."

"And he was probably too zipped on the snow to even notice I was gone." Held seemed to register something. "Hey, I asked you before, what're you doing here?"

"Can I sit somewhere, Jeanette?"

She collapsed back into the cushions of the couch, the T-shirt riding up, her seeming not to notice. "At this point, I guess I just don't fucking care."

Bowie watched me take a chair to the side of her. Once seated, I put my necessary question. "Have you heard from Malinda Dujong yet?"

"Malinda? No, and she can find somebody else to 'spiritually advise,' she doesn't even return my—"

"I was there."

Held looked confused. "Where?"

"At her condo, when the police and I played back her tape messages."

Confusion became concern. "The police?"

"Yes. No one seems to have seen or been contacted by Ms. Dujong for a couple of days now, and she's broken more appointments than just yours."

Held said, "Christ."

Bowie growled again.

"Jeanette, do you know anybody named 'Wendy'?"

"Wendy? I suppose I must have gone to school with some, but . . . nobody down here, if that's what you mean."

I nodded, feeling better about Pintana's and my speculation at the Homicide Unit. "Did Ms. Dujong ever mention the names 'Sundy Moran' or 'Ford Walton' to you?"

"Sunday . . . ?"

"Moran, a woman. And Ford Walton."

Held raked her hair again. "No. No, I don't think so."

"They're both dead, Moran close enough in time to your daughter that I thought they could be related. Now I more than think it."

"What . . . what did this Moran woman have to do with Very?"

I explained about Tommy O'Dell and Donna Moran.

"Christ. This wasn't bad enough as a nightmare, now I've got to worry about some dead guy Spi used to play with?"

"And write songs with, though I don't know whether that's another connection or not. What I suspect is that Veronica's killer used Sundy Moran to call Malinda Dujong as 'Wendy,' a friend of yours."

Confused now. "A friend of mine?"

"I think the killer thought of it as a play on words, Jeanette. Sundy like Sunday, Wendy like Wednesday."

"But what . . . what would this woman be calling Malinda for?"

"To keep Ms. Dujong away from the birthday party that day."

"Keep her . . . away?" More confused. "Why?"

"For the same reason that I'm afraid Ms. Dujong is missing. The killer somehow felt she could tie him to Veronica's death."

"Malinda?"

"Yes."

"And now . . ." Held shook her head. "And now you think something's happened to her?"

"I do."

"Well, I don't see how I can help you. Or Malinda. She never said anything about who killed my baby."

"Jeanette, once the person who murdered Veronica also killed Moran and Walton, I don't see a reason he'd have to silence Ms. Dujong, too."

"I . . ." A helpless shrug. "I don't follow you."

"Moran and Walton maybe could tie him to your daughter's death, but at most Ms. Dujong could recognize Moran's voice if the police ever had a lineup."

Held nodded, trying. "And if this Moran woman was dead, Malinda couldn't hear her voice as—what, the one calling her, you said?"

"Right."

"So?"

"So I think Ms. Dujong could have figured out who the killer was, even without being at the party to 'sense' something."

Held shivered, hugging herself across the chest as Bowie lifted his head and whuffed. "If Malinda had been there, Very might still be alive?"

Bad path to start down. "We'll never know that, Jeanette. But I think you may be able to help me."

Held sank back to confused. "How?"

"Ms. Dujong advised you, both before and after . . . the Colonel's birthday."

"Yes."

"If you can tell me how she goes about that, maybe I'll be able to see the way Ms. Dujong sensed who the killer was."

"You mean, like, how Malinda does what she did with me?"

"Right."

"Christ," said Held, losing it a little. "If I knew that, I wouldn't have needed her."

"Please, Jeanette. You're kind of the last hope for me."

"Hope." The woman in front of me seemed to regain some ground. "Not a lot of that going around anymore."

As I thought about Buford Biggs at the pool, Held said, "We're gonna go through all this shit, I'm gonna need coffee." She stood. "A bucket of it."

It smelled like Frangelico liqueur in the kitchen, but probably because Jeanette Held had emptied a coffee bag she called "Vanilla Hazelnut" into the fancy grinder.

Held brought a steaming mug with Disney's Goofy baked onto it over to the island counter, taking a stool diagonally across from me, as though the extra distance from the source of her current misery could ease the cumulative pain. I sat over a tall, cylindrical glass glazed the color of a Christmas wreath and filled with orange juice. Bowie lay on the tiles between us, chin on his white forepaws.

Held took a long, loud slurp from her mug. "How Malinda helps me."

"Or what she does, the process."

"Process." A shorter slurp, just as noisy. "At the beginning—months ago—I was just kind of thrashing around. My husband didn't seem too interested in our marriage thing anymore. My daughter was in her own world at school before Spi got his fucking brainstorm about bringing her into the band. I guess I was mired in the typical, 'I'm pushing forty and life sucks,' you know?"

"I think so."

Held set down her mug. "Well, Malinda was a real help

there. Cassie knew her from the club, said this spiritual-advice stuff had really helped some of her friends there. So, I decided to give it a try."

"What happened then, Jeanette?"

"First time Malinda came over, she had me talk to her in each room for like ten minutes."

"Each room of this house?"

"Right. I asked her why, and she said she'd tell me later. Well, an hour, hour and a half after we started, Malinda said, 'Let's go back to the living room.' And as soon as we did, I started to—I don't know exactly, but kind of . . . relax? It was like I suddenly felt that was where I ought to be talking to her. And when I said that, Malinda just smiled and told me she sensed it, too."

"Meaning Ms. Dujong was comfortable as well?"

"No, no. Meaning she could sense that I was comfortable there. And so we've had our little interludes in that room."

"'Interludes'?"

"Malinda's word for what the shrinks call 'sessions.'"

"What do these interludes involve?"

"Mostly talking." Held took some more coffee. "Sometimes we'll be sitting like we are now—across from each other, I mean, but facing each other, too. Other times, Malinda has me lie down on the couch—the way I was when you came in before."

"And still mostly talk?"

"Yes. Oh, maybe once in a while, Malinda will walk over and kneel down next to the couch, hold my hand. Or move her fingers in circles on my head."

"Circles?"

"Like so." Held put down her mug again, then brought both middle fingers up to her temples and massaged gently in a circular motion. "But mostly we just talk. Or I do."

"Ms. Dujong doesn't say much herself?"

"No." Held lowered her hands to the countertop. "Malinda's way of advising is more asking you to tell her how you feel, where the stress is coming from, and then finding out how you can vent it."

"The stress."

"Right. Exercise, diet, even confronting the people causing it."

"Confronting them, Jeanette?"

"Actually, that's my word." More coffee. "Malinda's always nudging me to talk things out with people, get their side and show them mine."

Pretty much common sense. "What's the spiritual part of it?"

"Not to keep things in. Malinda says it muffles the spirit, takes oxygen away from the flame we all have burning inside us. She's told me, you use your mouth to let out the bad feelings, the head and the heart won't burst."

"So, who have you talked with?"

A strange look. "Malinda."

"I mean, who were the people causing you stress?"

"Oh. Spi'd be number one."

I felt the ice under me getting a little thin, but I said, "Because?"

A resigned laugh. "He thinks he's this real liberated guy. 'Woodstock showed us the way,' you know? Well, I've seen videos of that, and it looked to me like everybody was just muddy and stoned. Besides, Spi's a throwback on the husband/wife thing. 'Stay at home, raise our daughter, and spend the rest of your time in the kitchen.' I told him, 'Wrong squaw, white man.'"

"Were there any other strains on your marriage, Jeanette?"

Another laugh, this one jaded. "What, you asking if Spi's been fucking around on me?"

Bowie seemed to sense the change in tone, but just lifted his head without making any sound.

I said, "If that's what you suspect."

Held started to drink more coffee, then spit it back into her mug. "Cold." She got up, went to the microwave, and put Goofy into the enclosure. As the timer beeped merrily along, Held turned back to me. "Look, Spi's been in a rock band since the time he was—what, fifteen? It's the only life he knows. Hell, it's probably the only life he thinks exists. Would Spi pork some teenybopper who came on to him at a club? Sure. That's how I met him, for Christ sake. But, was he ready to bail on Very and me for another 'tunnel of love'? No, especially not with Spiral's comeback and all."

"Wouldn't being separated from you make his life on the road . . . easier?"

"You mean, for fucking around? Maybe, but Very would have put the wood to him if she'd noticed, and he'd know that. She was my baby, but she enjoyed having power over people. And besides, Spi screws around too much, maybe the Colonel pulls out of the angel business, leaves us all high and dry."

The microwave binged a READY signal. Held didn't seem to notice.

I said, "Any other people beyond your husband who put stress on you?"

"Well, it's not the easiest thing in the world being in the same house as his brother."

"David."

"Yeah, David. I mean, he's like a ghost who's real, you know?"

"Meaning you're afraid of him?"

"Meaning he's just . . . there. Every time we'd go over to the Colonel's, you'd either see David ducking around a corner, or think you did."

I knew what she meant. "But no danger from him?"

"David? The only thing scared of him ought to be any bugs that try to eat his plants."

"Any other sources of stress, Jeanette?"

"On me?"

"Right."

She glanced out the sliding glass doors, toward where Buford Biggs was still lying on the lounge. "Try living with your husband and three other guys think they're twenty-one again. No." Held came back to me. "No, that's not fair. Ricky Queen's got his head on straight, even if he is queer. But at least he's got some maturity." A grunted laugh this time. "Think about that, will you? The most mature guy in the band is the youngest by a couple of decades."

"Have you talked about these people with Ms. Dujong?"

"Yeah. Well, not all at once."

"What do you mean, Jeanette?"

"I mean, I talk with her about whichever one's giving me the hardest time at the moment."

"And how often have you been seeing Ms. Dujong?"

"Before Very got . . ." Held cleared her throat. "Before, Malinda was coming over once a week for an hour or so." The binger sounded again, and Held finally seemed to remember her coffee, taking it from the microwave. "After Very . . . died, every day."

Expensive, even with a health . . . "Did your insurance cover that?"

Held blew on her coffee, apparently too hot now. "Spi's father did."

I guess I shouldn't have been surprised. "You said Ms. Dujong talks with you, and occasionally holds your hand or rubs your temples."

"Right, right."

"Anything else she does?"

A shrug. "Tells me stories sometimes."

"Stories?"

"About growing up in this little village in the Philippines, way out in the Pacific."

I thought back to Dujong's account of being paralyzed as a child. "What kind of stories, Jeanette?"

"Well, I don't know if they're real or not. More like fairy tales or—what does the Bible call them?"

"Parables?"

"Right, parables." A tentative slurp from the mug. "Those touchy-feely stories you'd hear in church about shepherds protecting their sheep or some girl's father arranging a wedding. Those kinds of stories."

"But Ms. Dujong's are from the Philippines."

"Yeah."

"Do you remember any?"

Another slurp. "There's a corker about her not being able to walk, but this witch doctor got the evil spirit to come out of her."

Having heard that one, I said, "Any others, Jeanette?"

"About this crab-monster-thing lives in a big, dark cave place, doesn't want anybody else to find out he's there, so he makes sure people get lost in it."

Knew that one, too. "Mrs.—"

"Or about these monks, and how the Spaniards tortured them."

"Monks?"

"Not Catholic ones. One of those weird religions from China that the Spaniards didn't like, although what people from Spain were doing all the way out in the Pacific Malinda's never said."

I decided to forgo a history lesson. "Anything else?"

Held seemed to return to the present, and not happily.

"What difference does any of this shit make? Fairy tales didn't kill my baby."

"Did Ms. Dujong act strangely before she failed to show up yesterday?"

"Strangely?" Now Held slammed her mug down onto the butcher block. "Ever since Veronica was killed, I've been lying in the living room like David the Zombie, losing the days. How am I supposed to judge strange?"

"Coffee. I gotta have some of that—"

Jeanette Held looked up at her husband, standing in the doorway, palms braced against each side of it. "There's probably enough left for you."

Spi Held had lost the wig and—judging from the way he lurched across the kitchen—most of his sense of balance as well. When he got to the coffeepot, his fist came down on the counter. "Mug."

"Try the dishwasher," said his wife.

He opened it, the door banging down so hard it nearly torqued into the tile floor. Pulling out one of the wire drawers, he found a mug with Pluto on its side and poured from the pot into it. The coffee overflowed, and Held dropped both mug and pot, screaming and running to the sink with his hand out as everything shattered on the floor.

Bowie bolted from the room, though more noise-frightened than coffee-scalded, I thought. Both Helds were cursing so hard, loud, and fast that you almost couldn't understand them.

Holding his hand under the water now running from the faucet, Spi Held finally overrode his wife. "I don't give a fuck about your fucking pot, your fucking mug, or the fucking floor. This is my fucking career, if I'm burned so bad I can't play."

"Your fucking career? What career? Last night—or *par-*

don me, five fucking hours ago—you said your fucking career was over."

"Get out!"

Jeanette Held slid off the stool, walking stiffly on her bare heels around the puddles of coffee, the shards of porcelain and glass. "Fuck you, and clean this up before Bowie comes back in and cuts himself."

"He can fucking slit his wrists with it, all I care."

Spi Held watched his wife until she disappeared into the corridor. He shook out his hand before shutting off the water and turning around. "And what the fuck are you doing?"

"Same thing I've always been."

A woozy grin. "Playing surrogate son?"

"What?"

Held reached for a dish towel. "Hey, don't go dumb on me, okay? The great 'Colonel Helides' was always off playing soldier with guys like you instead of home playing daddy with me. Or even fucking David. Then, when I told my brother the truth about how he killed Mom by being born, my 'hero' father throws me out, cuts me off without a dime. And if I let 'the Colonel' know I don't care how much he wants to play daddy now that he's old and sick. . . ."

I kept my temper as Held began wrapping the towel around his hand.

". . . the bastard'll cut me off again, especially with Very gone."

"Maybe not, if I can figure out who killed her."

"Yeah, well." Held looking up from his first-aid. "I don't see you've done anything more than the cops. Those pigs may suck, but at least they work for free."

"Like it's your money paying my bill?"

Held stared at me, a shadow of the drug haze creeping back. "Someday, maybe."

Stupid thing to say if he was the one who tried to trigger a terminal attack in his ailing father. "You ever speak with Malinda Dujong about Veronica's murder?"

"Yeah." Held finished with the dish towel. "I told her my fucking wife wasn't crazy enough before this, she's probably gonna crack like a fucking egg over it, so keep an eye on her."

"Did Dujong tell you anything?"

"Me? I don't need any of her oriental New Age shit."

"I didn't necessarily mean advice. Maybe more information."

"About what?" said Held.

"Your daughter's death."

"Very's . . . ?" Both hands dropped to his side. "The fuck could Malinda know about that?"

"I'm sorry?"

"She wasn't even there that day, man. What could Malinda tell you about Very getting drowned?"

That's when it occurred to me. The way I could maybe—

Held took a step toward my stool. "I said, what could Malinda—"

I got up and turned away from him. "I wasn't there either, but I've learned a lot about it."

As I went back through the sliding glass door, Held yelled, "Learned what?"

Leaving the door open so that Spi Held could follow me if he wanted, I stepped onto the patio. Instead, he stamped across the kitchen and rammed the door shut so hard, I thought its glass would shatter like his wife's coffeepot.

From the lounge, Buford Biggs watched me. Quietly, he said, "You not be brightening anybody's morning, babe."

"Just my own."

"What you find out, make Spi go bullshit like that?"

"The same thing Malinda Dujong did. And I finally know how to use it."

As I started walking away from him, Buford Biggs said, "What you talking about, babe?"

I didn't answer him this time.

Generally, I prefer to think things through more thoroughly before setting any kind of trap. Be a little more certain that the message would get circulated among all the people I'd want to have hear it. But the timing seemed just right, and if I didn't seize the moment, I thought another might not come along.

I also thought that the first person out of the Held house would be the one.

Drawing the Olds Achieva even with a sprawling shade tree three blocks away, I pressed all four window buttons to get some natural cross-vent. Then I waited, using the rearview mirror to watch the driveway behind me as I went over my logic.

Somebody decides to kill Veronica Held for a motive I can't isolate. The same somebody figures that the Colonel's birthday party would bring together a wide array of potential suspects to deflect attention from that motive. But the killer also has some fear—maybe founded, maybe not—that if Malinda Dujong were at the party, the "spiritual advisor" would be able to "sense" why Veronica might be a target. So the killer enlists or threatens Sundy Moran, a woman with a blood connection to Spiral from the old days, to call Dujong and thereby keep her away from the Skipper's house. Moran can tie the killer to that call, though, so Moran has to die as well. And, once she does, Dujong couldn't pick her out of a voice lineup.

Only then Nicolas Helides brings me into it. I start rattling cages on Tuesday into Wednesday, and Moran's boyfriend

Ford Walton comes visiting with a knife on Wednesday night, apparently believing I murdered his girlfriend. The killer must have given him my name, and that knife as well, because it had Moran's blood on it. Due to my ability to identify Walton, though, and the police lab's ability to match his prints on the knife used to kill Moran, Walton becomes a liability, too. And I might have softened him up enough for the killer to finish him, dumping his body in that warehouse district.

Which is where Dujong comes back into it. Somehow, she can link the killer to Veronica Held's death, despite the elimination of both Moran and Walton as potential witnesses. So the killer takes Dujong, too.

But maybe, just maybe, hasn't killed her. There's no corpse yet, and the murderer might keep Malinda Dujong alive to find out how she discovered the link to Veronica's death. Especially if word gets back that a hired investigator has stumbled onto the same link himself.

Of course, the only way that gambit could work is if it flushed the killer from the woodline. By targeting me as the next risk to that person getting away with murder.

TWENTY—ONE

Ten minutes turned into twenty, and twenty into thirty, but nobody left the Held house, either by car or on foot. I decided to give it another half hour, using the cell phone to call the answering service for my Boston office. There were a dozen condolence messages about Nancy and a few regarding cases up there. I returned only the business ones. The final message was from Drew Lynch, a simple, "Please call us when you get a chance."

I wasn't up to talking with Nancy's landlord either. Whatever he wanted, it could wait till I went back north.

After pushing the END button on the cellular, I checked my watch. Seventy minutes since I'd planted the seed with Spi Held and Buford Biggs.

I started the Achieva again and headed toward the southeast quadrant of Fort Lauderdale.

"You're always in," I said.

Mitch Eisen looked up at me from the big judge's chair as he slid a pair of earphones down over his jawbone, giving himself a high-tech necklace. "What?"

I pointed to the cord running back to some stereo equipment. "Last night's show?"

"Last . . . ?" He fingered the cord. "Oh, you mean the Alamo?"

"I thought the name of the place was—"

"Not the name. The metaphor."

"That bad?"

"Worse. At least the Mexicans had the decency to kill everybody they found there. Spiral, on the other hand, lives to suck another day."

I took a chair, asking a question I'd already heard answered. "Anything specific?"

"What, you mean about the band stinking the place out?"

"Yes."

"No. No, we're talking a real *team* effort. Gordo was high, Buford was nervous, and the kid, Ricky, tried for most of the first set, then just mailed in the second. But Spi was the real star of the show. Pissing off the houseman about the P.A., dissing the audience when they didn't leap to their feet in idolatrous enthusiasm, and sniffling so bad that you'd think he'd somehow figured out a way to snort a line off his microphone."

"So where does that leave them?"

"Dead in the water, far as doing warm-ups in this town." Eisen settled his narrow shoulders back into the chair. "Of course, if his old man's still willing to play Daddy Warbucks—hey, that's kind of clever."

"What is?"

"The Daddy Warbucks thing. I mean, his father was in Vietnam, right, and he did make a lot of money afterwards, so the name kind of—"

"Different name."

"Different?"

"Malinda Dujong."

Eisen's hair plugs did their march forward. "I didn't see her last night."

"Last night."

"At the gig. Shit, even Jeanette didn't bother to show, which kind of tells you her view of the situation."

"Mitch?"

"Yeah?"

"I know what she found out."

Another hair maneuver. "What Jeanette found out about what?"

"Not Mrs. Held. Ms. Dujong."

"Malinda? I doubt she ever even heard Spiral practice. She wasn't into music that I could tell."

Wasn't. "There a reason you used the past tense, Mitch?"

"The past tense?"

"In talking about Ms. Dujong."

"I don't even know what *you're* talking about." Eisen shrugged. "Okay, I grant you, Malinda might have heard them out at Spi's house, although that studio there is fucking state-of-the-art, accoustically speaking."

"Meaning soundproof."

"Right. Which is why I didn't think Malinda would've—"

"I'm talking more about what she found out regarding the murder of Veronica Held."

Eisen stopped, started to say something, then stopped again before, "We negotiating here or what?"

"Maybe."

He seemed to relax a little, as though the conversation had returned to more familiar ground. "Hey, Cuddy, granted I told you I could use any information like that. But, with Spiral going into the toilet last night, I don't know that who killed Very's going to be worth a bonus for you anymore."

A great act on something he'd anticipated, or maybe just innocence. "Well, give me a call if you change your mind on it."

"Sure thing. Hey, and good luck with the bad guy, huh?"

I'd parked outside the Mail Boxes, Etc., next to Mitch Eisen's office. Sitting in the Achieva, I watched the doorway to his building. In the lot to my right, I could also see about half of his orange-and-cream Corvette.

An hour later, I was still seeing it.

Thirty minutes after that, I turned the key in my ignition and headed for the next station down the line.

"Hello?"

Holding the cell phone, I said from the driver's seat, "Mr. Tranh, John Cuddy."

"I am quite busy at the—"

"I'll be there by one-fifteen."

"That is impossible for—"

"The Colonel will want to hear what I have to say, and I think you will, too."

No reply now.

I said, "See you shortly," before clicking off.

As he closed the gate behind my car, Umberto Reyes said, "The Colonel wants me to call him as soon as you arrive."

I waited until Reyes drew even with my window again. "Don't you always?"

"Always?"

"Call him about arriving guests who don't live here."

Reyes colored under the blond crew cut. "Yes, I do. What I meant was, he wants to be the first person you speak to, I think."

"Who else is in the house right now?"

"Mrs. Helides, Mr. Tranh, and my sister, Delgis."

"David Helides?"

"He left."

"How long ago?"

"An hour, maybe."

"To go where?"

Umberto Reyes turned toward his gazebo. "Mr. Helides never says."

"Lieutenant, you've caused quite a stir."

Nicolas Helides kept his mangled voice as steady as possible, but his eyes were afire. He sat in the den, blanket over his legs, brace within easy reach. Next to him stood Duy Tranh, wearing a black shirt and black pants outfit. Popular fashion today, though regardless of the race of the person wearing the clothes, they always remind me of the pajamas the Vietcong used as battle fatigues.

I said, "Mr. Tranh, I'm glad you could join us."

The Skipper didn't look up at him. "At your suggestion, Lieutenant." Then a different tone. "My son tells me you've discovered something important about Veronica's death."

"Your son?"

"Spiro. He called me several hours ago, claiming that you told him something you hadn't yet told your client."

A little edge there. "Colonel, it's a lead I've been developing for a while, but it just fell into place this morning."

"What is it?" the edge growing sharper.

Before I could answer, there was a knock at the door.

Helides called out, "Yes?"

Delgis Reyes opened the door with one hand while balancing a tray with what looked like three lemonades in the other. She hesitated, maybe sensing the tension in the air.

Using a gentler tone, the Skipper said, "Delgis, please come in."

As Reyes nodded shyly and moved toward us, I addressed Helides and Tranh. "I've found out what Malinda Dujong did."

Tranh started to speak, but the Skipper rode over him. "Did to whom?"

I shook my head. "No, sir, what she herself found out."

"About—Oh, thank you, Delgis," accepting a glass from her. Tranh and I did the same. As Reyes left us, Helides tilted his mouth to the left and took a sip of his lemonade, swallowing carefully before saying to me, "Found out about what?"

I was speaking with the Skipper, but watching Tranh. No reactions visible.

"Your granddaughter's death," I said.

Nicolas Helides drew in a breath. "Then let's have it."

"I can't, Colonel."

A jump in his eyes, like I'd just slapped him across the cheek. "I . . . I couldn't have heard you right just now, Lieutenant."

I looked up at Tranh, his eyes a little wider as he glanced down first at his employer, then stared at me.

"Sir, what I've found out is still just logic until I can put some proof to it, but I'll have that evidence by tomorrow."

"Mother *Goose!*" Helides tried to bring himself under control. "Then why did you come to my son with the information this morning?"

"Because it was something he said that closed the circle."

"The circle?"

"Of the logic, Colonel."

Helides moved his good hand up to the functioning side of his face. "Lieutenant, are you all right?"

"I believe so, sir."

"I mean"—the hand went back down to his lap—"that concussion in the fight you had with . . . His name again?"

"Ford Walton."

"Walton, yes. Are you sure you're now thinking clearly?"

"Reasonably, but I'm not absolutely certain. Which is another reason I want hard evidence before I spell out anything further."

Duy Tranh spoke for the first time. "If you are concerned about evidence, Mr. Cuddy, perhaps you should consult with a lawyer."

"I plan to call Justo Vega."

"If you can't reach him," said Nicolas Helides in an iron voice, "he'll be here tonight by seven, and so should you."

"Mr. Cuddy, wait!"

In the corridor outside the den, I turned around as Duy Tranh closed the door behind him. After six determined strides, he reached me.

"I have things to do, Mr. Tranh."

"In addition to what you already have done to the Colonel?"

"What *I've* done to him?"

An angry flash from the black irises. "He loved his granddaughter, for all her faults. And ever since Veronica's death, he has lived for the moment someone will bring him her killer. But just now, in that room, you . . . teased him."

"How do you mean?"

"I mean just what I said! The Colonel is a proud old man with one remaining, defining goal. And you play games with that, and with his feelings. Even in front of a house servant like Delgis."

An awfully good deflection, but then, I'd come to believe that Duy Tranh was a very clever player. "I'm sorry if it came off that way. Not every investigation progresses in a direct, linear—"

"I am not talking about your methods of investigation. I am talking about the spirit of an elder whom you serve in one way and I serve in others. That spirit must be nurtured, not . . . toyed with."

"Mr. Tranh, take this one to the bank: I'm not toying with anyone involved in Veronica Held's murder."

"God, talk about the bad nickel."

I watched Cassandra Helides come around the opposite corner at the back of the house. She wore a thong bikini bottom and not much more on top, the implants she'd mentioned standing unnaturally forthright under the faux-leopard fabric.

"Mrs. Helides."

She stopped two feet in front of me when, given that we were outdoors and not sharing a secret, three feet would have felt more comfortable. But then, I didn't think Helides was trying to make me feel comfortable.

Her left thumb and forefinger went up to the spaghetti strap of material running from her shoulder toward her breast. Then the fingers slid down the strap like a firefighter going down a pole. "I figured I missed you."

"Missed me?" I said.

"Coming here. After Spi called in a huff a couple hours ago, I waited to see you, but I had an appointment that I don't like to miss."

"At the tennis club."

A saucy smile. "At the spa, actually." The right hand stroked her thigh as she gracefully shimmied toward the grass, then back up again, the hand following suit. "Wax job. Go ahead, feel. Smooth as silk."

"I'll take your word for it."

"Your loss." Saucy gave way to coy. "So, what did you find out about Very, our little dead lesbo?"

"The same thing Malinda Dujong did."

"The fortune-teller? What could she know about it?"

"I thought you were the one who recommended her to Jeanette Held?"

"I did." Helides changed hands and straps, but the effect was the same. "A couple of girls I know at the club swore by her. And I even talked with Malinda a few times myself."

"Until?"

"Until she told me things I didn't need to hear."

"For instance?"

The left hand came over to me, its fingers doing the same thing they had been on her bikini. "That I should 'close' one chapter of my life and 'open' another. Love 'people,' not 'things.'"

"Meaning?"

"Meaning turn my back on a fortune and instead settle for short money that wouldn't last me five years." Her fingers pinched a little, playfully so far, urgently soon. "I've waited this long for the lottery, though, I can wait a little longer."

"For your husband to die."

"For nature to take its courts."

I stayed on the point. "Like it did with Veronica Held?"

Cassandra Helides withdrew her hand. "Mister, you didn't

know Very. I did. And given the way she acted, I'd say her getting killed was pretty natural." She turned and walked toward
the back door, each buttock rolling independent of the other
in her caricature of a showgirl. Reaching for the handle,
Cassandra Helides glanced back at me. "Nature's a fucking
dangerous place to live, you know?"

I didn't stay to watch her climb the steps.

One of the houses down the street from the Skipper's had the
look of a family off on vacation, though if somebody lived on
the Isle of Athens, it was kind of hard to see how they could
improve their recreational hand by traveling somewhere else.
I backed the Achieva into the driveway far enough that its
snout became hidden by some large, red-blossomed bushes.

I waited only thirteen minutes this time before
Cassandra Helides blew by in shades and a baseball cap,
the Porsche Boxster probably hitting sixty before I could
start after it.

I nearly lost her three times.

Once was thanks to a delivery truck that Helides almost
sideswiped but that pulled out after the Porsche and blocked
my view of it. I could hear the driver's curses, though, even
from fifty feet back and over his engine and mine. The second was when she came within a hair's breadth of clocking a
couple of kids on skateboards, other cars swerving to avoid the
chain reaction she'd set in motion. The third time was
another two miles on, when Helides started taking side streets
in a quartering way northwest. At first I thought she'd spotted
me, then I realized where we were. Chalking up her evasive
tactics more to a shortcut that avoided traffic lights, I arrived
at the gate of the tennis club just as her car bounced over the
most distant speed bump.

A different guard asked if he could help me. This one

was African-American and very polite, his nametag reading
BENJAMIN.

"I'm here to see Shirley Nole."

"And your name, please?"

"John Cuddy."

Benjamin dialed, waited, and spoke into the telephone.
Then he turned to me. "Ms. Nole wants you to tell me who
you were here with last time."

Cautious lady. "Police Sergeant Lourdes Pintana."

A nod as Benjamin went back to the receiver, and
another nod as he hung up. "You know her building, sir?"

"I do, yes."

. . .

"I don't, no."

We were sitting in Nole's apartment, and I'd just asked
her if she knew of any special relationship between
Cassandra Helides and Malinda Dujong.

"Shirley, how about between Cornel Radescu and Ms.
Dujong?"

"No. I mean, you say 'special,' and maybe that's what's
throwing me. We all know each other here, but Malinda's
so much better than Cassie, and Cornel's so much better
than Malinda that they'd never play together."

"Actually, I was looking for any relationships beyond
tennis."

Nole seemed troubled.

I said, "I already know about Mrs. Helides and Mr.
Radescu."

"Then what don't you know that you think I could tell
you?"

"Any arguments, or the opposite. Did Ms. Dujong ever
mention Mrs. Helides to you, that sort of thing."

"Well, no. I mean, nothing special, the way I think you
mean. But maybe you should talk with Mi Soo."

"Malinda's tennis partner?"

"Opponent, more." Shirley Nole relaxed just a little. "They're still young enough to play singles."

"You want a drink?"

"Iced tea would be great."

At the patio tiki bar, Mi Soo Temkin put in my order and hers, the male bartender saying, "You have time to let me brew some fresh?"

I nodded from my stool, and Temkin said from hers, "Fresh, Joe, thanks."

Then she tilted the sun visor back on her forehead. Early thirties and Asian, Temkin wore a conservative swimsuit under a short robe. I wouldn't have known how tan she was except for her bare feet, which were pale enough where anklet tennis socks must cover that they reminded me of the white paws on the Helds' Australian shepherd.

Temkin said, "Shirley tell me about you trying to find where Malinda is."

"Any ideas?"

"I don't see her for maybe three days now. I worry, because Malinda never break a match with me unless she call first."

"Any problems between Ms. Dujong and Mr. Radescu?"

"Cornel? Why he have problem? He have life of Riley."

I must have looked at her oddly.

Temkin smiled knowingly. "I too young for those shows, but in Korea, I learn English from Americans at Army base. I never read Shakespeare except in my language, but television, movies, I could be on *Jeopardy* game."

"So, no problems between—"

"—Malinda and Cornel? No, I think she tell me."

"How about Ms. Dujong and Mrs. Helides?"

"Ah, different story. I don't think they give each other Christmas presents."

"Do you know why?"

"I ask Malinda once. She tell me, Cassandra not like the way Very—her granddaughter—behave here sometimes. Cassandra think maybe Malinda tell her bad things."

"That Ms. Dujong told Veronica Held bad things?"

"Yes, but not about Cassandra. More like, advice for life."

"Advice for Veronica's life?"

A nod as our iced teas arrived in plastic beer cups. "I think Very talk to Malinda, ask her questions."

"About what?"

Temkin tried her drink, then reached for a sugar packet. "Malinda never say. She is professional, not tell on her clients."

"Veronica was a client of Ms. Dujong?"

A shrug as Mi Soo Temkin stirred in some sweetener. "That was word Malinda use."

When Cornel Radescu opened the door to his unit, I said, "No need to get me a drink. I brought my own."

He stared down at what was left of my iced tea, then back up at me. Radescu wore a dirty T-shirt and raggedy shorts. There was plaster dust in his long black hair, the kitchen behind and over his shoulder all torn up.

I said, "Renovating?"

"What do you want?"

A familiar voice behind him said, "Me, probably."

Radescu's eyes closed for just a second. "Cassie, I told you not—"

"Oh, Cornel, the bastard's a detective. He can probably sense I'm here, just like Malinda can."

I spoke to Radescu. "May I come in?"

He stared at me a little more, his features so blank I really didn't know what answer he'd give. "Why not? It seems to be the way of my life now."

The living room beyond the kitchen was a lot bigger than the one in Malinda Dujong's place. I didn't see any bedrooms, though there was a four-by-four hole in the ceiling that a man with an eight-foot vertical leap could have jumped through.

"Cornel's putting in a spiral staircase." Cassandra Helides had taken off her sunglasses, but was still wearing the ball cap. And, at least so far, a sleeveless mauve pullover and skin-tight white slacks. Rolling her shoulders against the back of the sofa in basically the same way she'd rolled her rump at the back of her house, she said, "Very romantic, don't you think?"

I took a barrel chair that contrasted nicely with the colors of the other furniture. Radescu stayed on his feet.

"Mrs. Helides, you mentioned Malinda Dujong."

"Yeah. That's your flavor of the day, right? I mean, when that call from Spi came in this morning, you'd have thought Nick finally got the word that those Vietdongs had won."

Only half-correcting her, I said, "They did win."

A flip of her hands. "Then whoever."

Radescu said, "You asked us yesterday after my match about Malinda. Now everyone around the clubhouse says she is missing."

"So far as we can tell, nobody's heard from her since sometime on Wednesday."

"We?"

"The police are involved, too."

Helides started doing leg lifts, knees locked, toes pointed toward the hole in the ceiling. "I wouldn't worry about the cops. They still can't figure out who dunked our little Very, and there weren't more than a dozen of us in the house that day."

I waited a bit before saying, "You don't seem worried about Ms. Dujong, either."

"Hey, like I told you back on the Isle, I didn't have much use for her advice, so I'm not exactly holding my breath till you find out what happened to her."

"What makes you think anything has?"

Dropping the leg lifts, Helides began rotating her feet while keeping the calves stationary. "The way you keep coming back here." The coy smile. "Unless it's just to see me?"

Radescu said, "Only Mr. John Cuddy comes to this unit, not yours." Then, in my direction, "What is it that you want, really?"

"To know who killed Veronica Held, and what's happened to Malinda Dujong."

"Very died five, six miles from here, and Malinda was not even at the party that day."

"But a lot of other people were," I said, "and maybe one of them was worried that Ms. Dujong would find out something."

"What?"

"The same thing I have."

Radescu stared at me searchingly, then finally smiled. "You're bluffing."

"Why would I?"

A broader smile. "He's bluffing, Cassie."

From the sofa, Helides said, "How would you know?"

"I crawl on my belly under the guns of border soldiers, I know when somebody can shoot you and when they can't." Radescu turned back to me. "And you don't have any bullets in your gun."

"We'll find out tomorrow."

A cloud came over Radescu's eyes. "Tomorrow?"

"When I'm going to get the hard evidence to back up what I've already figured out."

"It's still a bluff," but without the smile now.

"You'll be the first to know."

As I walked toward his door, I could hear Cassandra Helides say behind me, "Hey, Malinda's so into New Age shit, maybe she can just beam you a message from her brain."

There was a parking lot for some charitable organization fifty yards west of the tennis club's gate. A dozen or so people were moving boxes and clothes from car trunks and pickup trucks into a building. Most of the people were black, one white and one Latino. Two of the blacks and the Latino asked if I needed help carrying anything in for the "drive." I said, thanks but no, I was just waiting for someone to come back out.

And, in a way, I was.

Traffic ebbed and flowed through the club entrance, but I knew Radescu's Checker and Cassandra Helides's Porsche. I also figured her boyfriend would be pretty distinctive behind the wheel of any vehicle, even at my distance from the gate.

At least, that's what I figured.

After two hours, neither showed. I told myself I'd give it another.

When my watch read 6:30, I started the Achieva and headed back toward the Isle of Athens.

The January sun was long down, so sitting outside didn't seem a viable option. I was getting pretty tired of the den, but Nicolas Helides seemed to prefer it over his living room. And, given that latter area was where he'd last seen his granddaughter alive—despite what she'd been singing to him about, and how—I could understand the preference.

What I couldn't understand was Justo.

From his signature chair, the Skipper looked at a clock on the big desk for maybe the third time in five minutes. Seven-forty-five P.M. now, the news from it not getting any better.

Helides said, "I have never known Lieutenant Vega to be late."

Duy Tranh nodded from the corner of the couch, sitting himself for a change, though not looking particularly comfortable. "At least without calling."

At seven-fifty, I said, "You have Justo's phone number handy?"

Tranh stood up. "Office, home, or cellular?"

I locked my eyes on his. "We'll try all three."

The answering service at Justo's office told me he was gone for the day to an appointment and not reachable. His cellular number rang four times, then just forwarded to the service again. I dialed the home one and drew a familiar voice answering in Spanish.

"Pepe?"

"Who is this, please?"

"John Cuddy."

"Hey, Mr. Whatever, how you doing?"

"I'm doing fine, but we've been waiting for Justo at the Colonel's house for nearly an hour."

Very quietly, Pepe said, "Mr. Vega, he tell me he suppose to be there at like seven."

"You weren't driving him?"

"No. He don't like it so much when one of us not with his wife and little kids in the nighttime."

"And you haven't heard from him?"

A woman's voice spoke some Spanish in the background, Pepe answering her briefly with a laugh in his voice. Then he said into the phone, "Give to me your number. I cannot talk so easy here."

TWENTY-TWO

I was still exchanging stares with Nicolas Helides and Duy Tranh when the phone rang a minute later. I picked it up, Pepe speaking before I could.

"Talk to me about what you know, man."

I told him the same things about Justo that he'd heard in my call a minute before.

Pepe said, "Mr. Vega, he no tell you he going anyplace else?"

"No."

Only silence from his end.

"Pepe?"

"I got to think, man."

His voice was tight, like a dog wheezing while straining against a leash. When Pepe came back, though, his tone was more resigned. "Mr. Vega, he worry about the *comunistas* coming after him. Always he say to me, 'Pepe, I am gone with no reason, this is what you do.'"

"I don't see how Cuba could be—"

"Mr. Vega say, 'Pepe, you take my wife and my children, and you go to this place, soon as you can.'"

"Where, Pepe?"

"I no can tell you, man."

"Pepe—"

"No!" The tightness in his voice again. "Mr. Vega, he say I don't tell nobody."

"Pepe, listen to me, okay? I don't know what's happened to Justo, but another person involved in this case has also disappeared, and so I—"

"Man, you hear what I saying to you? Mr. Vega tell me to do something, I do it."

I remembered both Justo and Pepe making a point of that. "I'm not trying to—"

"And you hear something else, too. You got to find Mr. Vega, man."

"Pepe—"

"I do what Mr. Vega say, you do what I say."

That last was spoken with the resonance of a blood oath. "Is there anything . . ." But then I stopped, realizing that Pepe had broken the connection.

"Lieutenant?"

Hanging up, I looked over to the Skipper. "Pepe doesn't know where Justo is."

Tranh said, "What about the rest of your conversation with him?"

"Instructions that Justo gave him for security."

Helides shook his head. "And no help to us."

"I'm afraid not."

Now the Skipper glanced up at Tranh, who was looking only at me. "Duy?"

No reaction.

"Duy."

Tranh looked down now.

Helides said, "Do you have any ideas?"

"Just one, Colonel."

"What is it?"

Duy Tranh now looked back over at me. "That Mr. Cuddy seems to have made a bad situation worse."

* * *

"In a way," I said, "he's right."

Tranh had left us in the den, the Skipper asking me to pour him a scotch, straight up. As I extended the glass toward his chair, he said, "In what way, Lieutenant?"

I sat down across from Helides. "When I got here Tuesday afternoon, only two people were dead, your grand-daughter and Sundy Moran. Since then, Ford Walton's joined them. And now probably Malinda Dujong, and possibly even Justo as well."

The Skipper stopped the scotch before it reached his chin. "You're not certain Malinda is dead?"

"No," and I told him why I'd run the bluff on his son and the others.

A suckling sound as Helides tipped the glass toward the good side of his mouth. "So, you thought spreading the word that you'd discovered what Malinda had found out might spook our killer."

"Into going where he's holding her."

"Or making him come after you."

I nodded, and the Skipper nodded back.

"Colonel, anything at all that you haven't told me?"

His eyes showed over the rim of the glass. "About Malinda?"

"About anything at all."

Helides rested the drink on the arm of his chair. As I was about to ask him if he was all right, the Skipper said, "After I lost Nina—my first wife—I didn't go to any kind of psychotherapist. Or 'head-shrinker,' as I thought of them in those days. Then, when David's condition was . . . obvious, I couldn't see that the doctors he saw helped him much. Even Henry Forbes, who's top-notch in his profession. But after Veronica a . . . was killed, I asked Malinda if she'd speak to me."

"Malinda?"

"Yes. Through my . . . grief, I could see that she was helping Jeanette. Had helped her, even before . . . that day, in coping with Spiro and his lifestyle."

"So you thought Ms. Dujong might be able to help you as well?"

A slow exhalation. "At that point, Lieutenant, I couldn't see what harm it could do."

When the Skipper didn't continue, I said, "What did you two talk about?"

"My dreams."

He spoke the phrase so quickly, I almost missed it. "Your dreams?"

"Oh, not what happens when I sleep at night." A pause. "If I sleep. No, more what I had hoped for in my life. The grand strategy—my words, not hers."

"Sir, I don't mean to pry, but—"

"Prying is what I've asked you to do."

Almost a smile from him.

"Essentially," I said.

Helides suckled some more scotch. "My dreams, Lieutenant, were to grow old with Nina and have a son in Spiro that we could be proud of. Well, I think now my personality was more suited to being a commander than a father. It never really registered with me that you couldn't give orders—even good ones—to your son and still expect him to respect you. So I began to focus on the new baby God was about to give us. Then, when David arrived and Nina . . . died, I foreshortened those dreams considerably. Did what I could for David in terms of treatment, especially after Spiro ran out on us. Watched from a distance as my older son became more and more successful with his music. And all the while, I tried to keep my younger son out of the very institutions every well-meaning friend told me I should relegate him to. A few years later, after Spiro frittered away his success and crashed his life to boot, I kept him afloat financially. With Mitch Eisen's complicity, of course."

"I don't understand, sir."

Now an actual smile, small but genuine. "I asked Eisen to approach music halls, give Spiro a place to play."

I turned that over. "With you footing the bill."

"The only way. Eisen told Spiro that because of Spiral's former status, the smaller clubs were willing to pay a premium. Despite apparently poor performances and sparse audiences."

"Colonel, did your son ever find out?"

"That I was paying his . . . salary, so to speak?"

"Yes."

"Eisen assured me not. But, who really knows?" Another slow exhalation. "Nina and I had such . . . expectations for our sons. The first had the ability, but circumstances—what I've told you plus my being away at the wrong times and the unpopularity of our war—pretty well scuttled Spiro's turning out as I had dreamed. And David . . . Well, some life in *this* home is better than any life in *a* home, don't you think?"

"Yes." I hesitated, then, "And you told Ms. Dujong about all these feelings?"

"I did. Over three or four sessions. Sorry, that would be Henry's phrase for them. Malinda spoke of them more as 'interludes.'"

Jeanette Held had used the same phrase. "What would Ms. Dujong do?"

"Work me through my grieving. Give me a chance to meditate on what had happened before, what dreams had already not come true."

"The frying pan over the fire."

"Basically." Some more scotch. "And she did help. In fact, I suggested she work with David, too."

"David?"

"Oh, without telling Henry, of course. And without supplanting him, either. I can't imagine what my son would be like without those mood-leveling drugs. No, Malinda would be more a *supplement* to what Henry could provide David, an additional window into his situation."

As the Skipper drank again, I said, "Did Ms. Dujong ever speak with your son?"

"I don't think so." A cough that at first I thought came from some scotch going down the wrong pipe, but what I then realized was the verge of a laugh. "At least, she never sent me a bill for it."

After Colonel Helides went off to bed, I stayed in the den and on his telephone, confirming through a supervisor at the answering service that Justo Vega had not checked for his messages. I tried the house in Miami again, but got nothing.

Not a person, not a machine.

I pressed the plunger and dialed Sergeant Lourdes Pintana's cell-phone number. On the third ring, I heard a forwarding pickup and "This is Detective Kyle Cascadden."

Give it a shot anyway. "Sergeant Pintana, please."

"Out of the office." Then about enough time for the light to dawn before, "Beantown, that you?"

"Yes. I need to speak with her."

"Well, boy," the sneer coming across the wire. "I guess you're gonna have to settle for me."

"This is serious, Cascadden."

"So am I. Talk, or I'll go back to my dinner here."

Not much choice. "You know Malinda Dujong is missing?"

"Who?"

I counted to three. "The woman who was counseling Jeanette Held."

"Oh, right, right. That Chinese girl."

"Filipina."

"Same difference."

I let it pass. "Justo Vega seems to have joined her."

"Justo . . . ? That lawyer from down Miami with the stick up his ass?"

I counted to five. "Cascadden, he's a friend of mine, a good friend from the service, and I'm worried."

"He's probably just stuffing himself with some of that *cubano* roast pork and beaned *arroz.* Y'all have that rice plate up in Beantown, Beantown?"

"His security man and family and answering service haven't heard from him."

"So he's swilling some *vino* along with his meal. That's the way they get, you know?"

I counted to seven.

"Beantown, you still with me?"

I said, "Cascadden, you have any idea of what it would cost the city, you could have saved Justo Vega and instead just threw me ethnic slurs about him?"

"No, I sure don't. But I do know this. I took a bullet once for this here municipality, and there's people in high places remember that."

"Cascadden—"

"And besides, who's gonna know what we been talking about anyways?"

I heard the click before I could finish counting this time.

On my way to the back door, I heard it opening. When I reached the kitchen, David Helides was just closing it behind him. He still wore a sweatshirt and pants, but these were smudged with dirt, as were his hands and cheeks as he turned into the light.

And jumped back like a scalded cat.

"I'm sorry," I said. "Didn't mean to scare you."

One of the hands went to his chest, naturally rather than theatrically. Then his eyes cast down toward the floor. "I am just not used to . . . strangers in the house."

"I'm not so much a stranger anymore."

"No." A glimmer of smile. "No, you are not." Then it seemed as though a jolt went through him as his head jerked back up. "My father, is he . . . ?"

"He's all right." I decided to chance it. "But someone else is missing."

Helides squinched his eyes shut. "Who?"

"Malinda Dujong. And now Justo Vega."

The eyes opened. "Malinda . . . Mister . . . How?"

"I was hoping you might know."

"Me?" Eyes back to floor. "How would . . . ?"

I said, "I'd like to talk with you about that, but do you want to change first?"

"Change?"

"Out of those clothes."

"Oh." He looked down at himself, wiping both hands vigorously on the thighs of the sweatpants. "Oh, no. I always come back like this."

"Back?"

"From my plants." He gestured behind him. "But we can sit outside . . . if you want."

"Outside."

"I like it by the water . . . at night. When no one can . . . see who I am."

I watched David Helides drag a white resin chair from the perimeter of the external portion of the pool toward the Intracoastal Waterway. He positioned the chair in the shadow of a large-crowned tree, the big sailboat creaking against its dock.

I followed Helides with a matching seat for me. By the time I reached the tree, he was already sitting down, legs stretched out rather than bunched, shoulders loose rather than tensed.

Lowering myself into the second chair, I said, "You seem a bit more relaxed."

From the shadows, his voice was as hard to hear as his face was to see. "Like I told you, I enjoy it by the water. The tree"—he moved his hand over his head—"protects me."

"What kind is it?"

"An alien."

I paused. "An alien?"

"Not indigenous to Florida, an immigrant." Then some hesitation. "My father prefers simpler trees that need little care."

"He was always a low-maintenance kind of man."

"With a . . . high-maintenance kind of son."

I didn't reply.

"I am sorry," said Helides. "My comment probably made you uncomfortable."

"A little."

I could see his head bob once against the tree-line behind him. "We all strive to . . . please my father, each of us in his own way."

Somehow it troubled me that Helides was right. "The Colonel said that he thought Malinda Dujong might help you."

No movement of the head this time, and I couldn't read his eyes. "She tried."

"How?"

"By sitting with me. Only she did not want to play at the computer like . . . Veronica."

"What did Ms. Dujong do?"

"Talked. Or asked questions to make me talk."

"About . . . ?"

"What I did with my time, what I wanted to do."

"Such as?"

"My plants . . . my computer . . ."

When Helides petered out, I said, "When was this?"

"I do not know."

"Approximately?"

Almost a shrug. "Days ago, a week?"

"Before or after the birthday party?"

Helides waited a moment. "It must have been . . . after."

"Why?"

"Because Malinda asked me if I knew why Veronica . . . acted that way."

"But I thought Ms. Dujong wasn't at the party."

"She was not. But she wanted to know . . . anyway."

"And what did you tell her?"

"That I . . ."

"Yes?"

Another moment. "That I thought maybe Veronica was on . . . drugs."

"Drugs?"

"Yes. The way she acted was"—a cough like his father's laugh—"crazy, like my brother sometimes gets . . . on cocaine."

I thought again about the autopsy report on Veronica's body. About the video that Kalil Biggs shot at the party. About the other one of the recording session that Mitch Eisen showed me in his—

Helides said something from the shadows that I didn't catch. "I'm sorry, David?"

Slightly louder with, "John, what do you think . . . happened to Malinda and Mr. Vega?"

"I don't know. Did either of them ever say anything to you about being afraid?"

The cough again. "To . . . me?"

"I know it sounds unlikely, but I thought maybe Ms. Dujong might have told you something."

"No." A pause. "No, she just asked about . . . me. Sat where you did." The head turned toward the house. "In my room, I mean. It was easy to talk with Malinda, but now someone has probably taken her away."

"I'm afraid so."

Another bob of the head. "I used to wish . . . for that."

"What?"

"Malinda asked about my . . . dreams, what I really wanted in life. I told her . . . that what I really wanted was to die." A stirring in his chair. "Oh, I do not mean . . . suicide, though without Dr. Forbes and his pills . . . I think I could. I mean just for someone to take me away. . . ." His right hand came up and then down. "Away from here, from my life. To a place where I could start everything over again, all sound in mind and body."

My time in Boston after Nancy's death flooded back. "I don't think life works that way, David."

"No," came the voice softly from the shadow of the tree. "No, it never . . . seems to, does it?"

Duy Tranh yelled, "Mr. Cuddy, are you out there?"

Helides jumped as I turned toward the back door of the house.

I said, "What is it?"

"There is a telephone call for you."

Getting to my feet, I thanked David Helides for his time before breaking into a run.

TWENTY—THREE

We found her car," said Lourdes Pintana's voice on the other end of the line.

"Where?"

"Got a pencil?"

It was a big, park-and-lock lot near the beach, behind a string of restaurants and bars. I could see a marked cruiser and an unmarked sedan blocking the driveway, Pintana and a uniformed officer standing together at the dovetailing trunks. Nearby, an older man sat in a lawn chair and stroked the neck and back of an obese cat taking up most of his lap.

I left the Achieva at the curb and walked over to the police cars. Pintana pointed at a yellow Toyota Celica several rows away, then beckoned me to follow her toward it. Over a shoulder, she said to the officer, "Dundee, don't let anybody else drive in."

The older man looked up from his cat. "Oh, that's just peachy."

Pintana said, "Only until our tow truck arrives, Mr. Freeman."

A squirting spit from the lawn chair. "What I get for calling the cops in the first place."

Pintana just shook her head.

As we approached the Celica, I said, "How did you find it?"

"Didn't," she said. "I put it in the computer as a BOLO."

Meaning, "Be On the Look Out" for. "And?"

"And when 'Freeman, Arthur' back there noticed this

car was still in his lot a day later without the guy coming back to claim it, he called into the department to let us know it was going to be towed."

I said, "The 'guy?'"

We reached the Toyota. "*Sí.*"

"Description?"

Pintana almost smiled. "I'll let you ask Freeman when we get back to him." Then she turned serious. "I don't see any damage. You?"

I walked around the car. "No."

"See anything else?"

My hands clasped behind me so I wouldn't accidentally touch paint-job or chrome, I peered in through the windows. A beaded talisman hung from the rearview mirror. Some wadded napkins lay on the floormat, passenger's side, and a puddle of dark liquid had dried on the armrest, driver's side. The rear seat was clean, as though Malinda Dujong never used it.

I mentioned the stain to Pintana.

She said, "That all?"

"I saw something like the talisman on the rearview when we were back in Dujong's apartment."

A nod this time. "Me, too."

"You pop the trunk?"

"I thought we should wait till our truck got it back to the garage, let the techies do their thing in a controlled environment."

I said, "What if Dujong's in there?"

"I don't get any decomposition smell coming out."

"What if she's alive in there?"

"You think that's likely?"

I looked around the lot. "Seems to me there are plenty of places in your city where our killer could have left her car without its being found this quickly."

Pintana stared at me a long moment before turning toward the uniformed officer at the entrance. "Dundee?"

"Yo?"

"You got a tire iron in your vehicle?"

It took Dundee three tries, but he finally got the lock to spring. As the lid came up and the little light came on, I held my breath, but there was nothing inside the trunk.

Well, almost nothing.

Dundee started to reach for it, but Pintana said, "No. Let the techies deal with the thing. Besides," she glanced up at me, "we can read what it says."

The sheet of paper lay centered on the trunk's rug, a small flat rock as anchor. The letters were cut individually and pasted, just like the note I'd gotten back at my hotel.

Only this one said, "sHe'S Not HerE, cUdDy."

After Pintana sent Dundee in search of a rope or bungee cord to secure the trunk lid of the Celica, I said to her, "I've seen one of these before."

She crossed her arms. "Where?"

I explained it to her.

Pintana frowned. "You didn't report this note to me."

"At the time, I thought somebody was just trying to help my investigation without identifying themselves."

"Who?"

I looked back down at the paper. "That seems to be the question, doesn't it?"

When Dundee got back, Pintana and I walked over to Arthur Freeman. As we reached him, I thought the cat might jump down and run away, but apparently it was enjoying the petting too much.

Pintana said, "Mr. Freeman, this is John Cuddy. Would you mind repeating for him what you told me?"

Freeman blinked and frowned. "Might be easier, y'all arrived at the same time. I could tell about this fellow the once, get back onto my business."

Fellow came out "feller," and business, "bidness."

Pintana put a little syrup into her next words. "Please, Mr. Freeman?"

He cleared his throat, but you could tell Freeman was going to cooperate, because he stopped stroking the cat. "Yesterday, around five in the evening, this fellow come by in that yellow car. My sign there says five dollars to park-and-lock. Well, he had the bill already out in his hand. So I took it, and he drove into that space there."

The cat made a grumbling noise.

I said, "This man never spoke to you?"

"Not a word."

"How about describing him?"

"Didn't really look the fellow in the eye."

"When he got out of the car, though?"

The cat grumbled again, twisted its head toward Freeman. "I was already taking on somebody else."

"So you never saw him standing?"

"Not standing, not walking, not doing cartwheels if he could."

I smiled in spite of our topic. "But you did say, 'that' car, not 'his' car."

Freeman looked up at Pintana. "What, y'all train every cop to ask the same questions?"

I said, "Was there something about him that led you to—"

"That fetish thing."

"Fetish?"

Freeman now stared at me. "You're still a young enough fellow, you ought to know what a 'fetish' is. If not,

I'd bet the farm this pretty little detective can show you."

I tried not to blush. "Mr. Freeman—"

"Whatever y'all want to call it, I mean that thing hanging from the rearview mirror."

"I still don't see your point."

Arthur Freeman's cat grumbled a third time, and he went back to stroking it, the cat's eyes closing in ecstasy. "Didn't seem the kind of thing a fellow'd have in his own car. Felt kind of . . . feminine to me."

From behind her desk, Sergeant Lourdes Pintana said, "Justo Vega is missing as well?"

"I tried calling you. Unfortunately, Cascadden answered."

Her eyes closed like the parking-lot cat's, but I didn't think in ecstasy. "When was this?"

I told her.

"*Madre de Dios.*" Opening her eyes, Pintana picked up the phone like it was a flyswatter, then just banged it down the same way. "We don't know where Mr. Vega was when he got taken?"

"Supposed to be en route, Miami to Fort Lauderdale."

Pintana exhaled loudly. "So, city or county down there, city or county up here. Wonderful, just wonderful."

"And even better that Cascadden's caused you to lose a couple of hours getting on it."

Pintana glared at me, then shook her head and picked up the phone again. After punching in some numbers, she said, "Cuddy, Mr. Vega's car?"

"Cadillac coupe."

"Tag number?"

"You mean his license plate?"

"Yes," impatiently.

I told her I didn't know.

Sergeant Lourdes Pintana had to hang up and start over. Again.

Outside her office, I was walking toward the security door when Detective Kyle Cascadden entered through it.

"Beantown, you didn't come visiting without telling me first?"

"We found Malinda Dujong's car."

Cascadden stopped. "And?"

"Now your sergeant's looking for Justo Vega's."

"Still doesn't sound like Homicide's problem to me."

"After talking with Pintana, you might change your mind."

A grin. "Lourdes hasn't heard my side of whatever you're pitching yet."

I moved by Cascadden. "Call me later, let me know what she thought of your fastball."

Driving back to the Helides house, I tried to reason through the question of who would have sent both notes.

You think about it, the second note seemed pretty clever, anticipating I'd be there when the trunk was opened. Maybe the killer believed that, after I realized Malinda Dujong was missing, I'd drive around the city, trying to spot her car. But Fort Lauderdale is huge, and I'd have no reason to cruise any particular part of it. So, whoever left that note must have figured that the police would be notified of the yellow Celica and would contact me.

Which also made the second note seem pretty stupid, too: I could now tie whoever took Dujong—and presumably Justo Vega—to the person leaving that envelope for me at the hotel. If only Damon on the registration desk had noticed who'd delivered it.

But even if the killer knew he hadn't been identified

there, why leave anything in Dujong's car that connected her to the person telling me I should "ask the band about Sundy Moran?" And assuming there was a reason to make Dujong disappear because of what she could have "sensed" that day at the Skipper's party, why take Justo as well, giving me yet another connection I didn't already have?

None of it made any sense. Who in their right mind would plan so elaborately, and then tip—

Jesus. Their right mind.

I pulled to the side of the road and stopped. There was opportunity. In fact, the perfect opportunity, thanks to the party. But an apparent absence of means. And no motive.

At least, none that I could see.

Shelving means for a while, I went back over what people had told me about Veronica Held. How manipulative she was in getting her own way. How interested she was in things sexual, including, according to Cassandra Helides, coming on to her. How enticing she was, from Ricky Queen's "demographics" explanation to the videos I'd seen myself of the birthday party and Spiral's "dry-run."

How David Helides, the "resident expert" on drugs, thought Veronica was under the influence when she gave her performance at the party, an impression borne out by the autopsy report that found cocaine in her system.

Killing Veronica Held made sense if she really did have some leverage that—under the spell of chemical inducement—she might reveal to the wrong person. Like maybe to her grandfather, since Nicolas Helides held most of the strings to the marionettes of family and band around him. And since Veronica would want to appease the Skipper for having behaved so badly on his birthday.

Except that given the means, and especially the sexual violation with condom, the killing still seemed premeditated, not something done on the spur of the moment after

Veronica ran beyond the range of Kalil's camera. And why would the murderer tell me through the paste-up notes anything that would lead to Sundy Moran or her relationship with—

No. No, back up. When I got the note suggesting I ask the band about Moran, I assumed it came from someone other than the killer and pointed toward someone in the band as the killer. Then, when the person taking Malinda Dujong planted that second paste-up in the trunk of her car, the composer of both notes seemed to *be* the murderer.

Which went back to handing me connections I didn't have, scrambling the people potentially having motives.

I decided to shelve motive and go back to means. If you believe the killer was male, and exclude on . . .

Wait a minute. Could that be the key?

It would explain means, all right. And even motive. In fact, the one would beget the other. But I had to be sure, especially before telling Colonel Nicolas Helides what I suspected.

Picking up my cell phone, I dialed the Skipper's house. When Duy Tranh answered, I said, "Can you give me some directions?"

TWENTY-FOUR

It lay off a dirt and marl road that reminded me of the one going by Billy's, the roadhouse where Donna Moran worked. Only I hadn't seen a building or a light since leaving the paved state route about half a mile back.

Tranh'd told me over the phone to watch for a neon-orange surveyor's tape on the left, because a driveway into the

Colonel's tract had been punched through a little beyond it.
Another quarter-mile, and I spotted the tape knotted around a
stout trunk, fresh tire tracks curving into the hammock.

Which is when I turned off my headlights and engine.

I waited until my eyes adjusted to the dark and my ears to
the silence. After a minute, I could make out both the shapes
of trees against the cloud-streaked night sky and the sounds
of frogs singing in them. After another minute, the shades of
gray became relatively distinct, and I was hearing sounds of
creatures I couldn't recognize. High-pitched barking, low-
pitched chuffing, even a roar that belonged in *Jurassic Park*.

I opened the driver's side door and stepped out onto
mushy grass, my shoes squelching in the quiet around me.
I didn't know how far sound would travel, but I'd guessed
that anybody for a mile around could have heard the car
engine, so I didn't sweat closing my door.

Ten steps up the driveway—really just a cleared and
packed trail—the mosquitoes found me. I waved at them,
but didn't slap any, figuring that noise could be identified
as obviously human by somebody close by. And though
Tranh had said the driveway went on for nearly half a mile
into the hammock, he wasn't sure how many side-paths
might have been blazed, so I wasn't sure how close that
somebody might be.

I moved down the center of the driveway, since I hadn't
known him to use any distance weapons, and I wanted the
open space of the cleared brush around me to buy reaction
time.

Thanks to moonlight trickling through the canopy of
tree crowns above, I could make out a narrower path cut to
the right. The surrounding trees, ferns, and vines—some
thick enough for Kyle Cascadden to swing from—were so
dense, I didn't think anyone would use anything else to
move along, so I followed the path to a dead-end about fifty

feet farther down. On the way back out, I listened carefully. I'd learned in Vietnam that a human being could remain silent in the bush by standing stock still, but almost every motion in dense foliage gives off some sound. I was fairly certain no one was moving on either side of me.

I still trod very slowly, though, swinging my head left to right in a slow arc and then back again, letting what images there were come in at an angle to my retinas, my ears like radar dishes for any noise, any movement. The Skipper had commented a couple of times about the old days, and that sense of walking on a razor's edge came close to what I was feeling now.

Back on the driveway, I moved farther along, the peek-a-boo moon giving me glimpses of continuing tire tracks. I passed three more side-paths, one on the left and two on the right, but even though leaving them unexplored and to my rear bothered me, I thought following the tracks might bring me somewhere faster.

Especially since I seemed to be getting closer to the creature making the low, chuffing noises.

Another hundred meters by my stride count, and three more side-paths, all on the left this time. Passing them was even more troubling, but the chuffing was getting louder.

Fifty meters farther, and I could see the driveway curving for the first time, to the right. I stopped and listened as carefully as I ever had in my life. Nothing I could call human, but the chuffing sound was now less than a baseball toss away.

Just around the curve, in fact.

I stayed on the inside of the driveway arc, moving two steps, then stopping, then one and stopping, then three and the same. Enough times to pick up sound, but hopefully without any kind of predictable pattern for someone to spring an ambush or—

I saw her first.

I'd already stopped for a listen. If I hadn't, I'm not sure the change in the shape of this particular tree would have been apparent until I was a lot closer.

Not that it made any difference to Malinda Dujong.

This time, the cloying smell of decaying flesh hit me ten feet later, the process no doubt accelerated by the heat of a Florida day. And by some creatures in the hammock as well, from the strips of flesh ripped from her body.

Up close, the eyes and earlobes were gone, peck-marks on her cheeks. The lips had been saved by black electrician's tape over them. Her dress was torn in places, less like random slashing and more like careful cutting, as though the intention were to expose certain parts. Her forehead was lashed to the trunk of the tree, her wrists around the back of the trunk, and her ankles to its base, all by wire cable like a trendy outdoor café might use to secure its tables and chairs after closing time. I didn't quite understand the reason for the wire as opposed to rope until I could see her neck and shoulders.

The skin looked as though acid had been dripped on it, the flesh scoured down to the bone in some spots. Through the gaps in her dress, more burned areas. And on her arms and legs . . .

Anywhere that had been in contact with the tree.

Which is when I heard the chuffing noise grow louder, a little farther along the curve. Fighting the reflex to run, I stayed to the inside of the arc, but not stopping as frequently as I could have. Or should have.

Though I'm not sure that would have made a difference, either.

At each stop, I turned to look back at Dujong. She was still in sight as I rounded a protruding tree limb and saw Justo Vega, thirty feet in front of me.

He was lashed to another tree, his eyes bugging but still in their sockets. His left arm seemed to be tied around the back of the tree, as Dujong's had been, but his right arm was bound at his waist in front, what I thought was the little Cuban flag I'd seen on the dashboard of his car now dangling limply from that hand.

And given the way his chest heaved and neck strained in time to the chuffing sounds, Justo was the "creature" making them.

I watched and listened for as long as I could bear just standing there. Then I ran in a zigzag pattern toward Justo, finally coming into the range of his eyes beneath the band of wire that restricted his head movement. He began waving the little flag frantically, his eyes rolling up as though he were trying to gaze at the moon.

Reaching for the tape over his mouth, I managed to get out, "Justo, I'll get these off—" before a whooshing sound above and behind me made contact with the back of my head, and I felt the tree take a shot at me, too.

Nancy remained just beyond my reach, but this time she wasn't drowning. Somehow we'd moved from the Bay area to Hawaii, and she stood in the path of molten lava, flowing down the hill toward her. Nancy was tied to a tree, her hand extending out to me. But the faster I ran toward her, the farther she and the tree receded toward the lava flow. I lunged as the hair on her head caught fire, nearly exploding into flame. And then the flesh on Nancy's hand began to melt away, down to skeleton. I could feel the heat, her pain on my own hands.

"John?"

And when Nancy called out to me, it wasn't even her own voice, but that of a man, a voice I thought sounded familiar, though—

"John!"

I opened my eyes to deep-set, hooded ones staring back from less than a foot away, my hands and shoulders and neck all burning so intensely I nearly cried out.

David Helides said, "For a moment there, I was afraid you weren't going to wake up."

I tried to talk, realized my mouth had been taped shut. Just like Justo's.

Helides stepped back by executing a little dance step, a runway model at triple speed. He wore a dark shirt and pants, but not his usual sweats. These were fashionable, like something in a Banana Republic display window, and his hair was brushed and gelled stylishly back over his ears.

"The real me, John."

A searing flash on my left shoulder. I squeezed my eyes shut and tried to swallow the scream, creating that same chuffing noise I'd heard Justo making.

Could still hear him making over the sound of my own.

"You're tied to a manchineel tree," said Helides. "I mentioned them to you the first time you came to visit, remember?"

The torture tree the Native-American tribe used on their prisoners.

"You might recall that I described the sap as being 'caustic.' Well, I've come to think of it more as arboreal 'lava,' really. Perhaps you'd now agree?"

I probably would have nodded reflexively, except my forehead was lashed, and I realized that the part of my scalp against the tree felt wet.

Helides pointed toward his left and my right, but out of the field of vision I had. "Your friend Mr. Vega agreed with me on that, after he promised not to scream if I took the tape off his mouth. Though frankly, I doubt anyone could have heard him anyway." Helides cupped his hand behind his left ear, bending his knees and widening his eyes in a parody of a Swiss yodeler. "Listen."

I could hear the doppler sound of an approaching and then receding vehicle engine.

Helides lowered his hand. "And that's from the state route, nearly a mile from where we are, as the proverbial crow flies. The reason I could hear you coming up the dirt road in your car. I must say, though, that you gave me a bit of a scare with your silence afoot." Helides executed another dance step, this time a pirouette ending in a karatelike stance. "Yes. John Cuddy, skulking along my path like some sort of ninja warrior." Helides spun around, but didn't kick or strike out at the air. Instead, he seemed to relax. "God, it's so good to act out." He turned back to me, smiling. "Faking chronic, clinical depression is terribly enervating."

I watch Helides cavort around the clearing, like a hyperactive child after a long drive. He skipped and hopscotched, jumping front and back, then side to side.

Suddenly Helides stopped, turning to me again. "You figured it out, didn't you?"

I just stared at him.

He said, "Same deal as with Mr. Vega. No tape, no screams. Not for help, not even from the pain. Agreed?"

I blinked.

Helides came forward, bouncing, almost prancing, on the balls of his feet. He pulled the tape off my mouth slowly, clearly enjoying the sound of it, the feel of it.

"There now, John. Tell me, how did you deduce that I was no longer depressed?"

"I worked backward from the crime. The pool scene chosen very thoughtfully, so that forensics wouldn't come up with much. Or with too much, given the number of people attending the party."

"A quite wonderful Website for mystery writers helped me immensely there."

"And Veronica had told you about Kalil Biggs wanting to do a video."

"Yes," said Helides. "The perfect excuse for my father ordering Duy to turn off the internal security cameras."

"Then the—" I clamped my jaw shut, gritting my teeth against a surge of pain from my right buttock.

"Ah, exquisite, isn't it? I would love to have had this kind of conversation with Malinda, too, but unfortunately my specialty is flora, not fauna."

Tightly, I said, "And something got to her first."

"Turkey vultures. If it were daylight, you'd see them above, circling. After I took her on Wednesday night, and brought her here, I really had to get back to my father's house, so there was no time to speak with her then. And besides, John, even I didn't know how quickly the lava/sap would work, though I am glad to have had the foresight to use cable wire instead of rope. I think the sap could weaken even braided hemp to the breaking point." Helides shook his head. "But, I digress. Learning from Malinda—whose heart, I believe, must have simply given out from terror—I went back on the Internet, found that vultures are discouraged by movement of any sort in what they perceive to be carrion. So, I gave Mr. Vega a scarecrow of sorts, the flag of his country of origin." He looked toward Justo's tree. "Waving it in a patriotic fashion will keep the vultures away." Helides came back to me. "For how long, though, should prove fascinating."

I tried to focus. "I can understand how you killed Veronica, even why violating her would deflect suspicion away from you given the depression and the drugs you take. What I still don't understand is why—"

"—I had to kill the little bitch in the first place?"

Another surge, from my left forearm this time. "Yes."

"Quite simple, really. She found out."

"About what?"

Helides regarded me the way a teacher might when disappointed by an otherwise promising student. "That I wasn't really depressed, of course."

"And you took her life for it?"

"Not immediately. I was actually quite naive. When I realized about fourteen months ago that I was seemingly, miraculously coming out of the years—decades, John—of genuine depression, I didn't tell anyone. Not Dr. Forbes, certainly not my father. You see, I wasn't sure if my 'improvement' was just another cruel joke the illness was playing on me. So, I conducted my own experiments, with my mind and body the laboratory. I slowly weaned myself off the drugs—still getting prescriptions filled, of course, even palming a few pills when someone else might be in the kitchen to see me 'take' them. I applied for—and received—a driver's license. Then, as the weeks went by, I could feel genuine well-being for the first time in my life. Hiding it from Dr. Forbes was child's play, as he'd already made up his mind about the hopelessness of my prognosis and basically just played drug dealer on every visit until it was time for him to go fishing. Within a month, I discovered I had a rather strong sex drive after all, even disguised myself to visit bars and occasionally indulge that drive thereafter, though one-night stands are not as easy to manage as I've heard they were in my brother's—and your—time."

A surge near my left elbow kept me from replying, even if I'd wanted to.

Helides said, "Well, as I began to feel even better and more confident, I took to 'acting out.' At first, as a celebration of feeling human and only"—a sweep of his hand around the clearing—"out here, in the hammock, where I knew no one could possibly see me."

"At first."

A rueful smile. "Exactly. There were days when, despite feeling better, I had no desire to visit this place. The weather, sometimes a particularly fierce hatch of mosquitoes. On those occasions, and when no one else was in the house, I would slip into the control room and simply deactivate one of the security cameras. Can you guess which one?"

I thought about it. "The pool, because it gave you the largest working area to 'act out' in."

"Bravo, John. In fact, to extend the metaphor a bit, it was the largest and most desirable theater in the house, so long as no security guard could monitor it."

"How did you get into the control room, though?"

"My father had a key. He sleeps from time to time. Not so difficult really to slip it off his ring and have a copy made."

"I still don't see why you had to kill Veronica."

The hollowed features changed. "During one of my sessions in the pool area, she had Cassandra drop her off at the front of my father's house. For some reason, Very decided to stroll around to the rear of the house."

"I thought you always called her 'Veronica'?"

"Only for you, John. To bond us, once I noticed you used her full name. Out of your respect for the dead, I assume, no matter how badly misplaced."

"And you didn't hear her coming?"

"Not through the glass wall, and since Cassandra, of course, lived in the house, there was no telephone call from the gate guard. Which wouldn't have mattered, generally, since my father's new wife is not the quietest of people, and I therefore always heard her coming in time."

"So, Veronica saw you through the glass wall . . ."

"And sensed immediately that she had an advantage over me."

"One that she—" I clamped down again, this time feeling the sap eating into my neck below the hairline.

David Helides beamed a beatific smile at me.

I said, "One that she . . . cashed in."

"Blackmail. For a supposed 'child' of thirteen, Very already exhibited a remarkable appreciation of how leverage on another person could improve her own position."

"But how did the knowledge that you were recovering give her leverage over you?"

The disappointed-teacher look again. "She threatened to tell my father, John."

"That you were better?"

"That I was faking still being ill. I told her it was only a recent phenomenon—I said 'thing' at the time, of course. However sly Very might have been, she was ignorant as pig dung. But the little bitch knew how to play the card I'd so unwisely dealt her, and so she bluffed going to my father and . . . exposing me."

"Bluffed."

"To gain what she wanted." A grotesque caricature now of pelvic thrusting. "In a word, sex."

"With you."

"Me?" Helides seemed shocked. "I was Very's blood uncle, John."

"And that stopped her?"

"It stopped me, at least until it helped cover up my crime. But even then, the experience wasn't terribly pleasant, because I waited until she was . . . 'in extremis,' shall we say? And there were smells—" Helides shuddered delicately. "No, in any case, Very was more interested in the love that dare not speak its name."

I thought about what Cassandra Helides had told me about the incident in her car. "Veronica wanted a female partner."

"And an experienced one. On top of which—no pun intended—she expected me to find such a slut for her in exchange for not blowing the proverbial whistle on me with my father. Which expectation presented quite a problem for a man who hadn't been out and about much."

A drop of fire crawled down my spine, but I thought I saw Helides's solution. "Sundy Moran."

"Oh, excellent, John. I'd met Sundy at one of those bars, and her name rang a bell, a conversation I'd overheard between two of my brother's band members at my father's house. A conversation about one of their deceased druggie cohorts fathering himself a child with that odd name. I thought it might add some spice, Sundy being completely unaware of my familial connection to Spiral, of course."

"And so you started dating Moran."

"Dating her? Not at all. I said before that sex was not as available in these plague-ridden times, unless, of course, one is willing to have 'a relationship' with the woman involved, which in my position would have been awkward at best."

"Or unless you were willing to pay for it."

"My, John, we are on the same wavelength, aren't we?"

"I hope not."

Helides seemed not to notice my jibe. Or care about it. "The 'allowance' from my father was sufficient to cover biweekly visits—including the cheap motels Sundy would rent for a couple of hours—so I'd become rather a regular client of hers. Enough so that she explained to me—*com*plained to me, really—about her boyfriend Ford and her 'momma Donna,' and how Sundy thought they might be 'doing it to each other' and how disgusting that would—"

"So you took a thirteen-year-old girl to see a prostitute."

"The girl took herself. My only function was the arranging and the transporting. I didn't even have to pay, since Sundy was curious enough to service Very on the cuff, so to speak."

I thought it through. "But those visits weren't enough, were they?"

"No." Another change in the hollowed features. "No, Very wanted other 'trips,' as she called them, a term no doubt cadged from one of the drugged-out band members. So, she found where her dear demented dad kept his cocaine."

"And snorted some."

"Yes. Obnoxious as Very was 'straight'—no pun intended again—she was exponentially the bitch once under the influence. The first occasion she used cocaine, with Sundy, Very let slip about her becoming a rock star soon, and that she'd take Sundy with her on the road. Fortunately, I was in the room with them, and realized the bitch hadn't just compromised my anonymity but could just as easily blurt out my secret to her grandfather."

"So you staged Veronica's 'performance'"—a searing sensation over my kidney—"for her grandfather at the party."

A shake of the head. "I'm afraid you're wrong there, John. I of course intended to kill Very then, given all the masking reasons you've already recounted. But her decision to snort up was one she made herself. Probably wanted to show the old man what his money was buying in more ways than one."

"And her running from that room gave you the perfect opportunity."

"Exactly. People had used the pool earlier, but no one was interested in going there after Very's performance. Except for Very herself, whom I found already in her bathing suit. As soon as I entered the pool area, she began to snarl: that she was going to tell her grandfather about my faking the depression, that she thought it had been going on for years, and that I'd been threatening her if she revealed it to him. However, Very was so high on drugs, she couldn't sense my attitude toward her—at that moment or any other—as being anything beyond the simperings of a pathetic beggar."

"But Malinda Dujong might have."

"Yes. Malinda, Malinda." Helides looked toward her manchineel tree. "I'm sorry to say I believe she suspected something about me even during the few times we were in each other's company. She had a genuine gift, John, and I'm just extremely fortunate that she also was so empathetic as to agree to meet a woman she'd never spoken to before instead of attending my father's party that day."

"You had Sundy Moran as 'Wendy' make the call to Ms. Dujong."

"From a pay phone, shortly before slashing her in our little trysting spot. But I have to say, the sex with Sundy just after the call was the best I've ever had."

"Because you were contemplating killing her."

"Yes. I insisted she shower and clean up when we'd finished in bed, because I wanted to take her out for a great dinner."

"But more because you wanted to wash away any trace evidence."

The beatific smile again. "When Sundy came out of the bathroom, I'd already gathered up the sheets. She said, 'Huh?' and that's when I took out the buck knife and started with her throat, to reduce any screaming. There's an excellent Web-page on combat killing techniques, too, though its site address probably won't be of much help to you anymore."

"Quite a risk for you"—Jesus, now the sap ate at my elbow—"to carry that knife away."

"Ah, so I was right! The police were able to match it as the one Ford Walton tried to use on you."

"A nice way for you to tie him to both crimes."

"Yes, John, my thought exactly. And even when I discovered after killing Sundy that Ford had an ironclad—if rather embarrassing—alibi, I thought it still might work. I even told him that I'd found the buck knife a few blocks from the hotel, where I'd seen you 'pitch' it after running from that hotel room."

"And Walton bought all that?"

"Ford was not the brightest of bulbs, John, and the prospect of killing you with the same knife you'd used on Sundy was, I think, too much poetic justice for his mind to question."

"You drive Walton away from my hotel, too?"

"Yes. It was the surest way for me to keep tabs on him for the short period between then and killing him myself. Oh"—Helides bowed, as a Japanese business representative might—"and many thanks for 'softening him up' for me. Even with that other Website on 'the Knife in Combat,' I'm not sure I could have handled an uninjured man of his background so easily, though all those years on the exercise equipment did keep my muscles toned, and these last healthy months really have strengthened them. Watch."

David Helides leaped straight and high into the air, extending arms and legs so that, combined with his head and neck, they made a five-pointed star.

When he landed, I said, "But once you'd killed Veronica, Sundy Moran, and Ford Walton, why take Dujong?"

"Malinda?"

"Yes. She couldn't have identified Sundy Moran's voice from the grave, so Dujong couldn't have tied her caller to you."

"Ah, but Malinda had 'counseled' me once, a stab at her 'spiritual advising,' though it seems she never sent my father a bill. When he asked me about our supposed session, I said, 'I don't remember talking to her,' and apparently he never pursued it with her. However, I think the reason Malinda never billed him was because she really did sense something about me, and that's why I had Sundy draw her away from the birthday party, so Malinda couldn't sense anything more about me there."

I thought of Dujong's "crab-monster" in its cave. "But why kill Dujong if she never attended the party?"

"Loose end." Helides' voice sounded so casual. "If Malinda thought about Very's death long and hard enough, I was afraid she might go to someone with any suspicions she had. Someone . . . like you."

Dujong's call to me on my hotel voice mail. Around a burning near my left hamstring, I said, "So you dropped off that note about Spiral and Sundy Moran to point me back at the members of the band."

"Precisely."

"But then why leave that second note for me in Dujong's trunk?"

A smile, almost sheepish. "Hubris, John. Sheer gall. I was beginning to enjoy the game so much—a game I could never have played while depressed—that I simply didn't want to see it end."

"And so you took Justo, too?"

A smug smile now. "My ultimate reasoning, John. I knew from my father that you all had served together in Vietnam. I knew also that Mr. Vega and you seemed 'brothers' in a way Spi and I never had. After meeting you, watching you, overhearing you in the house, I began to fear that you might be capable of figuring out what the police had not. When Ford Walton's attempt on you went awry, I decided that a frontal attack by me might fail as well. So, I thought I'd give you a stronger motivation to fall into my trap than the disappearance of just Malinda apparently provided."

A trap I thought I'd laid. "Taking Justo should have been a little more trouble for you than someone Dujong's size."

"Mr. Vega's training is almost as old as I am, John, and over the last thirty years, he's not been in the situations I expect you have." David Helides inclined his head toward the hanging vine behind him. "Though, playing Tarzan, I was able to take even you, now, wasn't I?"

"It still doesn't wash, David. How do you account for all our bodies?"

"Account for them?" Helides lifted his face to the sky and laughed like a maniacal bird in the old jungle movies. His laugh spurred more of the dinosaur roaring I'd heard earlier. "John, there has to *be* a body first, and that bellowing sound you hear comes from a nearby drainage canal— or more precisely, from its resident alligators, garbage disposals both mobile and hostile." A more serious look. "Though before that stage, I plan to have rather an unparalleled—and extended—period of study involving the manchineel tree, with two remaining subjects who should tell me much about its already evident properties."

I swallowed the chuffing sound coming up my throat. "You can't fool the Colonel, David."

"Oh, John, I've fooled him for over a year now! My father can't have much time left—Very's little show on his birthday nearly triggered another 'brain attack.' And he once insisted that I sit through an explanation by his estate lawyer of the trust which will support me forever. Provided, of course, that no one advises the good Colonel of my duplicity while there's still time left for him to revoke the trust and effectively disinherit me."

"If you'd just gone to him when you began feeling better—"

"—the old bastard would have disinherited me on the

spot!" Helides nearly roared the words himself. "Told me to go out in the world, earn my own way. Which is exactly how he 'handled' Spi, after my dear brother told me I was the cause of our mother's death. Well, John, what little I know about the 'world' I've gotten from books, television, and more recently the Internet or Web, and I don't like much of what I've found. The thought of spending the rest of my prime struggling to learn survival techniques—after depression robbed me of what most of you take for granted—is simply not tolerable. No, John, I need the money my father will leave me, provided he believes his poor son to be the same damaged goods he's had to suffer and support since birth. And once he's gone, my miraculous recovery can be effected a week at a time, with all the credit going to Dr. Henry Forbes, psychiatrist extraordinaire."

David Helides was Malinda Dujong's crab-monster, all right, protecting his cave until he doesn't need it anymore. "I think I liked you better depressed than crazy."

Helides tore a fresh piece of electrician's tape off the roll near his feet. "I like me better when I'm neither. But I think the only further sounds I wish to hear from you should not be recognizable as words." He came toward me with the new piece. "And I don't believe I'll be bringing you any kind of scarecrow for the vultures, either."

Helides was square in front of me, perhaps two feet away. I couldn't see anything past his head as he raised the fresh tape toward my mouth. That's when I heard a faint whirring sound, followed by a chunking one directly behind him.

Still holding the tape, David Helides staggered forward and almost into me, his eyes wild. As he turned, I got a glimpse over his shoulder of a figure at the edge of the clearing, before a flash in the moonlight like a fish underwater came hurtling through the air, another whir/chunk combination reaching my ears.

It was only then that Helides stumbled away from me enough for my eyes to range down to the steel handle with the circular holes, sticking out near his spine. The blade was sunk into his body almost to the hilt, his right hand, still holding the fresh tape, scrabbling at the handle from a contortionist's angle around the blood soaking through the black shirt.

Now Helides staggered to the side, a twin handle sticking out of his stomach. His left hand went down to it, tugging once before his facial features twisted, and he dropped to his knees. Helides began making a hacking sound, like a man with the dry heaves. Then he struggled back to his feet, lurching toward Duy Tranh, who had crossed half the clearing, the third throwing knife from his suite wall in his right hand.

Helides grunted something at him.

I said, "He's disabled, Tranh."

"I am not so certain." He looked at Helides. "I think you can still kill me, David. If you really want to?"

"You . . . ?" and four more lurching steps.

This time I yelled. "Tranh!"

He kept watching Helides. "Do not quit now, David. You have nearly reached me."

Two additional steps by Helides, mechanical motions more than natural movements, and Tranh hefted his third knife by its handle, feet shifting into a striding stance.

I said, "Tranh, just back away from him."

One more lurching step by Helides, throwing arm cocked by Tranh, blade near his right ear.

I didn't say anything more. David Helides, after swaying dizzily, keeled face forward, no attempt by his now limp arms to break his fall. I could see the point of the belly knife pierce the black fabric just above the back of his belt.

I said, "He may live if we can get an ambulance out here. Cut Justo off that tree, and then he can do me while you run for a phone."

Tranh looked in the directions of Malinda Dujong and Justo Vega before coming back to me. "The binding material is metal cable."

I tried to keep the anger out of my voice. "And you have a knife."

He regarded the artifact in his hand now. "It might ruin the blade."

I gritted my teeth. "Use your head, then."

Tranh lifted his eyes toward mine.

"Justo and I can testify you saved us with the second knife, or that you murdered David Helides with it."

Tranh blinked once. "After your call about 'directions,' I venture out here to help, and this is the gratitude you offer in return? Why should I not just kill you both, blame everything on David?"

"Because then you won't have any credible witnesses to make you a hero in the Colonel's eyes despite killing his son, and you won't have my testimony on what David did to the little girl whose body you found in that pool."

Duy Tranh looked down at David Helides, then once around the trees again before holding up his knife, admiring the blade in the moonlight. "You are right," he said finally. "But I want you to know that for me, it is a very close question."

TWENTY-FIVE

Why am I not surprised to see you again?"

I looked up from my hospital bed on Saturday morning at the nice Haitian doctor. "They say three's the charm."

"I should hope so." She asked me to sit up, then gently pulled the strings on my johnny coat. "After we admitted you, I did some computer research on this 'manchineel tree.' Not much information, but all of it quite nasty."

As the doctor very gently touched here and there with latex-gloved fingers, I said, "How's Justo Vega?"

"I cannot comment, but his associate asked the nurse's station to call him as soon as you were able to receive visitors."

"Pepe?"

"I believe so." She retied the strings at the back of my neck. "A most persistent man."

"Do you know whether David Helides made it?"

The doctor moved toward the door. Without turning her head, she said, "Not my patient."

"Hey, Mr. Whatever, how you doing?"

Carrying a small paper bag, Pepe was dressed conservatively in a pale blue shirt and dark blue pants. His lips were smiling, but his eyes weren't, the bags under them the color of his pants.

"Pepe, have you seen Justo?"

Some rapid blinking. "I am with Mr. Vega maybe an hour after they bring the two of you into here."

I waited.

More blinking, and then a swipe across his eyes with the sleeve of his shirt. "He gonna be okay. The doctor, she say maybe they have to do a—how you say it, when they take skin from one part and put it on another one?"

"A graft?"

"Yes, graft. That's what she say. But other ways, he gonna be okay." Pepe swallowed hard. "You save him from the devil, man."

I waited some more.

He came forward, put the paper bag on my bed. "I don't know do you smoke the cigars, but these are Macanudos. Havana got no gasoline and no electricity, maybe, but cigars from there, they still the best."

I thought of Mo Katzen, back in his office at the Boston *Herald*. "Thanks, Pepe. I know someone who'll love them."

A nod. Then a pause before, "Mr. John Francis Cuddy, you save Mr. Vega when he cannot, and when I cannot, because of what he say to me about hiding his wife and little ones. You ever need anything, you call Pepe, understand?"

"I understand."

"What's in the bag?" said Sergeant Lourdes Pintana.

"Illegal contraband."

"I think that's redundant." She fished some papers from her tote and handed them to me. "I need this statement signed, but I thought it might be easier for you if I came over here."

"You have any information on David Helides?"

"Died on the operating table."

No emotion in her voice, and none on her face.

I looked down, read the printed pages. Duy Tranh getting full credit for a brave rescue, mostly in my words as dictated the night before. "Close enough. You have a pen?"

Pintana passed one over to me. After I was finished and extended the pen back to her, though, she folded her arms instead of taking it.

I said, "What, you want to check my spelling?"

Pintana gave me the amber eyes full-bore. "I think you need to realize that sometimes people who come to you are trying more to help than to hurt."

"With me, it's generally been the other way around."

"Maybe you should work on that." Lourdes Pintana plucked her pen from my fingers without touching them. "Let me know, you ever decide to try."

"Colonel."

Nicolas Helides limped with his brace into my room as Duy Tranh moved an armchair close to my bed for him, then backed discreetly toward the wall.

After lowering himself into the chair, the Skipper said, "Lieutenant, I wanted to apologize for what David did to you."

"You had no way of knowing that he—"

"I've spoken briefly with Lieutenant Vega, and he told me about Malinda as well." Helides shivered. "To think that my own son . . ."

"He was a sick man, Colonel."

"I know. But depression is one kind of illness, and depravity another."

I couldn't think of anything to say that would make it better for him.

The Skipper stared at me, across a gulf of years filled with things I've yet to learn. "A great deal of my time has been spent trying to affect people's behavior in a way I thought was improvement. Ultimately, those efforts resulted in my soul being covered by scars. And Lieutenant, I almost envy yours being mainly physical."

Now I didn't want to say anything at all.

Colonel Nicolas Helides reached his good left hand across the sheets and covered mine. "Thank you, son. You've performed every mission I ever gave you, including this one." He withdrew his hand and put it on the arm of the chair, but didn't try to stand. "Duy?"

Tranh came to the Skipper, helping him get to his feet. More wobbly than he'd appeared entering my room, Colonel Nicolas Helides made his way to the door. As Duy Tranh closed it behind them, he gave me a tight-lipped smile.

Of triumph, I thought.

I spent the rest of my time in the hospital tying up loose ends. Visiting Justo, who was still a bit groggy from painkillers. Meeting his wife out in the sunroom, Alicia thanking me for shortening her husband's horrors. I even shook hands and exchanged clipped, awkward sentences with their three little daughters.

After being discharged, I gave an exclusive interview to Oline Christie of the Fort Lauderdale *Sun-Sentinel* on the proviso that no picture of me or the Vega family would run in it. Duy Tranh took care of my medical bills and settled with the rental company's insurance adjuster about the damage done to my Chevy Cavalier at Donna Moran's trailer park. Sunday evening in my hotel room, I even watched part of the Super Bowl as I packed, putting the picture of Nancy and me in a protective envelope before sliding it into my suitcase.

The flight back to Boston on Monday was a nonstop, the discomfort from the manchineel burns manageable, and no problems with baggage on arrival. There were even plenty of cabs outside the terminal at Logan.

I told my driver to take me home rather than to the office.

When we got to Beacon Street, I was amazed at the lack of snow and a temperature into the fifties during the last week of January. I walked around to the parking lot behind my brownstone. The Prelude still rested in its slot, and upstairs, my rented condo looked the same as when I'd left.

And I felt just as empty.

I walked over to the telephone tape machine. Its little window glowed a fluorescent "9," and I realized I'd better start getting back into the real world. Replaying the messages, I registered two above the others.

Both were from Drew Lynch at Nancy's three-decker in Southie, the second saying he really needed to hear from me by four P.M., Monday. Kicking myself now for not returning his earlier call after I picked it up from Fort Lauderdale, I checked my watch. An hour to spare.

When I dialed the Lynches' number, a familiar male voice answered.

"Drew, John Cuddy."

"John—"

"I'm sorry I didn't get back to you sooner, but I've been in Florida, and—"

"Florida?"

"It's a long story, Drew."

A pause on his end. "John, I'm afraid we've got a problem."

Just what I needed. "Go ahead."

"Remember when you were here last time, and I told you about my mom being sick?"

"Some kind of flu, right?"

"That's what we thought, but when she didn't get better, we took her to the doctor, and it's not a virus."

"So what is it?"

"An allergy." Another pause. "To cat dander."

Shit. "Renfield."

"Right. I guess it wasn't so bad when Nancy was living above us, because the cat didn't stray much, given his legs and all. But we've been showing her apartment, so Mom's been carrying him down to ours. And now with the allergy, we can't have him here anymore."

I felt a tug behind my belt buckle. "What are you going to do?"

"Either give Renfield away or bring him to an animal shelter. And my wife says today is the deadline."

I thought about Nancy and how much she'd loved the little guy. About my nursemaiding him after his operation and how he'd imprinted on me.

About how Renfield had looked and sounded when I'd gone back to Nancy's place to clean out my stuff there.

"John?" from Drew Lynch.

"I'll take him," I said, before I could change my mind.

ABOUT THE AUTHOR

JEREMIAH HEALY, a graduate of Rutgers College and Harvard Law School, was a professor at the New England School of Law for eighteen years. He is the creator of John Francis Cuddy, a Boston-based private investigator.

Healy's first novel, *Blunt Darts*, was selected by *The New York Times* as one of the seven best mysteries of 1984. His second work, *The Staked Goat*, received the Shamus award for the Best Private Eye Novel of 1986. Healy has been nominated for a Shamus a total of twelve times (six for books, six for short stories). Healy's later novels include *So Like Sleep*, *Swan Dive*, *Yesterday's News*, *Right to Die*, *Shallow Graves*, *Foursome*, *Act of God*, *Rescue*, *Invasion of Privacy*, and *The Only Good Lawyer*. The last two were Shamus nominees for best novel as well.

Healy has served as a judge for both the Shamus and Edgar awards. His books have been translated into French, Japanese, Italian, Spanish, and German. Currently the North American vice president of the International Association of Crime Writers, he was president of the Private Eye Writers of America for two years. Healy has written and spoken about mystery writing extensively, including the Smithsonian Institution's Literature Series, the Sorbonne in Paris, and international conferences of crime writers in New York, England, Spain, and Austria. A member or chair of panels at twelve World Mystery Conventions ("BoucherCons"), Healy also served as the banquet toastmaster for the 1996 BoucherCon and as Guest of Honor at the 1997 Dallas mystery convention. In October 1998 he hosted the International Association of Crime Writers as part of the World Mystery Convention in Philadelphia.

Jeremiah Healy